"Gripping and brimming with chemistry, th[...] edge of your seat until the very last page. W[...] is accused of a crime she insists she didn't co[...], her determined professor steps in to do her best to unravel the truth—whether the hunky defense attorney likes it or not. With sharp dialogue, lots of tension and unpredictable twists, you'll be left breathless while devouring every word."

—Lynette Eason, best-selling, award-winning author of the
Lake City Heroes series

"*The Accused* has everything a reader could want in a suspense novel: a methodical courtroom procedural and murder investigation, sharp dialogue, tight prose, and a dynamic cast of characters. A brilliant novel that fans of the genre won't want to miss!"

—Tosca Lee, *New York Times* best-selling author of
The Line Between

"*The Accused* is Putman at her best! The layered, twisty plot had me holding my breath, and the courtroom scenes were riveting. Highly recommend!"

—Colleen Coble, *USA Today* and *Publishers Weekly* best-selling
author of *Fragile Designs*

"*The Accused* has everything I want in a legal thriller. A chilling crime, a challenging case, interpersonal conflicts, behind-the-scenes judicial wrangling, and a climactic courtroom finale. Cara Putman drew me in with her complex characters, and the intriguing plot kept me engaged through every unexpected twist! I couldn't read fast enough!"

—Lynn H. Blackburn, best-selling, award-winning author of the
Gossamer Falls series

"Cara Putman's ripped-from-the-headlines legal thriller will keep you riveted. Her inside knowledge of the justice system adds a vital authenticity to the courtroom action and taut suspense. Verdict: Highly recommended."

—James Scott Bell, International Thriller Writers Award winner

"Classic Cara Putman! This twisty reimagining of the Amanda Knox case will keep readers guessing until the last page!"

—Rick Acker, best-selling legal suspense author

THE
ACCUSED

SECRETS TO KEEP

The Vanished
The Accused
The Targeted

We Three Kings: A Romance Christmas Collection
by Crystal Caudill, Cara Putman, and Angela Ruth Strong

SECRETS TO KEEP

THE
ACCUSED

CARA PUTMAN

KREGEL
PUBLICATIONS

Published by Kregel Publications, a division of Kregel Inc., 2450 Oak Industrial Dr. NE, Grand Rapids, MI 49505. www.kregel.com.

Published in association with Gardner Literary, LLC. www.gardner-literary .com.

Library of Congress Cataloging-in-Publication Data
Names: Putman, Cara C., author.
Title: The accused / Cara Putman.
Description: First edition. | Grand Rapids, MI : Kregel Publications, 2025.
  | Series: Secrets To Keep ; book 2
Identifiers: LCCN 2024052284 (print) | LCCN 2024052285 (ebook)
Subjects: LCGFT: Christian fiction. | Detective and mystery fiction.
  | Romance fiction. | Novels.
Classification: LCC PS3616.U85 A64 2025 (print) | LCC PS3616.U85 (ebook)
  | DDC 813/.6—dc23/eng/20241115
LC record available at https://lccn.loc.gov/2024052284
LC ebook record available at https://lccn.loc.gov/2024052285

ISBN 978-0-8254-4805-8, print
ISBN 978-0-8254-7084-4, epub
ISBN 978-0-8254-6983-1, Kindle

Printed in the United States of America
25 26 27 28 29 30 31 32 33 34 / 5 4 3 2 1

*To all the teachers who ignited a love of learning in me . . .
from my mom through four degrees to the colleagues who keep
me seeking the next mountain of learning. Thank you!*

Chapter 1

MARGEAUX ROBBINS SPRINTED FROM HER parked Sonata toward the Loudoun County Courthouse, miles from her comfortable office on the Monroe College campus in Kedgewick, Virginia.

She crammed her empty Java Jane's coffee cup into an overflowing trash can, then crossed the street, dodging a late-turning car as she hopped onto the sidewalk. She waited for her turn in the security line while attorneys with court IDs bypassed the X-ray machines and hurried to the stairs. When through security, she hustled to the two elevators, the main one ornamental with its old-fashioned cage and sliding door. Unfortunately, the more modern elevator only held six or seven squished people. Based on the waiting group of suit-clad attorneys surrounded by clients in front of the elevators, she'd be better off clickety-clacking up the stairs, but she didn't want to reach the third-floor courtroom only to huff like an out-of-shape racehorse sucking air. Not the most flattering image, and exactly why she wanted to avoid it.

When the metal doors clanged open, and after waiting for a stream of people to exit, she pressed into the older elevator. As the doors began to shut, a masculine hand shot between them. A moment later a dark-haired man wearing a tailored navy suit and silver tie joined the crush within. There was an aura of familiarity about him, something that made Margeaux riffle through her mental Rolodex as she worked to place him. Their gazes connected. He dipped his chin in a slight nod as he stepped against the wall and the doors slid closed.

"It's good to see you." His deep words startled her as his smile sparked something inside.

Where did she know him from? She couldn't remember—a hazard of working on a campus surrounded by students and colleagues. She tipped her head slightly as she searched for his name, her lips slipping up at how much she wanted to remember. "Good to see you too."

She turned back to the doors, wondering when the elevator would finally move.

He pointed toward her chin, his piercing gray eyes taking her in. "You've got something there."

She touched her jaw. There was no way. All she'd had was coffee.

"Here?"

"No." He shifted closer. "May I?"

"Oh no." Someone behind her snickered and she waited for the floor to drop out from under her. "That's an old line. You'll have to try better than that." Why couldn't she place him? Must be that movie star vibe he had from the tip of his perfectly styled hair to sable wingtips.

A woman in khakis and a blazer leaned toward her. "He's right. It's a hint of whipped cream or something."

Margeaux felt heat climb her chest to her neck, knowing he had to see each moment the red hit her pale complexion. She blew out air in a slow, steady stream, praying the elevator would reach the floor and the stupid doors would open. What was taking so long anyway?

"It's only fair to warn you."

She refused to look his way. "I'm sorry?"

"The spot."

Her gaze betrayed her by turning back to him. "What?"

He quirked an eyebrow and pointed to the corner of his mouth, exactly where his lips tipped in a smirk. "It's still there."

Her gaze traveled to meet his, and she lost the ability to speak. Her mouth opened and closed like a carp stuck on one of her grandpa's fishing hooks. Then she swallowed and forced her shoulders back as she tipped her chin to better hold his gaze. Mistake—total and complete—as the words she'd about marshaled into order fully abandoned her. And she made her living with words.

Her fingers brushed the edge of her mouth.

"A little more to the left."

She edged her fingers over, and they collided with a speck of cream. She rolled her eyes.

"You're welcome." His words were laced with . . . what?

Margeaux quirked a brow at him. She knew him, but she still couldn't remember why—her brain was a complete blank.

"This isn't your usual haunt." He spoke as if he knew her, but he didn't. Did he? Why couldn't she remember? His wasn't a face one would easily forget with its Roman features.

"You know how it is. I leave this form of combat to others."

"Yep."

"What?"

"You like to teach while others do."

Those few words hit hard, an echo of every time her grandpa reminded her she only taught undergrads at a small school. "You know that's a ridiculous insinuation, right? No one believes that teaching isn't worthy of my time."

The doors clanged open. Finally.

He waved an arm. "Ladies first."

"Thank you." Margeaux stepped off the elevator and turned right rather than pause to gain her bearings, wanting to escape this man's watchful gaze.

"Court's the other direction."

"I know." She breezed past the people lining the walls and sitting on benches, scanning quickly for her student as her phone buzzed in her pocket. Juggling her bag and files to one arm, she used her right hand to dig through her pocket.

The alert for the class she'd canceled to be here.

"The hearing begins in fifteen minutes." The man winked at her and strode toward a courtroom.

Should she follow him? Considering she wasn't sure they were here for the same hearing, she'd confirm her destination first. Even so, she let her gaze trail Mr. Darkly Handsome until he disappeared. Maybe she'd catch his identity when the judge recited the names of the attorneys present into the record. It was the kind of mystery she didn't mind.

Where are you?

The number, the message, annoyed Chase Crandall. He was the attorney. He'd be there, and he'd be early. He always was. This college student was Exhibit A for why Chase was tired. His patience for irritations like uncertain clients had waned. Annoyance and impatience was a dangerous combination and made him wonder if he should move over for a recent law school grad filled with passion, if not experience, to take over his criminal defense work. They couldn't do a worse job than he felt he did with the press of too much work.

He'd prayed about it but wasn't sure what to do. Make the call and accept an interview? Stay where he was? He refocused. He couldn't solve the dilemma in the moment. Instead, he had to focus on David Roach, yet another college student who'd driven with one too many drinks in him and had found his way to Chase's firm thanks to a friend of a friend's referral.

They didn't warn you in law school how hard it could be to cobble together enough clients, especially paying ones, when you didn't work for a big firm. Of course, more than one of his classmates at the big boys had lost their positions in the last couple of years, so even those jobs might not be stable anymore.

He reached the outside of the courtroom and scanned the bodies packed there, pausing to hammer out a quick text to his missing client.

The Accused

Where are you? Looking for
you outside the courtroom.

Waiting inside. It's where all the
action is.

Chase strode into the courtroom and wove around attorneys huddled with clients behind the bar. The quick preliminary hearing should be speedy. Then he'd be back to the office for the next round of meetings with clients.

Finally he spotted David. The young man wore khakis and a hoodie topped by a denim jacket. It looked casual yet not dressed down. Not what Chase had coached him to wear but better than a lot of the defendants whispering with their attorneys.

"There you are." The young man's gaze darted around the courtroom. "What's going to happen?"

"Like I explained yesterday, this is quick. The prosecution has to prove probable cause that you were involved in the alleged incident."

"We can't dispute that can we? My car's totaled."

"That's hard evidence. What we can focus on is that the prosecutor charged you with the wrong crime. A felony is too harsh for what happened. A misdemeanor will have lighter long-term consequences for you, with less jail time too."

The young man's shoulders climbed toward his ears like he was a turtle crawling into his protective shell. "Dad thinks I should waive the preliminary hearing."

Great. The absent parent was interfering. "That would have been better handled at your arraignment." Chase kept his voice steady and low. "If you're sure that's what you want to do, I'll tell the assistant commonwealth's attorney."

"Whatever makes this go faster."

Chase considered the young man. "Look. I know you're overwhelmed, but rushing to trial isn't always in your best interest."

"I can't sleep or think right now." He held trembling hands in front of him. "Look at me. I'm a mess."

"That's natural after getting arrested."

"I won't be able to practice law if this ends up as a felony, but if they charge me with that, and you prove they were wrong, then I can't be charged later with a misdemeanor."

"Who told you that?"

"My professor told me it would be double jeopardy." He gestured across the room. "She's even here to support me."

Chase followed the gesture and stilled when he picked out the woman David pointed to. The petite dynamo from the elevator. Margeaux Robbins didn't remember him, but that was okay. Any interest that had sparked when he teased her earlier dissipated in the light of her interference with his client. He refused to roll his eyes at the armchair lawyering. "It's a big if. The commonwealth could also press forward with the felony and prove its case."

"Not with you as my attorney."

"You're sure?"

The young man gave a decisive nod, and the hood of his sweatshirt bounced.

"All right." Chase scanned the audience, his gaze colliding with the opinionated professor. He'd love to stomp over and tell her what her meddling was doing, but instead he narrowed his eyes, surprised when she responded in kind. Then he marched over toward the commonwealth's attorney. Better to get this over with than wait until they were called.

"Mr. Crandall." Judge Archibald Twain's voice stopped him.

He pivoted and addressed the judge. "Your Honor."

"A word."

"Certainly." He strode to the dais, keeping his stance open when he reached it.

"Disturbing rumors have reached me, Mr. Crandall."

Chase's breath caught, then he forced confidence. "There are always rumors, sir."

The man tapped his right hand against his desk. "That you're leaving criminal practice."

"I always have conversations with prospective clients, Judge. It doesn't mean I'm leaving criminal law." How had the judge learned of any rumblings in this direction? He hadn't made up his own mind or talked to anyone who would tell the man.

"You can switch fields, but I'll still appoint you to key criminal matters."

Chase nodded. "Understood, Your Honor."

As he walked away, he didn't doubt the judge's threat. And that left a new weight buried in his gut.

Chapter 2

As Margeaux gathered her class file and other detritus, she knew she had to hustle or be late for the last class standing between some of her students and their break. This section had a blend of undergrads who wanted to attend and those who'd been coerced by graduation requirements. Add in a handful of grad students, and it was an odd mix. They were each hers for this semester, though none really loved the scholarly purgatory between a late lunch and sleep. Stir in the fact that spring break commenced in mere hours, and Margeaux had her work cut out for her. The bigger goal today was the same one she embraced every day—connect with each of her students and their personal story. Some of those stories were laced with pain and others with grace. Each layered in unique ways.

A rap at the door yanked her attention from the frantic search for her phone. Without it, she couldn't log on to the classroom computer, which meant no slides or other bells and whistles the students expected.

"I'm going to be late for class." Then she noted her colleague Kelly Chupp's drawn face, her beautiful curly white hair straggling around it. "Are you all right?"

"It's David Roach." The words were choked as Kelly forced them out.

"What?" Margeaux sank onto her chair as she braced for whatever else Kelly needed to tell her.

"He was killed this morning in the jail. His name just leaked."

Margeaux rubbed over her heart as the words sank in. "I planned to check on him next week." Spring break had been the earliest she could slip away.

"I thought you'd want to know. Since he was in your class, I wanted to arm you with the information in case a student mentioned it."

"Thanks." Margeaux's mind spun as she considered the implications. How could this have happened? He would have been free in a few more weeks. And now he was dead? It didn't make sense. That young man had a bright future in front of him, one that had been snuffed out. What was she supposed to do with that knowledge? "What do I say?"

"There's no script for situations like this." Kelly wrapped her arms around her middle.

"It would make it easier if there were."

"Maybe, but then we'd miss what the students in front of us need."

Margeaux acknowledged that truth with a nod. "You're right, and they need me to show up fully." Sometimes it exhausted her, but it also remained her favorite part of the job. Being there for the students and authentically offering what they needed from her. "Thank you for letting me know so I wasn't blindsided."

"Been there and it's no fun." With a quick hug, Kelly was gone.

Margeaux grabbed her files and the phone underneath them and hurriedly left her office, closing the door behind her. How could she help her students process this information? *Father, help me navigate this situation, please. Guide my words.*

No one gave instructions for handling tragedies. What to say. What to avoid. How to address the new reality without causing trauma.

She swallowed as she felt the pain rising inside her. She pushed it down, just like she had every time she'd been injured on an apparatus in the gym. She didn't have time to deal with her grief now. Maybe later, but she had to get to the classroom.

The worst part was that David shouldn't have served any jail time, even ninety days. But the judge had been determined to teach him a lesson with the felony DWI, even if the largely suspended sentence was designed to catch his attention before his partying turned into addiction. That short sentence had converted to the young man's coffin.

She entered the classroom and moved to the lectern where she logged on to the computer.

Margeaux's heart hurt considering how David's mistakes had led to his death. The lowest level felony should not transform into a jail cell death, and that could have been avoided if he'd pled to a misdemeanor. But negotiating a plea would have required effective assistance of counsel.

She clicked to the class website and downloaded the slides she'd uploaded for the lecture.

Chase Crandall thought he'd had everything under control, but he'd been overconfident in his abilities to avoid the charge. She'd noticed him strutting around the courtroom, overzealous until the tables had turned in an instant when the jury found David guilty. The irony of the legal system was that the attorneys never paid. Their clients did.

Margeaux felt eyes locked on her and blinked.

She forced her thoughts back to her current students. The ones who came to class deserved her best efforts. She lifted her head, looked at the students, and cleared her throat.

Some days she taught from the zone and easily shocked them into a place they could learn. Other times she couldn't find that sweet spot of connection. Today was feeling like one of the latter.

"I wanted to make sure you knew one of your classmates died this morning. You may have heard that David Roach, who began the semester with us, passed this morning." She paused and tried to assess how each student was absorbing the news. Then she quickly explained the campus resources and invited students to talk with her if they wanted, though she didn't know what she would say.

She blew out a breath and scanned the students before picking up a whiteboard marker. A quick transition might be best.

"Who can tell me the four elements of negligence?" She leaned against the table that rested in front of the whiteboard and waited.

The sixty-some students in her introductory business law course shouldn't be surprised by her opening question. Margeaux had asked a similar one in the prior lecture, and she would repeat it in these hallowed halls of learning until her students could list *duty, breach, causation,* and *damages* without conscious thought. If she was fortunate and did her job exceptionally well, they might even remember the legal concept each represented.

The silence lengthened like taffy stretched to the breaking point.

She kept her expression firmly in place as she eyed row after row of students hunched over laptops or slouched against the black plastic chairs bolted to the floor in the Fairbanks School of Business at Monroe College. The large clock on the back wall warned her she had forty more minutes to make her point before the students were released to dash to their next class.

Monroe College was famous for having all buildings within ten minutes of each other across pastoral grounds, but whoever had timed it ran, not something her students liked to do unless voluntarily for fitness.

What would it be like to have a bailiff in her classroom? Someone to call the wandering minds to order when they slipped away. She considered clapping, turning off the lights, or doing magic tricks. Today deserved grace if any day did, but she also needed to help them focus through the distractions of the day. *Okay, we'll use the Socratic method.*

"Anyone been in a car accident?"

A few students reluctantly nodded. Apathetic. Oblivious. Seemingly concerned only about what would stream next to their multitude of devices. At thirty-two she felt ancient, even though she was only ten or so years older than them.

"What happened?"

Silence.

"Donovan?"

The young man filled a chair in the second row, his dreadlocks bouncing around his head in ordered chaos, a small smile tilting his lips to the side. He liked to pretend he was disinterested in class, but his quizzes exposed his sharp intellect and curiosity. Then he'd come to office hours and solidified his place in her mind as a potential law student.

"A fool sped in front of my momma's car and clipped us."

Margeaux grimaced as she imagined the crunch of metal. "Was everyone okay?"

He shrugged. "I got outta school for a couple of days thanks to the headache."

Margeaux looked at the class, noted the sympathy in other students' eyes, the way one of the girls rubbed her neck as if she'd experienced a whiplash-induced ache of her own. "How was her car?"

"Totaled. Momma was not happy to let that little Datsun go."

Margeaux could imagine what a setback that had been for the family. "Did the police come?"

"Yep. Said it was the other driver's fault for ignoring the stop sign. 'Course, he didn't have insurance, so we got to ride the bus for a couple of months while Momma worked to get a down payment on a new-to-us car." He shrugged. "Seems the law failed us."

"What do you think, class?"

There was shifting in the seats before Natalie slowly raised her hand. One of Margeaux's goals was to help Natalie and the other young women in the class fill their space, to embrace the truth that they had valuable contributions to make. Some days her efforts didn't make an impact, but she'd keep chipping away at the target.

"Natalie?"

"It depends."

The other students snickered as Natalie parroted Margeaux's answer to every question.

"What does it depend on?"

"Whether the driver was insured. Whether there was anything that Donovan's mother did to contribute to the accident." Natalie shrugged thin shoulders beneath a bulky navy sweater. "It's the law, so there's a lot that it depends on."

"I told you he didn't have insurance." Donovan rolled his eyes. "That's why I called him a fool."

"In Virginia, there used to be an option to pay a five-hundred-dollar fee to the state to avoid carrying insurance, but if you failed to either carry insurance or pay the fee, it's a misdemeanor." Margeaux hurried on as she noted a student slide lower in his seat with eyes glazing over. There was one way to attack that. "Josh, why do you think Virginia allowed an opt-out fee?"

"So people could drive without insurance. Seems dumb though. Why let people drive without insurance? It just hurts people like Donovan's mom."

"Maybe that's why the law changed. What do you think?" She tossed the question to the class and let the conversation build before bringing it back to the four elements. A glance at the clock and she wrapped up with a quick comment. "Next class we'll talk about the rest of the chapter on torts. We'll focus on intentional torts and how they're the flip side of many crimes. Have a great rest of your day and enjoy your break."

Students bounded up, hefting backpacks over shoulders with more energy than they'd exhibited during class. Margeaux took a minute to close the slides and log out of the computer before picking up the eraser and swiping the words and charts off the whiteboards with sweeping strokes. She'd survived the class, and maybe now she could find a corner to process and grieve David's loss. When she turned around, Anneliese Richter lingered a foot away, her arms clutching the straps of her backpack as her feet shifted.

The German student had arrived on campus in late August to launch her year abroad, and she still moved about like a mist that hadn't quite formed and stabilized in her new location. She'd spent several days with Margeaux and her family over Christmas, but their relationship had frozen there. Though Emma saw Anneliese on occasion, the young woman seemed to avoid Margeaux. This morning Anneliese's brown hair was brushed into a low ponytail that emphasized her high cheekbones and brown eyes. Her form-fitting turtleneck overlaid hip-hugging jeans and high boots with stiletto heels. Margeaux had to admire her skill at moving without a sound on those spikes.

"Do you have a moment?" Anneliese's soft voice held a musical tone that hinted at the wind flowing through the trees in the Black Forest near her home in Berlin.

Margeaux resisted glancing at the clock on the wall. There was always something next on her calendar. "Walk with me."

The boots weren't so silent as Anneliese followed Margeaux into the tiled hallway.

"Can you help me with the assignment? I do not understand the . . ." She waved her hand as if that would help her pluck the right word from the air. ". . . The orders."

Margeaux fought to keep her smile in place. She wanted to point Anneliese to the syllabus . . . again. "The key right now is to figure out your topic. The paper is what takes your work to the honors level, because it's the additional work."

"Yes, this I know. But the details? Those are unclear."

"Recheck the assignment on the website. Make a list of specific questions, and we can meet after the break." Her watch vibrated, alerting her to an incoming text. She glanced at its face. *The department head wants to see you. Now.*

"Sorry, but I have a meeting with my boss. Make that list, and we can talk."

"Danke."

"*Bitte.*" The German response brought a small smile to the student's face, and she paused while Margeaux picked up her pace and hurried across the lawn to the business administration building. What could Timothy Tobias want with her on the spur of the moment? Her mind spun like a carnival ride and her stomach tightened. It was Friday and she was ready for the weekend—a rare one that wouldn't be filled with grading. She wanted to climb in her car and drive the thirty miles northeast to Sugarloaf Mountain for a bit of hiking if it wasn't too cold. The exertion combined with the views and time outdoors was exactly what she needed to clear her mind and rebuild for the midterms after spring break.

Time to breathe. That's what she longed for more than anything.

But if this meeting was like the prior ones with Dr. Tobias, breathing space was the last thing she'd get. The department head would have his own ideas about what her time should be filled with. She'd hear words like *publication, student mentoring,* and *service to the department and college.* She could do those, but she longed to invest her time in teaching with the occasional bit of research rather than vice versa. To watch the light bulbs switch on over students as they realized what they learned in her class mattered in their future careers but also met their current needs. Unfortunately, that wasn't what was required to secure tenure.

After dropping her bag on her office chair, she slipped her keys and phone in her suit jacket pocket and grabbed a notepad and pen before walking to Dr. Tobias's office.

Climbing the couple of flights of stairs left her taking a deep breath before rapping on his open door. "You wanted to see me?"

He glanced from his computer screen to her, eyes glazed behind glasses and longish hair rumpled as if he'd gripped it while working a problem. Probably something within his specialty—finance and banking. His bent toward numbers rather than people turned her mind to mush and left her asking why—often wondering what to expect from him. He blinked, then gestured toward the chair in front of his desk. "Have a seat."

She shifted a pile of academic journals and papers onto the floor and perched on the edge of the leather chair as she waited. The man was brilliant in front of others, but when he was deep in thought, it could take a while to unearth what he wanted. Even after three years in the business college, she felt like an interloper who had sneaked onto campus and no one had noticed—yet. She needed to remain focused while she wrote and taught, until she had tenure.

"I've learned that Gerald McCormick will retire at the end of the semester." His deep words led her wandering thoughts back to the moment. "That leaves me in a pinch and with a need for someone new to become the assistant department head."

Her brow furrowed as she tried to read the meta-message. "Yes?"

"I'd like you to apply." He studied her intently, and she fought the urge to react.

"Why?"

"It will give you the administrative experience you'll need."

"Are you asking me to do the job?"

"Apply. Let's see how the process goes."

"Who makes the hiring decision?"

"I do, but others will have input." He leaned back and steepled his hands in front of him. "What do you think?"

"I haven't considered something like this."

"It would be a good move if you want to make your career in academia."

"I do." More than anything, though an image from January's hearing and trial flashed through her mind. If that's how attorneys performed in court, she could do better than what she'd witnessed. Then perhaps she could have prevented David's death. After all, she taught the law, and you couldn't do that if you didn't know it. But she wouldn't have worked so hard in law school and her clerkship if this, teaching, hadn't been the goal. She'd created the life she wanted despite what people told her was possible.

He dipped his chin, his hair flopping forward over his eyes before he brushed it to the side again. "You'll find the information waiting in your inbox. Give it careful consideration." He nodded again.

"Yes, sir. And thank you."

A moment later she hesitated in the hallway, slightly dazed as a couple of students brushed past her on the way to the faculty offices that lined either side.

Chapter 3

ONCE UPON A TIME, CHASE could walk into court with an idea and a prayer and things happened. Now? He didn't want to be there, and it went deeper than just an uncertainty about the job. He didn't know if his purpose aligned with the work anymore. That unsettled him at his core, making him wonder who he would be if he wasn't a litigator. He tried to shake free of the thought as he made the short drive to the courthouse in Leesburg.

Friday's hearing had been a disaster, followed by the terrible news his client David Roach had died in jail, the apparent victim of a wrong-place, wrong-time situation. Chase had spent the weekend trying to reconcile the loss and couldn't. He agonized over the idea that God could have stopped the tragedy and didn't. David should have had a bright future in front of him, but he'd heeded bad advice from his father and meddling professor.

The result had been deadly, and Chase couldn't reconcile why.

He parked and climbed from the car, the air slightly warmer than it had been over the weekend. He'd gone for a long, cold walk in the foothills of the mountains Saturday but hadn't found the peace he usually did while communing with God in nature. He knew he'd find what he listened for, but God had been frustratingly silent. Nowhere to be found as he'd hiked. Instead, Chase was bone-level weary. He couldn't keep fighting for clients who didn't know how to avoid trouble. If he didn't make changes, his practice would kill him. Then he tried to avoid that thought, because the fact was that David should never have been sent to prison.

If the kid had only paid attention to Chase, the one person in his life with courtroom experience.

So did he want to begin his week in court? The answer was no, even if this time he sat in Magistrate Hopkins's courtroom for a quick trial.

"Judge Hopkins, this witness is not qualified to serve as an expert under the *Daubert* standard." Chase leaned into the defense table with his arms relaxed at his sides, a confident thrust to his shoulders. The jury needed to believe he was right even if the judge overruled him.

This was all about planting a reasonable doubt in one juror's mind.

That's all it took.

Elaine Liddell, the deputy commonwealth's attorney, lurched to her feet. "Your Honor." She turned and glared at Chase. "Mr. Crandall obviously ignored the list of this man's qualifications."

As he hoped the jury had. The litany of degrees and board certifications the doctor had earned would weigh a person down. Or bore a person to sleep. Either worked for Chase. He loved the battle of the courtroom.

The judge tapped her glasses against the papers that rested on the raised bench in front of her. "Counselors, let's stay focused." She turned to the jury, the lace collar around the neck of her black robes shifting with the movement. "This court rules Dr. Lynch is eminently qualified to testify as an expert."

Chase hid a grimace at the use of the word *eminently*. Maybe no one on the jury would understand it. At least there wasn't a professor or high school English teacher serving today. "Thank you, Judge."

He unbuttoned his jacket and sank onto the hard wooden chair.

His client, Albert Trales, leaned over. "That go okay?"

He couldn't tell him no. "We'll know soon."

Each criminal defense client deserved a vigorous defense, but normal work was nearly beyond Chase's grasp today as he slogged through the grief and questions David's death had generated. What if the same type of accident happened to Albert? That fear, though outsize and ridiculous, still gripped Chase. He couldn't protect his clients in jail. Trials like today's could easily spin out of control with unpredictable moments. He could replace one expert with another, substitute one witness to the crime with another, but the risk and uncertainty remained the same.

Albert had gotten caught in the opioid culture, and some jurors wouldn't understand how unrelentingly the addiction could assert its grip.

What jurors could forget as they drove home was that each defendant deserved a fair trial, an opportunity to confront their accusers. That conviction had lit a fire in Chase's belly throughout law school and his first ten years of practice.

Albert elbowed him. "The judge wants you."

Chase smoothly rose to his feet and rebuttoned his jacket, a sequence of moves he'd made often in court. Had it become too rote?

"Judge?"

The woman eyed him carefully. "If we've regained your attention . . ."

He refused to flinch.

"It's time for cross-examination."

He glanced at the prosecutor, who smirked his direction.

The judge gestured toward the box. "The witness is yours."

Chase's gaze stole to the jury box, where twelve sets of eyes stared back.

Albert slumped back with a groan. "Come on, man."

Chase patted his client's hand in a placating motion. "Thank you, counsel, Your Honor." He squared his shoulders and studied the witness.

Dr. Edward Lynch held teaching privileges at James Madison University and claimed he could prove that Albert waving a gun in the face of the victim had caused the heart attack that killed the older man. If so, the charge would transform a misdemeanor into a felony and the sentence would multiply. He blew out a slow breath and collected his hard-won confidence.

"Dr. Lynch, did you examine John Lloyd?"

"Yes."

"How closely to the time of the heart attack?"

"As soon as I was hired by the prosecution."

"And that was?" Chase had seen the paperwork, but the jury hadn't. He liked to remind them the man had a pecuniary interest in the success of his testimony.

"Six months ago."

Chase riffled through a stack of papers on the table in front of him, then dramatically held up a set of papers. "Wasn't it July 10? More than a year after the heart attack?"

"Yes, I suppose so." The man shrugged as if the detail couldn't matter.

"Do you know the condition of John Lloyd's heart prior to examining him over a year after the heart attack?"

"Not personally, no."

"Did you take a health history during the examination."

"Of course."

"And did you learn anything about John Lloyd's heart during that history?"

"Like what?"

Chase rummaged through more papers before holding up a thick sheaf. "Like a diagnosis his attending cardiologist made three years prior to the heart attack, which stated after a series of tests that the man had less than twenty-five percent heart function."

"I saw that in a review of his medical records."

"Isn't it true that a diagnosis like that would leave him with a strong chance of a heart attack at any time?" Chase scanned the jury as he waited for the answer. The architect seemed attentive to the line of logic as she met his gaze.

"I suppose."

"You suppose?" He arched an eyebrow, then quickly continued. "Isn't it a medical fact that a heart that has compromised function at those levels will make someone more susceptible to a heart attack than you or me?"

Dr. Lynch's gaze skittered from Chase to the jury and back before swallowing and nodding. "Yes."

"So Mr. Trales here"—he gestured at Albert—"had nothing to do with the heart attack."

"No. In my expert opinion, the act of forcibly stealing Mr. Lloyd's briefcase contributed to the attack." Perched slightly above the rest in the witness box, the man raised his chin and looked down at Chase.

"But it's not assault and battery. No further questions."

He sank into the chair and felt the lift of what he'd accomplished. He'd taken a disaster and salvaged it. Albert slid down in his chair, and Chase elbowed him to nudge him back up. The jury didn't need to see his client disrespecting the court and them. Not when Chase had successfully questioned the expert's opinion.

An hour later the case headed to the jury. As often happened, the prosecutor was good, but Elaine had left too much riding on the testimony of the cardiologist. An attorney who consulted long enough with an expert believed the testimony or a piece of evidence held the key to the case and got sloppy. Sure, Chase had a momentary lapse, but he'd recovered well. Enough so the jury wouldn't let Dr. Lynch's testimony sway it.

Until they returned a verdict, coffee sounded like the ticket.

He gathered his notes into the rolling case. He saluted the bailiff. "I'll return this to my office and be back." The county courthouse wasn't in Kedgewick but twenty minutes away in the Loudoun County seat of Leesburg. Not as simple as walking across the street to the town square. But it wasn't a commute into DC either.

It wouldn't take that long to make the round trip to Kedgewick.

"I'll be here." The man gestured toward Albert. "I'll keep an eye on him and call when the jury comes back."

Chase grabbed the briefcase handle. "I won't be that long."

Not when his small storefront office filled a spot on the town square. He'd drop off the bulk of the trial documents and then grab a to-go cup of dark roast. At Java Jane's the baristas knew his name and prepared his order before the door closed behind him.

When he reached his office twenty minutes later, Leigh Lundstrom sat at the desk in the small reception area, a headset strapped on. His right-hand assistant, Leigh served as a combination paralegal and hall monitor. She also made sure his associate stayed on task, as Marcus Shell took each client's plight personally. Chase had originally appreciated that passion, but the pace of it now exhausted him. Marcus would have to learn to balance the highs and lows, or he'd burn out faster than Chase.

"How'd the trial go?" Leigh glanced at his roller bag. "Want me to put that away?"

"Trial was short and good. The best kind." He hoped. "And I've got it. I'm dumping it in my office before I grab coffee. Want anything?"

"And stay up half the night?" She raised an eyebrow in that way all mothers perfected.

"Right." They'd covered this script before, but he'd learned not to forget to ask in case she changed her mind. The one time he had assumed he understood what she'd say, she'd pouted for two days after a particularly rough night with a sick toddler.

"Jim Clary called for you. Something about a civil case or something." She shrugged as she slipped him a sheet of paper. "He was vague but insisted he speak with you. Soon."

"All right." He took the page and read it before placing it in his pocket. "I'll call him back."

"I know. Later or never." The light on the phone flashed, and she pasted on the perky expression she wore when answering in her friendly way.

Chase moved past the desk to the short hallway. An abstract piece a local artist created in her garage brightened the crisp gray walls. He found the slashes of color more interesting than the typical office walls lined with pastoral pictures or photos. He'd invested his funds in the small conference room and adjacent library but stuck to bare bones in his office, using a desk he bought at the college surplus store and a knockoff office chair that looked like it escaped an episode of *Junk Finders*. He didn't need a throne and appreciated the price.

He released the handle to the rolling briefcase, and it coasted to a stop next to his desk.

Might as well see what the man wants. He placed the call and waited for an answer.

"This is Jim."

"Hi, Jim, Chase Crandall returning your call."

"Thanks for getting back to me so quickly. I have a few questions for you and a possible business proposition. Do you have time to meet in the next few days?"

"Possibly. What's this about?"

"A client who needs an attorney and is considering bringing one in-house." Chase heard a few clicks. "I just sent you an email with pertinent details outlined." The man paused. "When can we meet?"

Chase leaned over and woke up his computer. What would it take to get it to move faster?

He heard the man tap a pen against something hard. "Let's get it scheduled and then you can read the details. If you hate what you see, you can always call and cancel."

"All right." After picking a time, Chase ended the call and glanced through the email. The details were sketched outlines but indicated a client who wanted a dedicated attorney to take care of all the company's legal needs. The work would be civil, not criminal, and the thought had a little appeal—enough to learn more.

As he glanced at the bare wall and sterile overhead light, he considered what would need to change if he moved into the corporate space. For those concerned about spending years behind bars, image fell off the priority list. Corporate clients paid better with the work more certain, but they also had different expectations.

He might not have a choice though. In the hours after David had died in prison, he'd received a rash of calls from current clients asking if he'd get them killed too. Some said they'd fire him if they had a choice, but since the court had appointed him to represent them, they didn't. It had been only two days, but he already sensed a downturn in non-court-appointed criminal clients, which could fast-track his decision to make a change.

Most importantly, he needed to get back in the game and back to court.

He slipped out the rear door and walked along the alley. A few steps later he walked into Java Jane's.

"Yo, Chase." Grayson, the prince of coffee, waved from his position at the oversized espresso appliance. It whirred and steamed like a fantastical steampunk machine. "Typical?"

"The usual."

"Nothing usual about you." The man worked his magic as Chase took his place in the short line.

After the mother with a toddler on her hip ordered, he stepped to the butcher-block counter.

He glanced at the new barista's name tag. Eva. "Chase Crandall."

Her smile was like the sun cracking through the clouds. "Nice to meet you. I'm new and so excited. Grayson's going to teach me how to make drinks." The man cleared his throat, and color climbed into her college-aged cheeks. "But first I have to take your order."

"It's a dark latte." Grayson intoned the words mournfully. "No whip. No sugar. No fun. Kind of like an attorney."

Chase kept a straight face. "If I really ordered like a lawyer, I'd take an Americano."

"Guess I should count my blessings." Grayson rolled his eyes as Eva tallied the order.

Chase tapped his card on the credit card reader, then glanced at his phone. "Gotta get back to court."

"Good thing I've got your drink." Grayson handed it across the counter. "Till next time."

Chase lifted the drink in a salute, then hurried toward the door and straight into a soft mass.

Spring break should have meant Margeaux could finally step into a corner of one of her favorite off-campus sanctuaries and catch up on work. Last week she'd asked students to bring an assignment on paper as well as submit it online so she could step away from the computer for a while.

Enough had complied that she could sit at a table in a coffee shop this morning rather than hunch in front of a monitor in her office, where myriad distractions awaited.

The breath oomphed from Margeaux's lungs as she rammed into some- one, and something warm splashed across her front. Seriously? All she wanted was a quiet corner to grade the stack of essays she had collected. Without a grading fairy who would magically take the stack and, with a wave of a wand, turn the papers into meaningfully commented-on ones that the students would actually read and respond to, she needed this time.

She glanced down and groaned at the brown liquid discoloring her silk blouse. There was no way to salvage this mess. Then she looked up into soft gray eyes and froze. Oh no. She did not need this. She blinked and turned slightly away, trying to ignore the familiar man.

"You." The word was an accusation, but she didn't stop it.

His mouth opened but no words came out. And that's when she put it together. Chase had been familiar because he was often at the coffee shop at the same time she was. They'd never had a need to speak since they operated in different circles, even if she'd caught him watching her on occasion.

"Adding careless with coffee to careless with my student?" Color rose in his face, but she didn't stop. "Did you miss the day in kinder- garten when they taught that caring for others more than yourself is a superpower?" Margeaux swallowed, feeling the warmth soak through her shirt. She knew she wasn't responding rationally, but everything felt raw. "Excuse me, but I need to deal with this."

He scrambled through his pockets. "Here. Send me the bill." He shoved a card at her. "I'm truly sorry." He glanced from her to the street and his lips slipped down. "I just got the call the jury's back. Sorry."

She stepped into the doorway at the same time he did, and they danced around each other.

Then he was gone.

The man was a menace. Parading around like he was good and on the side of justice like a real-life Captain America . . . except he was only watching out for himself.

She pinched the bridge of her nose and tried to breathe.

She needed to find a new third space, because she couldn't risk running into him again—not considering what he did to her nerves or her clothes.

Margeaux hesitated inside the coffee shop, soft jazz flowing from hidden speakers, and stared at the card. Chase Crandall. No way she'd call him. Instead, she spun on her heel and left the shop, dropping the card in the trash as she walked by. She'd replace the blouse herself rather than rely on the man who sent David Roach to prison to die.

Chapter 4

THE KNOCK AT HER OFFICE door tugged Margeaux from her thoughts and she bit back a groan. During spring break, if she didn't leave town, she tried to catch up on all the details that eluded her the rest of the semester. Many of her colleagues abandoned campus, but this year Margeaux had stayed with her pen raised and door closed as she worked.

Today the idea of pretending her office building was empty tempted her, but she quickly abandoned it.

It didn't take a 4.0 to recognize light filled the room, and she'd cracked her door. If she hadn't wanted interruptions, she should have worked from home or found a different coffee shop, but the walls of her cottage had pressed against her until she thought she might implode.

She rolled her neck and then forced a smile as a second timid knock sounded. "Come in."

A moment later the door opened and Anneliese stepped inside. Margeaux's smile stretched as she recognized her favorite international student. "Anneliese, how are you? I'm surprised you aren't traveling for spring break."

"I decided not to go."

Margeaux scooted closer to the wing of her desk that faced the chair rather than her computer. "What's wrong?"

"I do not know." An understated lift of one shoulder conveyed more than the most effusive shoulder roll from her other students.

Margeaux let the silence stretch, praying for guidance. Filling space with words came easier to her than silence, but she wanted to wait for Anneliese to find the right words, so she paused. She'd learned with each office-hour visit that Anneliese would speak what she needed, but it might take some time.

The younger woman's shoulders relaxed, which signaled to Margeaux that she should pay attention.

"I do not think I can finish this semester."

"But you're already halfway."

There was another small roll of her shoulders. "I know."

"Then what's happened?" Margeaux considered her carefully. "Has something changed with one of your friends?"

"Not really." Anneliese dropped her head into her hands and hid behind a veil of her light brown hair. "I am not welcome in my apartment."

"Can you tell me more?"

"It feels like there are always new people in the space and no room for me anymore."

"Are you unsafe?"

"No . . ." The word extended beyond the space a two-letter word should occupy. "I feel unwanted." She didn't hesitate as much as she grimaced—as if the word tasted bad on her tongue.

"Hmm." Anneliese hadn't indicated problems or challenges existed with her roommates before. In fact, she'd seemed content with them. The other three young women hadn't made much of an effort to welcome her. Over winter break Anneliese had flown to New York City, where her family had met her for a few days, before returning to campus early and spending several days with Margeaux and her family. Maybe that was the source of the new challenges. Anneliese missed her home, family, and friends.

Margeaux couldn't imagine making the decision to leave home for months at the same age. It would have overwhelmed her even if she could match Anneliese's language skills. "How can I help? Do you need a connection to someone who can help you talk with your room-mates?"

The student shook her head. "We will be fine. I am only tired and overwhelmed."

"Are your roommates home now?"

"No, they left for break." She waved a hand as if swatting a fly. "I should not bother you."

"It's all right." While Margeaux couldn't alter the roommate situation, she could help shift the focus. "Are you doing anything fun for the rest of break?"

"Catching up on classes." Anneliese wrinkled her nose and talked about a spreadsheet class that bored her and a philosophy class that failed to challenge her. Maybe she needed a course that pushed intellectually in ways her current classes weren't. Then she couldn't fixate on issues with her roommates. A small alarm went off, and the student startled, then collected her backpack from the floor. "I must go. Thank you for your time."

"Always." As she watched Anneliese leave, Margeaux sank against her chair. Had she accomplished anything for the young woman? She couldn't know if the conversation made a difference any more than the never-ending pile of grading did. With each comment, she threw ideas into the void and wondered if anyone took the time to open the documents and see the comments. Unfortunately, the software let her know the less-than-stellar student open rates.

Disheartening.

She had to believe what she did mattered.

If it didn't, she'd invested her life in a field that didn't value her and with a population that didn't care.

That depressed her, so she worked harder rather than second-guess her life choices—decisions that made it difficult to pivot into another field. She grabbed her coat and scarf. She desperately needed to escape her thoughts and refocus before she spiraled worse than Anneliese had. A quick walk to the Elliott Museum for a cup of coffee at its bistro would provide the excuse to escape her office. The change of venue could shift her perspective enough for her to give herself to whoever needed her next.

Maybe she could detour to something that mattered, like sharing legal expertise with the art museum director. Serving as a board member provided a good community outlet and interaction with adults—well, when her fellow board members chose to act like grown-ups and not feuding middle schoolers.

She slipped her wallet from her drawer, shoved her keys in her pocket, and escaped her office, easing the door shut behind her.

The numbers on the spreadsheet escaped their orderly rows, and Chase needed a break. Somewhere it was noon, which meant lunchtime. What was the benefit of being your own boss if you couldn't eat lunch whenever you wanted?

He slid into his coat and slipped his phone in the inside pocket. He tapped the reception desk as he walked by to catch Leigh's attention. "I'm going to grab a bite and clear my thoughts. Need anything?"

She pulled an ear of the headset free and looked at him. "Where are you going?"

"Flo's?"

"I'm good."

Marcus stepped from his office. "Want company?"

There was something about the eager expression on the younger attorney's face that made Chase tense. He should say yes. However, he'd spent the last forty minutes calculating how long he could make payroll if the county didn't pay its bill, and he couldn't pretend everything was fine. "Happy to bring back something for you."

"Sure. Not a problem." The thin man stepped back into his office. "I'm good."

Leigh looked at Chase with something like strong disapproval. "He wants to model you professionally."

"Then he hasn't seen the income statement or taken the calls I have this week."

"It'll work out. It's not your fault David got caught in that fight."

"That's not how the people calling see it."

"Want me to take messages?"

Tempting as it was, he wouldn't do that to her. "No, I'll take my lumps when I get back."

He headed out the door, no longer sure Flo's sounded good as he walked across Kedgewick's downtown. His goal remained gaining perspective before he returned to work.

While he couldn't utilize his current clients' retainers to pay the bills, he took some comfort in knowing limited money waited in trust accounts as he and Marcus worked for clients. Even so, the economics remained strained as long as the firm relied on the county paying its bills on time—which required cases to conclude so Leigh could submit the bills. Then he had to wait for the judges to review and forward the bills to the treasurer, where the money languished until the treasurer released the funds.

Most days he liked being in Kedgewick versus making his home in the bigger cities that dotted the East Coast. There was an appeal to living in a place where you knew most people by sight . . . and often were aware of their life stories. But other times anonymity and a bigger pool of potential clients would be nice.

Chapter 5

THE RINGING PHONE SLOWLY PENETRATED Margeaux's groggy dreams. She'd fallen asleep sometime around eleven, and images of a man with a penetrating gaze had slipped into her dreams. One moment he loomed next to David Roach, the next he doused her with hot coffee. Then he towered over a table with a Kiss Me sign. So confusing and intriguing. Now as she squinted at her phone, which read 12:34, she wondered what world she lived in. She wasn't someone who met a man and then dreamed of him—no matter how much he looked like he should occupy a movie set rather than a smallish Virginia town.

The phone rang again, jerking her back to the reality of the middle of the night.

Nothing good came from middle-of-the-night calls.

"Hello?" The word croaked past her dry throat. She swallowed and tried again. "Hello?"

"Professor Robbins?"

"Yes." She pushed hair from her face and tried to place the voice.

"I need help." There was a slight musicality to the words, a rolling heaviness that was unique. Margeaux struggled to place the voice through her fatigue.

"Who is this?"

"Anneliese."

Margeaux collapsed against her pillow and groaned. When the exchange student had spent time with her over Christmas break, Margeaux had enjoyed getting to know her, but she hadn't invited calls after midnight. "How can I help you?"

"The police are here, and I do not know what to do."

"The police?" That wouldn't make sense even if she hadn't been sound asleep three minutes before.

"One of my roommates is dead. Can you help?" The faintest tremor quivered the words.

Margeaux's thoughts moved more quickly as her synapses snapped awake. "What did you say?"

"My roommate is dead."

Margeaux shook her head. She hadn't misunderstood. "I can be in Kedgewick in twenty minutes. Where will you be?"

"I am unsure." Margeaux heard murmured voices. Then the student came back. "They say the station. Where is that?"

"Are they arresting you?"

"I do not think so. They say they want to talk. Away from the scene. I do not understand."

"Tell them I will give you a ride. Don't say anything else to them." Margeaux hadn't practiced law long before moving into teaching, but Anneliese talking to the police without someone to protect her interests couldn't be a good idea. "Maybe I can call a friend who is a practicing attorney to come."

There was silence for a minute as if Anneliese chewed on the words. "Not yet. Please."

Margeaux caught her lower lip between her teeth and worried it as she considered the options. Janae slept soundly, so a call might not wake her. "All right. We'll start with me and get someone else involved if needed."

"Thank you." There was a brief pause. "My family has limited funds. Sending me here was a sacrifice." Background noise intruded, and then Anneliese spoke again. "Hurry please. They want to take me now."

Only fifteen minutes later Margeaux hurried into her car and sped onto the highway.

What situation would she walk into?

She didn't know, so she couldn't what-if during the drive, playing out and preparing for different scenarios. Instead, she wondered what it would take to save a client from terrible accusations.

She'd had no criminal cases during her short stint in private practice. Most of the stories she told her students involved other people. Other lawyers morphed into the hero, and she remained the onlooker. Maybe she could change that. If she could help someone she knew rather than a stranger, all the better. That experience would equate to leaping a building in a single bound.

Her grandmother had graduated from the University of Virginia's law school and regaled her with stories about her work on behalf of women. The women Grandma helped still kept in contact with her ten or fifteen years after she'd walked them through a divorce or bad custody situation. The connection between these women and Grandma and the respect they carried for her was powerful to witness.

Margeaux hoped she impacted her students, but using the law as a vehicle to protect and transform lives?

Part of her wanted that. Longed to know what it felt like to have that ability.

When she arrived at the apartment complex, the twirling white-and-blue lights from Loudoun County sheriff's vehicles and a lone Kedgewick police car washed the parking lot in color. There was even a Monroe College Police vehicle next to an ambulance with its lights and siren off, which indicated that whomever it had arrived to aid was beyond help. The parking lot's entrance was blocked so she found street parking, all the time wondering what happened.

Why did police want to take Anneliese to the station?

She should call Janae. She was a practicing lawyer.

But Anneliese had called Margeaux and asked her to help. Not Janae. She straightened her spine and pulled back her shoulders as she considered her next move. This wasn't a textbook. Anneliese depended on her showing up and helping. Time to do rather than read and explain what others had done.

Margeaux could delay and stare at the apartment building, waiting until one of the deputies decided she merited an investigation—or worse, one of the reporters picked up on her presence—or she could take the initiative. She might not know exactly what constituted the right next step, but generally movement ended better than waiting and responding.

After a slow exhale, she turned off the car and grabbed the keys. Then she stepped from her Sonata and strode up the sidewalk until a deputy stepped in front of her, his hands planted on his hips.

"Ma'am. You can't be here."

"One of the women who lives in the apartment called. Anneliese. Richter." She placed an artificial pause between the words as the activity behind the man captured her attention. Although he filled most of the visual space, she watched officers move in and around the building. He expanded as if recognizing that she searched behind him, and she took a half step to the left, distracted and horrified to watch paramedics roll an empty gurney up the sidewalk. "The roommate's really dead?" The call had left her with questions, but the utter lack of urgency playing out around her hammered it home.

"You need to leave." He looked like an actor with a limited role in an episode of *Law and Order* rather than an officer in Loudoun County, Virginia.

She lifted her chin until she met his hooded gaze in the light streaming from the streetlight. "Not without Anneliese." She crossed her arms so her posture mirrored his.

"Do we have a problem, Andrews?"

Margeaux about jumped from her skin at the unexpected voice. Allison Erickson was here? This was worse than she thought if the commonwealth's attorney, the CA, had bothered to leave her bed in the middle of the night.

The flashing lights distracted Chase as he skimmed the edge of campus on his drive home from a fundraiser in the city. It was late, too late. He should drive home without stopping. He had no reason to get involved.

Not when his mind spun with glimpses of what his future could look like.

He could move from chasing lights like these that warned of another tragedy and instead focus on the puzzles and problems that harmed only bank accounts.

Jim Clary's words tempted him. Sure, the pressure would remain, but it would be contained within business hours. What an amazing change from his current experience.

No more waking up in the middle of the night, drenched in sweat and wondering if he'd get the CA to settle before the case went too far and passed the point where a trial was inevitable. That point where one errant word or expression by a client could lead to them spending the rest of their days in jail if they were lucky, or stabbed to death, killed by a cruelly crafted shank, if unlucky.

Which world did he want to operate in?

He had thought he'd invest the rest of his days in defending the criminal process, ensuring the Constitution and its protections were guaranteed. Now? He needed to get out before someone else got hurt or killed.

So why was he easing to a stop?

Why was he leaving his truck?

Why was he walking up the sidewalk, eavesdropping, and opening his mouth?

He should pivot, get back in his vehicle, and escape. Now. While he still had time. That's what he should do.

"What are you doing here, Crandall?"

Shoot. Allison Erickson had seen him. He pasted on a smirk and slowly scanned until he saw her. "Saw the flashing lights and couldn't stay away."

"Why not? Have a client here?"

"No client. Just driving home."

The commonwealth's attorney made a show of looking at her watch, some sort of exercise tracker. "At this hour?"

"Guess so. There's always something happening."

Another woman wobbled on the sidewalk as she glanced between the two of them and the deputy, taking a half step back as if she needed to create some distance from whatever was happening. Margeaux Robbins. Why was she here? Nothing he could do about that, so he returned his focus to Allison before she could attach too much meaning to his presence.

Chase tipped an imaginary hat at them. "I'll be on my way."

Allison tightened the belt of her coat and hugged her arms closer. "This isn't one you want to be involved with."

"Is that professional advice?"

She considered him. "I know better than to give you anything like that. Just consider . . ." She paused, then shook her head. "Never mind." Someone called her name and she nodded before walking away.

When he glanced back toward the deputy and Professor Robbins, she had disappeared. She had used the distraction to move into the shadows and toward the door, phone attached to her ear. Just like she'd popped into court and caused a disruption that ended up costing his client his life. Good things never happened when people interfered where they didn't belong.

Chapter 6

"I'M HERE, BUT THE POLICE won't let me up to your apartment. You'll have to come to me."

Margeaux looked around as she spoke into her phone, wondering when someone would force her away from the building. So far the deputy hadn't noticed she'd slipped away, but that could change any moment. Chase Crandall had been good for a distraction.

People, many in uniform, milled around, but not as many as she expected. Maybe because Kedgewick rested far enough outside the greater DC metro area to not have large city resources. Maybe the smaller swarm would allow her to slide Anneliese to safety.

The fact Allison Erickson had arrived after midnight bothered Margeaux. She didn't really know Allison but had met the sharp woman during the last election cycle. In fact, after meeting her, the CA had spoken in Margeaux's class. The fact that the woman hadn't acknowledged her probably said more about the late hour than anything else.

Her presence felt unusual, but Margeaux didn't know the proper protocol.

Kedgewick didn't experience many deaths without clear explanations. Although Janae Simmons, one of Margeaux's dearest friends, had been questioned in the death of a local attorney last year, murders remained unusual.

But what really bothered Margeaux was the CA's conversation with Chase Crandall. He might have contributed to David's death by failing to keep the student from jail, but the man had a reputation as a decent attorney. Why had Erickson warned him off?

Now that Chase was gone, she stepped off the sidewalk and around the overgrown hydrangea bush. Would she disturb a crime scene if she wandered to the back of the building? She needed to abandon her original idea of slipping up to get Anneliese and instead do the safe thing and wait for Anneliese to meet her.

No, if safety were what she sought, she'd have stayed in bed and referred the student to someone who practiced law. The moment she left her home, Margeaux had entered a path that diverged from the clear road of wisdom. Now she needed to figure out if she could return to it.

"Miss, you can't leave."

"I have a ride, and I will leave." The slightly accented words sounded muffled but grabbed Margeaux's attention.

Margeaux stepped back onto the sidewalk with a small wave. "I'm here, Anneliese."

The petite young woman gestured toward her but kept moving. "See, my ride waits there." There was a frantic edge, one layered with fatigue, to her movements. Her clothes were dark, shadows obscuring details, and she looked like she would shatter if she stopped moving.

The uniformed officer followed Anneliese as she approached Margeaux. Margeaux put an arm around her student. "When should I bring her to the station?"

"I don't know. The detective is on his way but hasn't arrived."

"All right." She reached into her purse and searched for one of her cards. It took her too long to find one, and she felt sure the man would grab Anneliese to keep her in place. Finally her fingers closed around the rectangle of cardstock. She pulled it out and thrust it at the man. "Here. I'm sure you have Anneliese's contact info. Now you have mine.

I will make sure she comes to the station when you, the detective, or whoever needs to talk with her is ready. Until then, I'll take her somewhere to get some sleep." Even the dim light from the streetlamps couldn't hide the shadows of fatigue and stress Anneliese carried. "My car's this way." She hugged Anneliese closer and executed a quick pivot even as the officer narrowed his eyes. She'd escape before he could formulate an argument about why they couldn't leave.

Though not overly cold outside, a tremor vibrated through Anneliese as they walked from the building and the flashing lights. "We're almost there." She urged their tempo faster, feet moving down the sidewalk and toward her sedan.

Anneliese bobbed her chin in a repeated gesture—as if once she moved, she couldn't stop. "I do not know what happened. There was so much blood."

"Shh." Margeaux's gaze darted around the area. An officer followed behind them and someone, maybe a reporter, chased along as well. "Not here." She lowered her voice further. "We'll talk more when we get to my home."

"Not the police?"

"No. Not yet." Margeaux's mind spun, but she knew taking Anneliese to the station wasn't the right move. Not until she had a better idea of what happened. She might be in over her head, but she was a licensed attorney and needed to protect Anneliese from the tactics the girl didn't know to avoid.

The ride was quiet as they left Kedgewick. Margeaux turned up the heater all the way, but Anneliese didn't stop shivering, her arms wrapped around her middle and her body rocking as far as the seat belt allowed. Margeaux directed the vents toward the young woman, then turned onto Highway 704 and headed the few miles north to her small home in Hamilton. The two-lane highway was narrow, and trees encroached on the passenger side—taking on the aura of eerie monsters and crowding the road in the middle of the darkness. She kept her brights on and the speed down, leery of deer or other wildlife dashing in front of the car.

Margeaux's eyes were on the road except for quick peeks at Anneliese, who had now curled into the door, her gaze fixed out the window.

"We'll reach my house in a few more minutes."

"I remember." The words whispered into the space.

"Is there anyone you need to call?"

"I do not have my phone. The police kept all my things when I left."

Margeaux frowned but supposed it made sense. Her thoughts felt slow.

The last time Anneliese had visited, Emma had joined them for a Barbie-themed sleepover. Laughter and silliness had filled the evening along with pink-marshmallow s'mores in front of Margeaux's gas fireplace after the movie. Margeaux longed for the zaniness of that night as she struggled to start a conversation now.

"Do you want to tell me anything about what happened?"

Anneliese shook her head even before Margeaux finished. "I do not think I should." Her voice dropped lower. "I am not sure what happened."

The words settled between them, heavy and unsure. A contrast with her earlier rush to speak.

Then she rubbed her hands together and whimpered. "The blood."

As she turned into her driveway, Margeaux didn't know what to say that wouldn't sound trite. "You can clean up and then we can talk or you can sleep. In the morning we can figure out the next right steps."

"She is dead." Anneliese finally looked at her, her face shadowed in the darkness. "There can be no right steps after that."

"I disagree. There's always a right approach. Sometimes it's hard to find." She opened the car door and gathered her keys and purse as she fought a yawn. "But right now we need to rest, and then we'll figure out what happened." If it weren't the middle of the night, she'd call Janae and ask for help, but for now, that would wait for daylight.

When they entered the house, Margeaux gathered a towel and washcloth from the small linen closet for Anneliese, who then entered the bathroom. While she showered, Margeaux made up a quick bed on the couch with a tie blanket Emma had made for Margeaux. She pulled out a toothbrush and sweats for her guest and set those by the bathroom door. Then she knocked. "I've set out some things you'll need for the night."

Was hosting Anneliese the right thing for this moment? This wasn't Christmas break when she'd wanted to be part of a family for a few days. Now her roommate had been killed. Likely murdered.

If this choice wasn't right, Margeaux didn't know what else to do. She couldn't imagine dropping Anneliese at a hotel and then taking her to the police station without knowing more information. She'd handle the fallout later.

Twenty minutes later, Margeaux was drooping over a cooling mug of tea at the small kitchen table when the shower finally turned off. The girl must have lingered under the stream until the water heater emptied. When Anneliese slipped from the room a few minutes later, she'd tugged on the navy sweats Margeaux had left inside the door, the color washing out her skin. Then she hurried to the couch and dove under the blankets.

Margeaux moved beside her. "We should talk."

"I cannot right now. I am too tired."

Margeaux covered a yawn she couldn't stifle. Maybe now wasn't the best time. "All right. I have to teach in the late morning." She yawned again. "You can ride with me."

"To the police?"

"I don't know. We'll see if the police reach out in the morning. I can't imagine it will be too long." They would want to interview her roommates. Anneliese likely topped the list.

Anneliese had left the clothes she had worn in a pool on the bathroom floor. The sweatshirt was sopping wet, as if she had showered while wearing it. Margeaux frowned at the puddle of water and grabbed it to wring out and hang. As she twisted it, she noted the rust-colored stains.

She froze, the liquid dripping over and through her hands.

What is that?

Her mind whispered a word it didn't want to process. At the same time, she knew what it had to be. The reality seeped through her.

Blood.

On the sweatshirt.

It had to be.

And Anneliese had tried to rinse it out.

Why?

Margeaux hung the sweatshirt off the tub's faucet and squared her shoulders. No more delays. She *had* to have the conversation with Anneliese and find out what had happened. Only then could she decide the best path forward to help her student.

Chapter 7

ANNELIESE HAD CURLED INTO A tight ball on the small couch, which was really more of a love seat so it could fit in Margeaux's tiny home. The young woman gave a good impression of being asleep, but she couldn't simply wash evidence from a sweatshirt and avoid the issue.

Margeaux needed answers, now, before she found out later that she'd harbored a murderer.

She didn't want to believe it, but what if . . .

Could it be true?

The student Margeaux knew had held herself slightly aloof until she'd stayed with Margeaux's family during winter break. Then a different woman had emerged from the tightly constructed cocoon of wariness and observation. This one had exhibited warmth as she became fast friends with the younger Emma, and Margeaux had known bringing Anneliese here rather than letting her linger in the apartment alone had been the right thing to do. A warm camaraderie built between Anneliese and Emma over games and puzzles and mugs of hot cocoa topped with mounds of whipped cream.

Margeaux touched Anneliese's shoulder. The girl continued to play possum, but Margeaux wouldn't be deterred. "We need to talk."

Anneliese finally opened her eyes. "*Was*?" Her German accent slurred the word.

"It's time to tell me what happened." Margeaux settled onto the small cream-and-blue-striped chair she'd thrifted and re-covered by herself on a rare weekend without grading.

Anneliese struggled to a seated position, brushing light brown strands of hair from her face as she did. "I am too tired."

"If you're staying here, I need to know what you saw."

"It was awful."

"I'm sure." Margeaux bit back a sigh, because everything in her wanted to equivocate that she didn't really need to have this conversation in this moment. It could wait for a better time. But that was wrong. She wasn't trying to be mean. She had to know facts and impressions to prepare for whatever came next. Caring in this situation meant getting to the bottom of what happened in the preceding hours rather than delaying their talk. "Tell me what you can."

Anneliese rubbed her eyes as if trying to wipe away a bad vision. "The night did not open well."

"Why?"

"Lauren wanted me to leave. She did not like me to be home when she had her male friends over."

"There was more than one?"

Anneliese gave a small move of a shoulder. "It depended on the week. Some days she favored one. Other times if he wasn't her preference, she would entertain multiple young men, sometimes on the same night."

Best to figure out if there was a language difference. "What do you mean by *entertain*?"

"They came. I had to leave." She shrugged. "I do not know for certain what they did while I was not there."

Fair enough. "Do you know names?"

"Not really. She did not care to introduce me." Anneliese looked away. "Maybe she thought I would be competition? A silly fear on her part."

"Are the men not good-looking?" She couldn't imagine that since Lauren was an attractive coed.

"They are fine. It is their personalities I do not find attractive. And I do not plan to stay after I graduate, so it does not make sense to get entangled."

"Really? In my experience many international students come hoping to secure employment and a green card while they are here."

"I want to take my knowledge home. Germany needs my help more than your country." Anneliese's fingers played with the fringe on the blue blanket Margeaux had set out for her. "Everyone said I should come to the United States. No one imagined this would happen."

"What did happen?"

Anneliese twisted the edges of the blanket in her fingers as she hesitated. "All was quiet when I reached home, but the lights were on. It was strange because one of our suitemates is religious about stopping the electricity use. She turns the lights off all the time. Sometimes when I am still in the room. I am that invisible to her." She shuddered. "Tonight, all the lights were on, but no one was about. I felt something was wrong, but it was unclear."

Quiet fell and stretched.

"What did you do?"

"I called, but no one answered. When the doors are closed, none of my suitemates like me to approach, so I waited, but it was late, and I could not shake the feeling something was wrong. It is not unusual for the two on the other side to be gone or ignore me, so I began with Lauren. That's when I knocked on door, but this time it opened."

"This time?"

"She always keeps it closed." She knotted her fingers in the blanket and didn't look at Margeaux. "There was so much blood. I screamed. I think she had already died. But I left to get my phone."

"Did you check to see if she was breathing? Had a pulse?"

"There was no point." She spoke the words so flatly and matter-of-factly. "When I leaned over her, I could tell she did not move. And the blood got on me. I could not stop it from spreading. No one could survive."

"Then why go get help?"

"Because I had to try. They do that on TV."

Her words startled Margeaux, sounding off somehow. Anneliese must have noticed the reaction Margeaux tried to hide because Anneliese looked up. "What else should I have done? Left her?"

"No, of course not."

"Then why was calling the police the wrong thing to do?"

Chapter 8

IF HE DIDN'T PICK UP his pace, Chase would be late to his appointment. Jim Clary had insisted on too early at 7:00 a.m., but that didn't mean Chase should arrive fashionably late. Especially when it felt like a stage in a job interview. His speed edged on the high side when he turned onto First Street and finally found parking near Flo's Diner. He could almost taste the Denver omelet and hash browns with a side of bacon that had been his standard order until his doctor warned him he needed to make some health changes. His stomach rumbled its demand for the protein overload, and he picked up his pace to get closer to the source of sustenance. Maybe ordering it today would be okay.

After he entered, he took a minute to look around the early morning crowd to see if Jim had arrived. A tall man who had the thin build of an athlete, slightly stooped from years hunched over a desk and computer keyboard when he wasn't on a golf course, Jim was hard to miss. In-house counsel for one of the technology companies flooding the area, he wore an impeccable suit and intense expression only to surprise you with a deadpan comment.

"Can I help you, Chase?" Daisy's friendly voice eased his attention back to the moment.

"I just spotted the man I'm meeting."

"All right. I'll bring you a cup of coffee in a minute." She held up her almost-empty pot of coffee in salute and moved behind the long counter.

Flo's was an interesting throwback to a '50s diner that hadn't been updated since *Happy Days* filled the airwaves. It felt like a greasy time capsule, the black coffee being one clue. You wouldn't find a latte on the menu. The tables were old with silver edging, and the vinyl seats were patched together with duct tape—except for the room that held community meetings. That one had newer tables and chairs, the gift of a patron who tired of being poked in the behind one too many times when she attended Optimist Club gatherings.

While the setting was chaotic, the food was fantastic. His mouth salivated at the aromas assailing him as he strode between the tables, navigating between chairs that edged into the narrow aisles.

"Right behind ya."

"Thanks, Daisy." He toed out the chair opposite Jim. "Morning."

The man grinned at him, then gestured to his plate of half-eaten eggs, running his toast through the egg yolk. "About time. I'm almost finished."

"I'm here now." Chase bit back his frustration with Jim as he sank to his seat and Daisy set a white mug with the Flo's logo stamped on it in front of him. He wasn't that late. "Thanks. What's the news?"

"Hear about the murder?"

Sure, the man would open with crime, dangle it like catnip in front of him. The guy really didn't understand him. The level of crime didn't attract him. He loved the chase. The opportunity to test his mettle against another attorney. There was something intense about going head-to-head with a worthy opponent. However, he was also weary of the clients who couldn't pay and the others who wouldn't. Add in David's death, and it was enough to break even the most tenacious man.

But that wasn't what Jim wanted to hear.

Then Chase stopped. Thought about what the man had said.

"A murder? I didn't know." Not from his short drive across town.

"Student on campus killed her roommate."

Oh, Jim really was looking for a response. "You know that's the wrong way to talk about it."

"Sure. She's alleged to have killed her roommate." Jim might as well have put air quotes around *alleged*.

"What happened?"

"Unclear." He stabbed the last bite of eggs on his plate and then ran it through the potatoes. "The deputies filled campus most of the night."

"Who's your source?" Jim hadn't been on campus last night, so he shouldn't know this detail yet.

"The paper."

"That's it?"

"A birdie in the sheriff's office."

"Why would they talk to you?"

"I wanted to make sure one of the judges wouldn't lure you away from my client."

And that was the crux of the conversation. "There's a lot I need to know before I make a decision."

"I know."

Daisy sidled back up to the table. "Ready to order, Chase?"

"I'll take my usual."

She rolled her eyes. "Sometimes I swear you've turned into an old man already. What happened to the Denver omelet with bacon?" As he opened his mouth to respond, she held up her hand. "Never mind. I don't want to know. Would you like some Grape-Nuts with your oatmeal?"

"What are those?"

"Something crunchy my grandpa ate every morning." She smacked her gum and winked at him. "One bowl of steel cut oats with blueberries coming up."

"Thanks." Chase waited until she walked away, then refocused on Jim. "There's nothing wrong with protecting the system our Founding Fathers put in place."

"Sure. But you have an opportunity to pivot and work on equally important cases from the perspective of going to war where dollars are involved rather than jail sentences. I've followed you a long time, and you're a talented attorney, but you're scared of the courtroom."

"I'm not afraid." The idea was preposterous.

"You are." The words dropped into the space between them. "That's a problem for a trial attorney of any sort, but especially for a criminal defense attorney." Jim studied him, something almost caustic in his expression. "When was the last time you had a good old-fashioned full-length trial? One that went to a jury verdict?"

"The David Roach trial and that didn't go so well." He sputtered as his mind spun through his calendar and list of clients. One after another had been a plea bargain long before trial or quick negotiation at the close of the state's case. The short trial Monday didn't count since it felt like a hearing with a jury of spectators. Since David Roach's death, that wouldn't change. "What does it matter?"

"You can't be great if you never fight to the end for your client."

Chase arched a brow as Daisy slid a bowl in front of him. "Thank you."

"Sure thing. Here's your pot of skim milk to go with it. Enjoy—if that's even possible with all that healthiness." She rolled her eyes but grinned the whole time.

Chase chuckled as he picked up the small pitcher and poured some of the liquid over the oats before refocusing on Jim. "Your point?"

"Which one is your future and which is your past?"

Chase stared at him, then set the pitcher down deliberately. "This wasn't what I expected for breakfast." He picked up his coffee mug and took a sip, buying time to think. "What happened to a friendly chat as I consider my options?"

"It's that, but last night changed the situation. We both know even with your distaste for trials, you're one of the best criminal defense attorneys in our corner of Virginia. That means you'll get a call soon about representing that student. Before you do, you need to decide what you want. Don't get distracted by a crime that can't do anything for you long-term."

"There's no reason to think I'll get the call."

"There's no one else to tap. I've checked." Jim studied him, hard lines forming at the corners of his eyes and mouth. "Accept and you'll lose your shot at this job and client."

The direct comment caused him to freeze with his spoon halfway to his mouth, oats and berries ready to plummet to his lap. All the background noise fell away as his attention telescoped to one place. He returned his spoon to the bowl and studied Jim. "Why do all this at seven in the morning? This is some interesting psychology."

"Not at all. If you know what you want, there's nothing confusing about it. Take the interview and offer when it follows." Jim leaned forward, elbows bracketing his empty plate. "But if you have any doubts, now's the time to back away. My client is used to getting his way."

This area of northern Virginia was laced with powerful men. Even out here in the foothills of the mountains, the influential congregated. The drive to the District wasn't that far, not when you had someone to navigate for you.

He glanced at the oatmeal, then pushed back from the table. "I appreciate your concern, but considering I don't have an interview or know anything about this murder, it's misplaced. If you'll excuse me"—he checked his watch—"I have to get to court."

He threw ten dollars on the table and wondered if he'd just boxed himself into a career he wasn't convinced he still wanted.

The knot in his stomach suggested he had.

Chapter 9

THE SOUND OF THE RADIO blaring some folksy ballad startled Margeaux from a deep sleep. She bolted up in bed and brushed her hair from her face.

Something was wrong, deeply wrong, but what?

She didn't startle awake.

Not like this.

Years earlier, she'd gotten used to living on her small piece of land. Her house was situated in the village of Hamilton, and she could imagine she lived in the country with the open grass and trees surrounding her small home.

This was her cottage.

Her oasis.

The place no one could sneak up on her. No one could take her by surprise.

Not with the security cameras and motion-detecting lights.

Emma laughed at her when a racing squirrel would trigger those lights in its dash to hide a walnut.

But Emma would never understand what it felt like to wonder if she was safe.

Never.

Margeaux had done everything she could to ensure Emma always felt safe.

But if Emma wasn't here—which she couldn't be, not on a school day—then who was? Margeaux grabbed her robe from the side of her bed and slipped it over her T-shirt and sweatpants before stepping into slippers. She loved her hardwood floors, except on cold mornings. She was delaying. She knew it as she caught another creak of something.

Then her slow thoughts finally caught up with the noise. "Anneliese?"

The petite woman turned from the cabinets where she rummaged. "I was looking for coffee."

"It hasn't moved from your last stay." She yawned and stretched. "Why are you up?"

"It is not so early."

"Really?" Margeaux glanced at her watch and her eyes widened. "Ten o'clock already?"

The woman gave a rolling shrug. "You were tired."

"Aren't you?" Anneliese had endured the trauma of finding her roommate.

"My thoughts would not stop. I keep waiting for the police to call and demand a talk." She paused, her posture stiff. "They can do that? Demand I come?"

Margeaux took a seat on one of the three chairs at the small IKEA table she'd pressed against the wall to save room. "Sit and let's talk about what happened." Last night they had wandered through the events leading up to finding the body, but Margeaux wondered if Anneliese had remembered more in the light of day.

Anneliese approached with halting steps, as if afraid of what Margeaux would ask. She tugged out the opposite chair and perched on the very edge. "*Ja?*"

"Did you remember anything more? About last night?"

"Is that a good idea? To talk about the details?" She clasped her hands and moved them below the table's surface. "Will the police want to know who I talked to?"

"I don't know. But I can't help you if I don't know what happened."

"Maybe I do not need your help." There was a new stiffness to her posture that felt defensive.

"But you're here."

"I had nowhere else to go last night." She said it as if now she did.

"Okay." Margeaux tried not to take the brusque words personally. She should be relieved that Anneliese no longer wanted her help. It allowed her to walk away without fear of sinking into a problem she couldn't handle. She didn't know anything beyond the textbooks about handling a criminal case, so she shouldn't pretend otherwise. She bit her lower lip. But she did know the law. She taught it, after all. And she knew Anneliese. The woman would need help navigating the US legal system. "Let's get you breakfast, and then I need to get to Monroe. I'll be late for my class if we don't hurry."

Half an hour later, Margeaux had a travel mug filled with coffee and creamer in one hand and her backpack slung over a shoulder. Anneliese trailed behind her, hair hanging in damp waves around her round face. She wore the same clothes she had the prior night. But when she glanced over to make sure Anneliese had fastened her seat belt, Margeaux noticed the splashes of red. It was the same sweatshirt she'd tried to wash out the night before.

Margeaux swallowed down the bile that rose at the back of her throat. "We can't leave yet."

"You will be late."

"There's still time, and you can't wear that." She gestured at the front of the sweatshirt. "I didn't notice."

"I did."

"I'm sorry."

"I had no choice."

Such a cryptic thing to say. "No choice?"

Anneliese kept looking ahead, through the windshield, as if she could will the car to move and the conversation to end. "The deputies let me take nothing."

"I have something you can wear." Surely a dress she had would fit until they could get into Anneliese's apartment. The student was about the same height, petite in frame, but rounded in a comfortable and cuddly way. Margeaux had never lost her gymnast's lean muscular frame. She hurried from the car and unlocked the back door before hustling to the office closet that held her extra clothes. A quick flip through the hangers, and she grabbed a sweatshirt dress she'd gotten for coffee dates she never had. Its forest green color would look great on Anneliese, so she handed it to the young woman who had followed her into the room. "Let me grab some leggings, then you'll have an outfit."

"It is too much."

"No, but we shouldn't wash your sweatshirt any more than you did last night in case law enforcement needs it for any reason." Or until she'd had a chance to confirm with Janae or another attorney that they wouldn't be inadvertently destroying evidence. Margeaux dug up a pair of leggings and handed them over.

"I will change in the bathroom." Anneliese took the dress and leggings and slipped into the room.

A minute later, as she set the few breakfast dishes in the sink, Margeaux detected the washer in the bathroom initiate another cycle. "No!"

She hurried to the bathroom and knocked on the door. "Anneliese, you can't wash your clothes."

"They are the only ones I have. You said I cannot wear them."

"I also said you can't wash them. Let me in." She rattled the door's handle but it was locked. She didn't want to break down the door even if she could. "Please stop the washer. I'll take you to buy more clothes, I promise."

A very long minute later the water stopped and the door opened. Anneliese's face was pale under her sprinkle of freckles. "Are you sure I cannot wash them?"

"Yes." Margeaux opened the washer and swiped the sweatshirt from it. "Please don't do anything else to it, okay?"

"All right." Anneliese seemed to shrink. "What is going to happen?"

While her question could be about the schedule for the day, Margeaux knew the context was so much bigger than that.

"I don't know, but you won't be alone if you don't want to be." Margeaux reached out and squeezed Anneliese's hand. "I'll help if you'll let me. I promise."

Chapter 10

BY THE TIME THEY REACHED Kedgewick, no one had reached out to talk to Anneliese, so Margeaux took her to campus. "You could use my office phone to call the sheriff's office or police and learn whether they are ready to talk to you, but until then you could talk to someone on campus." Surely someone in the office of the Dean of Students or Student Legal Services could help her.

Margeaux unlocked the door to her office on the second floor of Haverson Hall and waited for Anneliese to take a seat at the small circle table. Then Margeaux sank into the chair at her desk and rubbed her forehead with one hand as she woke up her computer by jangling the mouse. "I'm not sure who would be best."

"I will wait to see what the police want to do."

"You should talk to an attorney first."

"I am." Anneliese looked pointedly at her.

Margeaux turned from her computer and gave her full attention to the student. "While I'm an attorney, I don't practice. There's a difference."

"One that will cost much money, right?"

"Yes." But it could also keep her safe and out of jail.

"Then I will talk to you."

"But you need someone who understands the process intimately."

"You can learn."

The muscles in Margeaux's neck tightened, causing shooting pain, a remnant of landing awkwardly one too many times when throwing a new gymnastics skill. This was worse than when a student had approached her a week before the final and asked to take it a different time because it landed on his twenty-first birthday. Actually, this far outclassed that. She looked to the top of her credenza where she had lined up her Little People collection of Inspiring Women. She wasn't someone who broke ground like Rosa Parks, Amelia Earhart, or Maya Angelou. She couldn't claim the courage of Sally Ride. Neither did she have the skills of Wonder Woman, despite the toys she'd been given that lined the top alongside the Little People. Normally the row brightened her day at the whimsy of being a college professor with toys in her office, but right now she wished she had good advice or answers.

"I'm just a teacher." And not even at a law school. She couldn't help Anneliese. Not really.

"But you are my teacher."

The way Anneliese looked at her as she said the words, Margeaux wanted to believe she could make that difference. But she knew the truth. She didn't like the deadlines and stricture that were outside her control. She loved organization and controlling her future. She thrived showing up for the people who needed her here. On campus. Students who wondered if they'd survive a class, but it lacked the seriousness of life or death. What Anneliese could face had those types of odds.

Her Fitbit vibrated, a warning she should gather her things and get ready for class. "I'll be back in an hour or so." She pulled out a twenty-dollar bill from her wallet. "Here's a bit of cash if you need to get anything while I'm in class."

Anneliese accepted the cash. "Thank you for this and your help." Something shuttered on Anneliese's face that concerned Margeaux.

"Where are you going?"

"Nowhere. Where could I go?"

"Just don't talk to the police alone."

"How could I? They do not know where I am."

Margeaux didn't bother to comment it wouldn't be hard to locate Anneliese because, as she mentioned, where would she go? Margeaux had given the police officer her card, so it wasn't a stretch to look for Anneliese at the college or Margeaux's house. As far as Margeaux knew, Anneliese didn't have the resources to disappear, and the police might be digging through her finances at this moment. Maybe the student would use Margeaux's office phone to call a ride, but even to reach Dulles Airport twenty minutes away would take time and money. Then she'd need more money and her passport to get home. Chances were strong her passport waited back in her apartment. The one that likely remained a crime scene.

"Don't do anything rash." Margeaux closed the door firmly behind her before hurrying down the hall and toward the stairs. If she hustled, she might make it before class began.

Seventy minutes and a dozen student questions later, Margeaux returned to her office to find it empty. Anneliese wasn't there, and she hadn't left a note. Should she search for Anneliese or trust the young adult to make her own decisions . . . even if she'd never been near a violent death before? Margeaux whispered a prayer for the student's protection and then tried to settle at her computer for some of the grading she never quite caught up on.

Sometime later Margeaux had worked her way through almost a dozen short essays when her office door opened, startling her.

"Do you still like plain lattes?" Anneliese's nose crinkled as she spoke, conveying her disgust. "You Americans and your inability to drink real coffee."

"I've seen you drink it with all the add-ins."

"Only because you met me here."

Anneliese set a cup on Margeaux's desk with a small bob of her head. "I owe you an apology. I let my stress overtake me and took it out on you.

That was not acceptable behavior. Thank you for the help last night." She settled into the chair. "This is a peace offering that took longer than I expected to acquire."

"From the museum. One of my favorites." Margeaux took it gratefully, the short night catching up with her as she fought a yawn. "Thank you."

"*Bitte.*"

She took a small sip, surprised to find the coffee almost cold. They sipped in silence for a minute.

"Have the police asked for me yet?"

Margeaux shook her head. "Nothing yet. I can call a friend to see if we should expect contact soon or call them."

"Not yet. Maybe they found someone else to harass."

Possibly, but the detective would still need to talk with Anneliese and discuss what she had seen. One look at the young woman's face made it clear, Margeaux had to dance carefully to navigate the right way to help her. If she pushed, Anneliese might disappear, and that couldn't be the best thing.

Anneliese looked at her cup. "I will stay with an acquaintance tonight. I have bothered you enough."

"It isn't a bother. Then I can help you when the police call."

"I appreciate the offer, but no. I will check with you daily, but not burden you."

Margeaux considered urging her otherwise, but maybe it was for the best.

Back at his office, Chase had scheduled the day for focused research and drafting briefs and memos for various cases. Instead, he'd spent it in a flurry of interruptions that left him unable to enter any sort of flow. He stumbled into the afternoon, wanting to throw his phone out a window or tell his assistant to pretend he'd left the office. Unfortunately, that wouldn't accomplish anything except postpone the inevitable.

His back warned him he'd lingered too long in the same position, so he stood and rolled his neck and then his hips, trying to loosen the tight muscles. When that wasn't enough, he walked to the small kitchenette to refill his thermos with water. While there, he scrolled through the headlines in the short break that he gave himself. Police weren't saying much about the campus death other than there was an ongoing investigation, but that would change. The victim was the sort that would draw sustained media attention: a beautiful young woman whose life had ended well before it should have. Her photo vibrated with life, her expression—electric and intriguing—seemed to tease the viewer closer, inviting them to lean in for a secret or conversation.

What had she really been like?

He closed the tab. It didn't matter. He hadn't known her in life and shouldn't fixate on her in death. Instead, he would focus on the living clients he had.

Still, there was something about the way Jim Clary was so certain Chase would be asked to take the roommate as a client that had his attention.

No, he wouldn't.

He never searched the backgrounds of possible clients. He wouldn't change his process now.

The last thing Chase wanted was another case that would lead to media attention while David Roach's family threatened a lawsuit. He understood they grieved the death of their son and brother. The kid had been likable, if arrogant. News of his death had stunned Chase. He still woke in a cold sweat, sheets twisted in a mess, wrestling with demons who taunted that he could have and should have done more.

That case alone should have him racing away from criminal practice and into the arms of Jim's safe corporate client.

So why was he hesitating?

He needed to get away from his thoughts, and if he didn't have time to escape for a nature walk, then he could distract himself by engaging with Leigh. She'd get his head on straight in no time or chase him back to his office.

Leigh tapped her headset as he approached, curiosity widening her eyes. "What can I do for you?"

"Any calls I need to return?"

"If there were, I would have brought them to your attention."

"Emails?"

"Same."

"Motions to respond to?"

She crossed her arms and leaned back in her chair as she studied him. "What's bothering you?"

"Can't a guy make sure he's not missing critical work?"

"Sure. But that's not my boss." Her brows crinkled and she tapped her fingers against the desktop. "What's going on?"

"Know anything about the death on campus over the weekend?"

"You mean the murder?"

"Maybe."

"The scuttlebutt among the legal secretaries has landed on murder since a young lady can't stab herself." She paused dramatically. "Multiple times."

Chase winced.

"Yeah. Sarah in the CA's office says it would give a mortician nightmares."

"And she knows . . . ?"

"Because Allison Erickson promoted her last month. Sarah said if she knew she'd have to look at images like that she wouldn't have taken the position. No amount of money is worth it. Hindsight and all that."

He rolled the idea of the photos through his mind for a minute. "They must be bad."

"Terrible." Leigh shuddered. "The things we do to each other."

"Any rumbles that I'll be appointed?"

"Do you want the case?"

"No need to sound so incredulous."

"I thought after David . . ."

"Yeah." He fought to keep his features and posture neutral, betraying nothing. He wanted to whisper a prayer for guidance and hope, but God was on the other side of a chasm. Yes, the distance came from him, but he wasn't sure how to close it yet. "Over breakfast Jim suggested the judges want me on the case."

Leigh waved away the suggestion. "What does he know? It's odd for him to say anything this early. Rumor has it the police don't have a strong suspect."

"Interesting."

She shrugged as she looked at the blinking light on her phone. "I should get this."

"Sure."

"It's what you pay me to do."

"The lowest value part of the job."

She rolled her eyes. "Crandall and Associate." She listened a moment and her eyes widened, then she hit a button. "It's David's father. He's yelling about how he'll sue you if you don't help him sue the prison."

The nightmare he couldn't quite wake up from. He really needed to find a way to reconnect with God. Trying to do this alone just left him with a heavy heart and a headache. "If I take the call, he could sue me."

"And if you don't, he says he will."

"Guess I'll take it." What else did he have to lose right now?

Chapter 11

A COUPLE OF DAYS LATER, Margeaux tried to focus on the students in front of her in class, but she felt Anneliese's absence. Where was the young woman? Since leaving to stay with her friend, she hadn't been in touch with Margeaux. She didn't need to, but that didn't stop Margeaux from worrying about her.

Time to get her thoughts back in the game. Right now that looked like lecturing in an engaging way. "The Bill of Rights doesn't apply between you and another citizen. It only applies between you and the government." Her phone vibrated in her pocket, throwing Margeaux off her rhythm for a moment. Why had she put it there? Other than the fact she never got calls, there wasn't a good reason to have it on her person when she taught. She glanced at the clock as she refocused. Five minutes until class ended. "That's why a company can fire you because of something you say on social media that the company doesn't like or thinks reflects negatively on it."

"That's not right." Joelyn crossed her arms from her seat in the second row. "They can't fire me for that. That's not a good enough reason."

Margeaux tapped her chin as she made a show of considering the student. "Does a company need any reason to fire you?"

The students groaned and then chorused, "Not if you're an employee at will."

Her phone rang again, and her smile faltered. "That's a great place to stop today. I'll see you on Friday. Avoid trouble until then."

The students sang out their good-byes as they sailed from the classroom, and she took a moment to wipe off the whiteboards as she prepared the room for the next class. When she finished, she stacked her files and textbook, then glanced at her phone as she left the classroom. She squinted at the number she didn't recognize.

She hit dial and waited for someone to pick up as she walked across campus.

"Loudoun County Sheriff's Office."

Margeaux stopped and looked around. No one lingered near her as she hesitated on the sidewalk between buildings. Those who were out strode with purpose to their next destination. "I'm sorry."

"This is the sheriff's office in Leesburg." The woman's voice sounded weary, as if tired of crank calls. "Do you need assistance?"

"No, I'm returning a call from your number."

"Who called?"

"I'm not sure."

"Did they leave a message?"

"Not that I saw before calling back."

"I'm not sure how I can help then, hon. You'll have to call back when you have a name." The woman hung up before Margeaux could ask any questions.

Margeaux sputtered a moment before checking her voicemail. A man named Detective Phillips had left a message. "I'd like to have a conversation with Miss Richter about the night her roommate died. Please have her call me."

So the detective had finally called. Probably a good thing. But she didn't want to call back. The words sounded right, but there was something in them that made her wary. It was one thing to expect a call, and another to arrange a conversation between the police and Anneliese.

Maybe she was overthinking it, and her role began and ended at messenger. She didn't need to stay involved if Anneliese continued to fluctuate about whether she wanted help. Margeaux shivered as a breeze slid down the back of her neck. She needed to keep moving and get inside. Spring approached, but Virginia didn't waltz into the season with grace. It felt more like a cold plod.

She hurried to Haverson and up the steps. A crowd of students pushed out the doors, and she stepped to the side until the flood abated. When she reached her second-floor office, Anneliese waited on the bench that rested against the wall, across the hall and two doors down. Her hair was slicked back in a short ponytail, her jeans and sweater rumpled like she'd slept in them.

Margeaux slipped her key in the lock and twisted. "Where have you been staying?"

Anneliese stood and approached her. "With a friend. She has loaned me a couch and clothes."

"Anyone I know?"

"Have you heard anything?" All right, so Anneliese didn't want to share.

"The sheriff's office left a message. A Detective Phillips wants to speak with you. He also asked you to bring the clothes you were wearing with you."

"When?" Anneliese twisted her hands together.

"I'm not sure."

"Will you go with me?"

"If that's what you want. Or we could find someone else to go."

Anneliese looked down for a moment as if considering her options. "You are who I want."

"Fine." She couldn't get into trouble for simply attending the meeting with a student. She'd be careful if things morphed into law enforcement focusing on Anneliese as the person of interest. In that rare eventuality, Margeaux would distance herself since she didn't actively practice law. But showing up for an interview should be fine.

Two hours later they walked into the Leesburg station. Margeaux held her head high, but the certainty she strode outside her area of expertise pressed against her. They stopped at the front desk and waited for the uniformed officer to end a call and look up. "We have an appointment with Detective Phillips."

"Name?" The officer didn't bother to look up from his computer screen.

"Anneliese Richter."

"Ah, the elusive witness." He jerked his chin toward the empty chairs. "Have a seat, and I'll let the detective know you're here."

"Thanks." Margeaux followed Anneliese to the vinyl chairs and settled down.

"That did not sound good." Anneliese worried her hands in front of her.

Margeaux had to agree. "Not a great beginning."

Anneliese fidgeted in the seat, as if nervous energy bubbled through her. A few strands had escaped her ponytail, and paired with the jeans and rumpled sweater, she looked even younger than her twenty-one years. She tucked her feet on the chair and placed her chin on her knees. "How long do you think this will take?"

"I don't know."

"What should I say?"

Margeaux glanced around. The lobby was empty except for a man and his attorney in the far corner of the room. She leaned closer and lowered her voice. "Only and always the truth."

"What if they do not believe me?"

"Then you keep saying the truth anyway. It's imperative that you are always honest." She had to believe that was so. The system couldn't work on lies.

The door separating the lobby from the working part of the station opened, and a man in a creased suit walked toward them. He loomed over Margeaux, and she craned her neck to look at him. His clothes carried the scent of cigarettes, indicating his vice of choice. Margeaux nudged Anneliese to stand.

He extended his hand to Anneliese. "Hello, I'm Detective Jack Phillips, and you're Anneliese Richter."

She gave his hand a small tug even as she gave Margeaux a panicked glance. "Yes."

"Glad to meet you." He turned to Margeaux. "And you are?"

"Margeaux Robbins."

"Her attorney? She doesn't need one for this conversation."

"No, I'm her professor."

Chapter 12

THE DETECTIVE BARKED A LAUGH. "Well, that's a new one. In all my years here, I can't say I've had a professor come with a witness." He turned back to Anneliese. "You brought a regular comedian with you. Ready to come back? Dr. Robbins can wait here."

"I'm not a doctor."

"Good. Don't need one of those making things more complicated."

Anneliese grabbed Margeaux's arm. "I want her to come."

"There's no need. She's not your attorney, and you don't need one. Especially if you don't have anything to hide." His tone held a jovial note, but Margeaux sensed an underlying alertness to his every movement.

Anneliese froze, and Margeaux wondered if her language skills had abandoned her in the stress of the moment. Had her thoughts returned to German and she couldn't find the English words?

"You don't have anything to hide, do you?"

"No." The word squeaked out.

"Then you can come with me, and Professor Robbins can wait right here."

Margeaux struck a power pose as she prepared to defend Anneliese. "I'm here to support Anneliese in any way she needs."

"That's great, but you've already said you aren't her attorney. You don't need to clutter the interview room."

Why was he so determined to cut Anneliese off from any support? Margeaux looked between the two, then focused on Anneliese. "Do you want me to wait out here? I can if that's what you want."

"No." The word dripped with panic. "*Bitte.*"

"All right." Margeaux raised her chin as she met Detective Phillips's gaze. This was no time to be bullied even if done with a polite edge. "We're ready to follow. Do you have a warrant for her clothes?"

"Do I need one?"

Margeaux considered what the right answer was, then nodded. She wouldn't give up evidence without one. It was too risky. And the more time that passed the better. "Yes."

He patted his pocket, then pulled out a sheet of paper. "Here it is."

She scanned it, then handed it to Anneliese. "It looks like what you need."

"All right." Anneliese pulled her backpack off, unzipped it, and pulled a grocery store bag free. "Here you go. May I have a receipt?"

"Have it your way." He made a sweeping gesture with his arm. "Come on back."

The walk to the small conference room wasn't far, but Margeaux felt a suffocating sense that the walls closed in as they left the lobby and moved into the working part of the station. He opened a door and ushered them into a small, industrial-gray room. It reeked of fear and disappointment—that, and a sense of years-long abandonment.

"Here we go. Can I get you anything to drink?"

Anneliese gave a small shake of her head and then sank to a seat.

"Thank you, we're fine." Margeaux perched on the edge of a chair, fingers itching to take notes. "First we need the receipt."

"All right." He called in an officer, who put on a pair of gloves, took a couple of photographs of what was in the bag, pulled it out, took more photos, and then finally placed everything in a paper bag he sealed and stickered. Then the officer filled out a form that he gave to Anneliese. After he left, Detective Phillips settled at the table. "Let me get down to it. Anneliese, you're here because you called 911 about finding your roommate's body, and then before I or any other investigating officers arrived, you disappeared."

"I did not. I told the officer I had a ride."

He held up his hand. "Sure. But you left without talking to us."

"I did not. I answered many questions." She looked at her hands, flipped them over, as if seeing the blood on them still. "Then they left me alone." She shivered. "It was a terrible night."

"I'm sure." He settled, his hands clasped on the table, and Margeaux guessed there was a recording device hidden somewhere.

"Are you recording this conversation?" She gestured around the room. "Are there microphones somewhere? Because if so, you should alert Anneliese."

He glowered at her from his seat. "I thought you weren't her attorney."

"I'm not. I'm a concerned friend, but one who knows quite a bit about the law. I would be a terrible friend if I didn't ask that question." Then she glanced through the window that looked two-way. "And who's on the other side?"

"No one that I'm aware of." But his gaze skirted to the mirror before flicking back to hers, enough to make her think her instinct wasn't off.

Now Margeaux leaned forward. "I want to make it clear for whatever recording you have that Anneliese hasn't been Mirandized, and this is a noncustodial conversation. She came voluntarily to answer questions and has remained willing to do so since the evening of the death. However, she has not waived any of her rights and won't do so." She met his gaze with all the intensity she could telegraph. "Are we clear?"

His posture tightened. "Yes." Then he turned to Anneliese and his body language loosened. "Miss Richter, when was the last time you saw your roommate alive?"

"Around eight Sunday evening."

"What were you doing?"

"She had men coming over, so it was time for me to leave."

"Why?"

"That was normal."

"Where did you go?"

"Out."

"Can you be more specific?"

"I walked campus. Spent time at the library. When enough time passed, I went home."

"When was this?"

"When did I call 911?"

"Why?"

"Because I got home five or ten minutes before." The interchange happened without hesitation.

"The records show you called at 12:15 a.m."

"Then it must have been about twelve. You have my phone."

"Did anyone see you?"

"I do not think so. I did not see my other two roommates."

"What did you see?"

"A quiet apartment with all the lights on. So I looked for people. That is why I went to Lauren's room. It was too quiet."

"That was unusual?"

"With the lights on? Yes." Anneliese shrugged. "If she was gone, all the lights would be off. She wanted to protect the environment. At least with the easy solutions."

"When did you enter her room?"

"When she did not answer."

"Why then?"

"It all felt wrong." Anneliese shivered and rubbed her arms. "I knew something was wrong."

"What did you find?"

"Lauren on her bed, her chest wet with blood." She covered her mouth and closed her eyes.

Detective Phillips let the silence stretch. "What did you do?"

"I tried to see if she was alive. Then I called for help."

"Why that order?"

"What if calling would have taken too long? I wanted to try. She may not have liked me, but I never wished her harm."

"Come on. You were roommates. You want me to believe you didn't do more to help her?"

"I did what I could."

"The blood didn't scare you? You weren't concerned the killer still lingered?"

Anneliese paused as if searching for words. "I did not know what to do."

"Really?" There was such skepticism in his tone.

Anneliese trembled in the chair. "I did what I thought I should."

"Sure." He considered her for a long minute. Then he suddenly leaned forward, and Anneliese flinched as if he'd slapped her. "Did you really find her like that? Or did you stab her? Maybe throw her into the wall first?"

"No, why would I do that?" Anneliese's eyes widened and the color drained from her face. "I would not hurt her."

"Maybe you didn't mean to, but the neighbors got a load of yelling."

"It was not me."

"They definitely got an earful of Lauren yelling and were used to her yelling at you. So used to it they ignored it."

"Why would they do that? Could they have saved her?"

"Call it the bystander effect, I don't know. Smarter people can fill in the fancy terms. What I do know is you had an argument with her and it turned violent."

"I did not hurt Lauren." Anneliese yelled the words as she clutched the table with tight fingers.

Margeaux put a hand on Anneliese's arm and turned to Detective Phillips. "We're done for now. If you have evidence that supports your wild allegations, you can call me or you can give Anneliese her phone back and call her. Unless that happens, she won't sit for your badgering questions." She pushed back her chair and nudged Anneliese. "Let's go."

Detective Phillips let them stand, but when her hand touched the door, he laughed. "You think you're so smart. The professor with all the answers." He leaned back and crossed his arms. "Miss Richter, think carefully about who you trust to defend you. They might send you straight to jail."

Margeaux turned slightly to meet his gaze. He arched a brow as he stared right back.

"If you walk out now, this isn't over."

"It is for now." And she took Anneliese's arm and left.

Margeaux took her to get a pay-by-the-minute cell phone. Then, with reluctance, Anneliese shared the location of her friend's apartment where Margeaux could drop her off. Margeaux drove her back to Kedgewick and headed home to spend a quiet weekend, before she received her next call from Anneliese.

Chapter 13

CHASE'S WEEK STARTED WITH ANOTHER Monday morning motion hour. The courtroom buzzed with activity, the sort that was unusual during that time. Magistrate Judge Frank Beaver looked like he'd sucked on a lemon all morning as he looked down from the bench, and Chase wasn't eager to work his way to the front. Maybe he'd hang back and wait to see if anything put the man in a better mood. It didn't look like he could land in a worse one at this point.

A couple more people moved to the front for their turns, had low-volume huddles at the bench, and then the auxiliary consultations buzzing in the room quieted. There at the front stood Professor Robbins. Funny how he'd barely seen her two months ago, and now he ran into her everywhere. She grimaced when she made eye contact. Guess he wouldn't wander over and say hi.

He couldn't blame her for the reaction. Not really. But it would be nice if she could acknowledge that life had a way of causing mishaps and accidents. Then he sighed. His choices regarding David ended up being much bigger than a mistake. Chase still wondered if he could have done anything different, but reality made that unlikely. Sometimes there was only so much a lawyer could do. Once the client walked into jail, Chase's little bit of influence evaporated, but that concept would elude someone like the professor, who remained aloof from the real process of law. David's death didn't land at any one person's feet. Where he lived, the law got messy and erratic. It didn't fit in the neat pages of a textbook.

Ms. Robbins stiffened as if bracing for a body blow. Why? When he looked closer, he noticed she had a frazzled air rather than her normal perfect poise. Bags filled the area under her eyes, and her hair didn't fall in its classic twisty thing at the base of her neck. Instead, she looked like she'd gone a round with the wind on her way into the courthouse and hadn't come out the victor.

Suddenly the doors at the back of the courtroom opened, and a young woman in handcuffs walked in.

Chase didn't want to stare but did anyway, along with most of the people in the room. What was it about knowing what you would see? The local media had blazed with the news of the student's arrest on Friday evening, a cheap shot by the police and commonwealth. She couldn't get her initial day in court after business hours, so she'd spent the weekend in jail—unnecessary had she been arrested and processed on a weekday before five.

Anneliese Richter had a soft beauty the media would love. She looked like the wholesome girl next door, not someone who would have thrown and then stabbed her roommate violently. Yet police believed that had happened, at least as the media reported it.

Now as sheriff's deputies guided her forward, the white shirt and pants of the jailhouse garb lightened her pale complexion and made her seem like she hadn't seen the sun for years rather than a couple of days. She looked nervous, and he wondered if anyone had told her that criminal proceedings moved quickly in Virginia. She'd have her day to tell her story to the judge and jury within a few months if no one slowed things down in a dramatic fashion.

He glanced around, looking for her attorney.

Jim Clary's words came back to him from the prior week when the man had believed Chase would land the murder representation.

Then more movement caught his attention. Jim slid into a seat in the back of the courtroom, tucked in a corner where Chase could easily miss him.

Huh.

Had he come to make sure Chase didn't get assigned the German student?

It doesn't matter.

The student wouldn't face Magistrate Beaver on her own.

She couldn't.

That wouldn't go well on the best day, let alone on a day when the man looked like horseradish had climbed his sinuses. No one stepped next to her as if prepared to walk through this hearing with her. Chase hated the injustice of it. This would not go well for the international student. While both Germany and the United States were part of the Western world and had similar laws, she should not navigate this on her own.

But he wouldn't volunteer to insert himself into the mess either.

Not when he had questions about whether he belonged in criminal work or should step into the clean lines of corporate law. Jim Clary lingering behind pushed him closer to the edge too. He'd heard some corporate clients expected their lawyers to practically worship at their feet, but he hadn't even accepted the job. Could he deal with someone like Jim constantly monitoring him?

The deputies stopped her in front of the raised bench.

Judge Beaver cleared his throat. "Where's your attorney?"

Miss Richter looked up at him and then down at her hands shackled in front of her. "I do not have one."

"No attorney or any representation?"

"I asked someone to help, but she said she cannot."

"Why is that?"

"I have no money, and she is a professor. Says she does not practice." The young woman wrinkled her nose as she said the word, as if unsure what *practice* meant in that context.

The judge harrumphed. "You need a real attorney." He looked over his reading glasses at those in the large room, then back at her. "And you have not had an attorney appointed in a prior hearing?"

She bit her lip and looked down.

"You'll need to answer so the reporter can pick it up."

"No, sir." Her voice was soft and lightly accented, but it carried enough to reach Chase's ears. What thoughts cycled in her mind?

He turned from the scene playing in front of him and scanned for his client. Another DWI. If he didn't know better, it'd be easy to think the only thing students did at Monroe was party. The kid still hadn't shown up and, at this rate, risked missing the hearing slot altogether. That wouldn't go over well with good ole Beaver. The man ran a tight ship and reminded everyone he was the most important person in the room. That made him a small man, but a powerful one in that space—a bad combination.

"Crandall."

Chase kept looking. The judge had no reason to call his name. Not now.

"Mr. Crandall."

"Chase." Larry Neeley nudged him. "The judge is trying to get your attention."

Chase glanced back to the front of the courtroom. "Why?"

The other attorney shrugged. "Who knows? Good luck."

"Why does that sound like a benediction?"

"Maybe 'cause it is." The man's laugh sounded hesitant and forced.

Chase pushed to his feet and strolled to the front near the bench. "Your Honor."

"Crandall, this young woman does not have an attorney."

"I'm sorry to hear that." He glanced at the accused. There was something forlorn and wistful about her. Something a jury could lean into if guided toward her.

"Good, because I'm appointing you as her counsel."

"You can't do that."

"Yes, I can. You're on the county list, and you are below your full quota at the moment."

"The county hasn't paid its last bill." Another reason he needed to leave the criminal side of the law. It was a lose-lose situation in his experience, and his creditors circled like sharks sensing blood in the water, blood that wouldn't disappear unless he had actual money. Leigh could only work so many miracles robbing Peter to pay Paul in any given month.

"Take it up with the county clerk."

"That's what you said last time."

"And it's what I'm saying again." Something almost brittle shadowed his expression. "This young woman needs an attorney and you're it."

But he had to know Chase didn't have much fight left. He couldn't stomach the risk of a trial and another client ending up in jail where they could be caught in a terrible fight. He wanted to avoid the recurring nightmare that interrupted his sleep each night. Taking on a case this high profile and high-risk was the opposite. He couldn't just plead this one out. Not if he wanted to do a good job.

"She might have an opinion on it."

The judge turned to her. "Ms. Richter, do you have funds to hire an attorney?"

"No, sir, I still do not."

"Are you asking this court to appoint one for you?"

"If that is the correct process, then yes. *Bitte*."

"All right. Then meet Chase Crandall, your new attorney."

As her hopeful gaze settled on him, Chase felt a rock fall into his middle. Did he have the fire to fight when a plea might work better for a client in the long run by keeping them alive? But that wasn't right either, because if David had fought, he probably wouldn't have gone to jail. That's where his thoughts muddled.

He couldn't see how a plea would work in this student's favor.

There were times to stand and fight, and a murder charge was that unless the evidence was rock-solid against her.

When Judge Twain had mentioned appointing him to more cases, he'd planned to avoid them by steering clear of courtrooms when he could. Eventually someone else would be tapped and he'd escape. Now it didn't matter if his DWI client showed up. His day couldn't get worse.

Chapter 14

MARGEAUX SETTLED MORE DEEPLY INTO one of the fold-down chairs that reminded her of her high school auditorium. She already felt like she hadn't slept since the police had arrested Anneliese Friday evening, and now the judge appointed Chase Crandall as her attorney? The nightmare was exploding, and she couldn't escape.

The door opened, and a moment later a chair squeaked as Janae Simmons pressed on it and sank next to her. "Sorry I'm late." She set down her briefcase. "Why's Chase Crandall talking to the judge?"

Margeaux leaned toward her friend. "Your delay means the judge appointed that man as her attorney."

"Shh." Janae practically put a hand over Margeaux's mouth. "You're kidding."

"I wish." Margeaux sighed. "How can we fix this? Wait. You're here. Get up there and tell the judge you were delayed but want the case."

"That won't work."

"Why?"

"Judge Beaver likes me about as much as you like Mr. Crandall."

"That bad? What did you do?"

"Ran against him for bar president."

"And won." They whispered the words together.

Margeaux couldn't believe she'd forgotten that bit of bar scandal. "You're right. Anneliese needs every bit of help she can solicit."

"Chase is a good attorney. Great actually. He could represent her exactly the way she needs."

"I don't think so. His client who died?"

Janae waited.

"That was my student. I won't let him hurt another one."

"They aren't exactly yours."

"You know what I mean. David had his family and a swarm of people who could help him. Anneliese is in a country that isn't hers, and she's on her own. She needs someone to guard her."

"And you've appointed yourself."

"I guess." Margeaux shivered. "I don't want to see her get hurt too."

Janae took her hand and squeezed, grounding her in place. "What happened to David was tragic, but not necessarily Chase's fault. Anneliese will be okay. Besides, you can make sure Chase does his job." She sighed. "Though you really don't need to. There's a reason he's won so many Defense Attorney of the Year awards."

"I'm sure he'd love me poking around and noticing everything."

"He won't have a choice. Especially if you get her parents involved. They must be frantic, and I imagine it would comfort them to know someone helped them protect their daughter."

"I like the way you think." It would be messy but might work. She blew out a breath as she asked God to give her grace to let go of the bitterness that was taking root in her heart. She didn't like the press of anger building against a man she didn't really know.

Margeaux half tuned in as the judge walked Anneliese through some questions related to her financial status. After satisfying himself that she couldn't afford an attorney, he banged the gavel. "I appoint Chase Crandall as your attorney for purposes of this case. The commonwealth will pay your legal fees related to these charges."

"Or not pay." Chase probably meant to mumble the words, but Margeaux overheard them from where she sat.

"Excuse me, what did you say?" Judge Beaver leaned forward as if he'd like to crawl over and have a conversation with Chase.

Chase straightened. "Nothing of consequence."

"Then keep your editorial comments to yourself. Understood?" The judge glared at him, making Margeaux glad she waited a good distance away, so the heat didn't scorch her. "Bailiff, please escort Miss Richter to the side room where she can become acquainted with her attorney."

"What about bail?" Chase seemed at ease with what to ask.

The bailiff didn't move toward Anneliese, who waited for the hearing to conclude.

"What about it?"

"My client shouldn't wait in jail."

"Where will she stay? She was arrested after breaking in to an apartment."

"It was my apartment." Anneliese's voice was soft but firm. "I did nothing wrong."

Allison Erickson hurried up. "Sorry, Judge. But without a place to stay, the defendant needs to remain in jail."

Margeaux took her feet. "Your Honor, she can stay with me until the apartment is released. She's already done so over winter break."

"You are?"

"Margeaux Robbins. I teach at Monroe College."

"And you will accept responsibility for her?" The man turned his glare on her, but she refused to wither.

"Yes."

"Commonwealth?"

Allison turned and studied Margeaux. "No objection at this time, but we reserve the right to change our mind if we find evidence the defendant is a flight risk. She is from Germany."

"Fine. She can be processed and released to Margeaux Robbins, and I'll require the normal bond." He turned to Chase and the commonwealth's attorney. "Don't let this matter linger. Get your evidence wrapped up and the trial underway. Cases like this are better completed."

"Better for whom?" Chase's eyes widened enough to let her know he hadn't meant to speak up.

The judge's nostrils flared and his color heightened. "One more editorial comment, and I'll have you thrown in jail for contempt. You are warned."

"Your Honor, a race to trial isn't best for the defendant."

"You know this from seeing her for a minute? Then you're a mind reader."

"No, but I know that in a case like this, we should proceed with deliberation."

The judge arched an eyebrow. "You should every time."

"Yes, but even more when the case has international implications."

She'd give him credit for thinking quickly on his feet. It hadn't taken Chase Crandall long to read the complexities. A foreign exchange student caught in the host country's legal system was a nightmare for all involved. She'd been up for hours studying the documentaries on Amanda Knox in horror. Easy answers eluded situations like this.

Janae leaned toward her. "Told you he's good."

Margeaux had to agree, but kept her attention focused on the drama playing out in front of them.

"Meet with your client. You can lecture the court after you understand what's involved with your case."

"Who is the speedy trial better for?"

"The law is clear that a defendant is entitled to quick process."

"It's not in her best interests to have—"

The judge raised his hand. "That's enough. This isn't a hearing for oral argument." He turned to the court reporter. "It's time to call the next case."

Chase stared at the man a moment, then pivoted sharply on his heel. "I need to find my client. The one I came here to represent."

Anneliese hesitated a minute, her mouth open and hands still handcuffed in front of her. "Excuse me."

No one turned her direction.

She cleared her throat and tried again. "Excuse me."

Janae stuck her fingers in her mouth and whistled before quickly covering her ears as if she were innocent.

"Ouch." Margeaux hissed.

"It got everyone's attention." Janae showed no remorse, and the corner of her mouth twitched as if she fought a laugh.

Anneliese had frozen as all eyes fastened on her. "Can someone tell me what to do now?"

The court reporter leaned forward and waved her over. "Follow your attorney, honey." Then she frowned. "Well, if he's finished for the morning."

"My attorney?" Anneliese's forehead wrinkled and her shoulder scrunched toward her ears as if she couldn't comprehend anything more.

"The man who just argued with the judge." The woman lowered her voice, and Margeaux had to strain to catch her continued consult with Anneliese. "It didn't go well, but it shows he'll fight for you."

Anneliese acquiesced, then turned and scanned the courtroom, stopping when her gaze landed on Margeaux. She hesitated then moved toward them. "Hello."

"Anneliese, have you met my friend Janae?"

Janae extended her hand. "We met briefly this winter. I hope it's all right that I came. I wanted to be close in case you needed anything."

"Where did my attorney go?" She wrinkled her nose at the end as if the word tasted bad.

"We'll help you find him." Margeaux looked around and noted the judge scowling at them. "We should probably leave and talk out there." She took Anneliese's arm.

Janae led the way to the courthouse rotunda. "Judge Beaver can tip toward grouchy easily as a horse turns to bite at flies." She scanned the open space between the second-floor courtrooms. "I don't see Chase, but we can probably find him at his office."

A deputy walked up. "It'll take an hour to process this young lady from the jail and about that long for you to get the bail bond."

Margeaux groaned. "That'll be a new experience."

Janae turned to Anneliese. "Keep your chin up as they take you through the paperwork, and we'll see you in an hour."

Anneliese swallowed and then slowly followed the deputy away.

Margeaux watched her leave, and then looked at Janae. "What should I do now?"

"If Chase's hearing is like the others scheduled during these motion hours, it shouldn't take long. Otherwise it would have a designated time slot." She glanced at her watch. "We can use that time to get Anneliese through processing."

"Why do you think he's so reluctant to take on these cases?"

"He didn't used to be, but I've heard rumors the county has slowed down payments, and some attorneys are frustrated." Janae shrugged. "Personally, I think it's because attorneys aren't getting the paperwork submitted promptly, but what do I know? Chloe handled that for me the few times a judge assigned me a criminal defendant."

Margeaux considered the information. "Why don't you still get appointed?"

"I finally convinced the judges I really wasn't a criminal defense attorney. It takes a special person, and that really isn't my specialty. I didn't want to miss something detrimental." Janae looked at her watch again. "Do you want me to meet you at Chase's law office?"

Margeaux wanted her to come, but noted how she kept glancing at her watch. "I think we'll be okay. Thanks for coming to the hearing."

"Always." Janae gave Margeaux a quick hug. "Call if you need anything."

An hour later, Margeaux and Anneliese walked out of the jail and to Margeaux's car. Anneliese stopped for a moment to soak in the sunshine before slipping into the passenger seat and strapping on the seatbelt. She didn't say anything, and the silence felt heavy.

After Margeaux edged onto the street, she observed the young woman. "You okay?"

"I do not know. What is happening? Will I be all right?" She took a shuddering breath. "Will this man help me, or should I find someone else? I have no money, and they still did not let me take my purse and wallet from the apartment. Without that I remain trapped."

"Your parents can help get your documents and credit cards re-sent to you. The police will have to release your apartment soon. Chase should have answers to questions like that. Meeting with him can't hurt anything." She tried to infuse her words with positivity, but it took effort. Maybe he'd surprise her, and she could forget he'd been David's attorney. After all, he'd done all right in court. Performed an impressive tap dance with the judge, if she let herself be honest. Maybe she could see him and not want to ask why he hadn't done something more for David.

But she doubted it.

Because her first impression remained her strongest.

Chase Crandall was the last person who should represent Anneliese Richter, and it was up to Margeaux to make sure he couldn't harm this student.

Chapter 15

POUNDING TENSION RATCHETED THROUGH CHASE'S neck and shoulders as he pulled into his slot behind his storefront office. After parking, he leaned against the headrest. His phone buzzed, but he ignored it again. What would he tell Jim? The man had seen what happened. Chase had been appointed counsel for the accused college student.

Jim had lurked in the courtroom, but when Chase looked for him afterward, he had disappeared. He must have seen that the magistrate roped Chase in. How could any client hold that against him? Especially given the accused.

The girl seemed scared of her shadow, overwhelmed by every element of the small hearing.

What would she do if this proceeded to trial?

Unless he could prepare her well, she'd collapse in front of a jury.

Today's pressure was nothing compared to what would come.

He strode into the office and tried to relax. Here he ruled his domain—from the crisp gray walls with wood paneling and black paint details to the laminate flooring. He'd salvaged what he could when he made the decision to build his office in Kedgewick rather than Leesburg. Everyone asked why he didn't move to the more largely populated area. But he'd wanted the chance to stay closer to his roots and rebuild a portion of a dilapidated downtown block. He still had work to do on his apartment on the second floor, but that couldn't take priority when he had to serve his clients . . . even if they only sometimes paid the bills.

He felt the bitterness in his bones. The idea was that if he worked this hard, the rewards would come—or at least a living wage with enough extra that he could make payroll each month without stress.

When he'd started his practice, he'd believed this was the path God had placed him on, but each step had evolved into a bone-crushing journey. Was it wrong to want a little ease and relief?

He hoped not, but the twist in his gut made him wonder if he wanted the wrong things.

Leigh glanced up from the computer where some sort of superhero movie played in a small square while she worked on evidence. He didn't know how, but the movie she'd seen a hundred times somehow focused her mind while she flipped through the thumb drive of images. "How'd court go?"

"Got appointed to the campus murder."

Her mouth formed an O, and she slipped out her earbuds. "I'm sorry?"

"Seems like the right response." He flopped onto one of the empty chairs that he'd gotten at a church rummage sale. They'd seen better days but gave people a place to sit. "Judge Beaver wants everything fast-tracked. He acts like we're part of the rocket docket rather than small-town Virginia."

"He's not ready for semiretirement. Said he wanted to stay active while his youngest attended college."

"Then he shouldn't have stepped down." That statement wasn't fair. It had been more of a highly encouraged step, but Beaver had directed his time and frustration into the smaller domain of magistrate. As this morning had demonstrated, it didn't work well for many who appeared in front of him.

"What are you going to do?"

"Try to convince this young woman that anyone else would fill the role better for her."

"Then you might want to get ready. The young woman is strolling down the sidewalk. And if I'm not mistaken, that's my old teammate Margeaux Robbins with her. I babysat her sister a long time ago." A funny look covered her face, then she blinked and it disappeared.

Chase grimaced and turned for the hall. "Thanks for the warning."

"I'll stall them a few minutes, but Margeaux has always been no-nonsense in a protective way. She cares deeply about others but hides it under a tough veneer." She handed him a stack of mail. "I haven't sorted it, but it'll buy you a bit of time and distraction."

"Thanks." He'd take the opportunity to get a few minutes in his office to develop a strategy. Normally, each court-appointed client meant sure payment eventually, but the slowdown combined with the pressure from Jim Clary made him leery.

Why did Jim insist Chase stay away from Anneliese Richter?

Something about that made Chase want to dig in his heels and press forward with the student's case. Not a good idea.

When he got stubborn, bad things tended to happen.

He plopped the stack of oversized envelopes on his desk. Attorneys had to file most court documents electronically, so he wondered if anything other than junk filled them. He sank onto his chair and riffled through the pile, stopping at the second one since it was addressed to his attention without a return label.

He grabbed the letter opener from the center drawer of his desk and slit the envelope. Instead of a cover letter, a half sheet of paper was clipped to the packet.

Will file this with the court in two weeks if you don't agree to mediation. Client is adamant that something should be done regarding son's death.

Bile climbed Chase's throat as he yanked the note off and looked for the name of the plaintiff. David Roach Sr.

He leaned back with a groan and put his hands in his hair, elbows tented over his face as he swiveled his chair from side to side. He couldn't convey to the family how much he regretted not talking David Jr. out of his plan to stay in jail. The kid had thought that a few nights in jail would be better than asking his dad for more money. Especially after his dad made a big issue over the prior time. David had been determined to handle the rest of the "mess" on his own. It had spiraled beyond Chase's control so fast, he couldn't stop the tsunami, but it shouldn't have ended David's life.

No one expected he'd get caught in a jailhouse brawl. One misplaced punch and his life ended, but the impact continued to ricochet through many lives.

How could Chase show the family that David's death hadn't been anyone's fault but was, instead, a tragedy? Chase had advised the kid against going to trial with the felony charge, but also saw how the other options could have harmed David's career ambitions.

The fact was, Chase understood their need to blame someone, but coming after him wouldn't solve anything.

Leigh's extension beeped his phone, and Chase tapped the speaker. "Send them on back."

He had to get it together. As much as he didn't want the case, for right now Anneliese Richter was his client, and he had to give her the best advice he could.

Leigh kept up a running commentary as she led Anneliese and Margeaux to a small conference room. "Make yourselves comfortable."

"Thanks." Margeaux waited for Leigh to ask about Emma, but she stepped to the door.

"Sure thing." Leigh hurried back down the hall, and Margeaux stood until Anneliese picked a seat.

The young woman had the vacant look of someone in shock. At the same time, she couldn't stop fidgeting, as if nervous energy insisted on slipping from her twitching fingers.

From her seat next to Anneliese, Margeaux took in the exposed brick on the outside wall and rough painted plaster on the other three walls. She didn't want to wait here. Work continued to pile up in her office, papers and exams that wouldn't grade themselves, but she also couldn't leave Anneliese to navigate her defense on her own.

After what seemed like an hour—the wall clock timed it at ten minutes—firm steps came down the hall, followed a moment later by a rap on the doorframe. "I see you found my office."

"We did." She kept the phrase short because she didn't want to question him on why he hadn't interacted with Anneliese at the courthouse. Making them find him didn't settle well with her, but she had to let that go and focus on how he could help Anneliese. Everyone told her he was the best and the judge had appointed him, so maybe she should be relieved instead of fixating on what happened to David. Maybe there was grace in the appointment.

As she looked at Anneliese, she vowed she'd try to give Chase the benefit of the doubt.

Chase shoved his hands in his back pockets, then visibly relaxed his shoulders. "Look, we need to come to an understanding." He studied Anneliese. "I'm sorry about the situation you find yourself in, but I can't serve as your attorney."

She scowled at him. "You do not have a choice. The judge assigned you."

Chase settled opposite her. "You want an attorney who can do a good job. I have too much work to do to add a trial like yours."

"You mean you do not want to do the work."

"No. I couldn't."

Anneliese glanced around, and then focused on him. "You are not overrun. You could if you chose."

Margeaux tried to bite back the grin that wanted to grow. Anneliese didn't need her here for anything other than moral support. She defended herself just fine.

The young woman leaned forward, elbows planted firmly on the table. "You do not have a choice other than to work hard for me. Otherwise, you will be on the wrong side of a judge, which is bad."

"She has a point." Margeaux held up her hands in a placating motion. "We need to focus on what Anneliese needs."

"That's what I'm trying to do." He studied the student. "You need someone who can concentrate exclusively on this case, because the judge wants it fast-tracked. That won't be possible with the other cases I have."

Sounded like a stretch to Margeaux. "How about we focus on what should happen next." She noticed Chase's jaw clench and held up her hand to forestall his argument. "Listen, we can waste our time on why I don't trust you, and we can talk about whatever your issue is. Or we can figure out why the police targeted Anneliese."

"That's easy." Chase waved a hand in the air like he was flicking a fly. "She put herself at the scene and left incriminating evidence."

"You know this how?"

"Without evidence, they wouldn't have arrested her. Talking is one thing. Arrest elevates it to a whole 'nother level." He scrubbed his face and looked like he hadn't slept in a long time. "I need some coffee. Can I get either of you anything?"

"No." Margeaux turned to Anneliese. "You need anything?"

"Water?"

"Great. I'll be back." Chase lurched to his feet and fled the small room as if someone chased him.

A moment later, Margeaux followed. She spotted him turning into a doorway, and when she entered, he was hunched over the sink. Where had the cocky man from the courtroom gone? In this moment, he didn't look like he could defend anyone.

"I just needed a minute." The words were a growl, low and pained.

She hesitated but continued with tempered words. "There is a young woman in your conference room who needs you to show up in a serious way. She is about to have the fight of her life, and that judge this morning decided you are her attorney. You're her person. I can't represent her, but I can make sure you do your job and fight for her." David Roach's face floated into her mind, and she fought back a lump that wanted to block her throat. "You didn't do that well for my other student, but I will make sure you do your best for Anneliese. I will not let her fight this alone."

He snorted. "You don't know what you're talking about, and that can be deadly. Just ask David Roach."

She went still. "What does that mean?"

She didn't want to hear, even as she knew she needed to hear, what he thought he knew.

"Taking his case to trial was the worst possible decision. If we'd pled to a misdemeanor, I could have had him on a suspended sentence that would have never hit his record if he avoided a second DWI."

"That wasn't good enough."

"It would be better than being dead." His words barreled into the space between them, expanding until they pushed the air from her lungs.

"That's not fair."

"No, it's truth." He pointed at her. "You blame me for his death. Well, think about this. You're the one who gave him the bad advice that landed him in jail." He stabbed his finger toward his chest. "Not me."

Margeaux blanched, his words burning through her righteous anger. The edge of truth stung, but she pushed back. How dare he throw her in the fire? "I never gave David specific advice. That's unethical. But I can't prevent students from taking a lecture out of context. If he did, that's not my fault, and a good lawyer would talk his client out of foolishness." She pivoted and fled, the heat of guilt licking at her heels.

Chapter 16

THE SOUND OF RETREATING FOOTSTEPS echoed almost as loudly as the words that had been tossed at him. Margeaux had a petite frame but a large spirit, and she didn't hold back. But he should have. It had felt good to strike back, but now Chase could admire her fight even as he regretted the verbal punch. Then again, maybe he didn't regret it. Not really. Not when he knew she didn't take ownership for her part in the tragedy. They had each played a role.

He hadn't done one thing wrong with David Roach's case, but he lived every night with the aftermath of the young man's death. He couldn't close his eyes without seeing the images of David's battered face and body, and that left him thrashing with questions he couldn't answer. Could he have done anything different? Anything that could have kept David safe?

It hadn't taken David's father long to decide to extract a pound of flesh from Chase, all while the court forced him to take on the defense of another college student.

He didn't want to be here, but the law didn't provide an exit ramp.

He had no choice but to make this work. And he had to do it fast, before word got out that Chase Crandall was cracking. The only question was how to do it.

He breathed out a prayer for strength and peace, then waited for either to arrive.

How was he supposed to help this international student with an impossible case?

"You okay, boss?" Leigh's voice brought him back to the moment.

"Sure."

"Good, because your client doesn't look so hot, and I don't blame her. It's not reassuring to have your attorney bail before you've really met." She brushed past him and filled a glass with water. "Here. Drink this, then snap out of it, and go help that girl. She needs your best."

He gulped down the glass, then paused. "Wait. What do you know?"

"Nothing for sure, but I don't like what my brother isn't saying." Leigh's brother was a newer deputy and often inadvertently passed information to Leigh. She had a sixth sense for what was important.

"All right." He squared his shoulders and picked up a glass of water for Anneliese. He couldn't do a thing about David, but he could do something for Anneliese, and it began by hearing her story.

After introductions and a few minutes of awkward small talk, he launched into strategy. "We don't have much time if the commonwealth moves forward as fast as I anticipate. In Virginia we can go from an arrest to a murder trial in a few months."

Margeaux did an admirable job staying quiet, though her twitching and shifting telegraphed how difficult she found it.

"What do I do?" Anneliese's gaze bounced from his.

He waited until she looked at him. "What happened that night?"

"I already told her." She pointed to Margeaux.

"Now you need to tell me." He turned to Margeaux. "I'm hiring you for her case. If you're uncomfortable with that, you'll have to leave."

She glared at him. "Why? Weren't you the one just telling me I helped kill David?" Then her mouth bowed and she swallowed. "Attorney-client privilege."

"Exactly. With you here, anything she says is unprotected. I'm not certain this will hold up, but it does for expert witnesses. I just can't afford to pay more than minimum wage."

Her glare didn't soften.

"Either take the offer or wait in the lobby. I don't know what Anneliese will say, and I can't risk the police or commonwealth's attorney getting that information from you."

"When you put it that way . . ." She swallowed hard as she glanced from him to Anneliese. "And I can quit anytime."

"Or be fired."

"Fine. But my agreement doesn't mean I won't question what you're doing."

Chase shrugged despite the zing of annoyance.

Anneliese stood. "I am still here. Maybe I do not want you as my attorney if you were David's. Things did not go well for him."

"Then go back to the judge and tell him you want another attorney." Chase didn't back down. That was the outcome he wanted. Right?

She studied him. "He will not like that."

"Probably not, but now's the time if you want to ask for a change."

Margeaux focused on Anneliese. "You okay with this?"

Margeaux was obviously a caring woman and probably a good teacher. If only she'd see that he cared too . . . maybe a bit too much.

The young woman hesitated. "Do I have a choice?"

"I'll go with you to talk to the judge."

Anneliese shook her head. "I just want him to fight for me and not give up."

Chase stiffened his spine. "I'll fight."

"Then I am okay." Anneliese's eyes were shadowed as she spoke.

Margeaux blew out a slow breath, then stuck out her hand to Chase. "Looks like we're partners."

"Not the word I would use. You're my employee, along with my associate attorney." He focused on Anneliese. She was the person who mattered. "It's important that you tell me everything that happened."

"Why?"

"I can't help you if I don't know the full story." He studied her.

"Aren't you going to take notes?" Margeaux interrupted . . . already.

"Nope. That's your job." He slid a pad of paper and a pen toward her. "Your other job? Don't interrupt."

"Fine." She ground out the word and muttered something about not being his secretary.

She'd learn what it was like to be a practicing attorney, and maybe that'd knock her off her high horse.

He counted to five and refocused on Anneliese. "What happened that night?"

Anneliese shrank as if the bright lights shining from the fixture bore through her. "Everything felt wrong."

Anneliese froze, and Margeaux wondered whether she would continue. Margeaux fumed that Chase had relegated her to secretary and that she'd willingly stepped into that position. Why had she allowed that?

Chase pulled out his phone and appeared to open an app of some sort. Was he taking notes? Seriously? After he'd asked her to be the notetaker? But she didn't want to criticize everything. She reminded herself he was good at what he did.

After a long minute, he set his phone down and leaned across the table. "You have to tell me more than that. This is serious, Anneliese. Without information, I can't help you."

Margeaux glared at him and reached for Anneliese's fisted hands on the table. "What he means is that we can't effectively conduct an investigation without knowing what you saw."

"Not we. Me." Chase looked to Anneliese. "Judge Beaver assigned me to your case because I'm the best defense attorney in the area. But I need something to investigate." He paused and rubbed a hand along the back of his neck. "Let's begin with what you smelled. What about that felt off?"

Smell? That was an odd place to start, but Margeaux stuffed down the question. Maybe that was the sense that Anneliese would share. But as she observed Anneliese continue to struggle, she wondered if this was an example of a freeze response. Could the trauma of what Anneliese had seen have pushed her to a place no one else could go?

Then the young woman gave a shuddering breath. "Our suite smelled dank and heavy." She seemed to shrink even more. "Like the earth had come inside. I wanted to run, but the lights were on. It was strange. So I called for Lauren. She did not answer. It was quiet but not the way an empty room feels quiet. It felt heavy and solid. I did not like it at all. The room felt smaller and . . . not friendly."

She shuddered and wrapped her arms around her middle. "I did not know that what I felt was evil or that I smelled blood. Not at first. Lauren had been so mad at me the last time I saw her, I thought the silence was her anger. But it was heavier and different." She ran a finger along the edge of her chipped nail polish. "My feet froze as if they knew what my brain did not comprehend. Lauren had already died."

Maybe Chase did know how to obtain the right information from his clients. Margeaux wouldn't have expected a question about smells to tug those kinds of specifics from Anneliese, but he'd already gotten more detail than she had. Where would he take the young woman next?

"How did you know she had died?" Chase's question dropped into the room.

"I did not. Not really. Not yet." She sighed heavily and sagged lower. "It was a premonition." She shrugged. "I just . . . knew."

The silence ate time as Anneliese stared at her hands and then the ceiling in a repeating pattern, as if she swayed to her own secret music. Chase tapped his fingers against his phone in time with her bobs. Then he seemed to reach the end of his patience, because he scooched back his chair with a screech against the floor.

Anneliese winced.

"I don't know how things work where you're from."

"Germany." Margeaux bit her tongue as he turned to her with a glare.

"I need her to speak for herself."

"Sorry."

Watching him work with Anneliese felt like a master class in easing a reluctant witness toward the truth. Each time Anneliese hesitated and Margeaux wanted to step in front of a verbal bullet, she reminded herself he asked each question to help Anneliese. She had to relax and let him do his job.

She slipped her phone from her pocket and sent a quick text to Janae.

> You're sure Chase is the best?

> Absolutely. Why? Any
> concerns?

> I don't know. I guess I wish I
> knew more.

She stared at the words she'd typed. Maybe that hit at the antagonism that erupted in her when she saw him. If she'd known enough, maybe she could have helped David. And now, seeing Chase with Anneliese, fear pushed to the surface. What if she worked every day and something awful still happened to Anneliese? She'd have to live with the knowledge that she couldn't do a thing to prevent or change it, because her knowledge of the law remained more theoretical than practical and, in this instance, wouldn't serve Anneliese.

> Sorry to bug you.

> You aren't. He'll take care
> of her. As much as he can.
> Then you have to trust her to
> God. You should do that first
> anyway.

Margeaux slipped her phone back in her pocket, wishing she could push the words from her mind as easily. She knew she should trust God with the young woman. But she had seen how he didn't always show up in the way she needed. He had felt so absent when she was fifteen and sixteen. Part of her, as an adult, could accept that he had never left, but at the time she could not find any evidence of him. Reconciling what she knew with the ruins of what she experienced continued to wreck her.

Lord, I'm choosing to trust Anneliese to you. Help me know how to show up for her in a way that supports her without causing unintentional problems. I just want to help.

She refused to add a *but* or condition even though part of her demanded certainty or an exit clause. She blinked and refocused on Chase's words.

Chase had leaned into the table, his gaze lasered on the young woman. "While I'm appointed to represent you, I can only help as much as you let me. The US system of law is predicated on you making a defense. You have to tell me more than smells and feelings and move into more details so I have something to investigate. Without that, the state gets to show its evidence, and you will probably go to jail. Likely for the rest of your life."

Anneliese blanched as his words seemed to settle in. "But I did not kill Lauren."

The words whispered from her, a mere breath, and evaporated into the space between them.

"Then tell me what you saw. You have to give me something I can work with. What you smelled is good. But I need something I can go to the prosecution with—a convincing story that points them in a different direction." His focus never wavered. "Right now, you are their easy answer. We have to give them a better one, the right one."

"What if I cannot?"

"Then you are in trouble."

"That is why I am concerned." Her hands twisted together on the table, and she licked her lips. She looked at Chase and Margeaux and then down again. "I cannot tell you much."

Then she began talking.

An argument had erupted—a horrible one.

It hadn't been the first time Lauren had come back from a lacrosse practice ready to blow off steam and picked a fight with Anneliese. Most times, Anneliese slipped into her room and avoided Lauren until she was in a better mood. Not this time. Lauren had followed her into her small bedroom, trapping her and pressing in until Anneliese had no choice but to collapse on her bed.

Lauren had decided around the end of Christmas break that Anneliese wanted her boyfriend. No matter how Anneliese protested, Lauren refused to believe anything else. Her intense jealousy had taken a decent roommate situation and made it untenable. It didn't help that Anneliese knew Lauren's boyfriend was unfaithful, but not with her. She'd seen Dominic with another woman at a coffee shop and then again kissing in an alley next to an off-campus bar.

"Lauren told me to stay away from him."

Even though Lauren didn't want to be in a committed relationship with Dominic.

But she refused to let Anneliese near him—even if Anneliese didn't have an iota of interest in him.

"The truth did not matter to Lauren. She found it easy to believe I wanted Dominic, so she harassed me at every opportunity."

The intensity continued to build.

The argument chased Anneliese from the apartment—forced her from the small suite that night.

"Where did you go?"

"Out."

"You'll have to be more specific."

Anneliese shrugged. "I cannot." She bit her lower lip, then looked at Margeaux as if begging her to understand. "I wandered campus seeking peace. And when I got cold, I went into town."

"Who was with you?"

"No one."

"Someone had to see you."

"I do not know who." Her jaw firmed, signaling her adamance. "I wasn't anywhere specific. Just the gathering spots."

Margeaux recognized the euphemistic term for the campus watering holes. Anneliese continued to explain that while students filled every seat, she couldn't single out any she had interacted with. Instead, she waited on the periphery of the action at each bar until she warmed up. A couple of guys bought her drinks, but she didn't know their names. It was easier that way. If a good conversation developed, then she would have to invest in knowing them. Often someone would hear her accent and back away.

"People hear my German and are not curious to learn more. Instead, it makes me an oddity to avoid. All I wanted was to drift into the background without being alone. Ironic, no?"

Anneliese pressed her thumbs into the corners of her eyes and hunched over. A moment passed, and then she seemed to gather herself. "Maybe if I had found the courage to force conversations when out, I would not need your service. I could tell the police the names of people who knew I was not at home when Lauren died."

Chase concurred. "You'd have an alibi. Can you give me the names of those bars and approximate times you visited each? We might find people who saw you there."

"The night she died."

"Yes, but when that night?"

"No, you do not understand. While I usually wander campus when it is uncomfortable at the apartment, I do not usually go to pubs. That night is a blur to me. Things were so bad that I had to stay away from the suite. Hours I wandered looking for peace."

Margeaux's heart ached for what Anneliese had experienced. The fights had gotten horrible. Extensive enough that people asked her about them.

Would those who lived in the suites around them think the constant fights led to a breaking point that caused Anneliese to murder Lauren?

Margeaux feared it was possible.

"And I have no one to defend me." The bleakness in Anneliese's eyes almost broke Margeaux's heart. "Everything is superficial in America. Why invest time in knowing someone who will only be here a few months or a couple of years? People treated me like I wasn't worth really knowing, and it made it easy to reciprocate."

So Anneliese said she would have no one to vouch for the fact she had wandered from bar to bar, killing time until Lauren would either fall asleep or go to her boyfriend's apartment.

"Did the boyfriend ever stay over?"

She shrugged, a small roll of her shoulders.

"This could be important."

"Of course he stayed. They were completely obsessed with each other. Until he obsessed over others, but she always enticed him back. They were like oil and water. Mixing and repelling at the same time."

"Did they fight?"

"She fought with everyone. She called it being passionate. I considered it thoughtless of others."

"Can you tell me more?"

"I am tired." Anneliese wrapped her arms around her stomach as if to protect herself. It had taken months for Anneliese to warm up to Margeaux, and she hadn't sensed a real thawing until Anneliese had spent part of Christmas break at Margeaux's cottage. Even then, the moment they'd stepped back on campus, their relationship had reverted back to the formal professor-student distance. Anneliese had opened up more to Chase than Margeaux had expected, but she still wondered who had hurt Anneliese and caused her to be slow to trust people. She saw so much of herself and her past hurt in Anneliese that it made Margeaux more determined to do everything she could to protect her.

Chapter 17

THE RING OF HIS PHONE pulled Chase from his thoughts and he groaned. In the two days since his initial meeting with Anneliese he'd reached out multiple times to the police in an attempt to connect with the lead investigator but hadn't received a call back. If he didn't know better, he'd think the county had experienced a crime spree that had required all investigators to spend all their hours outside the office and far away from phones.

He'd also met with his associate and shuffled a few upcoming hearings to Marcus. The young man had asked for more experience, and this would give it to him.

He considered ignoring the call but hit the intercom button.

"Detective Phillips is here." Leigh's words were welcome.

"It's about time." Chase rubbed his hands together. Maybe he'd get some information he could work with now.

A minute later the thin man in an ill-fitting suit lingered in his doorway. Chase rose and gestured to the chair in front of his desk. "Have a seat." After the man sat, Chase sank into his desk chair, wondering what had brought the detective to town. "What can I do for you?"

"The commonwealth's attorney asked me to bring you a copy of the file."

"Thanks. I've tried to reach you the last two days, so I'm glad to get it. Which attorney has this case?" He would prefer to meet with the CA directly rather than a detective, but he'd work with it. Might be easier to get Detective Phillips to talk without the CA playing referee.

"Allison Erickson."

The two words left Chase biting back a scowl. The woman was dogged in her pursuit of the truth. That was all good until she bit into a version that didn't match the facts. Then it became almost impossible to convince her to look at the situation a different way. Her tenacity worked all right if everyone had the same take on what had transpired, but if anyone had differing opinions or facts, it didn't work so well for the dissenting party.

She could also hand the case off to someone else unless something made it appealing to her.

Allison had been at the scene the night of the death, so he wasn't surprised she'd kept Anneliese's case, especially with the media attention it was garnering. If she handled it right, her star would rise—helpful if she aspired to higher political office, as others whispered.

Time would tell, but her aspirations and personality combined to make her a formidable opponent.

He strove to keep his expression neutral as he met the detective's gaze. "Good to know."

"Funny. She had the same reaction when she learned you were appointed." Detective Phillips placed a slim folder on the desk. "Everything in here is a copy."

"Of course." It always was. No CA would let the originals walk away from the office. That would destroy the chain of evidence and result in a lost trial before it launched. She might be many things, but Allison Erickson was an excellent attorney.

"The originals are available for your view by appointment."

"Undoubtedly."

"I told her you knew the drill and would entertain a plea offer by tomorrow."

The certainty with which the man threw the words into the space between them rankled. "It'll take longer than that to review the file."

"There's not that much. You'll get through it fast. Trust me."

Based on the detective's smirk, Chase should expect nothing important or helpful. He reached for the file and hefted it, assessing its weight. "Well, thanks for the drop-off. I'll be in contact."

"This one is a good candidate for a quick negotiation. Your client's good for the murder."

Chase waved the file. "Thanks for the advice. Unless you have anything more to share?"

The detective studied him a minute, but Chase didn't blink. "This isn't the case to make a name for yourself."

"Funny, 'cause I'd say Allison thinks it is."

"You never know." The man pushed to his feet. "I'll leave you to it." He looked around as if expecting to find the wheels of justice spinning, nodded, then left.

As he disappeared into the hallway, Chase considered that the man had said more than he realized. Perhaps there was little to point another direction because the police hadn't looked. He could push and see what squirted to the surface.

If she didn't hustle across the campus to the coffee shop in the museum, Margeaux would miss meeting her friends. They'd grown up together, spending hours in the gym perfecting gymnastics routines and skills. There had been four of them before Libby Grainger committed suicide. Then the three amigos remained. Janae Simmons, Chloe Ainsworth, and Margeaux had stood together until Margeaux shattered. It had taken time to rebuild the trust she'd broken with Janae and Chloe, but having her friends back had been well worth the pain of sweeping away her fractured pieces.

When she'd gotten the text from Chloe asking if she could chat for a quick minute, Margeaux couldn't tell if Chloe had good or bad news. When she hustled up the stairs and through the large doors into the museum's lobby, she spied Chloe folded over a coffee cup on one of the second-level tables. She wore her usual black leather jacket and white T-shirt, but her blonde hair was ruffled. There was a heaviness to her posture that made Margeaux hurry across the lobby and up the stairs.

When she reached the table, Margeaux sank onto the free chair across from Chloe and tapped her friend's hand. Chloe startled, causing her matcha to slop over the edge of the mug and onto the oversized saucer.

"Are you okay?"

Chloe glanced up with a lopsided smile. "I think so."

"Oh?"

"I got in."

"In where?"

Janae strolled over from the counter with two steaming mugs and set one in front of Margeaux. She sank onto the seat next to Chloe, and the camaraderie between the two blondes reminded Margeaux she was the outsider. Janae nudged Chloe with her shoulder. "Our girl here got into law school."

"That's amazing!"

Chloe ducked her chin but couldn't hide her grin. "I planned to tell her that."

"Not before you and I turn thirty-one."

Margeaux tried not to flinch at the subconscious reminder she was older. Sometimes they forgot and it didn't matter, but if they remembered, they might remember to ask why she'd cut them out of her life for a season. She blinked back the memories that wanted to press into the present. "Law school." Her smile grew, and she felt it to her toes. "That's great news."

"Is it?" Chloe reached for the mug again, and Margeaux noticed the tremor in her fingers. "How will I pay for it?"

"Some of my students have had good success obtaining scholarships. Better than existed even when Janae and I attended. I bet you'll get one."

"Remember I'm not as smart as y'all are, so I can't expect anything."

"You'd be surprised what's available. It's definitely worth pursuing." Margeaux glanced at Janae. "Tell her."

"Who do you think got her to finish the applications?" Janae pointed her finger at her chest. "You have to decide whether it's really your dream, Chloe."

Chloe let go of the mug and clenched her hands as if afraid the matcha would disappear like her dreams had in the past. She'd always been the one who had to work harder than Janae and Margeaux, and she carried the scars. "I can't afford to not finish. I love working for you, Janae, but I don't know if I can be one of those students who work full-time and go to law school." She wiped her palms along her jeans as if they were sweaty.

Her two friends kept talking, but a man walked behind Chloe, completely distracting Margeaux. What was Chase Crandall doing here? Then she wanted to roll her eyes at the thought. The man had every right to walk in the museum.

"You're not listening." Janae's voice pulled her back to the conversation.

"What?"

"Exactly." Janae rolled her eyes. "We're planning Chloe's future for the next three or four years, and you're distracted by the hot attorney."

"Shh." Margeaux felt heat flame up her neck at the words. "Not so loud."

"What? Embarrassed?" A devious look popped into Janae's eyes, and Margeaux held her breath, wanting to wave her off. "What should we do about that, Chloe?"

"Leave her alone and help me decide what I'm doing with my future."

Janae batted her words away. "You know, but you need to give yourself permission to choose. Your mom will be fine without you."

Chloe leaned toward Margeaux. "You might want to quit staring."

Margeaux's gaze popped back to Chloe. "What?"

"You are so aware of Chase."

"How do you know him?"

She rolled her eyes. "Unlike you, I never left town, and I haven't cloistered myself on campus. I truly stayed connected to the community."

"That's not fair. I'm involved in the community."

"Yes, you serve on the board of this art museum. That deeply embeds you in the fabric of our fair town." Chloe laughed. "Thanks for the distraction. Don't worry, I'll figure out law school once I find out which other schools make offers."

"How may did you apply to?"

"Ten."

Margeaux shuddered at the thought of sorting through the options. "You will have some tough choices." She followed along as the conversation diverted to other topics but found her gaze tripping back to Chase working at a table across the area. He had his iPad out. She wanted to ask if he was working on Anneliese's case.

He needed to take good care of Anneliese and win her case. If he was as good a criminal attorney as everyone told her, this would be easy for him. Still, she'd pay attention. The stakes were too high for Anneliese for Margeaux to do anything less.

Chapter 18

NOW THAT HE'D HAD A chance to review the little bit of information the detective had dropped off, Chase called Leigh and Marcus into a meeting. Time would fly by, and they needed to outline a solid plan of attack. Once they were all seated in his office, he handed out a quick summary of what he knew. Not much but enough. "After talking with Detective Phillips yesterday, I think the commonwealth will try to fast-track the Anneliese Richter trial. To get ready, we should rearrange our cases for the next three months. The murder trial will consume our time and resources."

Marcus leaned back in his chair, his oxford shirt sleeves rolled up to his elbows even though it was only 9:00 a.m. "We've got lots of other clients. We can't abandon them."

"No, but we can triage." Chase glanced at the list he'd prepared. "Our priorities will shift while we figure out what's at stake in this one. We've got a lot of work to do before we know what really happened. My plan is to get you a lot of that lead trial experience you've wanted."

"All right." Marcus glanced at the page. "It's all here?"

"It's a beginning." Chase had drafted lists but had stopped when his eyes glazed over at midnight. He knew from experience he wouldn't do clients any good if he didn't get some sleep and come in fresh.

"I took time yesterday to update critical deadlines in our cases that have them." Leigh handed out a sheet that had a detailed flowchart of the next two months. "I've guesstimated a few, but you'll see we have a motion-to-dismiss hearing in two weeks in the Wilkins matter, a trial in four weeks in the Armstrong battery case that should take no more than three days, and an appeal in the Sommers matter that is due in three weeks. And that's just the next month. Rinse and repeat with others and you have the next quarter." She rubbed the back of her neck, her shoulders slumped as if she already carried the weight of all the discovery. "Add in a murder trial, and I don't know how we'll make it happen. It's a lot, boss."

Chase had felt the burden since Monday morning when Judge Beaver cornered him. He'd sensed the crushing heaviness as Anneliese told him she had no alibi and nothing concrete to help defend herself.

She hadn't provided an easy solution.

Finding the answers would fall squarely on them. He looked at his two employees and then bit back a snort.

"I may have bought us some help."

"You finally hired someone." The spark of something that looked dangerously like hope sprang to Leigh's eyes.

"Don't do that, Leigh."

"Do what?"

"Go getting all sappy and hope-ish on me."

"I'm pretty sure that's not a word." She turned to Marcus. "That's not a word, right?"

"Not unless it's a Chase-ism." The kid grinned at him.

"I hired Margeaux Robbins to help with the murder case."

Marcus stared at him, his jaw slack. "You hired a professor who hasn't practiced law in several years, if ever, to help on the biggest case we've had since you hired me?"

"Yeah, I guess I did."

"Why?" He plopped back against the chair. "I've told you we should expand before she bails on us." He gestured at Leigh. "You know she's the best part of us. You've always stonewalled me saying we didn't have enough money, so you hired a professor?"

"At minimum wage."

"And she said yes?" The man's voice rose.

Chase nodded.

"What made you think this was a good idea?"

"Look, she wasn't going to leave, and she couldn't stay in the interview room while Miss Richter told me what happened without some kind of attorney-client protection."

"Hiring her was your best idea? I can't believe it." Marcus pushed to his feet and paced. "Look at this list of cases and clients. We don't have the time or money for deadweight. We need someone who can do the work."

Chase turned to Leigh. "Wasn't Mr. Drama deadweight not long ago?"

"The worst kind."

"But you trained him."

"I sure did."

"You can do the same for Margeaux. Besides, she's not going to do much. She's got a full-time job already." He considered the sheet with all the cases and work. "I'll keep her out of the way."

She crossed her arms and considered him. "Why? With all this work, you don't need the distraction."

"She's tenacious and protective of Anneliese." He sighed. "We'll make it work. We'll work smarter, not harder. We have motions that are similar in our files. We'll use those and adapt them. Update the law, change the facts. We should never start from scratch anyway. We'll be highly efficient." He looked down at the Gantt chart and tried not to panic. "We'll work smarter, not harder."

"Already said that, boss." Leigh looked concerned. "Where's the priority?"

"I need to learn what the commonwealth has on Anneliese. The file the detective brought over was a joke. I want to believe that means Allison filed too early, but I think it means we don't have the real file. She's too good to file on what's there. Otherwise, this case will be simple to defeat, but I'm not relying on that." He turned to Marcus. "Let's hire a detective. See what we can learn about the victim. Our client only knows a part of her life, we need to know a lot more and quickly. I don't want to rely on whatever scraps the police let slip. We need to get our own investigation moving quickly. We also need to look into what our client was doing the night of the murder."

"All right. I'll get started on the detective. In addition, which of these cases do you want me to take over for you?" Marcus looked slightly less disgruntled at the thought he might take lead on a case.

"Let's see what you can do with the battery. We'll still strategize and plan everything together, but you can take the lead on trial prep. Depending on how the next four weeks go, it's your trial." He looked at his small team. "This will be a wild ride, but let's buckle up and find the truth."

The tap at his door interrupted his concentration, and Chase tried not to groan. It had been a fight to find it since the meeting, as his attention kept drifting back to the overloaded flowchart. It would take a miracle to get all the cases already on the calendar managed well, and now Anneliese's was added to the mix.

He had a small team, and adding Margeaux wouldn't help. The woman had no useful experience, so adding her to the payroll was an expensive exercise in futility. If someone wanted to get around attorney-client privilege, they'd find a way.

The tap repeated and he dislodged his morose thoughts. "Yep."

Marcus came in and took the chair in front of his desk. "I've been thinking about all the cases and work you have piling up. This isn't a perfect time, but I have an offer from a firm in Tyson's Corner, and I'm inclined to take it."

"Now? You just got this offer?" Wait a minute. "When did you interview?"

"It doesn't matter. You'd been acting weird, talking about moving from criminal law, and I don't want to work for corporate shirts. It's not why I went to law school."

"And this firm will let you work on all things criminal."

"Maybe, but the pay is significantly more."

"The hours will expand too."

"Sure, but have you looked at that chart? We'll work nonstop for the next four months or so before you go back to wondering where the next client is coming from. Me leaving helps you because it's one less salary to pay."

"How much do you need?" He was proud of how he gritted the words out.

Marcus looked at him, a hand pressed to his chest. "It's not about the money."

"It's always about money." He tried not to think about how low the firm's checking account had fallen. Maybe he could exercise that line of credit his buddy at the bank kept pitching before the hurricane brewing on the horizon reached him.

"Well, I wouldn't turn down an extra fifty dollars an hour."

Fifty dollars? The kid was crazy. Chase stuck out his hand. "I hope you love your new job. Tell them your first day is tomorrow. I'll have your last check mailed to your home. Wait, it's direct deposited. All the better." He turned to his computer, unable to stomach the thought of looking at his former employee another minute. Now he'd have to look for an associate or paralegal—no, he'd need an attorney—experienced in criminal law. Too many cases stared them down. He needed someone yesterday.

A minute later he realized Marcus hadn't left. "What?"

"You really aren't countering?" The young man looked shell-shocked.

"No." The word bit into the space between them, but Chase couldn't bother to care. "I don't have the time, money, or energy to entertain your ridiculous offer. If you'll excuse me, I have work to do and you have an office to clean out."

Marcus's Adam's apple bobbed as he swallowed. "What if it was thirty dollars?"

Chase began typing and ignored him.

"Twenty?"

Nothing. This kid couldn't hold him hostage. Not when his bank account sank to dangerous levels.

"Fine. I'll stay for ten dollars."

Chase turned back and looked at him. "Is there really another firm?"

"Yes. I can show you the offer letter."

"Then you should take it. If you got far enough in the process to receive an offer, you've already left."

"But you need the help."

"From someone I trust. Not someone who's trying to extort more from me. I can't pay big-city prices. If that's what you want, Tyson's Corner will get you closer, but you'll need the real city. Sounds like you've already made your decision, and I wish you good luck with your new firm."

Then Chase left his office before he could be betrayed again. He didn't need any more reminders that he was stranded on an island with no one he could rely on.

Chapter 19

THE WEEK HAD PASSED QUICKLY. Anneliese stayed at Margeaux's home while Margeaux taught classes and explored whether anyone would be willing to take the young woman as a client. It had quickly become clear that without someone who would pay for her defense, Anneliese would have to stay with the court-appointed attorney. And while Margeaux continued to learn only good things about Chase, anytime she began to believe he could save Anneliese, she'd remember David's fate.

She should do something, but the *what* remained elusive.

Each day since Monday, she'd walked by the law office of Chase Crandall and Associate but hadn't gone in. Without a scheduled meeting between Chase and Anneliese, she didn't know if she'd be creating a situation, and she had enough of her own work to do to not need his fake job offer. By Friday, though, she felt twitchy that she hadn't seen activity.

Shouldn't something happen?

Especially if the case was fast-tracked like Chase anticipated?

How could she force him to do the work? She had a growing urgency to find a way to get involved that filled her with adrenaline she didn't know how to channel. She liked to style it as consulting on the case, but his silence this week made it clear he didn't need or want her.

Even if he'd hired her.

Today she walked across campus, past the museum, and into downtown until she reached Margherita's, an Italian eatery that sat near the corner of Founders and Third. The brick-front building nestled between a boutique and a florist, the rich scent of tangy tomatoes and garlic spilling from the doorway whenever the door opened. Her stomach growled as she entered, emphasizing that the Greek yogurt with granola she'd eaten at her desk didn't make a big enough breakfast and she needed a good lunch now.

Chloe waited at a small table, a pile of garlic bread knots and a large bowl of salad resting in front of her. She raised one of the knots with a wicked grin. "These are still warm."

"Great. I can't wait to eat more than my share." Margeaux sank onto the seat. "Remember when we had to catalog everything we ate?"

Chloe grimaced. "Not the good ole days. I much prefer our current ability to make choices." She shoved the rest of the knot in her mouth as if afraid their old coach would come by and snatch it away.

Margeaux tried to shake the image. She'd loved the camaraderie of the gym and the ability to push her body to do crazy things that most people could only dream of attempting. Yet she'd grown into a healthier person in the years since then, through hard work, lots of prayer, and more than a little time. None of it erased what had happened to her, and as she observed Chloe, she knew the trauma still lingered for her friends too.

"You okay?" Chloe studied her as if concerned Margeaux would break.

"I'm fine. Just lost in thoughts." Margeaux shifted on the seat. "Any law schools get back to you this week with amazing scholarship offers?"

"Not yet. What was I thinking? Maybe I made a mistake, and I shouldn't have applied. My life wasn't so bad."

Janae hurried up to the table and collapsed into a chair. "Oh no you don't. You've worked hard to earn this opportunity, one you wanted for years." She reached for Chloe's hand and squeezed it. "I've noticed how you work with my clients, and you are ready. It's going to be great." Then she turned to Margeaux. "Don't give her a hard time. It's only been a few weeks. I've had to talk her out of changing her mind almost every day the last two weeks."

Margeaux held her hands up in front of her. "You'll be great. I only want to celebrate with you."

"I shouldn't let my nerves get the best of me." Chloe pushed the last knot around her small appetizer plate and then stilled. "I'll be fine. But let's change the subject. Tell us about your student."

"I haven't been very helpful. I don't think." Margeaux grimaced. "It's hard to tell."

Janae rolled her eyes. "I still think bringing you on was overkill."

"Probably. I'm not sure I can handle working in proximity with him even if it means helping Anneliese." She was still trying to forget his part, or maybe it was her part, in David's death. Maybe being near him put a stark light on the fact she could have or should have done something different.

Chloe placed her elbows on the table and leaned forward. "Really? You like him."

Margeaux recoiled and closed her eyes. "Um. No. It would be one thing if I thought he wanted my help. Instead, I get the sense he thinks I'm in the way but he needs to keep an eye on me."

"What's he afraid of?"

Janae snorted. "Chase is the type of attorney who bullies the deputy commonwealth's attorneys into pleading out cases. That's not someone who's afraid."

"Or is it the surest sign he is?" Chloe pulled a face. "Sometimes posturing is a cover for fear."

"He doesn't strike me as afraid of anything." But then Margeaux remembered the man leaning over the sink, sucking in deep breaths like he was trying to avert an anxiety attack. Maybe he was afraid. The question was of what.

"Detective Phillips is here for you." Leigh leaned in the doorway. "Want me to put him in the conference room?"

"Sure. I'll be there in a minute." Chase ran through his talking points. Leigh didn't move, so he refocused on her. "Yes, ma'am?"

"You still need to talk to Marcus."

"He's made his choice."

"Maybe not. He's a kid who may have made a mistake. It's something we all do, even you."

"Then maybe next time he'll think twice about when and how he 'negotiates.'" He used air quotes around the word. "Regardless, I can't deal with him now."

"You'll have to soon." She pushed from the door and returned to the lobby.

In general Chase was an expert at flying blind. Not that he preferred it, but he could handle it. Unfortunately today was just another day in a long string of bad days. He was trying to fly blind with his wings clipped. But if he could figure out a hint of the detective's game, it would give him important insight for the case.

He rolled his neck and shoulders and pushed to his feet. He considered grabbing a notepad, then decided to go in without one. Better to appear unconcerned.

Chase strode into the room and closed the door behind him. "Detective Phillips. Great to see you again. Have more evidence for me? Maybe the real file this time?"

The detective didn't rise from his position at the table. "Passing by, and thought I'd stop in about the Richter matter. You didn't like what I dropped off before?"

"There wasn't much to it."

"You know how these things go. I provided what we had, but more will come as we get reports back from the medical examiner and others. In fact, that's why I'm here now."

"I'm glad you came, since I've tried to reach you." Chase made a show of looking at his watch. "Unfortunately, I can only give you fifteen minutes."

"I won't need that long." The man didn't shift as he tapped the file in front of him. "I've got another gift for you from the commonwealth's attorney. It's something you'll want to look through soon." He took to his feet and buttoned his blazer. "See, a quick stop. Good day."

Chase felt his blood pressure spike as Detective Phillips met his gaze with a flinty expression. He leaned forward but refused to stand until he had a few answers of his own. "Why bother coming? You could have used a courier or sent it with a patrolman."

Detective Phillips's smile didn't reach his eyes as he stared at Chase and sat again. Then he spread his hands as if ready to elaborate on what he'd already said. "Your client murdered her roommate. I will prove it in court. Don't make the mistake of thinking she didn't. It'll be better for everyone if you cave without the farce of a trial."

Chase paused. Why was the detective pushing so hard this early in the process? "We don't even have a trial date."

"All the better. Plea your client out now. It saves us trouble and the taxpayers a lot of money."

"I need tangible evidence that connects my client to the scene."

The detective smirked. "A good kickoff is in this folder."

Chase considered him, looking for his angle. "Good, then slide it over. And I'll expect you to reveal all the evidence ahead of time. That's how we play the justice game in the United States. There're these things called the fourth, fifth, and sixth amendments, and that means you have to play fair with the defense."

The man remained relaxed. "Oh, I always play fair."

"Do you?" Chase leaned forward, elbows on the table, and gave his best wolfish grin. "Then it's simple. A case like this will be fast-tracked by the judge. Three months, maybe five at the longest, to trial. But if you don't get me everything you have, my client will walk, and I'll make sure the way you're treating her is on the front page of every newspaper."

The man held up his hands. "There's no need to be abrasive." He slid the file forward. "You should also know, patrol officers arrested your client again about half an hour ago, and she's being processed now." He tapped the file. "You'll see the arrest warrant on top along with the other evidence."

Chase grabbed the file and pulled the warrant out. Scanned the document. "I don't see anything that validates holding my client in jail."

"Other than the fact she tried to buy a plane ticket home the day after her roommate was murdered? That's up for the judge to decide. On Monday."

Chase paused a moment. Let the words sink in as he focused on what the detective had let slip. "If she didn't commit murder, then there's no need for her to stay."

"There is if we told her not to leave the country while we investigated." Detective Phillips settled against the chair as if that proved he was in the right.

"Sounds like it's your word against hers."

"Not when we recorded the interview."

Good. The fine detective called it an *interview* and not an *interrogation*. He'd file that helpful tidbit away. "Considering I haven't seen this alleged interview yet, there's nothing to confirm what you say."

"There is. And did I say interview?" The man's smirk deepened. "It was a custodial interrogation. She was Mirandized and given the full treatment."

Funny, that's not how Margeaux had explained it. "Then I expect a copy of that immediately."

"There are challenges to getting that to you."

"Yeah, I've seen the challenges in this technologically advanced day of forwarding an electronic file to defense counsel."

"We have to follow protocols. Rules of evidence. You know the drill." The detective studied him for a moment, his arms crossed, but not in a defensive way. "You don't want this to go to trial."

"What are you so afraid of? I'll do what's best for my client."

"Great. Tell her to be careful because she's been sloppy."

"What does that mean?"

"Don't worry about it. You should be considering the range of years she'll get in jail if she pleas."

"You've got this backward." Chase fought the urge to growl. There was a process to negotiations, and the detective knew it. "The CA brings an offer . . . and usually after you give me a preview of the commonwealth's case. You haven't shown me anything that makes me think the judge will hold her in jail pending trial, let alone have her convicted of any crime. When you're ready to make me an offer, let me know. Until then, I have a trial to prepare for." He rose, grabbed the file, and retreated to his office.

That had gone well, and he felt good about what the detective had revealed.

But he didn't know what waited in the file. And that could be the difference in his client avoiding a lifetime in jail.

Chapter 20

CHASE STARED AT THE FILE like it could turn into a rattlesnake and rise up for an attack. He hesitated to open it, something in him convinced bad evidence against his client waited between the covers. He didn't want proof she was guilty. At the same time, something was really off about the detective.

He didn't have to know what that was to make sure the detective didn't bully his way into Chase's psyche.

Chase huffed out a breath and ran his hands through his hair before lurching to his feet and flipping open the file. He thrust his hands on his hips and stared down at it.

There wasn't much there.

A binder clip held together a small packet of papers. The first sheet indicated it was the cover sheet for the police's interview with Anneliese.

He flipped to the next page expecting to see a typed statement.

But there wasn't one.

He kept flipping. Frowned.

What kind of game was Detective Phillips playing?

The folder contained a stack of blank pages.

He picked up his phone and dialed the number from the man's card.

When Phillips picked up, Chase jumped in without preamble. "You forgot something in the folder you left."

"Hello to you too."

"Usually when I get evidence from the police, it's actually evidence."

"That's what I left you." The man sounded put out, tense.

"No, you left me blank sheets of paper."

"I'm sure I didn't."

"I'm staring at a binder clip of nothing."

"Then it's an honest mistake."

"And I'm sure you'll be quick to bring the real evidence here."

"Sure, though it'll be faster if you come our way since I'm turning into the station now."

Chase gritted his teeth. Was this some sort of small-town power play or an honest mistake that deserved grace? He remembered his mom telling him to infer positive intent and his grandpa telling him only fools gave the other side an advantage. Too bad neither was here to help him figure out which side Detective Phillips rested on.

If he had to guess, he'd lean toward power play. But if his client had tried to flee, which he highly doubted, Chase needed the evidence.

He looked through his office window. The day looked decent, and stretching his legs to walk over to get the file and then a cup of coffee from Java Jane's wasn't a bad idea. "You'll be there long enough for me to walk over?"

The man snorted. "You can't walk over. I'm in Leesburg. But so long as there's not a public emergency, I'll be here for the next hour."

"Then I'll see you in thirty minutes. And I'll bring this file with me."

"I trust you. When I'm at my desk, I'll see if I grabbed the wrong file."

The thought made Chase cringe. That would mean the true evidence in the case had been left unattended on the detective's desk for as long as he'd been running around. And it still meant the man had brought a blank file. He had meant to play a game with Chase.

That said something about him.

Chase stopped at the receptionist desk long enough to let Leigh know he'd be out for at least an hour, maybe two, then grabbed a to-go dark latte from Java Jane's before settling in for the quick drive to Leesburg. Kedgewick was nestled between Purcellville and Leesburg, parallel with Hamilton and in the area of Virginia that felt rural and served as a commuter location for those who didn't want to live in the larger DC metro area. As he left town, he placed a quick call to Margeaux.

"This is Margeaux."

"Chase Crandall. I'm driving to Leesburg to meet with the police detective. He's playing some kind of game, but they've rearrested Anneliese."

"What?"

"That's all I know. While I'm working through details in Leesburg, do you have time to track down what's going on with the arrest?"

"I can try." Hesitation colored her voice.

"Call my office and ask Leigh for next steps. She can fill you in."

"All right."

"We can touch base later." He hung up and focused on the drive.

Traffic held steady on the two-lane highway, the pastoral scenery making it easy to forget how close he was to the city. Once he reached Leesburg, the view would change. But this area was famous for the occasional weekend fox hunts, rolling hills with rows of fences, and small communities lining the road.

As he neared the turn for the sheriff's office in Leesburg, his phone rang. Margeaux already? He clicked the button on his steering wheel to accept it. "Hello?"

"Tell me you aren't still driving, Mr. Crandall."

"Tell me who you are."

"Detective Phillips."

Chase kept his eyes on the road even as he wanted to say something that could get him in trouble. Instead he kept it simple. "Hands-free technology. All the cool cars have it."

The detective gave a short snort. "Touché. The CA thought we should meet at her office. Meet me there in ten?"

Chase hesitated at the change in plans, but didn't have a reason to say no. She was right, it would be good for them to meet. "Depending on parking."

"See you then."

He only had to circle the block twice before he found a slot for his Durango, then he stepped from his vehicle and locked the door. It took a few minutes to work his way through security, and then he paused at the directory to gain his bearings.

After winding his way down a couple of hallways, Chase pasted on a grin and sauntered into the commonwealth's attorney's office. He might love the court battles, but he stepped into enemy territory when entering the prosecutor's office.

It was exhausting.

Attorneys and their clients filled corners of the office lobby. Other people looked like they could be victims or witnesses who needed to be interviewed or prepped for trial.

He approached the reception area. "Hi, Shelley."

"Mr. Crandall. I didn't know you had an appointment today."

"I didn't until about fifteen minutes ago."

Her eyes widened slightly. "Ah, Detective Phillips. He blew in ten or fifteen minutes ago. I'll let CA Erickson know you're here."

"Thanks." He moved to a free spot along the wall and tugged out his phone. The building was an odd mix of brick Colonial on the outside and oppressively dated government issue on the inside. Add in the desperation of victims and their families for the commonwealth's representatives to do something on their behalf and he couldn't wait to escape. Even sitting in a small room with the enemy was better than lingering where he stood. He slid closer to the fake ficus, letting it shield him from the rest of the room.

The minutes dragged as he answered emails from clients and texts from Leigh about an appointment he'd missed while languishing here. At this point, she'd have to reschedule.

Finally, Allison Erickson came and waited at the door to the inner sanctum. Why did entering her office strike him the same way as walking into a medical specialist's lair for supremely invasive tests? It reminded him too much of the father who abandoned him for his medical practice and the pretty receptionist.

"Good to see you, Chase."

"Good to see you too, Allison. I was surprised to have Detective Phillips leave me blank paper."

"That doesn't sound like him, but if it gives us a chance to walk through the evidence with you, it won't be wasted time."

He'd reserve judgment on that, but followed her down a standard, nondescript hallway toward one of the small conference rooms. "What's this about arresting my client without informing me?"

"Detective Phillips was supposed to bring you the evidence."

"Hmm. So you have nothing."

She stopped and looked at him, a firm set to her features as she studied him. "Chase, your client killed her roommate. We can't let her walk free before the trial."

"You can if she's not a flight risk, and we haven't had a bond hearing yet."

"Well, that'll be on Monday. And she's a German undergraduate student accused of murder. Of course she's a flight risk."

"Isn't that like saying that you're a woman so of course you plan to get married and have kids? There's so much bias baked into both statements, they're ludicrous."

"Save it for the judge." She pushed into the room, where the detective slouched in a chair, another folder resting on the table in front of him.

Chase tried to slow the roar in his ears at the sight of the man. "Detective Phillips."

"Mr. Crandall. Thanks for coming this way."

"I would have appreciated avoiding the extra trip. What have you got?"

"Now that's the problem. I'm not sure you get to see it. Yet."

Chase glanced at Allison. What was with this power play? "You don't get to make that determination. And *you* came to *me*."

"All right, boys. Back down." Allison held up her hands as if she were the cop—ironic—and tried to get the detective's attention. "We agreed you'd give Chase the transcript."

"Guess I inadvertently left it here."

"So give it to him. It's not hard."

"Looks like I forgot it."

She looked between the two of them. "I'm not sure what's going on, but I'll get a copy for you. Then you can review it and let us know if you'd like to talk further." She glowered at Detective Phillips. "Be nice while I'm gone."

"Sure."

What's the deal here? The motivation for the shenanigans eluded Chase. Why play these games? Chase needed to figure it out, because any vendetta or agenda could be dangerous for Anneliese.

The man's obstruction had to be identified and neutralized.

Chapter 21

BY THE TIME LEIGH AND Margeaux got through the phone tree to someone who would confirm that Anneliese had indeed been arrested and
was in the custody of the sheriff's office, visiting hours had ended. When
Chase walked back into the office, Margeaux didn't know whether to
hug him or throttle him.

"Where have you been?"

"Killing time with the commonwealth. Good ole Allison is determined that our client is a flight risk, but I can't get them to explain why.
They tossed me this file finally." He threw the folder on the table, slowly
flipped through the pages, and then looked at her. "It's a transcript. Of
a meeting with Anneliese. Just her and them. Did she say anything to
you?"

"No." Margeaux's heart sank. "Can I see it?"

Leigh grabbed it first. "I'll make copies."

Chase ran his hands over his hair. "Did you have any luck tracking
her down?"

"By the time we did, they wouldn't let us see or talk to her." Margeaux
lurched to her feet and paced as panic welled at the idea of Anneliese in
the strange world of jail.

Leigh hurried back in and handed out the thin copies of transcript. "There's not much here."

Chase stared at her. "You read it?"

"Yep." She shrugged. "You're the one who sent me to the speed-reading course." She waited for them to scan it.

Margeaux's pulse sped up as the words sank in. "Does she really say . . ."

"Yes."

Chase held up a hand. "We can't panic."

"Then what do we do?" Margeaux stared at the words in the transcript that seemed to scream that Anneliese had prepared to flee.

"Tomorrow, you go see her. Learn what you can from her. We need to learn her side." Chase rubbed his forehead, and his shoulders slumped as if all energy had drained from him. "I'm going to reread this and catch up on some of the other cases and then get to the bars by the college as soon as they open. See if I can talk to people who would have worked that night. It's a long shot, but someone might have seen her."

"We could hire someone," Leigh looked at him. "You don't have to do it."

"I need to see what I can learn first."

"I can juggle the credit cards." Leigh chewed on the end of her pen a second. "I think I saw a new application in the mail this week and didn't throw it away. That'll buy us some time."

"I don't want to do that." The words growled from Chase.

Margeaux listened with growing horror. How bad were things that they openly discussed using credit cards to juggle the bills? As she watched, he closed his eyes and then relaxed.

When Chase opened his eyes, he seemed more at peace. "We'll be fine. I'll make sure of it."

"You mean God will." Leigh studied him with an intensity that showed her care. "Switching areas of law won't relieve this burden, Chase. You're trying to do it all on your own, and you're not supposed to. Let me work my magic with the credit. If it gets worse, you'll be the first to know. You need to focus your energy on the clients. You did not cause what happened to that young man." She lasered her focus on Margeaux for a moment. "Don't let anyone tell you differently."

He nodded, but it didn't have the same focus.

"I can't understand you. Your clients need you to speak up."

That caused the faintest crack in his facade. "Yes, ma'am."

"I'm not your mother, but that's better." She leaned back and glanced at Margeaux. "Know what you're doing?"

"Yes, ma'am." She flashed a small smile to note the irony. "I'll get to the jail as early as I can."

Leigh turned to her. "Wait until nine, but if you're after nine thirty the families will start lining up. There's a bit of a sweet spot for timing."

"All right. I'll let you know what I learn."

Chase bolted from the room, but Leigh stayed seated. Margeaux started to stand, but Leigh waved her down.

"Do you have another minute?"

Margeaux eased back to the chair. "Sure."

"I wanted to clear the air, since you and Chase aren't. I know you blame him for David's death."

"I don't."

"You do." Leigh sighed. "He does too. But he did everything he could. When that young man decided to ignore his advice and ran headlong into a trial, Chase fought hard for him. He'd even found an appealable issue, but David refused to move on it. He thought he'd be fine in prison for the short sentence, and that was better than asking his dad for more money." Leigh slumped over the table, but then caught herself. "Has Chase told you he was preparing the motion anyway? Knowing he wouldn't get paid? We were going to file on Monday, but then David died."

Margeaux let the words fall around her. "You were that close?"

"Yes. That's part of why it hit Chase so hard."

"Thank you for letting me know."

Saturday, March 29

The next morning as she graded more essays, waiting to go to the jail, Margeaux's thoughts kept turning to the weight Chase carried. She wanted to blame him for David's death, but maybe that was because she needed someone to focus her anger toward. The more she worked near him, the more she believed he cared. And what Leigh said had confirmed it. Chase cared deeply about his clients . . . all of them, including David.

She needed to think about that. Sit with it and see if it changed anything. Maybe it should. She could also do more to help. It wouldn't have taken much for her to offer to read the file when he tossed it on the table. She should have offered.

Margeaux arrived at the jail precisely at nine and easily slid through the security process. Then she followed the sheriff's deputy to the room where she could meet with Anneliese. The young woman didn't belong in the jail any more than Margeaux did, but she'd have to stay there until the bond hearing.

Margeaux's mind spun with the implications of Anneliese's arrest the day before.

What did the commonwealth know about the murder that led to them arresting Anneliese originally?

They couldn't get an arrest warrant without something.

But *what* remained a mystery.

She needed to tease any evidence from Anneliese that Chase hadn't found yet. Margeaux perched on the chair the deputy indicated.

He put his hands on his belt and studied her. "You should be safe, but if you need us, we're here the entire time. Knock on the door, and we'll let you out within ninety seconds. You'll have twenty minutes."

"I'm part of her legal team."

"Yes, and you get twenty minutes. Make the most of it."

She wanted to argue but could tell it wouldn't matter. She settled against the plastic patio chair, and a few minutes later a different correctional officer led Anneliese in. The girl's hair hung in greasy strands around her face, and her skin looked even paler than normal as she slumped in the only other chair in the room.

"When can I leave?" The words barely made it into the space between them.

"I don't know. The bail hearing is Monday. We'll know more after that."

"I cannot stay here. It is so loud and everyone is mean."

"Did you say anything when the police arrested you this time?"

"Nothing." She looked up and her gaze lasered through Margeaux. "I had nothing to tell."

"Are you sure?" She felt the weight of the transcript. Would Anneliese tell her the truth without it? "They had to have something to arrest you."

"They have nothing. There is nothing they could have. I did nothing."

"The police can't get a warrant without some evidence."

"Then they created it."

No, they had the interview. "Why would they do that?"

"They can do what they want. I am here, am I not?"

Margeaux studied Anneliese but didn't see anything except frustration on the young woman's face. "We don't have anything to talk about at the bail hearing. It's a routine hearing, and the police have sufficient evidence for the warrant."

"But I did not do anything." Anneliese bolted to her feet and paced in the small space.

Margeaux noted movement out of the corner of her eye. Anneliese had caught the attention of the officers. "Settle down or we're going to have company."

"How can I? You tell me there is nothing we can do, but I am trapped here. I am caged like an animal." Her shoulders slumped and she deflated in a moment. "You have no idea what this is like."

"I can imagine, but you're right, I don't know." The officer who had let her into the room appeared on the other side of the door, and Margeaux held up a finger. He met her scowl with his own. "Our time's up, but we have the transcript."

"What?"

"Of your meeting with the police. The one without me or Chase present. Why did you do that?"

"I did not meet with them."

Margeaux pulled it out and put it on the table. "You did. Here it is."

Anneliese's hand trembled as she reached for it. "I never met with the police."

"They have a transcript that says otherwise." Margeaux rose. "Is there anything I can do for you before the hearing?"

"What do I need to know?"

"Chase and I will meet you at the courthouse before the hearing. Hopefully we'll get this over quickly, but you have to be honest with me, with us."

"I am."

But as the officer led Anneliese back to her cell, Margeaux didn't know if she could believe Anneliese, and that shook her.

If that was all Anneliese had told Margeaux, then Chase didn't have enough to formulate a defense for Monday. He steepled his fingers and looked up at the ceiling. "You're sure that's everything she gave you?"

"She vehemently denies meeting with the police without us. But if she didn't, how do they have this transcript?" Margeaux clenched and unclenched her hands.

He sensed her frustration. She didn't like being challenged any more than the next person. Probably less than most, considering she ruled her classroom.

"There's not much in the transcript." He stood and twisted from side to side. "Detective Phillips tried to make it sound like they had gotten her to confess to all kinds of things, but I don't see it."

"Can I have another copy? I left mine with her."

"Sure. There's one in that folder."

She pulled it out. "Thanks." She stared at it, but he'd swear she didn't see anything. "How do we know they actually met with her?"

"What?"

"This is just a typed document. Where's the audio file?"

He smiled at the realization she'd started thinking like a defense attorney. "That's a great question. Time to prepare a request for the audio file. That might give us enough to keep this out of the hearing."

"Want me to draft it?"

He didn't have time to train her, and Leigh wasn't working on the weekend. "Well, I've got work to do until the bars open. I'm sure you have things to do too." He waited for her to get up and exit, grateful for the excuse to leave, but she didn't.

"You need help. More than me just reading this." She looked around. "Where's your associate?"

"He left."

"The way I heard it, it's a little more like you fired him. During one of the biggest cases of your career."

"I don't know about that."

"I do. Anneliese's case is going to erupt when it really hits the media." She stared at him as if imploring him to do something. "And you can't handle this case and all your others alone."

"Looks like I don't have a choice. Besides, I'm that good."

"Or that arrogant."

The words fell quietly into the space between them but still stung. He didn't want to think she saw something true in them. But what if she did? His job was to protect people in the criminal process. He had invested time and developed skill and expertise. Were others better? Sure, but not many in this part of Virginia. But he couldn't do it all. "What do you want me to do?"

"Ask for help."

"So you can let me down like Marcus did?"

"No, so you don't let Anneliese down like you did David." She bit her lip as if she wanted to take the words back. She stayed silent.

And there it was. "This was a mistake. I appreciate your willingness to help, but I can take it from here."

She made a show of looking around the space, then speared him with a look. "With all the people you've allowed in to work with you? You're really good at chasing people off, Chase. I guess your name is appropriate."

"And you're good at holding a grudge. Not giving people a chance. What's your deal anyway?" He tried to pause, but he could feel his frustration rising. He didn't run. He wasn't his dad. People chose to leave. "Look, I can't change the past. None of us can. And you don't know what happened."

"Neither do you." Her breath heaved in and out in large gulps.

"I know more than you do." There was nothing he could do to change her perception, and suddenly, he didn't want to try. What was the use anyway? He'd learned people didn't try where he was concerned. "I have work to do before I can try to find people who can corroborate whether Anneliese was in any of the bars the night of the murder."

She considered him a minute, puffing out air. "Maybe there's video."

"Maybe. And maybe it's not grainy. And maybe it wouldn't cost a fortune to hire someone to clean it up or watch it if we could find it. Or maybe the police already have it, but I doubt it. Or maybe a million other things, but I'm going to start finding out tonight after I do what I can for my other clients."

"I can help."

"I don't think I want the help. Not tonight." Not when he'd wonder what she was thinking and second-guessing each word and action. He didn't want to risk letting her get close only to have her leave. People tended to do that around him. Even his own father promised to come back and then betrayed that trust.

He and God were still working on that.

Tonight wasn't the night to dig deeper into those issues, and not with Margeaux. Too much pressed against him to open that Pandora's box.

Chase ignored her, and eventually Margeaux rose from her seat. He felt her presence looming in front of the desk.

"You don't have to look at me, Chase Crandall, but you should know I'm not a quitter. I'll keep showing up because I won't give up on Anneliese. And since she's stuck with you, you're stuck with me."

Her words formed a drumbeat in his mind throughout the afternoon and evening as he looked for anyone who remembered seeing Anneliese in one of the local watering holes. If she'd wandered through any the night of the murder, she hadn't made an impression. Other than compiling some names and numbers to call about getting surveillance video, he also hadn't had any luck on that front. Subpoenas might work, but he'd need to move quickly.

Each time someone denied seeing Anneliese, Chase felt a crashing wave that might swamp him. Anneliese needed his best work. He would just keep bailing and hoping that if he worked hard enough, he could stay ahead of the voice in his head that whispered he'd only ever be alone. Marooned on an island.

Chapter 22

AFTER RESEARCHING BAIL HEARINGS ON Sunday afternoon, Margeaux hurried into the courthouse Monday morning, hating the feeling she was the White Rabbit from Wonderland. There'd been an accident on the highway that had stopped traffic, then she'd struggled to find a parking spot on the square, and the line at security had made her even later. She'd hustled up the stairs, and that left her wheezing when she finally reached the courtroom. Chase's raised eyebrows didn't help as she slipped into position at the defense table next to him.

She didn't take time to look around as she leaned toward him. "Where's Anneliese?"

"Fortunately for you, the correctional officers are running late." The door behind them opened and he turned. "Here she comes. That means the hearing kicks off in a minute."

Margeaux had read and reread the code in an attempt to understand what would happen at the hearing, but she still didn't know what to expect beyond a lot of questions. The rules made it seem straightforward. The judge would question Anneliese about her ties to the area and whether she would flee. The fact she was a student should help, but the fact she was a German national and didn't have family or a job in the country could count against her.

Shuffling steps neared them, and Anneliese stopped next to her. Anneliese leaned into her. "Good morning."

Margeaux resisted the urge to give the young woman a hug. She seemed to shrink a bit more each time Margeaux saw her. They had to get her free before she disappeared. "Are you okay?"

"I am surviving." Anneliese's gaze didn't rise from her toes. "Do we sit now?"

Chase glanced to the front, where the court reporter settled behind her monitor. "I'll make sure they're ready for us." A minute later he returned and beckoned toward the bench. "The judge will be out in a minute."

This courtroom was smaller than the ones used for trials, its white walls bare of the oil paintings of prior judges that graced the rooms upstairs. Instead of a gallery with thirty seats, this room had space for maybe twelve observers, and a partition separated the office from the courtroom rather than a separate room. The overall effect was spare and unassuming, without any pretense or airs found in the larger courtrooms.

She watched the second hand sweep the face of the clock hanging above the judge's chair as they waited. The minutes dragged but only ten elapsed before Judge Beaver swept into the room. The bailiff yelled for all to rise before the man settled into his chair and gestured them all back down.

A man slipped in and sank onto a chair at the other table but didn't do anything more than nod at Chase.

Margeaux wrote a note that she slipped to Chase. *Who's the CA? Deputy Ryan Mitchell. Pretty new.*

The name didn't mean anything to her, but she'd research him.

Anneliese's chin tipped up and she kept her posture perfect as she sat between Chase and Margeaux at the defense table. Judge Beaver seemed unmoved by her display of bravado as he stared down his nose at her. Judge Beaver had slightly large front teeth and round, squinty eyes that seemed determined to ferret out truth as he hunched over the bench.

He turned his attention to the side and swirled a finger in the air at the court reporter, then swiveled back to the papers in front of him. "We'll go on the record." He recited the cause number followed by all the relevant names. "We're here today to set bond."

The deputy commonwealth's attorney leaned forward. "If I may, we have evidence to present that Miss Richter is a flight risk and accordingly should not be granted bail."

Margeaux resisted the need to act, but she didn't know what to do. When Chase didn't move, she rose. That woke him up because he bounced to his feet.

"Your Honor, she's a college student, and the commonwealth shouldn't detain her in jail."

"She's also an international student, and if she leaves, she'll be extremely hard to get back for trial." The deputy CA rose and picked up a file from the table. "May I call a witness?"

The judge leaned back and waved. "Proceed."

"Your Honor. We had no notice of a witness." Chase tried to keep the intensity from his words, but this was sabotage, the worst start to a hearing. He had no notice about who the state planned to call even after meeting with them on Friday. He couldn't prepare for what he couldn't anticipate.

"No need to act surprised that an international student might want to flee. Amanda Knox can't be far from anyone's mind." The judge rubbed his chin. "Have a seat, Mr. Crandall. You may proceed, Mr. Mitchell."

"Thank you. The commonwealth calls Detective Phillips."

Anneliese put her head in her hands. "Not that man."

Margeaux nudged her. "Sit up."

"I cannot."

"You must show strength."

"I have none."

The judge cleared his throat, and Anneliese and Margeaux finally fell silent. Margeaux might have meant the words to encourage and quiet Anneliese, but Judge Beaver didn't miss anything. Anneliese had to behave like each moment in court mattered toward her ultimate release. It only took a moment for Judge Beaver to decide someone disrespected him or the court and he would turn against them. Chase had seen him order crazy things like overnight jail visits for disrespecting the court, and no one challenged him. Everyone was too afraid.

It wasn't right, but it was reality.

Mitchell looked their direction, and then back at the judge. "If I can begin?"

"You may."

A minute later Detective Phillips swaggered past the bar and toward the witness chair. He sank into the seat and adjusted his jacket with an obvious movement of his gun and belt. The man was putting on a show, and Chase knew Anneliese caught every movement as the color leached from her skin. For once Margeaux didn't say anything but simply reached for her student's hand and squeezed it under the table.

After being duly sworn in, Detective Phillips recited his name and address before giving a brief statement of his title and history with the police force.

"May I approach?"

Judge Beaver dipped his chin, though he still looked supremely uninterested. "You may."

Mitchell took the folder with him and slid a piece of paper from it, holding the page in front of the detective. "Please tell the room what this is."

"It's a printout I gave you Friday."

"Printout of what?"

"As is customary when a bond hearing is coming up, we do a quick search to make sure nothing pops up on the suspects. Due diligence about being a flight risk. Usually nothing comes up, but with murder charges, things can get more interesting."

"What did you find yesterday?"

"I popped Anneliese Richter's name into the databases and out came a notice that she had entered her passport number to purchase a ticket to leave the country."

"You're sure it's the defendant?"

"I am." He settled back and crossed an ankle over his knee as if he had no concerns.

"How so?"

"There aren't many Anneliese Richters who would be flying from Dulles to Berlin in three days on a one-way ticket with her passport number."

"And how did you get her flight information?"

"Once we had the alert from the credit card company, it was enough to get a warrant from the judge, and that was all it took to get the specific details on her flight." He tapped the paper. "These are the details. She booked the flight on Scandinavian Airlines, but we still found it."

The man acted like he was the greatest detective since the Thin Man or Sherlock Holmes.

"No further questions." He turned to the judge. "I offer this as Exhibit A."

"Fine." Judge Beaver was being lax in his form, but Mitchell handed it to the court reporter, who marked it as an exhibit.

"Your witness."

Chase stood and buttoned his jacket. How could he poke a hole through this testimony? It felt airtight but staged, and he didn't like it. "I'd like a moment to look at the exhibit."

Judge Beaver glowered but nodded. "My next hearing is in twenty minutes, so make it quick."

Chase approached the court reporter. "Can I have it, Shelia?"

She slid it toward him. "He should have had a copy for you."

"We both know that." Still, making a fuss now wouldn't solve anything. He scanned the paper as he returned to the table, then slid the paper in front of Anneliese. "Notice anything?"

"What do you want me to see?"

"Everything look right?" He didn't dare ask her if she bought a ticket because if she had, it was an automatic go-to-jail admission. He wanted to avoid that at all costs, but not knowing what she'd done or if this was real made asking questions challenging.

"I do not have my passport number memorized. I do not fly Scandinavian Airways. But I do not know how to prove a negative." She frowned again. "Maybe it's like the papers for the meeting they said we had. But we did not."

"Objection, Your Honor. She's going beyond the scope of the question."

Judge Beaver frowned at Anneliese. "Stick to the question asked."

"Look at the credit card number." Chase pointed and Anneliese followed his finger. "Do the four digits there look right?"

"Yes, but someone could have stolen my card, right? The police did not let me take my purse, and it was in my apartment when I could not be there."

She had a good point, but she also raised a good point about proving a negative. He picked the sheet up and scanned it again. AI could re-create this receipt in seconds and make it look like hers. The larger question was why Detective Phillips would do it. Judge Beaver would not easily accept the idea that the police participated in entrapment, so Chase would need to set this up for a quick appeal if needed. That would be equally difficult.

"Today, counsel." Judge Beaver's voice and posture remained relaxed but his gaze watchful.

"Yes, sir." Chase took one more look at the sheet, then turned to Detective Phillips. "How did you say you came across this ticket?"

"A standard search before this hearing."

"Yes, but what was the timeline?"

"The commonwealth's attorney's office alerted our office to the hearing. Because this is my case, I ran the financials and got the information from her phone." Detective Phillips smirked like he'd done the smartest thing.

Chapter 23

CHASE SENSED AN OPENING. HE kept his face neutral at the admission. "How long have you had her phone?"

"Since the night of the murder." He uncrossed his leg and put both feet on the floor. "As we were clearing the apartment, we discovered the phone in the victim's room and took it as evidence."

"Where did you say it was?"

"The victim's room."

Chase let the admission sit. "When did you obtain my client's permission to search the phone?"

"We didn't need it."

"So you had a warrant?"

The man opened his mouth, then shut it. Chase let the silence linger a minute, then rephrased the question.

"Since you did not have my client's permission to search her phone, when did you obtain a warrant to do so?"

"Two weeks ago."

"Really? So immediately after the murder and before you talked to her?"

"Yes."

"And you've had the phone since then?"

"In police custody."

Chase paused to let the words linger. "Then how did she use the phone to order plane tickets? Either the day after the murder or over the weekend in jail?"

"What do you mean?"

"If you had the phone, she didn't."

The detective stared at him but refused to speak.

"Did she have the phone the day after the murder?"

"No."

"Did she have the phone in jail?"

"No."

"So she couldn't use it to buy tickets."

"She didn't need to." The detective straightened. "We only used the phone to access her emails. She could have bought the tickets on any computer or phone."

"And you can file that warrant with the judge to show that you properly accessed the phone and thus this document was fairly obtained from her phone and within the scope of that warrant you claim to have obtained?"

"Sure."

Chase turned and looked at Anneliese, who looked ready to faint. He spun back around. "And when did you serve my client with that warrant?"

"We didn't."

"Rookie mistake."

"Excuse me?"

"I said, that's a rookie mistake. Without a warrant, anything on that phone is inadmissible. Exigent circumstances doesn't apply since the phone was already in your possession. And without service, you didn't properly give my client notice of the intent to violate her rights. The use of anything you obtained from that search is fruit of the poisonous tree, and Judge Beaver can't admit it."

Judge Beaver's face turned red as color climbed up his neck into his cheeks. "Save your grandstanding for the jury."

"This isn't grandstanding, it's making sure an injustice isn't done." He took a breath and looked at Anneliese again. "I'm prepared to put Miss Richter on the stand to testify." Margeaux mouthed *no*, but he kept going. "You don't need that. The exhibit shouldn't come in because the police did not have a warrant, and even if they did, they didn't serve it. So the information, even if it were hers, was improperly obtained and cannot be used by this court."

"I've already admitted it as evidence."

"You didn't give me an opportunity to object."

"I don't have to provide an invitation, Mr. Crandall, as you are aware. Your job is to object in a timely fashion. My job is to rule only on those objections that are made effectively. You failed to object."

"I object to the exhibit coming in. It's improper and should be excluded as fruit of the poisonous tree."

"Overruled."

"I'd like to present evidence."

"Too late."

"Not on something this critical." Chase took a breath and forced himself not to rush into a mass of words. "Detective Phillips, when did you first know that Miss Richter had a ticket for home?"

"I don't know."

"Did you ask her when you interrogated her without representation?"

"I wouldn't do that." He smirked. "Not without her waiving her Miranda rights."

"Funny. That wasn't on the transcript you gave us."

The man's jaw clenched slightly, but he didn't speak.

"You told me you knew she'd bought a ticket the day after her roommate was murdered."

"No, I didn't."

"You did when we talked. Why would you tell me that and then present this receipt that is for a later day and time?"

"I didn't say any such thing." The man crossed his arms and his lips twitched, but his eyes were cold.

Chase considered him but decided to leave it alone for the moment. They had his sworn testimony going one way if they needed it later. "Judge Beaver, I reserve the right to recall him, but would like to call Anneliese Richter, the defendant, as a witness to testify about this exhibit. If Detective Phillips is alleging this came from her phone, then she should be allowed to testify as to whether she used her phone to purchase it." An impossibility if the police had it in their possession.

"Your Honor, she wouldn't have to use her phone to purchase the ticket. This receipt was simply sent to her email account." Mitchell made it all sound so reasonable, but he was wrong.

"Which you didn't have a warrant to access." This was why defending people mattered. A simple twist here and another twist there and suddenly constitutional protections disappeared, lost in meaningless legal wrangling.

"You don't know that." Mitchell turned to the judge. "If I may redirect with a couple more questions?"

"Since I seem to have lost control of this hearing."

"Judge, can I call Anneliese Richter?" Chase bit out the question.

"Not yet. Mitchell."

"Thank you." The man considered Detective Phillips. "Did you have a warrant for the phone?"

"We obtained one after discovering it at the scene."

"Did you need one?"

"We didn't think so, but after consultation with you and the commonwealth's attorney, we decided to err on the side of caution and get one."

"Did you serve it on the defendant?"

"Didn't see the need, since we already had the phone. We also had exigent circumstances because she could wipe the phone with the click of a button if she had another device."

"Objection." Chase was back on his feet. "This is conjecture, not actual knowledge. It also doesn't relieve the police of the necessity of serving the warrant. Having a warrant isn't the same thing as putting the defendant on notice and serving it."

"Not when we have the Uber driver telling us she set up an appointment for him to take her to Dulles." Phillips smirked at him. "Pretty cut-and-dried."

"Objection. Hearsay." Chase couldn't let the judge use that without hearing it from the driver. At this point Phillips might say whatever he thought expedient. The why remained elusive to Chase.

"Overruled. I know enough to ignore it." Beaver leaned forward and stared at Anneliese. "Is this true?"

"Your Honor!" Chase sputtered as the man ignored the rules of evidence.

Anneliese turned to Chase. "Do I answer the judge?"

"No."

The judge waved his hand. "Keep it moving."

Mitchell shrugged. "Nothing further, but I reserve the right to recall Detective Phillips."

Chase rose as Detective Phillips took to his feet and exited the witness box. "Your Honor, I call Anneliese Richter."

Anneliese trembled as she walked to the chair. Margeaux had watched the young woman slowly emerge from her shell over weeks and months in class. Now she turtled as she sank onto the chair that Detective Phillips had vacated.

After the judge swore her in, she looked at her lap while Chase approached.

He didn't have a script, and that made the next minutes dangerous. Without knowing what Anneliese would say, this could be a disaster for her. All Margeaux could do was pray for grace as she braced for what came next.

After walking Anneliese through stating her name and address for the record, Chase picked up the printed receipt. He walked over and handed it to Anneliese. "Have you seen this before?"

"No." Her word was small and muffled.

Chase paused as if giving her space to add to her answer, but she didn't. "Do you have plans to fly home?"

"As soon as I am allowed, yes. This country is no longer welcoming to me." She looked up and a tear trickled down her cheek. "I am sorry about what happened to Lauren, but I am ready to go home to where people know me and care."

"Did you buy this ticket?"

"No."

"Are you certain?"

She looked at him with such disdain, Margeaux wondered how he continued. "I already answered your question. I did not buy the plane ticket. I did not have my wallet, and without that I could not buy the ticket."

"You did not buy one the day after your roommate was killed?"

"No. Even if I had wanted to, I had no way to do so."

"Or over the weekend?"

"No."

"You did not use your credit card?"

"No. I could not. I did not have it."

"You haven't replaced your credit cards?"

"No." She looked down at her hands and her hair fell like a shield in front of her face. "I did not think I needed to."

"Then who bought the plane ticket?"

"How do you know anyone did?"

"What do you mean?"

"As you said, anyone could have created this. It does not mean I purchased a ticket or that any ticket was purchased."

"That's a lot of effort to create this and make it look like you plan to flee the country."

"Yes." She shrugged and finally looked up with a bit of fire in her eyes. "Why would anyone bother? I am insignificant. It does not matter who I am or what I do."

"Let me put this bluntly. Did you purchase a plane ticket?" He looked at the paper and rattled off the details.

"No. I did not." She said it with so much vehemence Margeaux believed her.

He glanced at the phone, then back at Anneliese. Would he raise questions about it?

Then she caught a smirk on Detective Phillips's face, and he leaned over and had a conversation with the deputy commonwealth's attorney. There was nothing hurried about it. Instead it seemed focused and dragged the attention of the room toward them.

"Do you have anything to add?" Judge Beaver's displeasure came through loud and clear as he frowned from his perch.

Mitchell hesitated, then straightened. "No, sir."

The judge grimaced as he took off his glasses and pinched his nose. "This hearing is scheduled for eight more minutes and then there are four more cases behind it. Will you finish presenting your evidence in that time or will we need additional time?"

Chase watched the judge a moment as the deputy apologized for the interruption. "Your Honor, I renew my objection to this exhibit and ask you to remove it. I also ask you to strike the testimony of Detective Phillips that references it because he has not proven that it's a business record."

"Overruled. Again."

"Judge, if you let this document in, it's telling a false story."

"Then what would you like me to do? Ignore it? It's paper documentation that your client, a woman who resides in another country, purchased a ticket to leave the country." He leaned on the desk. "Do you have any further questions?"

"No." Chase spat the word out.

The judge looked to Deputy Mitchell. "Do you have any cross?"

"No. But I do have a follow-up for Detective Phillips."

The judge made a show of looking at his watch. "You have four minutes. Can you do what you hope to in that time, or do we need a continuation?"

"Four minutes should be sufficient."

The judge sighed and then waved at Anneliese. "You may step down."

After Detective Phillips sauntered back to the chair, Deputy Mitchell dove in. "Did you watch the defendant's testimony?"

"Yes."

"She testified that she did not purchase the plane ticket, correct?"

"Yes."

"Is that accurate?"

"No."

"So she did in fact purchase the plane ticket?"

"Objection, Your Honor." Chase launched to his feet.

"Yes?"

"Leading the witness."

Mitchell didn't bother to hide his exasperation. "It's a yes or no question, Judge, on cross."

"You may answer." The judge leaned back.

"Could you repeat the question?"

"Did Miss Richter in fact purchase a plane ticket?"

"Yes."

"What evidence do you have to back that up?"

"A fraud alert on her phone from her credit card company."

"That is not true." Anneliese spoke the words too loudly, and Margeaux couldn't stop her. "I did not buy the ticket. How could I without my phone and from jail?"

"Order!" The judge pounded the bench with his gavel. "Keep your client under control, Mr. Crandall."

"But I did not do it. If I thought I could leave, I would already be gone." Anneliese wilted next to Margeaux. "Tell them. Please. I do not want to return to jail."

Detective Phillips had a smug expression as he waited for the chaos to calm. "There's nowhere to hide, little girl."

Chapter 24

Monday, March 31

ANNELIESE SWIVELED IN HER SEAT. "Your Honor, please do not make me return to the jail. I did not kill Lauren. I did not buy the plane ticket. I do not know why this is happening, but I did not do these things. Please, you must help me."

Her impassioned words rang in the small room, and Judge Beaver watched her with his mouth slightly open. Then he closed his mouth and banged his gavel. "I'm setting bail at a quarter of a million dollars. If the defense can provide any evidence that contradicts that provided by the commonwealth, I will reconsider." He tapped on his keyboard. "We will set the next hearing to determine trial and other key dates for two weeks out. I want this case to move quickly. No artificial delays, so come with your calendars and be ready to set the schedule."

When the correctional officers came to collect Anneliese, Margeaux stalled them. "Is there a room where we could meet with her for a few minutes? We need to discuss bail."

The woman officer glanced at her watch. "We've got some time before the others will finish their hearings. Follow me." She led them down a side hallway. "You can use this room."

Once the officers left them alone, Margeaux waited for Chase to take the lead, but he seemed disengaged. She focused on Anneliese. "Do you have anyone who can post bond?"

"What is bond?"

"It's the money that promises you won't leave between now and your trial."

Anneliese lurched to her feet and walked back and forth, arms swinging and eyes wide. "How can I do that? My parents barely had money to pay for me to be here. I cannot ask for more."

"They know about your arrest, right?" She'd considered calling them but hadn't. Maybe she should have.

Anneliese barely paused before she sucked in huge swallows of air and then folded at the waist. "What am I to tell them? That the police believe I killed my roommate?"

"You have to tell them something. The media will find them, if they haven't already." She looked at Chase and motioned while mouthing *say something*.

He shrugged, and she didn't know what to do that wouldn't make things worse.

Fine, she'd handle this herself, since the girl couldn't stay in jail. "Let me see what I can do." Then she grabbed Anneliese's hand as the girl tried to pass by again. "But Anneliese, you have to tell your family. I'd be surprised if someone hasn't already tried to find them. You don't want a stranger to be the one to tell them you're in trouble."

Anneliese shifted and looked like she wanted to bolt, but she nodded. "Can I leave? Please?"

"The officers will return you to jail."

"Yes. I cannot do anything from there."

Wait? Was she running to jail to avoid calling her parents? "Anneliese, you have to talk to them."

"You do not understand. They will be so disappointed."

"But they will want to help. That's what parents do." At least the good ones. The ones like Janae's parents, who helped when life overwhelmed and you needed a place to land while you rebuilt your life. Margeaux's parents had thought they did, but they had forced an impossible decision on her. "Give them a chance to help you."

Anneliese walked to the door and knocked on it, like she needed permission. Margeaux looked at Chase, but he ignored her. "Do something."

"She's an adult."

"One who needs support and help."

"No, she needs us to focus on her trial."

"Is that why you left David in jail?" She took a deep breath, knowing the words weren't true. "I'm sorry."

He stiffened as if electricity had jolted him, and she knew her words had landed harshly. She felt a desperate need to save Anneliese. "Help me."

The door opened and the female officer filled the doorway. "Yes?"

"I would like to leave now." Anneliese's voice trembled, but she waited with her head high and her arms stiff at her sides.

"We don't need to take you to the holding area yet."

"Please. Take me now."

The woman looked to Chase and then Margeaux.

Chase shrugged again. "If she wants to leave, you can take her."

"All right." The officer put handcuffs on Anneliese and then led her from the room.

Fury boiled inside Margeaux. "Why did you let her go?"

"She has to want our help. If she doesn't, she'll get in our way. This way we can focus on what we need to do." He finally looked at her, and there was a hardness to his face that had her retreating. "That does not include trying to get her bail. The worst thing that could happen right now is her fleeing. We need to focus on clearing her, not waste energy on where she spends the next three months. To that end, I'm returning to my office. If you would like to join me, you're welcome. Or if you have academic work to do, go do that." He pushed from the table and collected his briefcase. "Either way, I'll be busy proving Anneliese didn't kill her roommate."

And then he left. Without a backward glance. Margeaux didn't know whether to be angry at his dismissal or elated that he seemed so focused.

One challenge of a murder scene being on a college campus was that access couldn't be gained once the police cleared it. It had been two weeks, and the police hadn't allowed Anneliese to return to her home even though they had let her roommates return recently. Chase could stay in his office and look at the little evidence he had, or he could take another pass at getting into the apartment and locating witnesses. He couldn't sit still after that bail hearing, so he drove to the apartment complex. Because the campus wasn't closed, he could hang out in front of the apartment building and see who he could talk to. He timed his exploration for 6:00 p.m., after classes and before the evening activities. The challenge was he couldn't simply walk into the apartment and take a look around. Approaching the landlord wouldn't be enough to sweet-talk his way into the apartment. With his client waiting in jail, he couldn't have her walk him through either. It meant he was a bit stymied on how to gain access to a crime scene that wasn't one anymore.

One could argue there wouldn't be anything to see that he couldn't see on the crime scene photos, but he liked to visit the space. See the actual rooms where the crime happened when he could.

Then he could get a sense of how events occurred, a spatial appreciation lacking on flat 2D images.

One of the roommates might let him in if they'd returned to the apartment. And if that didn't work, he might learn key information by knocking on doors.

Unfortunately for Anneliese, neither of her other roommates had been around the night of the murder, and each had solid alibis according to the police—though he still wanted to confirm them—so law enforcement had focused on her.

The apartment building was only three stories and sprawled over a city block. The look reminded him of an old hotel set for a Hitchcock movie, as it surrounded an interior parking lot. Minimal landscaping revealed the clear focus on no-frills housing that had angles and shadowed alcoves everywhere. Anneliese's apartment was on the third floor, a corner unit. He imagined the young women had felt safer being off ground level, and it would be quieter without neighbors on top.

From the online floor plans, it looked like the typical unit was four small bedrooms, two roommates sharing a bathroom, with a small kitchen and living area in the middle. A good space, but nothing extravagant—designed for basic needs and privacy. Based on news accounts, Lauren and Anneliese shared one bathroom while the other two suitemates had the other wing, a standard housing option for students.

Despite what Margeaux seemed to think, he'd tried to reach the roommates without success and would keep trying. But he'd also see if he could find anyone else who knew any of the four who'd lived in apartment 321.

After he parked in an open spot across the street, he took a moment to assess the activity level. It felt fairly quiet, but few would linger outside in late March.

The complex had been built in the '70s and had open access, which meant he didn't have to talk his way onto the third floor. Maybe he would have an easier time than he'd feared. As he climbed the metal stairs, his shoes clomped, and anyone nearby would hear his approach. He knew he didn't really work on a movie set, but part of him expected someone to leap from a corner and question his presence. It would be nice to slip into the place unnoticed, but that wasn't an option.

It didn't really matter where he knocked, but the beginning seemed like a good place. As he waited in front of unit 321, he took in the details. A corner of crime scene tape still fluttered where someone hadn't bothered to pick it free. Were the roommates that lackadaisical about the details?

Or had they not come back? He couldn't blame them really.

A wreath on the door had a Valentine's Day heart on it that said Be Mine, and someone had written Permanently over the top with a black marker.

The fact no one had taken it down or claimed it as evidence both-ered him. It wasn't a shrine, but disturbing. As he studied it, he realized he didn't remember seeing anything in the media or online about any-one holding vigils or turning an area of campus into a gathering spot to mourn and remember Lauren. Surely he hadn't missed it. But if there hadn't been a vigil, why not? Didn't that typically happen when a young life was violently cut short?

A collective coming together in an attempt to make sense of the senseless?

He knocked on the door and waited. When he caught no movement inside, he knocked again then checked the time on his watch. A little before six should still be a decent time to catch college students at home.

A door opened behind him as he unlocked his phone and snapped a photo of the door and wreath.

"I doubt you'll find anyone there."

He turned and met the cautious gaze of a coed. She had the soft edges of someone who was still used to home cooking and other care from a watchful mom, yet there was an alertness in her expression that said she was also very aware of what had happened near her.

"Do you know any of the students who live here?"

"No."

"Never talked to them?"

"Not really." She crossed her arms and stared at him. "Who wants to know?"

"I'm Chase Crandall, an attorney."

"You represent Anneliese."

"I do." He cocked his head as he watched her. "You know her."

"A little. I was curious about her because she's from somewhere else. That takes courage."

"Yeah." He waited, wondering what else she'd say.

"The other two moved out as fast as they could. You won't find them here."

"Do you know where they went?"

"No. They didn't take time to meet the neighbors." A phone rang somewhere inside the apartment, and she looked that direction. "Good luck."

"Wait. Can I get your name?"

"Ava."

"Last name?"

"Lawrence. Ava Lawrence." She disappeared inside before he could get any more information, but it was a beginning.

Chase made a note, then considered the other doors on the floor. Since it didn't matter where he launched the effort, he shifted down one door and knocked. He made his way down the hall, but no one else was home. He wrote notes on business cards and tucked them in the doors and mailboxes. Not that the notes guaranteed a response, but maybe someone would contact him.

Chapter 25

LATE MONDAY NIGHT AFTER EMMA'S choir concert, Margeaux had noticed the lights on at the law firm as she drove by, but when she'd stopped, the door was locked and no one answered her knock. Guess if she really planned to help with the case, she'd need to ask for her own key. Of course that was a potential nightmare situation. Chase didn't give in to anything easily. She'd need to decide if she really wanted to take the bumps and bruises she'd acquire by forcing her way in.

Today had felt like April Fools' Day from the moment Margeaux stepped into the classroom, and it quickly became a lost cause of a day. No one was ready to study the finer points of insurance and why it mattered to the legal stability of a company. She could do a roundoff back tuck and no one would wake up long enough to applaud. Some days were just like that.

Instead, students huddled in twos and threes over the student paper.

Margeaux didn't read it like some of her colleagues did. In fact, some editions circulated without her even noting a headline. She simply didn't find it relevant to her daily life. She didn't have time to wonder what students thought about random campus occurrences, but after she had the computer up and slides ready for the day's lecture, she struggled more than usual to capture the students' focus.

"Hello, everyone." When that didn't work, she came around the table at the front of the room, leaned against it, and waited. Maybe a minute or two would get everyone's attention.

"Professor Robbins." An eager student in the fourth row waved her hand as if afraid Margeaux would somehow miss her question.

"Yes, Natalie?"

"Is it true that Anneliese stayed with you over winter break?"

Margeaux blinked a few times. How had that become public? She considered all possible ramifications of a student staying with her, then gave a mental shrug. Sounded like someone already knew. "Yes, she did for a few days. I didn't like the idea of her staying alone on campus."

"You let a murderer stay with you?" The young woman's upper lip curled in a sneer.

"That's leaping a bit, isn't it?" Margeaux fought to keep her stance open. The last thing she needed was to look defensive. "What's the first principle we talked about when covering criminal law?"

Natalie raised her chin, her dark hair brushing her shoulders, but didn't say anything. Of course not. This student's quizzes indicated she didn't like focusing on the details of the law as much as she liked gossiping.

Margeaux turned her attention to others in the class, but no one would meet her gaze.

"It's a concept that is foundational to our legal system."

"You want us to say, 'innocent until proven guilty,' but that's not how things really work." The young man Arthur practically spat out the words. "Innocent people go to jail all the time. I think that's why her attorney became one. His dad turned his uncle in for a crime the dad did. But then the dad disappeared. With his receptionist. Some story, huh? So much for innocence."

Margeaux just looked at him. "How would you know that?"

"I went to school where Chase is from. Asked some questions. Talk about a betrayal." Arthur leaned back. "I wonder which is more important to the attorney. Justice? Or the truth? Because sometimes they get in the way of each other when we're trying to live by 'innocent until proven guilty.'"

The words were so cynical, Margeaux wondered who had hurt Arthur. "I don't deny that. Never have. In fact, we talked about that during class. Justice is an aspirational goal and one we don't get right all the time, but at least we're striving for it. Imagine what our country would be like if we didn't care about guilt and innocence. Can we do better?" She let her voice rise on the question before intentionally giving the silence space. When it had settled in the room, she jerked her chin emphatically. "Absolutely. And we must. It's not okay to have an innocent person spend even one day in jail." She wanted to pound the table, get their attention, break through their social media perfection. Instead, she forced herself to hold back.

"So that makes it okay that a murderer stayed with you?" Arthur crossed his arms and leaned back as if he couldn't get far enough away from her.

"What if she's innocent?"

"How can she be? The police found her covered in blood."

"No, they didn't." Margeaux fought the chill that wanted to shake her at the words.

"They did." Natalie looked at her phone. "Here's a picture."

"She's still innocent."

"Until proven guilty. But pictures don't lie." The young woman held up her phone. "All you have to do is look. And then you'll see what the rest of us already know. She is one cold woman."

Another student nodded. "She needs to stay in jail."

"Maybe someone created the photo." As murmurs greeted that statement, the student who spoke it clammed up.

One of the male students crossed his arms. "Bail is too good for her. She needs to wait in jail and think about what she did. Lauren didn't deserve to die, and definitely not like she did."

"We aren't safe if Anneliese is free on campus." Natalie shivered dramatically.

What had they found that turned them so harshly against her? Margeaux didn't want to look. She didn't want them to change her perception of Anneliese. But she also knew she needed to see what they had found. What was out there? What was polluting the potential jury pool? She walked over and held out her hand for the phone. Natalie held it out with a smirk.

Someone had turned a photo into a meme.

One that cast Anneliese as a killer turned vampire with blood dripping from her incisors. The creator had gotten Anneliese's background wrong trying to draw a connection to Vlad the Impaler from Romania rather than Germany, but it wouldn't matter.

Not ultimately.

The result was the same.

Anneliese wasn't a young college student who was innocent until proven guilty.

She was now a bloodthirsty villain who needed to stay behind bars where she could do no more harm.

In that instant Margeaux knew they had to get the trial moved. If her students were this adamant that Anneliese was guilty and had seen photos that convinced them she was, how could she get a fair jury anywhere near Kedgewick and Monroe College?

The email message filled Chase's screen, a glow of warning that he'd refused to open when it arrived the prior night.

> We're concerned about the visibility you're gaining in the trial. This case was never supposed to make it to trial. Remember our offer was contingent on the status of this case. Jim

Why was Jim Clary so concerned about this case?

It didn't make sense. Never had.

A straitlaced corporate firm shouldn't care about his court-appointed criminal case. That left him unsettled and with questions.

Did the firm expect him to throw the case? Not do the work that was required to win a not-guilty verdict if that's where the evidence led? Throwing the case might commit an innocent woman to life in prison.

The idea burned inside him. Surely that wasn't what Jim meant, and even if it were, he wouldn't be foolish enough to put it in writing. Yet the words blinked on the screen.

He decided to ignore the message. For now.

Still, he didn't like the cloud the message created. Why threaten his future? Either the company wanted him or it didn't.

He pulled up the browser and did a quick search for Jim and then the company, but he couldn't find a connection to either the victim or Anneliese. Any association hid below the surface. He'd need to stay aware, but he couldn't focus on that, not when the trial raced closer.

The murder of the student had raised emotions. More than the tragedy of a life lost too early, it had morphed into the story of someone who didn't belong stealing what wasn't theirs. This story could infiltrate the jury and would be difficult to shake. How did you counter a narrative based in fear and closed minds?

The United States was a country birthed from a heritage of people coming and finding a fresh opportunity through hard work and ingenuity. But the letters to the editor and posts he read and that Leigh forwarded to him betrayed a gut-level shift that demonstrated a lack of openness and instead a vision of sameness and uniformity.

His phone rang and he picked it up. "Yep?"

"It's that firm on the line."

"That firm?"

Leigh sighed. "The one you think you want to join." She smacked her gum and blew a bubble that popped. "I don't know why you have to change things up. We're doing fine here."

If you didn't mind wondering if the clients would pay on time and running a volume business. "Sometimes it's time for a change."

"I don't think so, Chase. I think you're tired."

"What if I am?"

"Then you'd better return their email rather than avoid it. They think they're more important than you or a client."

"You've been reading my emails again?"

"You know it. It's the only way to make sure you don't skip the important ones."

"I haven't decided yet."

"Remember: No decision *is* a decision."

"I hear you." And he understood the truth in her words. Could he really work for Jim or Jim's client? Make the switch away from criminal defense? He went to law school to do criminal defense work. Had the dream changed because of a few bad experiences working for spoiled rich kids who had daddies who tried to buy get-out-of-jail-free cards? He considered Anneliese, who was completely lost on her own. Wasn't she exactly the type of client he'd wanted to help?

She needed his help in a way others hadn't in a long time.

He sighed and hit the Talk button. "Hey, Jim."

"Chase. How are the negotiations going?"

"Negotiations?"

"Don't be coy. Related to settling this case."

"I can't talk to you about a client. You know that."

"We were pretty clear in our conversations with you about this position. There can be no controversy."

"I understand, but I don't see how doing a good job with this case could cause any harm—assuming you mean the Anneliese Richter murder trial."

"What other case would I call about?"

"Why are you so interested in this one? You're a corporate firm with a corporate client looking for assistance. And to follow up an email with a phone call within a few hours seems pushy."

"Excited to get this locked up. We're convinced you'll be a great addition, but we need your undivided attention."

Chase tapped his fingers on the desk as he considered the words. "So there's an issue that needs my time now?"

"I didn't say that." Jim had a hold-up tone in his words. "We're ready to use your skill."

"I see. Well, the trial launches in two months, and then it should wrap in a week. I'd say I'll be ready after that—about the middle of June."

"I'll have to see if that still works with the partners."

"Why don't you see if it does." As he hung up, Chase's suspicion something more was at work seemed confirmed. Something he couldn't see or understand, but something he needed to identify.

He couldn't do anything about whatever shenanigans Jim manipulated right now, but he could make movement on Anneliese's case. He emailed Margeaux and arranged a time to go back to the apartment building the next day. The two of them working together could accomplish more than he could on his own. And later he'd consider why the thought of her working with him didn't bother him anymore.

Leigh bounced into his office, waving a piece of paper. "You won't guess who Marcus found."

"Does he work here anymore?"

She stopped waving the paper and frowned at him. "No."

"Then why would I care what he found?"

"Because the kid's trying to fix a mistake, and you need to learn a concept like grace." She sashayed up to his desk and slapped the paper down on it. "I'd suggest you get off your high horse regarding Marcus and call this number."

"Why?"

"It's one of the victim's last boyfriends. And Marcus located the man for you."

Chapter 26

THE DEPARTMENT HEAD HAD BEEN waiting for Margeaux when she'd arrived at her office that morning, wanting to know if she'd decided to apply for the assistant position. She didn't tell him she hadn't considered the job offer since the campus murder, but it had swirled in the back of her mind all day, vying for time opposite her concern for Anneliese. Then Chase had called to ask if she minded accompanying him on a potential witness interview instead of knocking on apartment doors.

With information like that, how could she say no?

Now, after she'd killed herself to get to his office after her class ended, she hurried to keep up with Chase as he hustled up the sidewalk to the apartment building where the murder had occurred. Hustling through her days wore her out, and she didn't need to pursue him. She'd hit the part of the semester where she lost her patience for all bustle. "Is the apartment on fire? I don't see any smoke or flames."

"Time's the one thing we don't have enough of."

"Tell me about it." She mumbled the words, but his popped eyebrow made it clear he'd understood. "Look, I know you're busy, but so am I. I've got classes to teach and students to meet." And it all mattered to her.

"Then go meet with them. Mold those impressionable young minds. This simple attorney"—he gestured broadly toward himself—"will handle the mundane details of the investigation. You know, the straightforward things that might prove our client didn't commit the murder." He huffed a breath and pinched the bridge of his nose. "Sorry. That went too far."

Her mouth dropped and she stared at him, hands planted on her hips. "You think she did it."

"Do you have a sliver of evidence that she didn't?"

She wanted to scream at him but forced herself to breathe slowly through her nose as she counted to ten, then counted again. Maybe if she counted to one hundred she would make it without wanting to strangle him. Then she blanched as she realized the direction of her thoughts and how wrong they felt moving into a potential witness interview.

"You know everything I know, Chase."

"So? Are you ready to admit she might not be as innocent as you believe?"

"Why?"

"Because you have to approach this like the police. You have to attack this like she's guilty and then prove all of their evidence is wrong or misinterpreted. That's the only way to get the jury to go along with an alternative theory to the one the police have."

"Really? That's the only way? That seems like a narrow interpretation."

"Maybe, but it works." Even as he stated it forcefully his gaze slipped from hers and he moved up the sidewalk. "Let's get in there before he leaves."

"How do you know he's in there anyway?"

He glanced over his shoulder with an arched brow. "I made an appointment."

"He'll have an attorney."

"Maybe, but he'll be there. And an attorney won't stop him from talking if he wants to. If he doesn't want to, an attorney isn't much of a barrier." Chase hustled up the couple of steps and held the main door open for her. His arm brushed her shoulder as she slipped past him into the entryway, and she shrugged away. She knew he was right. Just like he'd been right about getting Anneliese to talk and leaving the young woman in prison. But it didn't make her like it any more than she'd liked her coach telling her to push harder and throw one more routine.

The bare-bones apartment building was a common choice for students attending Monroe. First-generation students and privileged legacies created a blended population, and she found it interesting to watch them mix in the housing. This was the great equalizer. Everyone had to haul their furniture up the stairwell when they moved in, and the groceries didn't magically march up the flights on their own. Everyone found common ground in the requirements of self-preservation. Sometimes in the middle of the semester, on weekends or game days, the units would carry a clear aroma of alcohol and vomit, even weed. But that was missing now.

Margeaux glanced up the stairwell, wondering how many levels they'd have to climb. "Which unit is his?"

"215."

She gave a slow nod. A floor below Lauren. "All right. We can do this."

"Yep." Chase regripped his attaché case and stalked toward the stairs as if striding into battle.

She hurried after him, her heels clicking against the cement floor. She wheezed as they finally reached the student's door.

"Dominic Strand. God's gift to women. At least that's what my research tells me." Chase rapped on the door, paused a moment, then rapped again.

As they waited, she wondered if Chase knew the same words could be said about him . . . though he never acted that way. She imagined in college he'd worn the carefree look of a young man who caught the coeds' attention.

"Coming." The lazy voice was filtered by the door, but still came through with clarity. A minute later it opened to reveal a young Tom Holland wannabe. He leaned against the doorframe and looked at them. "Yeah?"

"Dominic Strand?"

"Who's asking?"

Margeaux bit on her lower lip to keep from grinning. So much for scheduling ahead.

"Chase Crandall. We had an appointment."

"Oh." The young man snapped his fingers and straightened. "You're the attorney. Wanted to talk about Lauren. Not sure what I can tell you, but come on in."

"Thanks." Chase met her gaze and gave a half eye roll before gesturing for her to precede him.

In the living space, a leather couch rested in front of an oversized flat screen mounted on the wall. Nothing else was hung on the beige backdrop, but a bookshelf was underneath, the lowest shelf filled with a few books, the rest sports game cartridges. A bag of expensive golf clubs sat in the corner of the room farthest from the door. It was an upscale bachelor pad. Which meant Dominic fell in the legacy camp. That would explain the entitled air. Margeaux glanced to him. "Have you gone golfing recently, Mr. Strand?"

"You can have a seat." He gave her a careful appraisal. "Not this year, but if you want to go, I'll be glad to make time."

His actions weren't those of a grieving boyfriend. But everyone reacted to death differently, so maybe she misread him. It seemed callous to essentially ask out a woman you'd just met when that person was here to ask questions about your recently murdered girlfriend.

"I'm busy. Thanks." She perched on the edge of the couch and waited as the men each took a seat.

Dominic held up his hands. "Hey, just being friendly. You have to understand Lauren and I weren't exactly an item anymore."

Chase leaned forward. "What do you mean by 'not exactly'?"

"Just that. She wanted to see other people." He shrugged like it wasn't a big deal. "I didn't love the idea at first but came to see her perspective. We were young to get tied down. Early twenties? What did we know about the rest of our lives? Nothing."

"Is that why others said you threatened her if she left you?" Chase dropped the sentence so nonchalantly it was almost possible to miss the meaning.

Almost.

But the man's flared nostrils and widened eyes suggested he'd caught the subtle thrust.

"She was a grown woman and knew her mind." Dominic slouched against the leather recliner. "I couldn't make her do anything. Wasn't going to do me any good to wonder if she was out with other guys when she wasn't with me. Might as well make it official that we weren't exclusive."

"Then why didn't her friends understand the change in your status?"

"I'd say that was hers to tell. Not mine."

He had a point. He wouldn't be much of a gentleman if he was talking about her in a negative light. "What changed between you?"

He gave a slow shrug as if he didn't know or care, but wasn't as casual as he probably thought. "I'm not sure."

"Come on." She leaned forward, wanting to cajole him to abandon his safe answers. There was more there, and he wasn't as intelligent as he thought. "You're a good-looking guy. I bet you're smart too."

"My grades seem to think I am."

"See? The world's your oyster."

He grinned along with her.

"Why wouldn't she want to stay with you?"

Chase took up the pursuit. "You must have asked yourself that question a lot. Developed some hypotheses."

"You might as well tell us what you think. Why leave us to our imaginations when that could be way off base?" Would he go where they were leading?

Dominic steepled his fingers and considered them over the top. "There had to be someone else, but she kept the secret really well."

"That must have driven you crazy," Chase said.

"You have no idea. It's impossible to beat a ghost."

"I bet you wanted to. You're, what, captain of the golf team?" Chase sank back on the couch like he had all the time in the world to chat with the man.

"Yeah. Competition's in my blood. I love it, but I need an opponent."

"So when you didn't have one?"

"Oh, I had one."

And then it clicked for Margeaux. "You found him."

"Sure did. It wasn't that hard. Lauren thought she was so smart. Putting me off and telling me she couldn't see me for our regular nights. But I figured it out." He crossed his arms and a muscle in his jaw popped. "It was easy to follow her."

"How'd you do that?" He just looked at her, and her mind raced to fill in the gap. "Did you have Life360 or something like that on her phone?"

"We had it on each other. I can't help it if she never removed me from her circle." His innocent expression didn't fool her. "I wanted to protect her."

Somehow Margeaux didn't think stalking a girlfriend counted as protecting her.

Chapter 27

MARGEAUX AND CHASE KNOCKED ON a few more doors, which provided some conversations but no leads. As soon as they climbed into Chase's car, Margeaux strapped in and turned his direction.

"He must be the one." Margeaux's excitement almost made Chase wish he wasn't the guy who had to disappoint her.

"One what?"

"Don't be so obtuse." She nearly growled the words. "He killed Lauren."

"That conversation was all it took to convince you he's a murderer?"

"Yes. And the jury will believe it too."

"And he's going to give that testimony on the stand?"

"Of course." Her forehead crinkled. "Why wouldn't he?"

"Because then he'd be looking at jail time. Now he was just feeling us out. Seeing what we know, as much as we felt him out." Chase put the car in drive and eased onto the street. "I'm hungry. Let's get some food and go to the office."

Margeaux looked at her watch and grimaced. "Much as I'd love to continue this enlightening conversation, I've got to get back to campus." Her stomach growled a protest, and she sighed. "Maybe a sandwich first."

After they were seated at Flo's Diner, she stared at a Reuben over-loaded with corned beef and Thousand Island dressing. "When did I let you order for me?"

"When you left the table before the waitress arrived."

"Right." She cautiously picked up the greasy sandwich and took a bite. An array of delicious flavors exploded in her mouth.

"Not bad, right?"

"It's unexpectedly good." She dabbed at her mouth. "Without a confession from Dominic what's your next move?"

"We keep poking. Usually there's no magic witness."

"There has to be. And he did admit to stalking Lauren. That must mean something. Give us something we can use with the jury. All we need is reasonable doubt."

He dragged a french fry through ketchup and mayo—yuck—and watched her. "Maybe, maybe not."

"Why do you do that?"

"Do what?"

"Mayo? Really?"

"Yep. Don't knock it." He shoved several more in his mouth and made a show of chewing.

She looked away in disgust. "I don't want to know. Back to what matters."

"It all matters. Look, I know this case and this client are all you can see right now, but in four months, life will have moved on. You'll be frantically getting ready for the fall semester, and I'll have fourteen more clients or will be on to another job. What's consuming us today doesn't matter in a few weeks."

"But it will to Anneliese. This isn't a game to her."

"Right now"—he gave a sad smirk that she wanted to wipe off his face—"that's all it is: a game. The highest level of competition. The kind with maximum stakes, because if we lose, she'll spend the rest of her days in jail." He swiped another handful of fries through the disgusting combination. "But we can only work with the evidence we have."

"Not if we find some."

He paused and gave her a hard look. "It might be a game, but we do not create false evidence."

"We can't simply work off what the police have found. They think they have their woman, so they stopped digging. We know they have the wrong person, so we need to keep hunting." She tore a corner of the crust away from the bread, then brushed the crumbs from her fingers. "We can't be passive about this."

"We also can't go off creating what doesn't exist."

"Maybe we can give it a little push."

"Not a good idea."

———

Chase knew she taught this material, and if she had a student voicing the statements she'd just said, she'd be livid, and rightly so. "Once you blow the jury's trust, the entire case is shot. Not to mention your credibility with the judge."

She sighed and tore another corner off her sandwich. If she kept this up, she wouldn't have much left to eat. "I know you're right, but the police had to miss something. Dominic stalking Lauren would give any woman on a jury the creeps."

"And the police will follow up on that. If he volunteered it to us, it'll come up with them."

"Now who's being naive?"

"The police are professionals."

"And they've gotten it right every time? With every one of your clients?" She raised an eyebrow as if daring him to deny she made a point.

"No one's perfect."

"Exactly. So we have to help them find what they missed."

"Or we have to be willing to admit they didn't miss a thing."

"You can't give up on her already."

"It's not giving up. It's being a realist. I'll keep talking to people because that's what a good attorney does. I'll keep looking for rocks to peek under, but sometimes you have to admit there's nothing there.

Sometimes even when we hate it, we must go with the answer, acknowledge what exists and what doesn't." He let his mind run through what they'd learned. "I'll try to track down some people who knew Dominic and Lauren as a couple. Learn what they saw in the relationship. I guarantee Dominic is not giving us the full story, but it'll take some work to flesh it out."

"Where will you begin?"

"Usually Lauren's friends and roommates, but that will be a bit muddled because I imagine they'll have strong opinions about Anneliese and Lauren."

She leaned into the table, and it was a good thing she couldn't really laser him with her look. "You've talked to them without me."

"Not yet, but I'll find them, and when I do, I can't wait for you for every conversation. We'd never learn anything." And her intensity would scare some people away. She had to learn to scale that back.

"I'll talk to some students too. See what I can learn."

"Please don't."

"Why?"

"You aren't an attorney of record or a hired investigator. You could really make a mess of things."

"Then I'll make sure I don't." She tossed her dark hair. "Thanks for lunch. I'll walk from here."

He watched her leave, then studied the pile of Reuben she'd shredded that filled her plate. She'd eaten maybe four bites before tearing it to bits.

Margeaux's stomach tumbled as she speed walked toward campus. She'd probably be late for the faculty meeting, but right now she didn't care as her thoughts ricocheted and pinged in anything but a straight line. She needed to think about who she knew that had been friends with Lauren Payge. As a student athlete, the young woman would have spent most of her time away from the academic buildings—not because she wasn't a committed student, but because her time had to be invested multiple places. So which student athletes did Margeaux have strong relationships with?

A volleyball player leapt to the top of the list. The young woman had attended office hours frequently and done well in Margeaux's survey law class. Blake Dillon was a senior and applying to law school, so she'd spent time in Margeaux's office talking through her options a couple of times earlier that semester. Maybe she had known Lauren. The campus was small enough that Margeaux hoped Blake or some of her friends had more than a passing familiarity with the lacrosse player.

There was one way to find out.

She sent a quick email to Blake and half an hour later had a reply. Blake would pop in the next morning.

Chapter 28

When Blake entered Margeaux's office the next day, she towered over Margeaux with the easy grace and athleticism of a powerful setter. She leaned over to give Margeaux a quick hug, then slouched into an extra chair, a posture Margeaux had come to recognize as the young woman trying to mask her stately height. "What would you like to know about Lauren?"

Margeaux appreciated Blake's no-nonsense approach. "Did you know her well?"

"There's a relatively small group of student athletes on campus. And since there's a lot of testosterone to wade through, we women watch out for each other." She laced her long fingers into a fist on top of the round table. "It's not all bad, but a couple of times, Lauren and I banded together along with Aren Folgyers, the women's basketball captain, to remind the sports director that we have different needs than the guys."

That reminded Margeaux too much of her experience in high school before she'd had to quit gymnastics. She pushed the memories from her mind before she slid down a rabbit hole that would distract her from the moment she lived in now. "What was Lauren like?"

"A competitive leader. She could entice people to work with her. It was great to watch. But she also loved a good party, sometimes too much." Blake's shoulders sloped forward as her gaze roved the book-shelves. "Is that a new Wonder Woman toy?"

Margeaux glanced over her shoulder at the shelf. "Yes. The Women in Business club gave her to me at the holiday party."

"I like it. Good to see you've embraced the nickname."

"Embrace it or fight it. Accepting seemed easier." Nice try with the distraction, but that meant something bothered Blake that Margeaux needed to probe . . . carefully. Margeaux let silence settle for a minute to see if Blake would return to the topic on her own. When she didn't, Margeaux redirected. "What was Lauren's reputation outside of the ath-lete circle?"

"I didn't know her well outside athletics." Blake blew out a breath. "Look, I don't know what you want me to tell you, but Lauren was com-plicated. She competed and played hard. She also partied and fought hard. She did everything one hundred and ten percent. She was all fire and ice. She loved you or ignored you. Period. You didn't want to move from her friends to enemies list because she made it nearly impossible to move back. But if she liked you, man, she fought for you as a fierce defender." Blake nodded toward the Wonder Woman dolls. "A lot like Diana."

"What can you tell me about her boyfriend?"

"Which one?"

"How many did Lauren have?"

"She didn't like to commit." Blake paused as if reconsidering the words. "That's not quite right. Lauren had really high standards and lit-tle tolerance for people who didn't match them. If you didn't live up to those ideals, then she settled for a good time. When it wasn't fun, she moved on. Fast. Sometimes too fast for the other person. She gave a few guys whiplash."

"So she had a lot of boyfriends?"

"She had a lot of boys who were friends. Intimate friends." Blake shrugged. "She seemed to be searching for something she couldn't find. But she didn't have any patience when I tried to tell her that she couldn't find what she needed in guys. A few times when she seemed really frustrated, I even told her that if she wanted to be genuinely loved, she should come to church with me. That there was only one man who could fill the dead spot inside her. She scoffed when I told her that was Jesus. Something had happened to scar her to those conversations. I never could figure out what."

Margeaux swallowed against the flash of pain because she thought she knew what had made it impossible for Lauren to hear—the same thing Margeaux had struggled with for years. She had felt unworthy anytime someone had mentioned that God loved her. First, she'd felt she had to earn his attention with perfection. Then she'd believed he could never look past her failures. It had taken so much work to come to a place of resting in the reality that there was nothing she could do to earn God's love. That lesson had been hard-won, but the truth moved from her head to her heart when she finally grasped it. Even now, some days she could easily slide back to a place of believing all God saw were her mistakes, even though she knew that wasn't truth.

She blinked once, twice, and stepped from the past. She gave Blake a wan smile and asked the question she'd waited for. "Was Dominic Strand one of her boyfriends?"

"He wanted to be."

Margeaux straightened. That certainly wasn't how he characterized it. "What do you mean?"

"He thought they were serious. And at one point maybe they could have developed into something, but then he looked at another girl on the lacrosse team and that was it. Lauren wrote him off. He thought he should get a second or third chance. But that wasn't how she worked."

"She was one and done?"

"That's a good way of putting it. Once her trust was violated, that was it. She didn't want to waste her time or emotional energy trying to figure out if you were going to break trust again."

"Sounds like you knew her well."

Blake paused as if really considering the sentence. "I thought we were acquaintances, but . . ." Her eyes filled with tears. "I guess I knew her better than I thought." She twisted her hands together in her lap. "It's hard to imagine Anneliese killing her."

Margeaux stilled. "Why do you say that?"

"I only met Anneliese a couple of times, but she seemed nice, if quiet. She was an observer, not a doer. Her big eyes took everything in and catalogued what she saw." Blake shrugged and then swiped under her eyes. "She's nice enough, but not overly invested in anything. It felt like she wanted to engage but didn't quite know how."

The aptness of that description touched Margeaux. "Anneliese struggles to bridge the gap."

"Exactly. I am sorry she got entwined in all this." She looked away. "It makes me wonder what would have happened if one of the other roommates got home first." She met Margeaux's gaze. "You know? Then they would have found Lauren's body rather than Anneliese."

That question plagued Margeaux.

Where had they been?

Why had they arrived home even later than Anneliese?

Or had they? Could one of them have killed Lauren and then slipped away to create an alibi, leaving Anneliese to find the body and look guilty of murder?

Chase had tracked down one of the roommates, and even though she might lie to his face, he found himself in front of her friend's apartment. He needed to take this carefully. Right now the police weren't considering either roommate a viable suspect, but he had to see what he could learn.

His job required turning over stones or he would risk committing malpractice by not effectively advocating for his client. He was good at chasing down threads and finding loopholes. It often kept him from taking a bad case to trial. He'd developed a good sense of the evidence the state had, but this case still felt obfuscated. He would probably have to risk a trial. He didn't have enough to force the commonwealth to offer a plea and ensure the outcome. If he did, it would be a win for the state—no expensive trial—and a win for the defendant—no risk of a jury giving a bad verdict. Everyone won.

He'd been surprised when Renee Jacobs invited him to the place she was staying. It was an apartment on the other side of the complex, and when he arrived, she matched her Instagram photos, which was more revealing of her coed lifestyle than her staid LinkedIn profile was. College students didn't think about how easily people could see what they were up to thanks to social media. An average-size college coed who hadn't bothered to put on any makeup before the meeting, Renee didn't have Lauren's athletic confidence or Anneliese's world-worn air. Instead she looked put out and annoyed.

Once they were seated in the small living area, she turned to him. "I don't know why you want to talk with me. I already talked with the police."

"This won't take long."

She made a show of looking at her smart watch. "Good. I have class in thirty minutes."

Nice. That was one way to limit their interaction. Chase took a moment to stuff his irritation as he grabbed a pad of paper and pen.

"Don't you have a laptop or tablet?"

"That's what this is."

"Yeah, if you're a caveman." She crossed her arms and smacked her gum. "In this day and age, we like to use technology."

He ignored her and straightened the pad of paper. No need to tell her that if the power grid imploded, all her gadgets and gizmos would fail but his trusty notes would still be available. "What was it like living with Lauren?"

"She wasn't there much." She slid a device into her backpack and then fiddled with the zipper. "Athletes keep a crazy schedule." She gave a shudder. "Not one I would want."

"What was it like?"

"She was out the door hours before I woke up, and most days she'd get back after dark. She had practices, classes, and then study hours at the success center. Even in the offseason, coaches had lots of expectations."

"Was she easy to live with?"

"Easy enough, I guess." She looked away as if thinking. "She had high expectations about what the place should look like." Renee scanned the space as if seeing it through Lauren's eyes. "She wouldn't be happy to see all the dishes around here and the blankets thrown around. She didn't like it looking lived-in. She came from money and wanted it to look like we were in *Southern Living* or something."

"Southern living?"

"The magazine. Her mom would pop in unannounced, and it stressed Lauren out. There were crazy expectations there. Lauren transferred those to us. I didn't like it, but I appreciated the extra food in the fridge, so put up with a little bit of crazy."

"You said she came from money."

"Yep. Lacrosse, buddy."

"What's that mean?"

"You ever seen a poor school with a lacrosse team?"

"Interesting choice for Monroe."

"Monroe has its haves and have-nots. Look at my suitemates. We had Lauren, the German girl, and the two of us. Lauren was a have. So's Anneliese, and then there's the have-nots."

Was that a note of bitterness? "Anneliese is a have?" That wasn't how she'd described herself to the court or to him.

"Yep. Her dad's a sixty-year-old doctor. Mom's an executive. She can afford to spend a year abroad as a student. That's a definite have. Why she chose Monroe is a mystery, but she has money. She and Lauren deserved each other . . . until they didn't. No one deserves to be murdered."

"How did you and Lauren get along?"

"Well enough, I guess. We didn't see much of each other. Different schedules, and we didn't share a bathroom like Lauren and Anneliese did."

"How about Lauren and Anneliese?"

"They were like oil and water. I got the sense Anneliese tried, but Lauren refused to get along. I'm not sure why. Anneliese was quiet and didn't want to be a bother. If anything, she tended to disappear. It was almost annoying how easily I could forget she lived there. Then I'd look up and find her watching, like I was someone to study." Renee gave a small shudder.

"Anything unusual about that?"

"I don't know. It made me feel . . ." She didn't answer right away. "Not unsafe. More like a specimen she observed. It was weird, so I ignored her." She looked down for a minute and he let the silence breathe. When she looked up, her expression had sobered. "Maybe that was the problem."

"What do you mean?"

"Maybe if we'd been friendlier, she wouldn't have killed Lauren."

How committed was she to that statement? He needed to probe to see if it was hers or something she'd adopted from someone else. "Do you know she killed Lauren?"

"She had to."

"Why?"

"The police said she did."

"You weren't there."

"Noooo."

"You're sure?"

Her spine stiffened and she stared at him. "Of course. I was at the library studying."

"What were you studying?"

"Statistics, I think."

"You think?"

"I had a test the next day."

"If you're going to accuse one of your roommates of murder, you'd better be certain."

"Who else could have done it?"

"You tell me. You knew Lauren and her friends. Who came around?"

"She always had guys over."

"Always?"

"Yes—a different guy all the time."

"Did she ever argue with anyone?"

"Anneliese and one of her guys."

"Which one?" This was like pulling teeth. She was making him tug each word out.

"Dominic. And there was another one too. Near the end." She grimaced. "I don't remember his name if she ever told me, but he was older. Too old, if you ask me. Gave creepy vibes."

"Can you describe him?"

"How about a picture?"

"Even better." Sort of. Though a name would be best. He didn't love the idea of walking around town with a picture asking if anyone knew who the person was.

She eased her phone from her hoodie's pouch and scrolled. Then she clicked a few buttons and turned the screen toward him. "Here he is."

He looked at the screen and saw a photo of three people, two young men on either side of Lauren. She had a radiant smile as she flirted with the camera. The older of the men gazed at Lauren with a possessive air. The other, an unkempt Dominic, stared at the first man, hand fisted at his side. "When did you take this?"

"It was a couple of weeks before Lauren was killed. At a pre–spring break event of some sort." She slid the phone back into her hoodie. "I don't remember."

Guess he'd have to ask for the photo and more details. "Can you send me the photo?"

"Sure. What's your number?"

"Just email it." He took her phone and quickly entered his work email address and sent the photo before handing the device back. Then, with a nod, he left.

Chapter 29

AT THE END OF THE week, as Margeaux tried to get grading done, someone knocked on her office door. She didn't bother to look up. "Come in."

"Margeaux Robbins?"

"Yes?" She glanced up and her heart stilled when she noticed Detective Phillips standing in the doorway.

"You need to come to the police station with me."

She was getting seriously tired of this man and his attitude. "Why?"

"I'd rather not say in public."

"Then you'll have to wait, because you're here in the middle of my work."

"Not possible." He said it with such adamance, she needed to get him out of the hall where anyone could overhear.

"Do you have an arrest warrant?"

"No."

Good. Whatever he thought he needed, she wouldn't go with him. "Then you should have done the professional thing and called." After all, this wasn't the first time they'd had a conversation. "Now I'd appreciate it if you wouldn't make a spectacle. We can schedule a time and accomplish your goal."

He pasted a stiff grimace on his face. "Then this is your invitation to come downtown with me." He glanced over his shoulder and shooed a student along. "I'd suggest you come now before more people notice."

"I've got a class in an hour."

"This one's getting canceled."

"Can it wait?" Her mind raced with what he thought couldn't wait for two hours until after class.

"No."

"This is a custodial conversation?"

"No."

"That's what this sounds like. Otherwise, I could have Janae meet me there at the end of class. Surely a couple of hours won't matter?"

"I'd prefer to wait in your lecture."

"I'm sure you'd love to learn all about white-collar crimes."

"That'll be fine."

He plopped into the chair in her office and waited while she sent Janae an email. Then she picked up an essay to grade, forcing herself to ignore the man taking up space in her sanctuary. This was her place to be in charge when everything else spiraled out of control, so she did not appreciate his bullying his way into staying. Should she call campus security? What would the dean think if she did? She picked up her phone and looked at him. "I'm going to call campus security if you don't leave now. I can meet you at the Leesburg office within half an hour of my classes ending."

"Who's your police chief?" He held up a hand and examined his nails. "Joe Grainger? We go back a long time."

"Great." She firmed her posture. "That doesn't give you the right to come here and intimidate me. I will come to whichever location you tell me as soon as my last class ends."

He stared at her, as if waiting for her to buckle under his intense glare, but she held her ground. Finally, he nodded. "Fine." He handed over his card. "Meet me here." Then he stood and walked carelessly from her office.

An hour later, she ignored the detective as she left her office. He'd lingered at the entryway to the building. She tried to pretend she wouldn't meet with him after the class but knew it distracted her. It took effort to stay focused on her students.

"All right. Now that you know everything about white-collar crime, I'll see you next week. Don't forget to prepare for the final. It'll be here before you know it."

The volume in the classroom rose as the students threw their textbooks in bags and talked about their plans for the rest of the day.

Margeaux slowly turned off the computer and collected her whiteboard markers and presentation clicker while the students lurched to their feet and hauled backpacks over shoulders. After most had left, Donovan approached the lectern.

"You okay, Professor R?"

She forced a smile. "I am. See you next class."

Donovan studied her a second, then nodded. "All right." He strolled to the door, then turned as if to check on her again.

When she reached her car, she tried not to be unnerved to see Detective Phillips waiting in his unmarked car. The man seriously needed a hobby. He followed her through town and along the short drive to Leesburg and the sheriff's office.

After she parked, he filled the space outside her car door as if he thought she'd bolt. There was no reason for him to think she would. He escorted her to the front door, which he held open for her, then walked her inside, past the woman stationed at the front desk and through a door to the back. She'd been here a couple of times before, but this was so much worse. "I'm not saying anything without an attorney."

"That's fine, but a bad decision. I haven't Mirandized you. This is just a friendly conversation."

She felt the walls closing in on her in the narrow hallway. "There is nothing friendly about being stalked and threatened at my place of work."

He opened a door and waited for her to enter the small interview room. She reluctantly did so, unsure why it felt like the moment the door closed she would lose the ability to leave.

"Have a seat."

"No." She crossed her arms and stared at him. "What is this about?"

He smirked at her, and she tightened her lips, determined not to say anything else. Instead she tugged out her phone and hit a few buttons.

"What are you doing?" He reached for it, but she jerked it away from his grasp.

"Recording this conversation. This is Margeaux Robbins. I'm with Detective Phillips who has me at the police station and won't tell me why." She rattled off the date. "I've asked for an attorney and refused to answer any questions without an attorney present." She stared at him.

"Your friend has named you as part of the conspiracy to murder Lauren Payge, and I thought you should have an opportunity to explain your side of the story before we arrest you."

Panic ripped through her as she fought to keep control. What did he mean Anneliese had accused her?

He slipped a small recorder from his jacket pocket and set it on the table with the click of a button. "And now I'm recording the conversation too."

There was something slightly sinister about the way he did that. Like he saw her bid and raised it.

Margeaux's knees gave way, and she sank onto a chair. She stared at him but refused to say anything. She had to stay silent. No matter what he said or did next, she couldn't let him bait her. If she was quiet, maybe he would tell her what he thought he knew. Without understanding what was going on, there was too much that she could say or do that he could misconstrue.

"I find it interesting that you were in here helping that student and now she says you were involved in the plot to cover up the murder. It's curious to me how you thought you'd get away with it." He smacked a hand on the table, and she jumped. "We're not small-town police who don't understand how to investigate a murder."

She bit the inside of her cheek to keep from asking a question or engaging with the craziness. He leaned into the table, and she felt his looming presence but refused to retreat.

"Why not call us when she told you about the murder? Why get embedded in the plot?"

She fisted her hands, letting her fingernails push into the palms of her hands, the pain grounding her in the moment.

"Ms. Richter said you were a help to her from the beginning. That you understood how to keep her from getting in trouble, but that your ideas weren't very good after all." He leaned back and put his hands on his stomach. "Nothing to say in your defense?" There was a knock at the door, but Detective Phillips ignored it. "If I were innocent, I'd want to clear up any misunderstanding as quickly as I could."

Margeaux met his gaze but refused to say a word. He needed to keep talking because so far, she didn't understand how any of this was an accusation against her.

The knock came again—this time more insistent. "Excuse me a moment." He moved to the door, and Margeaux sent Janae a text.

> I'm at the police station. I think it's not custodial, but I wasn't given a real choice about coming. What do I do?

> Don't say anything.

> I'm trying but it's hard to stay silent. I'm also recording.

> Good. Do everything you told me to do when I was there for Mark Ashby's murder. Stay quiet. Don't engage. This too shall pass.

Margeaux rolled her eyes. What had Janae been thinking when she sat in this chair?

Thanks.

Detective Phillips turned back with Allison Erickson next to him. Rather than wait, Margeaux took the initiative.

"While this has been enlightening, I have nothing to say, and I'm leaving. You know where to find me if you have any real questions." She paused a moment to gather her courage. "And next time, call first." She tightened her stance as she looked at the detective. "I'm not fond of bullies."

Allison looked between them. "What did you do now, Phillips?"

Margeaux paused long enough to throw a comment. "He harassed me by coming to my office and lurking for hours. Then he followed me here. Some of my students saw him, and he made at least one concerned. If he does that again, I'll file harassment charges. And if he brings me in here with baseless allegations and hurled threats, I'll sue for more than that." She focused on Allison. "I'd make sure he's busy with real cases in the future."

Margeaux didn't stick around to see how he responded as she brushed from the room. Maybe Allison could keep him occupied while she made her escape.

"I told you to leave Ms. Robbins alone. We weren't ready."

Weren't ready? The words didn't comfort Margeaux as they followed her down the short hallway. Tempted as she was to stay and learn more, she was even more interested in getting far away from the police while she could. She didn't like the sound of what the CA had said. *"Weren't ready."* That didn't sound like they didn't have anything. What had Anneliese said?

As soon as she was safely in her car, she texted Janae.

You at your office?

Yes.

I'm on my way.

When she entered Janae's small office thirty minutes later, Chloe looked up from the reception desk. "Everything all right?"

"I'm not sure." Margeaux couldn't make sense of what had happened. "Detective Phillips insisted I come to the sheriff's office, and then didn't tell me why he needed me to come there."

"He's fishing." Chloe made it a firm statement, but Margeaux didn't share her confidence.

"He thinks he has something. On me. I can't imagine what." Margeaux glanced around. "Janae in her office?"

"Yep." Chloe followed her down the short hall, and soon all three concentrated on the recording.

"What do you think he was trying to do? Why come to my office, lurk, and then do that nonsense in the interrogation room?"

Janae considered without rushing into an answer. "You didn't give him anything."

"No filling the space." Chloe agreed. "You let him do all the talking."

"Why focus on me?" She'd felt so alone and unsettled. Maybe she should have waited and insisted someone come with her. Gotten Chase involved. What would it be like to have Chase defend her the way he defended his clients? She'd never had anyone who stood up for her. Would he? She wanted him to . . . but if he didn't? The disappointment would crush her.

"Earth to Margeaux." Chloe waved a hand in her face.

"Sorry. Guess I got lost. Maybe I should have insisted that you or Chase be allowed to join me."

"Ah." Chloe grinned. "That explains the look on your face."

"What?"

"You were dreaming about Chase. He's pretty dreamworthy."

"No. I'm trying to figure out what's going on and why Phillips pivoted to me." She rubbed her forehead, wishing she had some aspirin.

"It would have been a good idea to have him or me there. Chase would make more sense though." Janae looked up from her notes. "Do you think Anneliese really said you were involved?"

"Considering I don't think Anneliese killed Lauren? No. And why would she say I was? It doesn't make any sense to try to implicate me. What would anyone gain by making me part of this mess?" Margeaux felt adrenaline trembling her arms and legs. "This case makes less sense each time I turn around." She rubbed her forehead. "The other odd thing occurred when I overheard Allison Erickson chastising Detective Phillips for bringing me in too early."

Chloe's nose crinkled as she made a note. "What does that mean?"

"I don't know."

Janae sank onto her chair and steepled her fingers in front of her as she considered Margeaux, a move that had Margeaux poised to fight although Janae hadn't said a word. "Why are you certain Anneliese isn't involved?"

"What?"

"Have you considered she could be?"

Margeaux looked between her friends. "Do you think she could be?"

Chloe held her hands up in front of her and looked like she wished the phone would ring, calling her from the room. "I don't know her."

"Yes, I'm the only one here who does. That should mean something."

Janae didn't relent. "Have you carefully evaluated the possibility that she might be part of the murder?"

"No." Margeaux noted the sharpness in her voice, but there was nothing she could do to dampen it.

"Then have you thought about why? Why are you so determined to avoid going there?"

The questions were valid and chased Margeaux from her friend's office. When had she allowed Anneliese's innocence to become so entwined with the rightness of the world? It bordered on irrational, and Margeaux prided herself on being one of the most rational people in any room.

What had changed?

She needed to clear her head and answer the question. Leaving her car here to walk back to her office would give her the chance to transition as she collected her things. As confused as she was, the walk to campus and back might not be long enough.

Chapter 30

"YOU MIGHT WANT TO GET out here."

Leigh's voice pulled Chase from his work editing the Wilkins motion-to-dismiss response. That hearing was sneaking up on him, and it'd be an automatic win for the other side if he didn't get this response filed.

He groaned but pushed to his feet. "We've got these fancy things called phones."

"Those make sense when there's more than two of us here." She turned back to the plate glass window. "The media's camped out front."

Chase shoved his hands in his pockets as he watched the cameraman set up. "Any idea why?"

"None, but I'd guess something to do with your international client. There's been no movement on our other cases." She gestured to the outside. "You going out there? Get your moment of fame?"

"No interest."

His flat words caught her attention. "What?" She reached out and touched his forehead. "You feeling okay?"

He pushed her hand away. "I'm fine. Just not interested in a feeding frenzy." But he watched a minute. "I'm getting back to work. We've still got deadlines to meet in the Wilkins case as well as the Sommers appeal. If I don't get that work done, I'll have some angry clients."

"Maybe you should have kept Marcus. At least for a while."

His jaw clenched and he tried to relax before he broke a tooth. "I won't be held hostage."

"I understand, but you can't do all of this on your own. There's a reason you hired an associate."

"Place a want ad. We can hire another."

"Not in time to make a difference for these cases." Her brows creased as she studied him. "I'm worried about you. I know you lost your passion for this type of work. I can call Marcus and probably get him back for a few months."

"I wouldn't trust him. Without that, it's not worth having him here."

"I think he got caught up in the idea of making a little more and thought he could stay here and do that." She sighed. "I know he didn't take the other job."

"Good for him. Maybe he'll learn something about how to approach his next employer in situations like this."

"You're going to stubborn yourself into an early grave, Chase."

He couldn't argue with her. Just looking at the calendar made him tired, but he didn't know what else to do. Marcus had violated his trust, and he had to trust the people he worked with or he couldn't do his best work for his clients. Even if he was drowning in work, he'd find another solution. "Surely we can find a recent grad who's struggled to find a job. The market's overrun with new attorneys."

"Then you'd better pray one is waiting to work for peanuts in Kedgewick. I'm not sure that's a thing, but maybe you'll get lucky." Leigh rolled her eyes and turned back to the street. "I still think you're a fool, but it's your funeral." She hesitated, then took a step toward the door. "Isn't that Margeaux talking to the reporter?"

Chase felt his blood pressure rise. "You've got to be kidding." He huffed a breath and then strode to the door. Would she know how to talk to them? And why would she even be out there?

"Don't say anything you'll regret."

"Don't worry. What would I say in front of the media?"

"I can imagine."

He ignored her as he opened the door and stepped outside in time to catch Margeaux trying to put off the reporter.

"Look, I'm just passing by. You should be talking to him. He's her attorney."

Great. Maybe he should have stayed inside after all.

The reporter pounced. "Brad Evans with the local affiliate. Do you have a response to the latest charges filed against Anneliese Richter?"

"No comment. We'll make our statements in court." He put a hand on Margeaux's arm and guided her inside.

"Is the reporter going to follow us inside?" Fear skittered across her face, so Chase flicked a glance at the rabble at his door. *What happened out there?*

"I don't think so." He locked the door just in case. "What did you say before I came out?"

"Nothing." She paused, her eyes a little glassy, as if replaying the conversation or considering what to say. "Nothing usable."

"Guess we'll wait and see." He hoped she was right, but he had a feeling the reporter would find a way to use a clip from someone as photogenic as Margeaux. "What are you doing here anyway?"

Her gaze sharpened, making him regret his short tone. "I wasn't stopping. I just wanted to walk back to campus."

"Why stop?"

"I—" She pressed a hand to her forehead and closed her eyes. *Was going back to the office too much for her?* "The press made me." She stepped around him and headed toward the back door. She opened her mouth and then closed it, as if weighing each word. Why couldn't she just spit out? "I'm sorry, but I don't have time for this. I'm going home."

"All right." There was something she wasn't saying. "Are you sure you're okay?"

"I'm fine."

But as she walked out, he didn't believe her. He turned to Leigh, but she just shrugged.

"I have no idea, Chase."

Saturday, Margeaux buried herself in her office. She'd stayed up half the night rewatching the clip the reporter had aired of her protesting that Anneliese was innocent, and the police had made a horrible mistake by arresting her. She firmly believed it, but the video made her look deranged in her advocacy. Chase had texted her one word, *nice*, with a rolling eye emoji.

As much as she'd at first been tempted to melt into Chase's capable defense attorney persona, his reaction had affirmed her decision not to tell him about her interaction with Detective Phillips.

She needed to, but right now Chase didn't feel much safer than the detective. She and Chase were on the same side, but it felt like they were on different ships attacking each other. It seemed that his caring attitude toward his clients didn't extend to her.

Would that change if she let him know what had happened?

She didn't know, and she wasn't sure it was worth the risk of him deciding she was as incompetent as he already believed her to be.

She'd gone for a quick run as soon as she woke up, then showered and moved to the office. Might as well pretend to get some real work done. With all the distractions, she'd let herself get behind on the work she was paid to do, and that needed to change. After four hours of focused work, she wasn't disappointed when her phone rang. "Hello?"

"Please tell me you're doing something fun on this beautiful Saturday." Chloe's voice had a tone of chiding to it.

"Sure, that's exactly what I'm doing."

"You're at the college, aren't you?"

"Busted."

"You have to leave your office. All that grading makes you a very dull person." Chloe's voice had that tone that let Margeaux know there wasn't much she could do to sidetrack her friend.

"You have no idea how much I have to do."

"You've said that so many times, I could say the line along with you."

There was a huff of breath. "Meet me at Chapters and Sips in thirty minutes or I'm coming to get you. You can even bring your laptop if you must. I'd recommend walking. The sunshine and exercise would do wonders for you."

"Thanks, Mom. I did go for a run this morning."

"Let me guess. Ten minutes. Barely enough time to break a sweat."

"Maybe. See you soon." Margeaux ended the call and sank back.

Chloe wasn't wrong. Margeaux knew she could hunch at her desk for another five hours and still be treading water on all that needed to happen. Maybe a quick break would help her focus better. And as her stomach growled, the thought of a fresh muffin with a mug of tea sounded good.

She could do better starting now by heeding her friend.

She didn't used to be so sedentary. A gymnast approaching elite levels trained hours a day for five or six days a week. Though grueling, she had loved it. Then her life had derailed for a season, and she'd never recovered. Her trauma had been an injury too significant for quick recuperation, and she'd struggled to find her new groove.

But she couldn't focus on her past now. She tucked her laptop into her backpack and threw a notebook and textbook in the front pocket.

Margeaux slipped down the hallway to the stairs and then out the main stairs to the double doors. Some students were sprawled on blankets across the lawn between buildings. She tipped her face to the sun as she reminded herself to enjoy the hints of spring and the reminder why she'd thought the professor life would be a great one. Theoretically, she could work from anywhere—though most days she filled the chair in her small office. Showing up in the room that had her name on it transported her thirty years into the future. A plus in academic circles. And she loved her cozy space. In fact, when many of her colleagues were slow to return to their offices, she couldn't wait to escape her small home and get back to the open expanse of campus. Going in on the weekend was overkill, though.

She passed the Union and then the Elliott Museum. One of the banners hanging on the front reminded her there was a new exhibit of Georgia O'Keeffe paintings she needed to make a point to visit. It wasn't enough to serve on the board. She wanted to enjoy the art as a patron too.

Another block later, she reached Chapters and Sips. For a season, Chloe had worked its shelves as a second job, and she still would, on occasion, take a shift to help her friend and former boss. There was something cozy about the blend of new and used books and the carefully placed chairs and love seats inviting people to linger and peruse the books. With the small coffee and tea bar, there was nothing urging people to scurry in and out, but instead an open invitation to sink in and enjoy the space.

The list of book club meetings was encouragement to do exactly that, only with bookish comrades.

Chloe's voice filtered in from a room around the corner, the one that bridged romance and suspense with a thread of travel books. The arrangement was interesting but created the perfect place for readers to tuck away and escape.

Margeaux waved at the young woman behind the counter and moved toward the tables at the back. Then a deeper voice spoke and she paused.

"I wondered if she liked books."

Chloe's laughter was musical. "When we were in high school, Margeaux read when the rest of us would have our headphones on at meets. She would escape the pressures by flipping through the pages of a book. I can thank her for my interest in them."

Margeaux hurried around the corner. "I hope you haven't been waiting long."

Chloe made a show of looking at her fitness watch. "You had five more minutes."

"I took your advice and walked." Then she shifted her attention to the person Chloe had been talking to. Chase Crandall, in the flesh.

"Hello again. It's good to see a local semi-celebrity." Margeaux stiffened, but he laid a steadying touch on her hand. "The press is impossible to deal with in the best of circumstances. Don't worry about it."

A shiver of electricity slipped up her arm, and she hated how much she wanted his approval.

She did not need her body snapping to attention like this. Not with the man she wasn't sure she could trust and needed to work with at least for a while. But as he gave her a slow grin, she had a feeling she was a goner. She'd need to do something to curtail her reaction.

"Were you working in your office? Or is your friend exaggerating?"

"Oh, I don't exaggerate." Chloe raised an eyebrow as she looked between the two of them. "I think I'll go make a London Fog. One for you too, Margeaux?"

"Thanks." She blinked, trying to slip free of the spell Chase seemed to have cast. "What are you doing here?"

"Looking for the latest Steven James or Daniel Silva novel or something." He shoved his hands in his pockets like a little boy who was embarrassed.

Where had the overconfident attorney wandered off to?

He scooped up a book like it might save him from his awkwardness and flipped it over.

"You won't like that one." Margeaux wanted to laugh at the novel he'd picked up.

Chase looked up. "Maybe I love this type of book."

She looked him up and down with a tip to the corner of her mouth. "Possible, but doubtful. While many adore Jennifer Deibel's historical Irish books, I think you'd prefer one of the books from Daniel Silva's older series. A little more action and a lot less romance."

"So you teach literature at Monroe." He waggled the book in front of her.

"Only when it's necessary to save fancy-pants attorneys from themselves." She reached for a small green volume. "Try some Joyce. He'll satisfy your need for Irish literature."

"I also need a book for my mom. It's her birthday."

A man buying a love story for his mother? Margeaux's body threatened to melt into an undignified puddle. "Either of those would fit the bill then," she croaked, and glanced over her shoulder for a distraction. "Is my tea ready, Chloe?"

"Almost. Making it myself." The voice came from somewhere near the front counter. "Now quit harassing the customers, or I'll never get to fill in again."

Margeaux gave Chase a quick perusal. "He doesn't look too abused. I'm going to go get my tea." And she hurried to the counter. When she got there, Chloe startled.

"I'll bring the drink over in a minute."

"I don't mind waiting here. I didn't want to stand there."

"Admit you're attracted to him." Chloe filled a pitcher with milk, then stuck it under the wand and turned a knob.

"What? That's not it. At all. Not when I've got bigger issues."

"There is that." Chloe looked up from steaming the milk. "You do need to talk to him about it."

"I know you're right, but he was a grouch the last time I saw him."

"And you're not?"

"Not as often as he is."

Chloe raised one eyebrow, and Margeaux laughed. "Fine, I can be prickly."

"Just more so for him." Chloe grinned at her. "Because you've decided he's attractive after all." She slipped the pitcher free of the wand and mixed the steamed milk in with the tea.

"I don't trust him." Then she sighed. "His superhero act doesn't feel honest."

"That again?" She stopped and swapped out pitchers of milk. "Margeaux, you need to admit that there is something attractive about a man who puts everything on the line day after day for someone he has no obligation to protect. It isn't an act. It's what Chase does every day." Chloe twisted another knob. "If he does that for strangers, imagine what he would do for the woman he decides to love."

"That's deep, Chloe."

"Of course it is. Deep waters, and all that. But think about it. You sense it's there in him. You've worked with Chase for a couple of weeks now. Has he done anything that makes you think he's not what Anneliese needs for the best defense?"

Margeaux paused and made herself consider before responding.

There was something compelling about the picture Chloe had painted, and it fit Chase so well. As she thought back over their interactions, nothing made him a villain. "No."

"Then give him a chance. And don't let your pride get in the way of discovering what might be possible." Chloe set two drinks in front of Margeaux. "This is a good place to start. Here's yours and one for Chase. I'll make another for me and join you in a minute. Maybe you can let him in where you haven't let me or Janae. Let someone in behind the walls you've constructed. There's a woman in there we all want to know."

The words stung, but only because truth filled them. Maybe it was time to take the risk. And maybe Chase was the one to take it with.

"Okay." Margeaux squared her shoulders and returned to the area of the bookshop she'd fled. But when she got there with the two drinks, Chase had disappeared. As she walked around looking for him, her cheeks pinked at the thought he might have caught any part of that conversation.

Chapter 31

MARGEAUX GRABBED HER TEXTBOOK AND markers and slid them into her bag, glad to have another class behind her. The satisfaction of another well-delivered one filled her as she walked toward the door, ready for a small recovery time in the quiet of her office.

As she stepped from the classroom, cameras flashed and Margeaux was blinded.

What was happening?

Her watch vibrated and she wanted to glance down to see what the message could be, but the media in front of her crowded toward her. She didn't know which way to turn but felt her breath hitch in her chest as she tried to inhale.

Something must be wrong.

"Were you involved in the murder?"

"What part did you play in the killing?"

"Did you tell Anneliese what to do?"

The reporters shouted the questions at her but they made no sense. Why was anyone asking her these questions?

She shouldn't stop, but she couldn't move forward either. "What do you mean?"

"How were you involved in the murder of Lauren Payge?"

Cold moved through Margeaux as the reporter's words ricocheted through her mind. "I . . ."

She couldn't force more words out, the shock paralyzing her.

Then a student burst through the crowd. Donovan. He snatched her arm, shielding her with his body as he pushed through the mob of media. "Where do you want to go?" His words were low and barely reached her as he hurried her down the hallway, away from the classroom that had always been her sanctuary.

"I don't know. Not my office." If the media had found where she was teaching, surely some were camped out near her workspace.

"How about the library? We can call an Uber for you from there."

"Good idea." Anything was better than staying where she had frozen like prey in front of a crowd of predators. "But how do we slip away to get there?"

"We'll have to get creative." Donovan hustled her down a hallway, took a turn, slipped down a stairwell, around another hall, and back up a flight of stairs. Then he hurried her into a men's restroom. "Sorry, but they won't look for you here."

"It's all right. Good thinking." And it was. Eventually she stopped sensing the reporters behind them. "Maybe we won't need to go to the library after all."

"I bet someone's still waiting and watching for you out there." He yanked his hoodie off and handed it to her. "Slip this on. They won't expect to see you in this. Slouch a bit and you'll look more like a college student than a professor."

"I play one on occasion."

"Now's the time to pretend you're back in school." Donovan moved to the door and opened it. He peeked out, looking more like Ferris Bueller than Jason Bourne, then waved her over. "Looks clear. If we go to the basement, we can walk the length of the building and come out on the side of the library. Then it's a short dash and you can hide there until we can get you a ride. Think about where you want to go."

That was a great question. She slipped out her phone and texted Janae.

You in the office?

She stared at the app, willing the blinking dots to appear, indicating Janae was texting back. After a minute of nothing, she texted Chloe.

You or Janae in the office?

A minute later a response popped up.

I am. What's up.

I need a place to hide. Media
is here and it doesn't make
sense.

☹ Come on over.

It felt too cloak-and-dagger as she waited until the end of a class period and tried to blend in to a flow of students leaving the library's computer lab and escaped the building. She kept her chin down and Kate Spade bag low, hoping she didn't attract attention.

The walk took longer than she wanted, but eventually she wandered past the Elliott Museum of Art and into the small-town square of Kedgewick. She picked up her pace. Janae would know what to do.

Margeaux had wanted to make a difference for Anneliese, but she'd had no idea what she called down on herself.

She was in over her head.

So far over her head.

But what could she have done differently? Anneliese needed someone to fight for her. Margeaux couldn't give up, but what should she do now?

Janae would know. That thought was the only thing keeping her calm as she strode down the sidewalk and opened the door to Janae's office. The bell tingled as the door opened, but no one was at the receptionist's desk. Where was Chloe?

"I'll be right there. Have a seat." Janae's voice filtered down the hallway from her office.

"It's me, Janae." Margeaux hurried past the desk, down the hallway, to the office. "I thought Chloe was here. She said she was when I texted."

"She was but had to run something to court on a last-minute deadline." Janae launched to her feet as Margeaux came through the door. "I wasn't expecting to see you."

"I texted."

"Sorry, it's on vibrate so I can focus. You look terrible."

"Thanks. The media ambushed me outside my classroom at the college." She took a shuddering breath as their words crowded back into her thoughts. "They asked if I was involved in the murder. I guess the allegations have leaked."

Janae tipped her chin as the words landed. "I'm sorry."

"Me too. Detective Phillips or someone else must have leaked something to the media."

Janae leaned forward, staring at her computer as she clicked away. "Have you done any online searches?"

"No. I was focused on escaping campus without anyone following me."

"I don't think it will be a stretch for them to find you here."

While their friendship wasn't hidden, it also wasn't necessarily something people would immediately know without research. "It'll buy me a little time."

"Looks like your student decided to talk without the benefit of counsel present. And she named you as someone who was involved in the murder." Janae swiveled her monitor around as Margeaux hurried forward.

"Why would she do that?" It made absolutely no sense. She was beginning to wish she'd never met Anneliese, that she'd never taken a step toward her when she arrived in the United States. At the same time, the part of Margeaux's mind that wasn't panicking knew that wasn't true.

She'd always been drawn to the international students who were brave enough to take the step she hadn't had the courage to take as an undergrad and catapult themselves into studying in another country for a semester or year.

Why would Anneliese take the friendship and mentoring Margeaux had offered and in turn suggest to the police that Margeaux knew anything about the murder? Would she really have done that?

But if she hadn't, where would the media have gotten that message?

Because someone told them she was involved. Why else would the media be at the classroom?

Was this Detective Phillips's way of getting her attention?

"Last time you needed an attorney, and now I do? What is happening to us?" Margeaux had meant the statement as a joke but couldn't quite pull it off. The words spiraled through her mind in a tightening corkscrew of panic. She tried to breathe but couldn't inhale enough oxygen.

"We could go to the police first. Tell them the media said you're involved, and you want to clear up that misconception right away. Or we can wait and see if the police want to talk. The media doesn't get it right all the time."

"Do you think Detective Phillips would go to the media?"

"I don't know."

"This wasn't one reporter, Janae. I had to sneak down to the basement and then through the tunnels to the library to get away. There were enough that I'm not sure how my students pushed through them to get to their next classes." She sank into the chair in front of Janae's desk and groaned. "What am I going to do?"

"Don't say anything." Janae shrugged, then nudged her monitor back around. She kept clicking, her gaze glued to the monitor. "The story hasn't been picked up outside the area so maybe there aren't any facts to back this up."

Margeaux wished she could believe that were the case.

But she had an unsettling awareness that things would get worse.

"You could ask Chase to help you deal with the media."

"Why would I do that?"

"Because he's experienced with them. He also needs to know about this so he can help you figure out where the leak occurred."

"What if I don't want to bother him with any of this?"

Janae crossed her arms to match Margeaux's tight posture. "Then you're crazy. It's too late for that. He needs to know. He's good at what he does, and it's time for you to acknowledge it, Margeaux. He has sound legal strategy. What if knowing you're being harassed helps him unlock a key piece of Anneliese's puzzle. Wouldn't it be worth it?"

Chapter 32

THE SPRING HEAT WAS BEGINNING to press Chase's shirt into his skin, and he was more than ready to find some air-conditioning, or at a minimum a fan. But he was stuck on Margeaux's tiny porch until she showed up. So far the press hadn't arrived, a fresh scandal in Congress distracting them, but that could change at any time. He'd expected Margeaux to arrive—he checked his watch—twenty minutes ago.

When she finally pulled in and slowed to a stop, Margeaux didn't immediately hop from her car, but waited a minute as if fortifying herself. Then she slipped from the car and took the offensive. "I've had a day and really am not in the mood for anything from you. I'm not even sure how you found me."

"I've got resources you'd never understand." He said it as a joke, but from the look on her face, it didn't land that way. "Sorry. My paralegal knew where you live."

"Leigh? How?"

He shrugged. It hadn't seemed strange to him. "It's on your employment paperwork. I'm paying you. For your time."

"Did you notice I live in a different town?"

"They're maybe four miles apart. It's not far."

"But they are separate." She rubbed her forehead, telegraphing her fatigue. "I don't have the energy for this. What do you want?"

"I thought a change of venue would help. I also thought you'd need a distraction." He pointed to the bag by his feet. "I brought snacks."

She jerked a fistful of keys out of her briefcase. "Whatever. Come in."

That wasn't as enthusiastic as he'd expected, but he'd take it. He'd been churning his wheels unproductively at work, and at the time it had seemed like a good idea to come brainstorm with Margeaux. She might not be a practicing attorney, but he thought she would have a good perspective and fresh approach. Something was off, though, as he followed her inside.

The rooms in her home were tiny. Even smaller than he'd expected based on the outside, but the white here was almost blinding. "You took the white-makes-everything-bigger vibe seriously, didn't you?"

"It's perfect for me." After setting her bag on a petite hall table, she turned and crossed her arms. "Why are you really here?"

"Trial is in about two months, and we have nothing."

"So?"

"So we need to make something happen. I hoped together we could generate some ideas." He waggled the bag. "Let's eat while we talk about why the detective is harassing you too."

"How do you know that?"

"Leigh heard about it from her contact in the sheriff's office. I don't like it." In fact, the shift in the commonwealth's tactics to come after her was interesting. It upped the stakes in a way he couldn't ignore.

"I don't want to talk about it."

"You can't ignore it."

"Yes, I can." Her jaw tightened as her eyes reddened. She must've had a horrible day. "I need a break. We can't make anything happen, not today."

This wasn't the woman who had been on him to fight hard. "Wait. You're the one who's been after me from the beginning to make something happen. And now you don't want to? That doesn't make sense."

"You want to know what doesn't make sense? Getting dragged down to the police station Friday. Being told that my student accused me of being part of a plot to kill Lauren Payge, but not being given enough information to know what to believe or even know if I was really named." She seemed to give up on him and swiveled to the small kitchen. "Then today after I finished teaching, the media was waiting outside my classroom. I really don't have anything to give you right now. I'm all volunteered out."

"You aren't a volunteer. I pay you."

"Minimum wage."

"But that means you can't quit."

"Watch me. It's called employment at will. You know what that is, right, Mr. Crandall, Attorney-at-Law?" She snatched a glass from the cupboard next to the sink.

"No need to get snippy."

"Snippy? That's something my grandma would say. And I have every right to resign." She filled the glass with some water from the tap. "I don't think it's helpful for me to give any more time to the case. My quitting is what you wanted, right? You never wanted me sticking my nose in this case. You kept telling me I didn't belong."

"Is that what you do?"

"What?"

"Abandon ship when it gets hard?"

"Does it matter?" She pivoted, then turned back as if she couldn't decide what to do or where to go. "You win. I'm done."

"You can't do that."

She turned so fast, she almost flung water all over him. "I am. You won."

"What if I don't want to?"

"Too late." She set the glass down. "You know where the door is." And she stalked out the back.

What had she just done? Her hands trembled as she tried to catch her breath. She hadn't felt this out of control and scared in years.

She felt her pulse racing as she thought of all the times people left her.

This time she hadn't successfully kept her distance, and there was no way he'd stick by her if things got dicey. It was better to exit gracefully than get pitched overboard to drown. And now she'd taken all of that out on the man who had shown up to ask for her help.

After all the time she'd invested in trying to prove to Chase that he needed her help, the impromptu visits to see if she could help, the hours invested in Anneliese and her case, she'd just walked away?

The tension from the afternoon wrapped around her like a boa constrictor, and she could hardly drag in a breath. She lifted her face to the sky and wished for sunshine to warm the chill that wouldn't let go. There was too much happening and nothing at the same time. Life charging ahead and stopping simultaneously.

What was she supposed to do?

She needed to forget about the crazy interview with Detective Phillips, but she wanted to understand what he'd tried to do. He'd wasted a couple of hours on campus waiting for her. Why? Why would he go through the exercise?

He had a reason.

Was he trying to create the internal chaos she was living with right now?

If so, it worked.

And when she didn't cooperate with the wannabe interrogation, had he then sent the media after her? While she might not understand his purpose, she didn't doubt he had a clearly defined reason.

And why had Allison Erickson been displeased that he hadn't waited? Waited for what?

The door opened and closed behind her, and she bit back a groan. She didn't need Chase pretending he understood. She also didn't want his sympathy. That was the last thing she needed.

She plopped down on one of her Adirondack chairs. "Please."

He eased next to her but didn't say anything.

The tulips were drooping but the peonies stood tall. In a few weeks their large blooms would bring her joy for a few days—a week or two if she was lucky. Maybe she'd even be home to enjoy them.

She had to shake off the pessimistic fog that had followed her home and draped over her.

Chase tipped his chin up as if trying to catch the last of the sun's rays over the top of her tree line. "Want to tell me about it?"

"Not really."

"It might help."

"I doubt it."

"Try me."

"Have you ever been questioned by the police?"

He slowly turned toward her and lowered his sunglasses. "No. Tell me about it."

"Yes. On Friday." She closed her eyes again.

"Why didn't you mention that on Saturday?"

"Didn't think there was a need." No way she'd admit she might have been distracted by his attention.

"So Phillips harassed you?"

"Maybe. I don't know. Aren't you glad you asked?"

"I am, because if he's harassing you, then we need to make a record and stop him."

"I did record the rather one-sided conversation."

"You did?" She turned to catch the grin on his face. "That was smart."

"I did go to law school."

"True, but not everyone who did would have thought to do that."

"Bully for me."

"Teddy Roosevelt."

She closed her eyes again. "Sure."

She felt more than saw his fingers waggle in front of her. "Hand it over."

"What?" Margeaux opened her eyes and straightened.

"I want to listen to the conversation."

"Already having lived through the enlightening experience, I don't care to."

"All the better to give it to me so I can listen with fresh ears."

She wanted to give him her own version of a fresh take, but instead handed over her phone. "I'll be inside."

"No, I'll go in. You stay out here. Looks like you need nature more than I do."

"Thanks." She didn't bother moving. Let him poke around all he wanted. She was done with playing trial attorney and trying to help some ungrateful student. Trying to do the right thing wasn't worth getting called into the police station and the disruptions to her day, not for the pennies Chase paid her and certainly not for someone who implicated her in murder. What must her students think? Detective Phillips hadn't worn a uniform, but he hadn't belonged. At all. And then there was the media circus.

Explaining any of it wouldn't come easily. She needed to make sure the detective didn't have a reason to show up again. That would be the easiest way to avoid giving an explanation.

If it meant distancing herself from the investigation and coming trial, then she'd have to do that.

Anneliese didn't need her. Not now.

Not when she had Chase.

And if he wanted to get Anneliese to plea out, fine.

He was the real attorney after all. Not Margeaux.

Margeaux would ignore the tightening around her heart and the sense that she had given up. She'd learned long ago that walking away was the safest thing to do.

As he concentrated on the recording, Chase marveled that Margeaux had kept her cool. It would have taken a lot for him not to fight back as the detective kept poking, but she'd managed to hold her tongue. Then Chase rewound and played it again, this time listening for what wasn't said.

Why had Detective Phillips called her in? Why now? He had a reason. Was he fishing for what Margeaux knew? Shaking her up through borderline harassment? He hadn't interacted with Phillips much, but the man's actions were shifting beyond committed cop. What about this case had the detective pushing so hard?

The second listen didn't reveal the answers, so he made a copy and forwarded it to himself. Better to have a copy and pay attention when he wasn't distracted by the hurting woman out there. He studied her through the small window, trying not to notice how unguarded she looked. She often had a slight edge to her, one that said beneath that beauty was a firm do-not-cross line. One that wouldn't let anyone get too close. But as she leaned against the chair, her head resting against the back, she looked vulnerable in a way he hadn't encountered before. There was a softness and youthfulness to her expression that made him wonder what had caused the underlying steel that she usually showed the world.

She shifted in the seat and wiped at her cheek. The gesture about broke his heart for her. He hadn't known her long, but she was a fierce defender of her students, so being threatened in her domain must be the worst sort of intimidation. He couldn't pretend it wasn't a big deal to be called in and interviewed. Nothing like that had happened to him during his years in practice. He imagined it would upset him too. Probably make him question what he could do to stay off the detective's radar.

He considered what he knew about Detective Phillips. The man had been on the force for a number of years but wasn't a lifer in their community. He'd moved to the area. What had brought him to their small corner of Virginia? There were more exciting places to plant oneself. More interesting places to round out a career, unless one was in the middle of a retreat. Then there was the way the man had given Chase the runaround and his odd demeanor in court. Added together, all the pieces made Detective Phillips a person Kedgewick didn't need.

Chase made a note to dig into the man's background. Someone knew why he'd shown up. That information might give some insight into what was happening to Margeaux and maybe Anneliese.

Chase stood. That had to be enough time for her to wallow. If he was right about her, what she needed was a nudge to get back to work. Then he reconsidered. She stiff-armed him every time he came near, and he didn't think she'd appreciate knowing he'd seen her weakness. Maybe the kindest thing he could do in this moment was honor her need to be alone and figure out what was really going on. Someone knew Detective Phillips. Maybe he could learn more about the man.

So he walked out the front door and drove away, even as part of him wanted to gather her in his arms and tell her she wasn't alone.

Chapter 33

THE SUN HAD BARELY SNEAKED over the horizon when Margeaux made the drive from Hamilton to campus. She still stung from the way Chase had disappeared the prior night. There had been something sweet in the way he'd fought her on quitting. She'd even thought she'd seen a spark of interest in his expression. She hadn't even realized he was gone until the sun's last rays had slipped behind the trees and she began to shiver in her chair. Then she'd entered her home and found it empty, just like her heart.

Emma's call asking for help on an English paper had been the welcome distraction she needed for the balance of the evening. Margeaux had then worked until her eyes couldn't focus, and this morning she'd gotten up before her alarm. She'd wanted to avoid the craziness of the prior afternoon and slip into her office before others could corral her. She needed to find a way to focus on her job and not the trial. If she could do that for even one day, she'd be in a better position for the finals that were barreling down on her.

As she locked her car and found her ID to swipe into the building in case it hadn't been unlocked yet, she paused long enough to look up and take in the view.

She couldn't forget that this was her calling.

Teaching students.

Mentoring them through advising student organizations and independent studies.

This would be her place long after the trial ended.

But if she didn't get back in the game here, the trial would end, and she wouldn't have a job to return to. She owed her students her best, and that was slipping. Not to mention that she couldn't be an effective professor when her worried thoughts constantly darted to Anneliese. Margeaux would do better. She would not let the distraction of one student supersede the needs of all her others.

Today she'd keep her door closed, if necessary, but a few hours of intense work would be enough to get back on track.

After a quick swipe, she hurried into the building, past the shadowed study areas on the first floor, and then up the stairs to her floor and hallway. She set her backpack on the trash can outside her door and dug out her keys but noticed something under her foot as she stepped inside. After setting her backpack on the small table in her office, she turned back and picked up the envelope that was on the floor.

Someone must have slid it under her door, and when she turned it over, she noted the dean's handwriting. Why would he put something in writing rather than send an email?

That seemed very unnecessary.

She turned it over and slit the back of the flap. She slid out the paper and her heart dropped as she read the words.

She was being called to a meeting.

At University Hall.

No explanation.

No reason.

Just a demand to show up in three hours for a meeting.

Margeaux set the letter on her desk and plopped onto her chair. She had a bad feeling about this, but there was nothing productive she could do until the meeting.

Several hours later, Margeaux scurried up the stairs to University Hall, one of the older buildings on campus. It had been built to house the president's office and a large recitation hall. She'd always found it an interesting mix of uses and purposes while also loving the blend of architecture. Monroe College wasn't as old as the University of Virginia, which had been established by Thomas Jefferson. Instead, Monroe College had the dubious honor of being founded in honor of the fifth president but without much funding. It had puttered along for forty years in the mid-1800s until a donor had gifted enough money for University Hall to be built. Now the campus housed approximately four thousand undergraduate students and more than a dozen academic buildings. But University remained the stalwart landmark plastered on memorabilia and the image alums and friends associated with the campus.

Once she hauled open one of the imposing wooden doors, she stepped inside an interior space that needed a new donor to refurbish it.

She wasn't clear why the dean wanted to meet here, so her steps were slow. She hated walking into an unknown situation.

It felt like an ambush.

One she couldn't anticipate or prepare for.

The hall stretched out in front of her, punctuated every few steps by an oil painting of a stern old white man. The former presidents and storied professors seemed to frown at her with whispered challenges that she didn't belong. That feeling bled through the years, yelling that she didn't move fast enough and wasn't good enough.

She knew it wasn't true. Margeaux had fought hard and earned the right to teach at the school. She shouldn't have to prove herself every day and semester. Resisting the urge to tiptoe, Margeaux strode down the hall to the correct room.

At the door, she paused, putting her hands on her hips in a power pose. She stood tall and breathed for a minute, glad no one watched in the hallway as she tried to trick her brain into believing she was okay when the tremor of adrenaline flowed through her arms.

She waited another two breaths, then decided it was time. Whatever was on the other side of that door, she needed to face it now.

She opened the door and marched into the room, hoping no one caught the way her fingers opened and closed as she released the tension flowing through her. Then she paused as the collection of people seated around the table registered in her mind.

The group of people clustered there could intimidate her if she focused on the individuals. A dean. A vice provost. People who set the policy and direction of the college. Someone in a campus police uniform. A member of the counseling center staff. Someone from the student health center. Another person she didn't recognize but whose name tent indicated she worked at the local hospital in Leesburg. Someone from residential life. It felt a bit like a who's who of those who touched students. Even a member of the student government sat at the far end of the table.

"Am I in the right place?"

The dean looked at her. "This meeting is wrapping up, so you're a bit early for yours. Wait a moment, because we need a word with you, Margeaux."

Vice Provost Fox shifted the papers in front of him, sliding a folder from the bottom of the stack. "That's right, Professor Robbins." A minute later everyone had left except the dean, vice provost, and Margeaux. Vice Provost Fox glanced at her. "We're ready now."

"Yes?" There was something in the set of their faces that put her on edge. "What can I do for you?"

The dean unbuttoned his shirt cuffs and rolled first the left and then the right one toward his elbows as he watched her. "Care to fill us in on what happened yesterday?"

"Sir?"

"The media circus you brought to campus. It disrupted several classes."

"And we've had a nonstop stream of calls from parents and important alumni asking if it's true that one of our faculty members was involved in the campus murder." The vice provost tapped the file. "As of the beginning of this meeting, the dollar amount at risk thanks to your involvement tops ten million dollars."

"Excuse me? I didn't do anything."

The vice provost shook his head. "As the adage goes, where there's smoke there's fire."

"We have no choice, Margeaux." The dean met her gaze steadily. "You are on paid leave until an investigation can be conducted."

"What?" Margeaux pushed from the table. "You can't do that this close to the end of the semester. Putting me on leave will hurt the students."

"Don't worry, you will be paid while we figure out whether you can continue or if we'll end your contract."

Her thoughts spun as she tried to catch up with the turn of events. "I don't understand."

"Yesterday's attention put this university and its reputation, staff, and students at risk. You cannot continue teaching while accused of helping to murder a student." The dean leaned forward and his gaze never wavered. "You have twenty minutes to gather what you need from your office, and then you are not to come back until you receive a letter from the college's attorney clearing you."

"What happened to innocent until proven guilty?"

"This isn't a criminal matter." There was such a hard edge to him. Why wasn't the vice provost stopping him? "The clock has started."

Chapter 34

CHASE HAD BARELY SETTLED AT his desk before Leigh poked her head into his office. "Before you get too deep, here're a couple of messages that came in while you were out. One's from that Jim Clary. He's determined to have you call him back. Sounded adamant you call him back today or else." She handed him a couple of notes.

"You could email these."

"And have you ignore them? I don't think so."

He reluctantly accepted the notes. "Thanks."

Once alone in his office, he glanced at the papers but didn't hurry to pick up the phone. He needed to decide what he wanted to tell Jim.

The truth was he felt alive when he worked on Anneliese Richter's case. This one wouldn't be a slam dunk. In fact, it had the marks of a case that would need all his effort and attention to have a chance of success. It also had the real threat of failure, and at a size that could take down his firm. The risk of working for himself was that he was always only one case away from potential bankruptcy. At the same time, he was also only one case away from making a significant difference in a person's life, and that mattered.

There was an allure to doing something new—especially when it came with a guaranteed paycheck and didn't bear the weight of paying the bills. Lifting that weight from his shoulders would make his days so much less intense, yet the trade-off would have a unique burden.

Did Chase want to owe favors to Jim or any stuffed shirt?

What had sounded really good when the conversation was initiated in March now felt like he'd be committing to be the man's slave rather than doing good for people in hard situations.

He needed to put a pause or a full stop on the pressure to make the move. It wasn't what he wanted anymore. Maybe he'd never wanted it, he'd just needed hope that an end to the tunnel of never-ending work existed. Instead, maybe he should rework how he approached his current clients. After the trial. Until then he had plenty to do.

He picked up the phone to call Jim, but the ding of an incoming message on his computer stopped him before he dialed.

Female hurricane inbound. Batten down the hatches.

Chase stared at the text. The office messaging system was great when it made sense, but this message didn't.

Thanks?

A minute later he heard something tossed on the makeshift desk outside his office, the one that Margeaux used. Should he let the storm blow over or brave the winds?

He'd never been one to back down from a fight . . . until lately.

He'd have to figure out how to fix being gun-shy in time for a trial in June or he'd have a problem. Maybe he could open with the problem right outside his office. He rose to his feet and rolled his neck, then stretched his arms up. No time like the present to see what had happened today. He glanced at his watch. Ten thirty in the morning. That was early for Margeaux to make an appearance.

Especially since she'd threatened to quit yesterday.

He kept his steps quiet as he moved through the door. It would be insightful to learn what he could before she knew he was there. What he saw alarmed him.

Her eyes were puffy and red, black streaks running down her cheeks. Her usually carefully arranged clothes were off-kilter, with the slit of her skirt toward the side rather than its usual place. One side of her button-down shirt had come untucked, and Margeaux didn't seem to notice as she rubbed her forehead and turned away from him. "Please don't."

"What?"

"Don't look at me. I'm a mess, and I don't have the energy to care." She plopped into the chair.

He'd never seen anyone who looked like they needed a hug as much as she did in that moment.

Instead, he leaned into the door and slid his hands into his pockets. "What happened?"

She gave a shaky laugh as she set her purse on the carpet. "What makes you think anything did?"

He gestured at her face. "You don't normally look quite like that."

"I don't want to know. It's the least of my worries right now."

"Okay." He considered her as she pulled a laptop from her larger bag. "What do you need?"

"I need my job back."

That stopped him as he cocked his head. "What do you mean?"

"I've been put on paid leave." She finally met his gaze, streaked cheeks and all. "Do you know how hard it is to let someone on the tenure track go? You have to have cause and go through a process. Especially when they're an attorney, you want to make sure you follow all the proper procedures and processes."

"I'm still not following."

"The media circus yesterday is causing the college some serious heartburn, so I get to wait on the sidelines while they decide whether I might be innocent. Right now my dean seems determined the answer is no."

"That's crazy." She fit the definition of intense, but she wasn't a murderer.

"Higher education is a crazy place. Has its own rules, and I'm caught in the middle." Then her eyes sparked with pain as lines tightened around her mouth. "What makes me mad is that my students are the ones who will be hurt. They'll get some random instructor for the rest of the semester." She wilted onto the chair. "But it doesn't matter, I don't have any power."

Chase let his mind take in what she'd said. "Wait a minute. That's not true."

"It is."

"No. You just have to prove that you weren't part of the murder."

"Right. It's a simple matter of walking over to the police, getting the file, and showing it to the vice provost and dean. Problem solved."

He pushed from the doorframe. Time to nudge her to action. "You've got ten minutes to wallow, and then it's time to get to work. I'm not paying you to waste time."

"What?"

"Meet me in the conference room, or you'll have lost two jobs in a morning."

He hid a grin as he went back to his office to the sound of her sputtering.

Yep, she had needed a bit of a push to revive her inner spitfire.

As he walked away, his cell phone vibrated, and he eased it from his pocket without looking at the number. "Chase Crandall."

"Chase, this is Jim Clary."

"Jim, what can I do for you?" Chase strode to his desk. He just needed to grab his notebook and laptop and then he could get to the war room. That sounded so much more impressive than calling it a conference room. With Margeaux on the team full-time, they might make something of Anneliese's defense.

"The firm's tired of waiting. What's your decision?"

He pinched his nose as if that would push the pressure back. "Jim, I'm sorry, but where's this coming from?"

"We've given you time to decide if you're ready to get off the hamster wheel and come to the easy side of the law. Make some real money and not have to do it all yourself."

"Like I told you in our last conversation, I can't do anything until after the trial in June."

"Then you'll miss this opportunity." The man's voice had hardened, and Chase didn't appreciate the tone.

"Then I guess that's your answer. I won't walk away from my clients. Thank you for the opportunity, but it's not the right time." As he hung up, Chase knew he'd made the right decision, but it didn't lessen the feeling that a noose tightened around his neck.

Margeaux leaned on the counter in front of the bathroom mirror, shocked by how ravaged her face looked. She leaned over to splash water in her face. It would take more than that to restore her to a woman who wouldn't scare small children with a glance. Good thing none hung around the law office of Chase Crandall and Associate.

She patted her face dry and then stretched as tall as her frame allowed.

The dean might think he'd boxed her into a corner, but he was wrong.

If anything, he'd made her more determined to prove that the police had wrongly accused Anneliese. By doing that, she would clear the shadow cast over her own reputation.

She left the bathroom and strode down the hallway to the small conference room. If she had an abundance of free time, she would put it to good use. The best way to do that would be working—full-time—on the case.

When she walked into the conference room, Leigh waited, but no one else. Margeaux sat across from her. "Do you think Chase would let me work here full-time on the case?"

Chase walked into the room with a stack of files.

"I need someone who's focused and running with logic, not emotion."

"That's fair." She took a breath as she tried to see it from his perspective. As she took in Leigh and Chase, she noted the dark circles under both sets of eyes. "We're all running on too little sleep. I know Anneliese isn't your only client, and you're doing this on your own. Let me try this. If it doesn't work, you can fire me. I did try to quit yesterday."

He considered her for a minute and then turned to Leigh. "I don't know."

"We need help."

"You're the one who called her a female hurricane."

"What?" Margeaux didn't know whether to laugh or cry.

Leigh shrugged apologetically. "You looked a little crazy when you blew in here."

"It had been a rough morning."

"And that's what I mean." Chase ran his fingers through his hair. "Trial work has a lot of rough moments. I need someone who can put their head down and work through them. Not pressure me for a pay raise or have an emotional breakdown. Can you do that?"

She forced herself to meet his gaze steadily . . . and then saw the cracks in his facade. Had she been so absorbed in what was happening to Anneliese and then in her own world that she'd missed the fatigue weighing him down? Did that come from a depth of caring for his clients? "Does that mean I can stay?"

"Leigh?"

"You know I'm up for some help, though I still think you should give Marcus another chance. The kid made a mistake, but we all do."

"Leigh." He growled the word.

Leigh cleared her throat. "Fine. Let's get to work." She held up a sheet of paper. "This list isn't getting shorter, and since Marcus left, we haven't made much progress."

Chase stood and walked over to the Post-it pad that rested on an easel. "Let's start with a list of potential witnesses."

Margeaux raised her hand, feeling like she was on a bit of an emotional roller coaster. "Can we stop for a minute? Am I on the team or not? After the morning I've had, I need clarity."

Chase arched a brow at her, all challenge in the expression. "Can you abide by my rules?"

"Yes."

"Do you want to be on the team?"

"I said yes."

"Are you sure? Because after this, there's no exit. I'll need your full commitment of time and energy from here through the trial. I need you to trust me."

Her hands shook like she'd had a dozen espressos chased by a large bag of her favorite tropical-flavored Skittles. This was a ridiculous show of nerves, given what it meant to work here. Maybe because she knew he was asking something important of her . . . something deeper.

But could she trust him?

There was a challenge in Chase's gaze that made Margeaux wonder what he was up to. But this wasn't raised eyebrows that clearly communicated skepticism about her value and abilities. There was a twinkle there too. An expression that suspiciously mirrored the one Janae wore when she was purposefully pushing a teammate from her stupor. She met him stare for stare. "I'm in."

"Good." He turned back to the easel as if she hadn't just made one of the biggest commitments of her life. "As I was saying."

Margeaux shot a look of desperation at Leigh, who shook her head with an expression that said, *It's easiest to go along with him*. Leigh picked up her pen and pad of paper and made a show of preparing to take notes.

"Wait. Don't we need to set some terms first?" Margeaux said.

Chase groaned. "Leigh, can you give us a minute."

"Sure thing, boss." She left her things on the table as she hurried to the door. "I'll be back in five minutes with a fresh latte. Anyone else want anything?"

"My job back."

"I'll get right on that." She pointed a finger at Chase. "Be nice while I'm gone." Then she disappeared.

Margeaux settled into the chair with her hands placed loosely on the table and waited while Chase studied her.

"Are you always this difficult? Is that the real reason you were put on leave?"

She flinched. "Thanks for that."

"Anytime." He pointed at the blank pad of paper on the easel. "We have to get to work. There's so much to do, and I turned down a job that would pay me a nice fixed income between holding your hand and walking in here." He hung his head a moment. "Sorry, I shouldn't have brought that up, but I'm committed to fighting for your student—who can't pay me anything, in case you wondered. So my paycheck is dependent on the county paying its bills in a timely fashion. Sometimes they pay me. Sometimes they don't. But I don't get paid until all the bills are. And neither do you. I'd say that makes me committed, probably more so than I have been in a very long time." His stare began to smolder through her. "Do you understand?"

What she understood was that Chloe had been right. There was something intense and attractive about a man who put everything on the line for someone he had no personal obligation to protect. It made her think Chase would brave the world for someone he cared about. And the thought of that kind of loyalty sparked a deep curiosity inside her.

Margeaux walked around the table toward Chase. His eyes flared as he watched, telegraphing his uncertainty about what she was up to. "Why didn't you take the job? If so much is on the line for you personally, why not take the easy course and the sure path?"

"Sometimes you have to do what's right even when it could cost you everything."

She stepped closer. "Even for a stranger."

"Even so." His answer was steady and sure—a superhero in plain clothes.

Margeaux stopped within arm's reach. A thread of tension stretched between them, growing taut like taffy being pulled as it began to cool. Her breath caught and she took a step back, snapping the connection. "Then I think we should get to work. Anneliese needs us to find the real killer since the police won't."

And she needed to deflect from whatever pulled her toward him.

She couldn't lean into it. Even if she could trust him for the case, she couldn't trust him with everything else. No matter how much a part of her wanted to see what might be possible.

Chapter 35

A TORNADO HAD STRUCK THE conference room, but that wouldn't be enough to identify what had really happened on that Sunday night in March.

The Armstrong battery trial was barreling toward him, but he needed to focus his energy on Anneliese's case.

Chase felt like he was caught in a storm. The facts swirled around him, just out of his grasp. Still he spun, trying to lay hold of any detail. But instead of helpful organization, he'd ended up with a disaster area. Margeaux had moved in a small refrigerator that she'd filled with bottled iced tea and sparkling water so it was only an arm's length away. She also had a basket with clementines, pretzels, and popcorn for brain food. Chase had brought in Coke and Flamin' Hot Doritos for balance, and then promptly remembered how much he hated things that spicy.

None of it really mattered, because without a viable candidate for who had murdered Lauren Payge, any jury would find the easiest perpetrator guilty—and that was Anneliese. If the police packaged her as the murderer, then most jurors would believe she had to be the one who thrust the knife. After all, the police wouldn't lie.

While Chase didn't think the officers in the area purposefully framed people, something niggled him about this investigation. But no matter how many times he studied the thin file of evidence the commonwealth had shared, he couldn't put his finger on it.

The scheduling hearing on April 14 had left them with a trial date of June 2, and he'd lose at least two days with the Armstrong trial and even more time preparing for it. Leigh was right. It was time to give in to her demands and let Marcus come back to help with a couple of criminal trials in April and May. Not that he would personally interact with the associate if he didn't have to, no matter how much Leigh sighed or poked. He couldn't help that he didn't trust the young man after he'd been so quick to try to leverage an offer into more money. The fact he seemed chastised didn't change what he'd done.

He knew Leigh wanted him to forgive and forget, but he couldn't make any promises. Not yet.

The murder didn't lead the newscasts or fill headlines above the fold on every newspaper, but the stories hadn't disappeared either. Lauren's photo would reappear often enough to make sure no one forgot her.

"That was a big sigh." Margeaux didn't bother looking up from the sheaf of paper she held, a pen in one hand ready to mark it up.

"We're missing something." He balled up a piece of paper and threw it at the trash can, watching as it ricocheted off the edge.

"Of course we are."

"Then what are we going to do about it?" He balled up another piece and threw it. This one didn't land any closer to the trash can as his question hung in the air.

"Find some witnesses. Because I don't think we'll have any luck moving the trial to another court."

He fought a smile. "I told you that was a nonstarter."

"Is this where I tell you I hate it when you're right?"

"Yep."

"I still think that meme the students had was prejudicial." She shuddered as if seeing it for the first time again. "So many biases are baked into that one image."

"But it's one image. It's not enough."

"And I think the courts agree with you, so we're back to witnesses."

"We haven't found any great ones yet."

"Then we keep looking. The boyfriend's not a bad one. And we have a student athlete I know. It's a start, and we aren't quitters."

"Maybe we should be." He took a piece of paper, and this time after he balled it, he chucked it her direction. It bounced off her ponytail, but she still ignored him. "Come on. Work with me."

"That's what I'm doing. Every day . . ." She kept her gaze firmly on the paper. "Even when you're annoying . . . and I miss my students."

"Then don't come in."

"I have work to do, Chase." Reaching for a piece of paper on the bottom of her stack, she slid it toward him. "Here's a list of possible witnesses for you if you need inspiration. Blake is the student athlete I interviewed who can fill in that piece of Lauren's life. But we've got holes."

The way she wouldn't look at him was infuriating. Okay, it was aggravating. He needed someone to argue with, and Marcus had always been willing to go a round with him. Margeaux clearly hadn't figured out that was part of the job. Each day she showed up looking like she worked at a big-city firm or was still ready to teach. Her narrow skirts and blouses gave her a polished look that didn't necessarily fit a legal war room, but it caught his attention and made him want to catch hers. He'd had to up his game to match her business style, to the point Leigh had commented on it.

Margeaux waggled the list at him, her gaze finally finding his above the papers. "Are you going to take it?"

"Tell me who you've listed."

"It's not so much specific whos as it is categories. We need to leave the office and wear out some shoe leather. You confirmed the one roommate's alibi, but have you found Lauren and Anneliese's other roommate?"

"Just the one."

"We need to keep trying. And we should interview the neighbors."

"Tried that before, and no one was home." He shook his head. "Scratch that. One talked with me, but she didn't know them."

"So we go back. I didn't know you were such a pessimist."

"I'm not, life just got busy." That sounded terrible, but he didn't have anything to say in his defense. He'd dropped the ball by relying on Marcus and not picking up the pieces after Marcus left. "Let's go."

"No."

"No?"

"We need a plan. The problem is we go off in all directions, but never stop to create a good strategy. That has to change because we're seven weeks from trial." She sifted through another stack of paper. "This is what I could compile about Lauren online. I'm not a detective, so I'm sure others could do a better job, but I noticed several reports of domestic disturbances at the apartment. Anneliese hasn't mentioned them, so we need to ask her and the roommates about them and get a copy of the police reports."

For someone who had never been a trial attorney, she wasn't doing bad. "What else would you do?"

"I would hire a PI to dig deeper into Lauren and figure out who her other boyfriend was. Statistics indicate murders are often perpetrated by someone the victim knew, and if there were reports of domestic violence involving her, that would increase those odds. We have that photo of her with Dominic and another guy, maybe the other boyfriend. Regardless, we need to track down the other boyfriend as a possible person of interest."

"That's one way of putting it."

"Anneliese hasn't given us names, so we'll have to look other places. Maybe the police reports will help. I would also try to talk to some of Lauren's professors and friends back home. I may have identified a few friends through her social accounts. Whether they'll talk to us is a different matter." She stopped and color slid up her neck. "What am I missing?"

"This is a good list." Chase ran his hands through his hair in a rough motion. Hadn't they hired a PI already? He ran through the steps they'd taken. Wait. Marcus had added that to his list right before he talked about the firm in Tyson's Corner. Unfortunately, the moment Marcus took it on, Chase would have taken it off his list. He groaned. "We should have hired the PI a few weeks ago, but it got dropped and . . . honestly, I refused to admit I needed help." He'd managed the caseload, but now he had to refocus on this trial. He glanced at his watch. "We need to think about who else could have something to gain. What if it's not a boyfriend? Who else could benefit by Lauren's death? If it's not Anneliese in the heightened emotions of an argument, then we need a motive. And if it isn't love gone wrong, then what else would motivate that kind of violence?"

"If we think about who was impacted when she died, it might give us some ideas."

"What do you mean? Who attended the funeral? Or who inherited from her? Because I doubt she had a will."

Margeaux picked up a pen and doodled on the paper in front of her. "I'm not entirely sure what I mean, but there's something bothering me about the way the police focused only on Anneliese. Why didn't they look at anyone else? Shouldn't they have considered others? The fact she had Lauren's blood on her when she found the body doesn't mean we can ignore other possibilities, right? Anyone who found her would have looked the same. So why use that as the deciding factor?"

He'd sensed it too. That there was a singular focus on the international student. "They focused early and hard on her."

"Almost like they had picked her out and decided she fit." Margeaux sighed. "I don't like saying that. It makes me so uncomfortable." She stood and paced the edge of the small room, then stopped and looked at Chase. "There's something wrong here, but I have no idea what. So helpful, right?"

"But not incorrect. Sometimes we open with the sense something isn't right." He leaned back. "The question is what do we do with it?" He snapped to his feet and patted his pockets. "Time for a field trip."

"We haven't finished our plan."

"Plans are great until they become a barrier. Sometimes you have to move." He waved for her to precede him through the door. "This is one of those times. We'll finish filling out your chart after we see what we can learn from a field trip to the apartment building."

After all, that was where the best witnesses were likely to be. "No time like the present to solve this mystery."

Chapter 36

TWO HOURS LATER THEY WERE back at the office, Margeaux with sore feet and a list of questions. "How could someone like Lauren Payge have left such a small impression on her neighbors?"

"Maybe it's part of the college lifestyle." Chase threw his notebook onto a corner of the table where it joined the scattered debris.

"Maybe." But something didn't sit right with Margeaux. She'd seen her students form tight bonds with each other, and Lauren should have had her group. Where were they? "She was a student athlete, and Blake explained her role there. Where else did she make an impact?"

"I don't know. She may not have had any time left after sports and academics."

Margeaux sank into a seat at the conference table and tapped the pencil against her mouth. "We're going to need help. You know, Marcus looks like he could be a college student. Maybe he could talk to students. He might not be as intimidating as you are."

Chase acted like he was affronted, with his arms crossed against his chest, but she was beginning to know him better and rolled her eyes.

"You said it yourself, we're leaking time, and we don't know enough about her."

Chase leaned out the door. "Leigh?"

"Coming." A minute later the woman stood in the doorway, her pencil poised above a tablet. "What's up, boss?"

"What was the name of the private investigator you found?"

"John Charles."

"Really? That's his name."

Leigh shrugged. "It's the one he gave me."

"Huh. That's pretty generic."

"A good one for an investigator." Leigh checked her notes. "I got his name from a friend when our regular investigator told me he didn't have time right now."

"All right. See if he has time to dig into a few people for me."

"Lauren Payge and her roommates?"

"Yep. That's the list."

"It's about time." Leigh jotted a line.

Margeaux watched with amusement as the two zinged back and forth.

Chase scrubbed his face with his hands. "Add anyone else that pops up as he's digging, especially boyfriends."

"Got it, boss. I'll make the call right now." Leigh stopped taking notes and looked at him. "We should have done this at the beginning of the month, but I'll make this a priority for him."

"Thanks. I knew there was a reason I value you so highly."

"Any time you want to match my pay to that value, feel free." Leigh grinned mischievously at him. "Need anything else?"

What was it with the people who worked for him constantly raising the price he paid them? "I'll keep that in mind." Maybe he should have moved to the corporate world. Taken Leigh with him and raised both their standards of living.

"Don't go there, Chase," Leigh said. "You're right where you should be. And I wouldn't want to wear a suit every day. That sounds miserable."

"I'm not going to ask how you read my mind."

"Worked with you too long." She tapped her pad of paper with the pencil. "Now I'm going back to the reception desk so I can make that call and do the real work while you look pretty decorating the white-board."

"Thanks." He chuckled as she left, then looked at Margeaux. "She's the best."

"She is."

This was exactly why Leigh was worth her weight in Ghirardelli peppermint bark each Christmas. "Are you going to ask for a raise too?"

"Nope. My raise is to get back to my real job. This has been an interesting experience, but I'll be glad to leave the trials to you in the future." She paused. "Were you really going to leave criminal work behind?"

"I seriously considered it."

"To do what?"

"An acquaintance had arranged for me to join a firm to work with a dedicated corporate client."

"Who?"

"Nosy, aren't we?"

"Curious."

He hesitated, then decided it was okay to share. "Jim Clary."

Margeaux blinked. "Which company?"

"I don't remember. It had something to do with sports, I think, and some other things."

"Monroe Alliance?"

"That sounds right. Why?"

"I need to think about it."

Chase crossed his arms and stared at her. "Not how this works. Brain-storming is a shared activity."

"I've heard a couple of students mention it. Especially student athletes. I think it has something to do with NIL."

"Name, image, and likeness?"

"Yes. I can ask Blake."

"I turned down the job. But if you remember it, I am curious about the company."

"I'll let you know if I remember." Margeaux jotted a note. "What's next, boss?"

He rolled his eyes, then caught her smirk. Played right into that one, but eliciting a smile like that was worth it.

Saturday, April 19

Four days later, Chase was regretting his decision to turn down the job. It was Saturday morning, and after insisting that it couldn't wait, the private investigator slouched in a conference room chair as he looked at a tablet he held. The man wore faded jeans and a polo with Adidas shoes, giving him a business casual air along with the impression he could chase someone if necessary. "There's not much to tell you. Lauren Payge was pretty well-liked by the students I talked to. She was a popular student athlete with a bit of an ego but hadn't made many enemies outside the team."

Chase straightened. "She'd made some on the team?"

"The normal rumbles about someone getting more playing time than maybe they should, but the coaches discounted it. A couple of people mentioned she liked to have a good time on the weekends and after matches. Nothing that seemed to suggest she'd made someone mad enough to kill her. I've got two names for boyfriends. Dominic Strand and Jordan Lewis. Still running down more information on them. One's a student athlete with a couple of domestic disturbance complaints but nothing that seems to rise to this standard of concern. Jordan Lewis is an outlier. Not a student, so trying to determine how the two connected."

"Anything on the roommates?"

"Not really." The man looked up from his notes. "On the surface of the internet, there's no reason for them to be concerned. But both were spooked enough that they threatened to call the cops and sic lawyers on me. That only made me more curious."

"All right. Keep digging and let me know if anything pops up on either of them or the boyfriends."

"Will do." The man began to put his tablet in his bag, then stopped. "Do you want me to investigate your client?"

Chase considered the question—a good one he had wrestled with for a bit. He needed to know ahead of time any dirt the police might have on Anneliese, but at the same time, he really didn't want to know if she was the murderer. In some ways it was easier not knowing. "I'd like to know how she's perceived by other students. She's a bit of a black hole right now. She was perceived as nice but an observer. No close friends."

"On it."

"Last thing, see what you can track down about any sort of student-led shrine, vigil, or service for Lauren. When I was at the apartment, I didn't see anything like that at the time of her death, but maybe I missed it. I also don't remember seeing articles or anything else in the news about a vigil. That strikes me as odd."

The man rubbed his chin and looked toward the ceiling. "I don't remember one either. Those seem typical in a situation like this."

"I agree, so it makes me curious. Maybe we missed it. But if we didn't, I'd like to know why there wasn't one. That might give us important insight that will help Anneliese."

"On it, boss man." The man stood and walked out.

Margeaux knocked on the door with a quizzical expression on her face, and something hesitant in her eyes. "What did I miss and should I have been in the meeting?"

"Not much to it." Chase gathered his files to take back to his office.

"Other than hearing what the detective learned."

"I can't pay you to review the exact same information."

"I might catch something you missed."

"Or it's a redundant system I can't afford."

Her mouth formed an O. "Maybe I shouldn't be here, then."

"No. That's not what I meant." Why was everything more complicated with her here? She seemed to sift everything through a layer of distortion that he didn't understand. "What did you learn in your search?"

"Not enough." Margeaux had dug through Anneliese's financial records and educational notes to see if she could find anything that would point to Anneliese having any motive. "I don't see anything, and not just because I like her." Her phone rang and she looked down with a frown. "I'm sorry, but I should probably take this."

"A boyfriend?"

Her cheeks colored in a way that suggested embarrassment and innocence. He wanted to know more. "No. It's . . . my sister."

Margeaux stepped from the room, easing the door closed on his adorable grin. The call was a reminder of why she could never trust a man. She hated the myth she'd created, but it was meant to protect the innocent. The question was, Had it worked? She'd long thought the lie shielded Emma, but she wasn't so sure now.

"Hello?"

Guess she'd let her thoughts capture her. "Hey, Emma. What's up?"

"Have you gotten Anneliese out yet?"

"No." She pinched the bridge of her nose as she prepared for the onslaught.

"Why not?"

"It's complicated."

"You know she couldn't have murdered anyone. She's not that kind of person."

"I agree. But why are you so certain?"

"We spent time together after Christmas."

"Doing what?"

"I don't have to tell you everything." An edge crept into Emma's words.

"I . . . sure. Emma, she's quite a bit older than you."

"And I'm mature for my age. That's what you and Mom and Dad always tell me."

True, but not something Margeaux had the energy to delve into. "It's been a while since I've seen you. Maybe we could get a pizza or something." Silence greeted that idea. "But we don't have to."

"I'd like that, but why now? You usually don't have time to spend with me."

"It's not that I don't want to." Time together felt wonderful and painful. How could she love someone so much that she willingly lived a lie every day for her benefit? Over time that lie became heavy and didn't fit like it once had.

"Hey, you disappeared again."

"Sorry about that." Margeaux leaned against the wall. "What else can I do for you?"

"Nothing. I just wanted to see how things were going for Anneliese." There was a sigh. "I'll let you get back to your important adult things. Since I'm only a high school kid."

"No, wait." Margeaux scrambled with something Emma had said. "When you hung out with Anneliese, did you meet any of her roommates?"

"Not really. They weren't the type to hang out." A voice spoke in the background, and then Emma giggled. "I've got to go. Bye."

"Bye." When silence greeted her, Margeaux glanced at the screen. She wanted to do more. Ease Emma closer. But that would only cause trouble. So she kept a distance that Emma noticed and attributed to an older sister too busy to spend time with her.

It was safer to let her think that.

Could Margeaux keep up the ruse forever? And the bigger question: Should she? What would happen, what domino would she knock over if she shared the truth with Emma?

She looked up to see the door cracked and Chase watching her, something thoughtful and sweet in his expression, as if he wanted to reach in and fix what was broken inside her. She couldn't lean into that, even if part of her hoped he truly saw her.

Enough of that. She pasted a professional expression on her face and moved from the wall. "What's next, boss man?"

He groaned. "I really hoped you hadn't caught that."

"No such luck." Her watch vibrated, and she glanced down and saw Janae's name, grateful for an excuse to create distance. Life was safer this way. "Sorry, I have an appointment I forgot about." She grabbed her things and hurried for the hall, relieved he didn't push to ask about the appointment. "I'll see you Monday morning."

As she left, she felt the loss of what could have been a fun afternoon as they wrestled to find the right next step preparing for Anneliese's trial.

Chapter 37

MARGEAUX HAD LEFT SO FAST, Chase wondered if he'd done something wrong. After replaying the scene, he decided he hadn't said anything offensive, so he refocused on work until his grumbling stomach reminded him he had to stop for lunch. He strolled across the block to Java Jane's for a smoothie and sandwich.

When he entered, his gaze was drawn to three women sitting at a table near the front window, but the woman with long dark hair drew his attention most. Looked like Margeaux's appointment was here for lunch with friends. He considered walking over to tease her but decided against it. What purpose would it serve other than flustering her? While fun, it wouldn't be productive.

After placing his order for a smoothie and loaded club sandwich, he leaned against the wall and scrolled headlines.

He felt a prickle at the back of his neck and looked up to find Margeaux's attention ping-ponging from him to her friends and back. He gave a small smile and then refocused on his phone.

Anytime he glanced up, her eyes would skitter away as if she didn't want to be caught staring. He would laugh if his mind wasn't busy trying to find a way to approach that wouldn't end in her embarrassing him.

She needed to make up her mind on what she thought about him, because he was getting whiplash from their interactions—even the silent ones like this.

That gave him an idea.

Maybe he *could* have a little fun—perhaps even bring a smile to her face. She needed some joy in her life after the week she'd had.

He strode toward her table, which didn't take long in Java Jane's. She almost melted under the table. It would have been funny, except he thought they'd reached a point where they were past the awkwardness.

"Ladies."

The platinum blonde looked at him directly. He liked that. With her ripped jeans and black blazer, she had an edgier look than the other two. "Can we help you? Don't you have a trial to prep for?"

So much for having a little fun. "Chloe, right?"

"Yep. Good memory." She smirked at him. "Care to join us?"

Margeaux clapped a hand over Chloe's mouth and fake grinned at him. "Chloe."

He slapped a hand over his heart. "What? Don't want me to join you?"

"No." She tossed her head, sleek dark waves bouncing. "It'll just be girl talk."

Janae Simmons shifted her attention between the two of them. "Margeaux, be nice."

"I try, but I'll try harder." She deflated just a bit, but then her direct gaze met his, and the connection made him take a step back. "In fact, we spent the morning talking about the case."

He might not have wanted to work with her initially, but her stubborn advocacy had grown on him. Now that the case was personal to him too, he understood and admired her commitment. Interesting how the sparks flew when they were in the same space. "She's brought some great ideas to the team, though she has a bit of an avenging Joan-of-Arc personality."

"Do not." But at Janae's knowing look, Margeaux shrugged. "Well, not really. Anneliese just needs someone watching out for her. She doesn't have anyone who cares about her best interests." She shredded the last bit of her sandwich. "Besides, I'd call it Wonder Woman rather than Joan of Arc."

"Anneliese is not a child. She's an adult who may have killed her roommate." Janae held up her hand as Margeaux sputtered. "I carefully phrased that."

"She didn't do it."

"Then the two of you need to work together and fast. That trial will be here in six weeks, and I haven't seen anything that refutes the building presumption that she committed the murder."

Margeaux pushed to her feet. "You know, I'm not so hungry after all. And I have an event tonight I need to get ready for."

"That's right. The one you needed to take someone to." Chloe waggled her eyebrows and made a sweeping *ta-da* gesture toward Chase. "I bet he'd go with you. Especially since it's for a good cause."

"Chloe . . . pushing." Margeaux growled the words out. It was almost cute how much she didn't want her friend's interference.

"Not at all. You need a plus-one, and I'm sure Chase would enjoy the fundraiser. Right, Chase?"

He looked at Chloe blankly, then blinked and nodded. This wasn't going at all the way he'd imagined when he started this direction. "Sure, we've been working hard. Maybe a break is exactly what our brains need."

"You don't need to do this."

"Just tell me when and where."

As Margeaux gave him the details, color crept up her cheeks. The blush meant she felt something other than what she normally displayed, which veered between hard as stone and raging anger. Now she was alive and engaged, and he loved seeing that. Maybe he'd have to thank her friend.

"I'll pick you up."

"I'll meet you there."

The barista called his name, so he said a quick good-bye. As he left to collect his food, he noticed Margeaux turn toward Chloe. "What have you done?"

"Given you a bit of a nudge." Chloe's voice was buoyant. "You can thank me later."

Later that evening, Chase waited outside the Elliott, not sure he liked feeling relegated to the role of a teenager waiting outside the theater for his date to arrive. When the Elliott had pitched these small showings of artsy films, he'd known they would flop, but then the museum had partnered with local nonprofits to raise funds, and the events had become quite popular. When Margeaux had been tricked into inviting him to join her in her role as board sponsor for that evening's event, saying yes had been a no-brainer. An opportunity to spend time with Margeaux while enjoying an evening at an event she would like. A little offbeat and a lot unique.

At the same time, attending with her allowed him to be a buffer if she needed one.

He hadn't wanted to ask if she was sure the museum would still want her to attend or if she would be persona non grata like she was at the university. He didn't want her to face the media alone if they showed up again. Maybe she hoped to slip in and out unnoticed, especially since no one had paid her any attention at the coffee shop—but there she'd worn jeans and a baseball hat. Here she'd be more dressed up.

He'd done some quick research on tonight's black-and-white movie, and it sounded interesting. *Casablanca* had been nominated for eight and won three Academy Awards, but he'd never seen it. He'd offered again to pick Margeaux up, but she insisted on meeting him at the museum. Maybe because she served on the museum's board, this didn't qualify to her as a date but a casual outing. He hadn't known how to change her impression without making a fool of himself or risking rejection. He wasn't ready to do that. Not when he needed her to believe he could do anything and win.

The thaw had been subtle, slow, occurring in inches rather than miles, and he didn't want to lose ground.

Would an old movie with Humphrey Bogart and Ingrid Bergman do the trick?

He couldn't see how. But there was art. And she liked art.

Chase tried not to fidget like a kid while he lingered at the top of the stairs by the large doors. He was too exposed waiting in front of the Georgia pink marble facade, so he sidled backward and leaned against one of the four massive pillars that supported the portico above him. Such an impressive building. He'd never quite understood how a community the size of Kedgewick had inherited a museum like the Elliott.

A woman hurried up the steps, her hair swept up in some sort of twist and her gown—a bell shape that hit mid-calf in a rich midnight blue—looking like a concoction from another time. He didn't want to look away even though he knew he was staring, and when she looked up and met his gaze a shock flowed through him.

Margeaux.

She was stunning.

And the hint of mischief in her eyes as she winked?

It made him want to hurry down and gather her in his arms.

Instead, he leaned against the pillar and waited as she skipped up the stairs. He offered his hand, and she took it. Instead of letting go, he spun her and watched her skirts billow as she twirled in front of him. Her smile glittered with joy.

"You clean up well."

"You do too. Thanks for agreeing to join me." Looked like she'd gotten over the coerced nature of her ask.

"Don't thank me until after the movie. It might not be any good."

Her mouth opened just a bit. "You haven't seen *Casablanca*?"

"Nope."

"Then why did you agree to come?"

"I don't know. Because you reluctantly invited me after much prodding by your friends."

"You are such a Neanderthal." She hooked her arm through his and practically dragged him to the doors. "It's a wonderful movie. You will love every minute of its Academy Award glory."

"I don't know about that." But as they walked in together and he looked down at her on his arm, he knew he would enjoy every moment he got to spend with the effervescent Margeaux Robbins. Soon enough the night would end and they would go back to sparring over legal strategy. But tonight, for this moment, they could pretend they weren't fighting to save a young woman's life, and he could enjoy imagining what could be. "Where's the theater?"

She steered him subtly toward a hallway he hadn't noticed. "It's not large, but it's nice for classes and when we have speakers or artists come in to talk about their works. The director, Carter Montgomery, is planning a symposium with Mrs. Seeger for the early fall."

"Who?"

"The heir who found some of her family's stolen art here late last year. It was quite a process to decide what to do with it." Her soft expression made her look younger and less like she felt she needed to leap tall buildings in a single bound in order to save the world. "I felt really good about helping to bring that to a resolution."

"You have quite the soft heart." Chase squeezed her hand. "And of course that's all bundled up under that Wonder Woman exterior. Makes you a rather remarkable woman, Margeaux Robbins."

She gaped a minute, letting him steer her forward until they turned a corner. "Here we are."

When Chase didn't move to enter the door, Margeaux looked up at him. "Thank you again for coming with me." And she leaned up and placed a soft kiss on his cheek. Then she stepped back, pink coloring her cheeks, seeming as surprised as he was by her gesture.

That kiss lingered on his cheek even as the movie opened, and left Chase wondering if they could become something more than reluctant colleagues. Because as he felt her head resting on his shoulder, he thought it might be worth the risk to explore.

Chapter 38

Wednesday, May 7

THE NEXT WEEKS HAD BLURRED together for Chase and the rest of the team.

Most people thought all the movies and TV shows featuring overwhelmed defense teams were wrong.

But they weren't.

In the days leading up to the trial, Chase dropped a steady blizzard of paper in front of Margeaux. If this was to be her only criminal defense trial, he wanted to make sure she got the full experience, but he couldn't shake the feeling they had missed something critical.

Each morning he arrived at the office and stared at the array of words and connecting lines that filled the whiteboard in the conference room, searching for the elusive something missing. Yet each day he would glower . . . and see nothing but gaping holes.

The PI had no luck getting the roommates to talk to him on the phone, but he did send a link to a campus newspaper article about a vigil. The piece was short with a grainy image, making it easy to understand how everyone on the team had missed it when it ran.

Margeaux had turned her focus to the roommates, who they may need for trial, but couldn't discover where the girls had moved. Even though Chase had talked with Renee, she'd vanished. Leigh couldn't track either of them on social media. It was like the commonwealth or their parents had spirited them home or to some secret location.

The why eluded him. His client remained securely behind bars. She wasn't going to hurt anyone. In fact, he'd stretched the time between his visits to jail because Anneliese seemed to disappear a bit more each time he saw her. His stomach roiled with the pressure to find an alternative story for the jury, but he kept coming up empty. He wanted to salvage the situation for Anneliese, but each time he asked, she failed to provide an alibi and continued to deny that she'd implicated Margeaux.

He needed leverage.

Some way to force the commonwealth to drop the charges.

At a minimum, he needed to get Anneliese out of jail before she disappeared and took Margeaux down with her.

Bottom line was, they needed to offer someone as an alternative suspect.

The evidence the police had accumulated was largely circumstantial. Anneliese's DNA on Lauren was easy to explain because she had found Lauren's body. Lauren's blood on Anneliese's clothes made logical sense for the same reason. You didn't check for life without getting covered in the blood.

So why had the police focused on Anneliese?

What had made them decide to quit looking in other places?

There was something. Something important that he didn't know yet.

He shoved his hands in his back pants pockets and kept staring at the whiteboard. He needed the connection. The trail to follow. The trial launched in a few weeks, and then time would be up. But if he could narrow it down now, there would still be time to find a winning strategy. He had to believe that, because Anneliese and Margeaux depended on him.

Margeaux walked in and handed him a cup of coffee. "Latte like you like it."

"Thanks." He took a cautious sip. "You're early."

"Not as early as you." She raised an eyebrow at him.

"True." This case was enough to push him over the edge and send him plummeting to the ground. If Anneliese was right, there was an alternate ending.

But this wasn't a Choose Your Own Adventure, where the flip of a page revealed a new answer or path forward.

And although he loved working with her, Margeaux Robbins was a distraction—not the solution he or Anneliese needed.

Like right now. She was saying something, but all he noticed was the way her perfectly colored lips moved. How did she do that?

His every thought needed to focus on the trial date that closed in with each passing moment. Instead, he could hardly think straight when she was in the room. It's what drove him to arrive earlier each day. The scent of her perfume wasn't heavy or cloying like many women's but was an enticing combination of clean and floral. It drew him to lean closer when he should be looking for the piece of evidence that would unlock the mystery of what happened March 16.

Why couldn't he fire her like he'd fired Marcus? Though the way Marcus had boomeranged, Chase hadn't exactly gotten rid of him either. Leigh had been right. Marcus had worked hard and redeemed himself on the first small trial and prepared well for the second one that loomed.

As Margeaux flipped another page, Chase wondered what she'd say if he told her she had to leave because he couldn't focus with her around.

He barely bit back a snort. Yeah, that would go over well. She would have him written up and in front of the bar committee in no time flat, and he wouldn't blame her.

"Are you focusing?" Her words penetrated, moving past his chaotic thoughts.

"Sorry, can you run that by me again?"

She heaved a sigh in dramatic fashion like he'd wasted her time. "To think I could be grading."

"That sounds stimulating."

"You have no idea. And it's important."

"Right up there with solving cancer or stopping a war."

"To my students it is."

"I'm sure." Then he matched her drama with a deep sigh of his own. "Too bad you're still on administrative leave."

"Low blow." The color flew up her cheeks. "Why do I bother?"

"Because you can't get enough of me."

"You wish." She practically vibrated across the table from him. "What would you do if I walked out of this room?"

She probably wanted him to say he'd be lost, but he couldn't. He'd miss the company, because she was more interesting to spar with than Marcus and certainly more beautiful by far, but he didn't *need* her. He must have waited too long or just long enough because she lurched to her feet.

"I can't decide whether leaving or staying will punish you more."

"Why would you want to do that?"

"You are infuriating." She bit out each word. Clear. Distinct. Chewed off and spit out. Yep, he'd made her mad. Did she have any idea how beautiful she was when frustrated? The color filled her cheeks and her eyes sparked. She was alive, and something inside him flared, pleading with him to lean toward her instead of running away.

Instead, he looked for a way to poke her further. How far could he push this time? "Maybe, but you need me. More than Anneliese needs me. We need to talk about Anneliese taking a plea."

Margeaux went still. So still he wanted to check her breathing. And then she spoke. "You can't do that."

"We have to be prepared." He rubbed the back of his neck as he watched her. She was taking this even worse than he'd expected. "What if it's the best option for Anneliese? With a plea, we might get the commonwealth to agree to a five-year sentence. Then she could be out in two and a half years."

"What are you afraid of?"

He stepped back, her words practically a body blow. "I'm not afraid."

"Yes, you are." The words exploded in the room. "You can't abandon her. Have you seen how she's deteriorating in jail? She can't survive there for years."

"Exactly. That's why we can't risk her being found guilty and spending ten, fifteen years there. I don't think she'd live through that." In fact, that had become his recurring nightmare. "I want to open a conversation with Allison. See what she's willing to offer."

"That's a mistake. You can't show them any weakness."

"It's not weakness if the alternative is our client being devoured. We haven't identified a single person to offer the jury as a suspect."

"That doesn't mean we give up." She waved her hands in the air and paced. "It means we work harder. Do more."

"Yes. We'll keep doing that too."

"You don't understand. If you give up on her, you're giving up on me too." And she fled the room, leaving him staring at the empty doorway.

Why hadn't he considered that Margeaux would take his words that way?

A plea for Anneliese could be the same as admitting Margeaux was part of a murder plot.

Chapter 39

IT WAS FINALS WEEK, AND she missed her students.

That's what Margeaux blamed her heightened emotion on as she fled the law firm.

She'd been caught off guard by a phone alert that the final for one of her courses was taking place that morning. The grief of potentially losing her job had slammed her all over again. Who was taking care of her students? Had the dean left them adrift at this crucial point in the semester? She bolted from the law office with the thought that if she visited Anneliese in jail, there was one student she could still help. She'd stayed away since being accused, but she couldn't do that any longer.

"We need to talk about Anneliese taking a plea." The words cycled the back of her mind as she processed through security. Twenty minutes later, when Anneliese shuffled into the small room and sank onto the chair across from her, Margeaux tried to push the phrase far from her thoughts. One glance confirmed her fears. Anneliese was wasting away. "Are you eating?"

The young woman gave a small shrug. "What I can."

"You have to try."

"I am." She looked down at her hands, which trembled on the table. "It is hard."

Margeaux reached across the table and put her hand over one of Anneliese's cold ones, trying to press her warmth into her student. "We're doing everything we can."

"I know." The words were so small. "I have tried to think of anything more to tell you."

"Why?"

"Why what?"

"Why would you tell the police I helped kill Lauren?" Anneliese tried to slip her hand free, but Margeaux didn't let go, though she kept her hold light. "I need to know, Anneliese."

"I did not say that."

"You must have, and it's upended my life. Do you understand that I can't teach right now? The college is keeping me away from students because the police and media have been on campus and in my classes."

"I am sorry. But I did not do it." Anneliese yanked free and rose to her feet. "You do not have to believe me. But it is the truth." She moved to the door and knocked on it.

"Before you go, Chase thinks you should consider a plea agreement. It would make sure you don't get a long sentence."

Anneliese didn't turn to look at Margeaux, but her words reached her. "What do you think?"

"I want to fight, but we don't have much to fight with."

"I guess it is good the battle is not tomorrow."

The corrections officer opened the door. "Are you done?"

Anneliese nodded. "I am."

He ushered her out and Margeaux stood. She didn't have any more answers, but she hadn't expected that anyway. What she did have was confirmation Anneliese struggled the longer she stayed in jail. By the time Margeaux reached her car and started the drive back home, her mind was racing. Between missing her students and the tumult with the upcoming trial, she couldn't imagine going back to the law firm.

Her mind flitted from one thought to the next like a hummingbird hyped up on the sweetest nectar, unable to transition from what was happening with the case and how it impacted her future at Monroe College to anything else.

By the time she reached her driveway, she was trembling. She pulled back out and kept driving, thoughts swirling on a prayer for peace as the miles clicked by.

What if the best thing for Anneliese was a plea?

As she wrestled with that idea, she found herself driving for hours.

She tried to tell herself there was still time to prevent that result, but either Chase didn't believe Anneliese was innocent or didn't believe in his skills enough to take the risk of going to trial.

Margeaux wanted to force him to fight for Anneliese.

But she didn't have the influence to make him do what she couldn't. He was right. She didn't know how to fight in a courtroom.

This was the reason she taught. She had a few good trial stories to tell. But she'd borrowed them from other people's experience. She read incessantly about what other people had accomplished. Learned from their wins and failures. It was safer that way. Less chance of making a critical error that cost someone millions of dollars or possibly their life.

When she returned home, she was exhausted from the mental gymnastics. Her shift from litigation to academia meant Chase was right about her and all the knowledge and experience she couldn't bring to the case. His words from one of their many meetings echoed through her mind as she stomped from her car and up the slate path to the front door.

"You don't know how to run a trial. Making split-second pivots and decisions is very different from neat, prepackaged thoughts in a book."

The closer they got to trial, the more his words rang true. Though she wanted to know more, she didn't know enough. But she hated to admit he'd been right.

Her hand shook so hard she dropped the key ring as she tried to insert the key in the front door lock. She squatted to reclaim it, her bag swinging off her shoulder and slamming into her head as she did so. What a great feeling.

Finally, she got the key in the lock and twisted it to open the door.

The warm scent of citrus and cinnamon reached her as she stepped inside, the leftover benefit of burning a candle that morning while her coffee brewed and she scanned the news.

She glanced at the small clock on the wall. Twenty minutes until Janae and Chloe arrived. Though normally she loved time with them, she wasn't feeling it tonight. But she knew if she canceled now, it would be easy to do the same the next time her schedule felt overloaded.

Spending all her hours working was too easy. She needed these scheduled breaks to keep any semblance of balance, especially as the trial barreled closer. She couldn't work constantly.

She only had a little bit of time to get ready before Chloe and Janae arrived. They'd chat from the floor cushions around her coffee table.

She hadn't changed much since she'd bought the house four years earlier, fully furnished. The area rug in the living room was more of a hall runner. The second bedroom barely had space for a desk and a blow-up twin mattress used when Emma stayed over on occasion.

As she turned on the fireplace, she glanced at the brass horse on the mantel. Someday she should make the space her own with decorations and details that were more her style. Until then it would do, because it still felt cozy and more like home than any other place she'd lived. She loved the space because it was hers. The open yard around the home kept her from feeling claustrophobic. She could see people coming, and that was what she valued most.

This was her safe space, and she loved every inch.

Margeaux set her bag on the floor by the desk, hung her coat on the hook, and then kicked off her boots and stepped into slippers. Returning to the kitchen, she grabbed a package of salami, a jar of mixed olives, a wheel of Brie, and a round of Gouda. It took only a minute to form a couple of flowers from the salami by placing the slices around the edge of a glass and pressing them in place on the board. Then a few more minutes and she had the cheese arranged, with olives swirled between the two cheeses. After she'd added a few crackers, the board met with her approval just as someone knocked and opened the door.

"We're here." Janae's voice reached Margeaux before she saw her former teammate.

"Just in time." Margeaux carried the board to the small oval coffee table and shifted a magazine to make space for the food.

"That looks too good to eat."

Chloe closed the door behind her and looked at the table. "Over-achieving again?"

"Not really. I saw a photo and wanted to try it." Margeaux clasped her hands behind her back, fighting the need to fidget. "I needed to create something beautiful. It was just that kind of day, you know?"

"You don't have to spoil us each time we come." Chloe gave her a quick hug. "I can pick up a pizza like you wouldn't believe."

Margeaux tried not to wince at the thought of all the grease and bread. "I don't mind." And she didn't. There was something therapeutic about creating beauty with food. It wasn't worth it for only herself, but for her friends? Yes.

"Too bad we couldn't have a fire outside." Janae moved to the cupboard to grab a glass and filled it with water. "There's something so peaceful about watching the flames."

"Maybe another night." She gestured to the fireplace. "You'll have to settle for the fake fire."

"To be precise, it's not really fake." Chloe popped a black olive in her mouth. "It's still a flame even if it's from gas."

Janae rolled her eyes. "Technicalities."

"You're an attorney." Chloe sank onto the small love seat and shifted her attention to Margeaux. "Speaking of the law, how are things going for your student?"

"I can't say much other than I don't like her court-appointed attorney."

Janae set her glass down and then slid one of the floor pillows over from its spot against the wall. "I thought you'd gotten beyond that."

"He wants us to consider settling."

"You don't settle in a criminal case."

"See? You're just like him. He's constantly telling me I don't know what I'm talking about. Like I didn't go to a top-tier law school and don't teach the subject. It's frustrating."

"But it wasn't top-tier while you were there."

"And you don't teach at a law school."

Her friends spoke the words on top of each other, and they echoed the words that already filtered through her mind, exposing her deepest fears.

"I know." And that was why she had to prove she was capable of winning a trial. This was her opportunity to do what no one thought she could. But first she needed to convince herself.

Chapter 40

Friday, May 16

THE NEXT FEW DAYS PASSED in a slog of searching for witnesses and readying Anneliese for what the trial would be like. Margeaux and Chase spent hours on strategy, ultimately deciding that Chase would handle most of the trial since he had the experience, but he would work off the earlier outlines she had created. That left Margeaux feeling like a glorified paralegal, but it also put her in the middle of the preparations. She organized files and tried to poke holes in legal theories during the long hours when she and Chase tried to anticipate what the commonwealth planned for its presentation of evidence.

Margeaux invested hours in preparing Anneliese while Chase kept digging with the PI. The end of the semester and students leaving for home or internships made it more challenging to locate them for in-person interviews, but that's why John was on the team. He could track them down.

Chase didn't mention pursuing a plea again, but she kept waiting for him to bring it up.

It had already been a long week, and while Margeaux knew she should look forward to the weekend, she dreaded the open space on her calendar and wondered if they should work on the case instead. She flipped to another browser tab, pounding search terms into her laptop while Chase stood staring at the board.

Then she felt his gaze on her. "What?"

He didn't say anything, but she would wait him out even as she sensed his intensity.

"I heard a rumor."

"One that will help Anneliese?" Otherwise she wasn't interested.

"I'm not sure."

As the silence lingered, she looked up, and the intensity of his gaze compelled her full attention. She pushed her laptop to the side and focused on him. "What is it?"

"A former client of mine called earlier today. Said he ran into someone who mentioned Lauren Payge. It got him thinking."

"Okay." She needed him to talk faster, because they were too close to the trial to waste time on rumors. Her foot tapped against the chair leg, but she tried to keep the rest of her body still.

"What if one of her boyfriends used Lauren to sell drugs to college students?"

She gave her mind a minute to examine the idea from all sides. "Lauren played on the lacrosse team."

"Yes."

"So that gave her and, by extension, her boyfriend access to all the student athletes."

"Probably."

"She was also more popular than I originally thought." She slid her laptop back in front of her and then flipped it around. "I found an additional profile that used an online name not clearly tied to her. I'm not sure why, because with name, image, and likeness deals, student athletes usually want to be easily recognizable. She didn't."

"What was she trying to hide?"

"I don't know. Or did she have a reason to value her privacy? I don't know that there's a market for professional female lacrosse players like there is in other sports. But I found a website that indicates the demand is pretty low."

"Makes sense." As Chase leaned closer to look at the small screen of the laptop, his woodsy aftershave wrapped around her.

Margeaux blinked and fought the urge to run from whatever was coming.

"I think I'm going to have John Charles dig into the rumor," Chase said. "See what he can unwind, if anything."

"To what end?"

"If he finds drugs, that could give us a host of potential suspects with motives."

"That's a jump." But maybe not as much as she wanted it to be.

"All we need is reasonable doubt."

"Yes, but we don't want to do it in a way that ruins someone else's life." She felt this to her core. "We're working too hard to find a way out for Anneliese to throw someone else into this position."

"Don't forget it also helps you."

"How could I forget since I still can't go back to campus?" She'd emailed the dean earlier in the week, and he'd been firm that she had to wait for the college's attorney to clear her. "This is very personal to me, and it's unsettling that you hold Anneliese's life in your hands. Mine too. I don't want her to be another David Roach."

Chase inhaled sharply, like he couldn't draw enough oxygen after being sucker punched.

She slapped both hands over her mouth. "I'm sorry. I didn't mean that."

"I don't need you throwing that into this." His voice was devoid of any emotion.

"I'm sorry, Chase."

"You might be, but David's father isn't about to let me forget . . . even if I could."

The admission landed hard in Margeaux's gut. "Look, I know you aren't at fault. I'm just scared."

"Emotion is dangerous in my line of work." Chase held her gaze, his jaw working beneath the shadow of his beard. "I have to keep a tight grip on logic to defend my clients."

Margeaux watched his anxiety bubble closer to the surface in the tight lines of his shoulders. She knew he cared but also needed distance. Maybe shutting down was a way to protect himself. She'd certainly tried it more than once. If so, she'd just hit him where he was most vulnerable.

"Janae says you're one of the best defense attorneys she's ever met."

Chase shoved his hands into his pockets and stared at the board as if she hadn't spoken.

Margeaux rose and inched toward him, watching his gray eyes darken. "Being an island doesn't make you good at your job, and it certainly can't make you happy."

"And what would you know about that?" Chase threw his pen on the table. "Are you happy? I've watched you, you know. You don't let anyone near enough for them to really know you. You push us away before that could possibly happen." He dropped into a chair, facing away from her. The suit coat hanging over his chair crumpled to the floor, and he ignored the wadded material as he stared at the stack of files in front of him.

Was that what she was doing? Pushing people away? But she was here, wasn't she? Helping Anneliese no matter what she had said or done to her. That meant Margeaux wasn't an island. She couldn't be and still help someone else. Right? Anneliese needed them to bring heart, passion, and logic to win her case. Of course, Chase had other cases that needed him as well. How did he manage them all when this one case exhausted her emotional reserves?

"We've got two weeks to finish getting ready." Margeaux stabbed the stack of cases in front of her on the table with her finger and felt her nail break. "We can work on our own issues after we save Anneliese."

"You believe she's innocent even after she implicated you?"

"She told us both she didn't. Why would she harm the one person who believes in her?" Margeaux rubbed her eyes, feeling the pressure of a weighted blanket of fatigue settle over her. "Besides, whether she did or didn't, the only way I'll get my life back is to prove who really killed Lauren."

Chase was fairly certain Margeaux had no idea how commanding she was when she was fired up. Definitely could give Wonder Woman's Diana a run for her money, even if she made him see double for a minute. But Margeaux was also naive if she thought passion would be enough to save either Anneliese or herself. So he did the only mature thing. He rolled his eyes. "You're back to that."

"Yes, I am. And I will keep coming back to it until we have definitive proof that Anneliese is the murderer."

"And her DNA at the scene isn't enough proof for you, with Lauren's blood all over her clothes?"

"No. She lived there. Her DNA would be everywhere. If it wasn't, *that* would be problematic."

"Then I hope the jury agrees with you, because from where I sit, that's the only evidence they have, so the jury will convict based on that if it wants to."

She crossed her arms and clenched her jaw like a stubborn toddler—a look he couldn't decide whether to love or hate. "Your clothes would have been covered too."

"No, they wouldn't."

She arched a brow at him. "Really? You would seriously leave her there and not check to see if she could be alive? I don't believe it. Not for a second."

He knew she was right, but admitting that would be like letting her storm his island. Especially when she already looked so maddeningly sure of herself.

"Let's focus on getting this right so that I don't have you or anyone else threatening lawsuits if it doesn't end the way you hope." Chase still hadn't played the latest voicemail from David Roach's dad. He didn't need the mental noise when he was trying to save someone else.

Chapter 41

ALL NIGHT MARGEAUX HAD ROLLED first one way and then the other, catching glances of the time on her digital clock. It was the night before the trial and she desperately needed to sleep, but her hyperalert mind seemed determined to prevent her body from resting.

As one and then two o'clock rolled by, she was sorely tempted to crawl out of bed and take a melatonin or Unisom. Anything that would stop the need to count more sheep. Surely she'd counted enough to fill Scotland, yet all she'd done was add to her tension.

She was excited and terrified by what the morning would bring.

Too much rested on responding to what the commonwealth presented, but she'd done what she could to prepare Anneliese. If she was honest, Chase had worked relentlessly with the private investigator and spent hours digging on his own too. The fact they hadn't found a clear alternate suspect didn't mean they hadn't tried.

In fact, Chase was still digging into the rumor of drugs even though she thought it was futile at this stage. The trial started in mere hours. And yet, she kept cycling through everything they'd investigated and researched over the last two and a half months and wondering which stones they'd missed.

At six she finally rolled out of bed, feeling like she hadn't slept.

She was facing a long day.

Somehow she had to find the strength to show up for Anneliese, but her attempts to get ready were a slog through quicksand. She wished Emma had spent the night so the teen could have hidden the dark circles under Margeaux's eyes with some influencer magic in the makeup department. Margeaux gave it a shot but knew it would take a small miracle for people not to notice she wasn't at her best that morning.

When she finally reached the courthouse, she was ready to take second chair and let Chase do the work. It felt like she'd already run the gauntlet. After hustling up the stairs, she saw Chase pacing outside the courtroom.

"You ready?" he asked.

"As I can be. Where's Anneliese?"

"The deputies just escorted her in. She's in a holding cell, and we can meet with her there. Remember, it's not a private setting, so be careful what you say."

"All right." Margeaux followed him into the elevator and to the holding area where Anneliese waited, wearing the pants and blouse Margeaux had purchased for her.

Anneliese didn't rise as Margeaux and Chase entered. Instead, she slumped at the table, her hands clasped and her gaze firmly fixed on them.

Chase sat across from her. "As we discussed, today will be jury selection, possibly opening statements. It depends on how quickly jury selection goes."

His client had that slightly glazed look in her eye. The one that made him wonder if she was all there or she was somehow okay with her roommate's murder. He'd seen flashes that made it clear she was upset about Lauren's death. But the slight smirk of her mouth made it seem like she couldn't be bothered with real life. Let reality impact everyone else—it didn't touch her.

That attitude wouldn't settle well with the judge and eventual jury. It came across as callousness. Some might even take it too far and believe it an admission of guilt, because no one who was innocent could appear untouched by murder.

That type of bias was compounded by the small, relatively rural setting. Yes, the metropolitan area of greater Washington, DC, was less than an hour away, but here in the rolling hills of northwestern Virginia, people were more country Southern than they were urbane city folk. That was not good news for his foreign client.

How much of her response to the situation stemmed from the fact she was from Germany? That was a question he couldn't answer. He needed to, but so far the explanation was elusive.

But Anneliese was his client, and that meant he would do his job. He owed her excellent representation.

How can I do that when I don't understand her?

That wasn't the right question.

He'd had lots of clients he didn't understand. What he really needed was an indication that she took this seriously. She might not comprehend, despite the number of times he'd tried to explain it to her, that a Virginia jury could decide that she should ultimately get the death penalty. Yet even early on, Anneliese had walked through her days with a blankness, as if the seriousness of the charges didn't penetrate. Was it a protective barrier? A coping mechanism of sorts?

Then she'd been put in jail and faded even more.

He was an excellent judge of character. It was what allowed him to do his job well. He could defend people because he could assess in a matter of minutes how a jury would take to them. Would a group of their peers decide that the person on trial was likable despite the charges? Or would the jury refuse to accept that the accused was fundamentally good regardless of the evidence the commonwealth presented? The question mattered—a person's life and freedom weighed in the balance.

With Anneliese, the fact that he wasn't sure how the jury would read her bothered him to his core.

A knock on the bars jerked Chase out of his thoughts, and the guard caught his attention. "Time to go upstairs."

Chase looked at her. "Any last questions?"

"No, danke."

"Then we'll see you upstairs."

Twenty minutes later, Anneliese fidgeted in her seat between Margeaux and Chase. Before Chase could move, Margeaux placed a hand on Anneliese's leg where no one could see. Anneliese stilled, and while her facial expression didn't shift, the young woman seemed to become preternaturally calm. It was almost unsettling.

"I'll be okay. I have to be." The words, though whispered on a breath, were important. They showed she understood how serious this moment was.

"Of course you will. Chase won't let you down." Margeaux's words speared through him. They felt like a promise.

He couldn't control how a jury would see the evidence.

He couldn't guarantee how a judge would rule.

And he couldn't prevent disasters from happening at the jail. But he could lean into the confidence of Margeaux's convictions.

"All rise. The court is now in session."

Chase stood, and then nudged Anneliese. She finally struggled to her feet, watching the judge walk to the bench. He glanced behind her and met Margeaux's gaze with a raised eyebrow. She shrugged before looking back to the front of the courtroom.

"The Honorable Rhonda Waters presiding."

The judge took a seat, adjusting until her robes settled just so. Judge Waters had a reputation for being firm but fair. In prior cases he'd tried before her, she'd kept the case moving forward quickly and in a way that kept everything focused and as impartial as possible. He'd been relieved when he learned she would preside over Anneliese's trial.

She shifted a few files on the bench, then looked up and motioned down with her hands. "You may be seated. We're here today to seat a jury. I want to set a few ground rules. I will not have the jury tampered with in any fashion, and that means from the moment we begin seating prospective jurors. I expect each to be treated with the respect they are owed as they fulfill their service obligation to our state and community. Am I clear?" She focused first on the commonwealth's attorney and then on Chase. Allison Erickson nodded and Chase responded affirmatively. Only then did she give a firm nod. "We've spent time in the pretrial hearing arranging the ground rules, and I've reviewed your preliminary motions. I will ask all questions of the prospective jurors. After each has answered, we will have a sidebar, and you may raise any objections at that time. Nothing will be stated in the hearing of that juror."

"Yes, Your Honor," Margeaux said.

Allison nodded along. "Of course, Your Honor."

Chase didn't have to like it, but he'd abide by it until the commonwealth's attorney violated. It wouldn't take long for her to break form. In fact, he gave her exactly one juror. "I understand."

The judge considered him carefully. "Understanding is not the same as complying."

"I will advocate for my client as required by law."

"I would expect nothing less. That's why you were appointed as her attorney." The judge tapped her files together on her bench. "Let's begin."

Chapter 42

NARROWING THE POOL OF TWENTY potential jurors to the twelve who would determine the case had taken less time than Margeaux expected. Why did it feel so monumental in books like *The Runaway Jury* or *The Justice Game*? The real event quickly evolved into a break for lunch, and then the twelve newly sworn-in jurors followed the bailiff to their seats. The two alternates waited with them. Each had a notepad and looked ready for whatever would come their way in the next days.

The jury consisted of seven women and five men. They were as old as Janae's grandmother and as young as a recent Monroe College graduate.

These people held Anneliese's destiny in their hands.

Unanimously they had to agree on her fate.

They were supposed to be her peers, but only a couple had traveled outside the country. None had experienced study abroad. None knew what it meant to live outside their home country.

They could not relate to Anneliese's experience.

But they would judge it.

The underlying unfairness hit Margeaux and knocked the breath from her.

Anneliese glanced at her. "Everything all right?"

Margeaux nodded because words wouldn't come. Not without air.

"Good." Then the young woman set her chin and gazed resolutely in front of her as if no one else were in the cavernous room.

The media did not exist. No one waited in the audience. They might as well have lingered in a classroom, counting down until Margeaux started her next class.

The judge made a few notations on a paper in front of her, then looked up over her reading glasses. "Ms. Erickson, you may begin."

"Thank you, Your Honor." In a navy sheath and jacket, Allison looked like she'd stepped from central casting as she found her feet. Without any sense of hurry, she collected a legal pad and moved to the podium. She settled her notes and took a moment to connect with each member of the jury as if she'd personally invited them to serve. "Thank you for being here."

After all the hours they'd spent preparing, Margeaux should know exactly what would come next.

Chase had explained that a trial was a well-scripted dance.

The commonwealth moved. Then the defense countered.

Instead of feeling prepared and ready, all she noticed was a wedge of terror locked inside her core. She'd count it a victory if she could keep the fear from spreading to her face and other nonverbals. But she wasn't sure how to master that when everything in her warned her to dash to the bathroom and lose the soup she'd forced herself to eat for lunch.

Apparently eating during a trial was not a recipe for success. So she pressed a hand to her stomach and forced a placid expression in place.

She prayed that Chase was right and somehow their preparation would make a difference for Anneliese. But in that moment, she couldn't imagine how.

Chase watched as Allison Erickson paused and several members of the jury leaned in. Already they seemed trained to anticipate anything she would say. "Today you've accepted an important responsibility. One that is foundational to the contract our country and our society are built upon. I know this wasn't convenient or easy timing for any of you. In fact, it's probably difficult for you to be here. You have people depending on you to care for them. And each of you could make more than the fifty dollars a day the state will pay you."

Several of the jurors shifted uncomfortably, and he had to admire the way she dealt a blow to the issue.

"Here's the thing. This is your civic duty. Once every three years, the state of Virginia can ask you to serve in this way. To lend your experience and your time to the commonwealth to reach a determination of whether we have proven beyond a reasonable doubt that someone is guilty of the crime with which they have been charged."

A moment of silence stretched, the words sinking into the space. "The work you will do this week is of the utmost importance."

Chase kept his face impassive, knowing this was where her tone would shift.

None of the jurors had a choice about whether they filled those seats, but she would let them think they were each about to do something critical. And it was a weighty task. But he wouldn't pretend she wasn't a shark who would create blood in the water when necessary.

"For the next week or ten days, you will have the singular purpose of deciding what happened in the residential suite of apartment 321 on Monroe College's campus on the evening of March sixteenth. Sometime that night, Lauren Payge's life was brutally stolen from her, and the commonwealth will prove beyond a reasonable doubt that the woman sitting at that table"—she thrust her arm toward Anneliese—"was responsible for that death."

Allison waited a moment until each person in the jury examined Anneliese like she was a bug that had been stepped on, and then she lowered her arm and picked up a clicker. With deliberation, she pushed a button, and a smiling image of the victim flashed on the screen at the front of the courtroom—all grinning, vibrant perfection. She looked like the poster child for student athletes. Blonde, beautiful, ready to change the world when she graduated. The attorney stared at her a moment, a downcast expression on her face, looking like an aunt examining the photo of a child who'd been taken from her family too soon. Then she suddenly turned back to the jury and pointed dramatically at the image.

"Lauren Payge was not only a gifted lacrosse player but also a talented student. In May she would have graduated with honors and then moved to Washington, DC, for a job with the State Department—an entry-level program for future diplomats. Her professors told me she had the potential to chart a course to become a country-hopping public servant. That's why she was excited to be assigned a roommate who was a student from another country."

"That's not true." Anneliese said the words too loud, and Chase put a hand on her arm and squeezed. "She didn't want me."

The judge studied Anneliese over her glasses, and Margeaux scratched a note and slid it toward her.

The young woman would have to remember not to react, or she would be her own worst witness without ever reaching the stand.

The commonwealth's attorney continued. "The future stretched wide open and bright for Lauren until that night. Then everything ended in the most brutal way possible. She was stabbed not once but multiple times. Past the point that she could recover from her wounds and the savage blood loss."

She paused, and Chase wondered what she'd say next.

She let the silence stretch as she considered Lauren's beautiful image. Then she turned to the jury. "I was advised by colleagues to show you images of Lauren's shattered body. To bring that into this space from the earliest moments of the trial. I've chosen to wait. I want to honor her, to remember who she was rather than glorify what was inflicted on her."

"Objection, Your Honor." Margeaux leapt to her feet before Chase could stop her. And now there was nothing he could do to stop what she'd launched.

Judge Waters looked down her nose at Margeaux. "Reason?"

Margeaux's gaze darted around. He knew she needed help, but he also knew that giving help would undermine their representation in front of the jury, and from the first minutes of the trial. He worked hard to keep his frustration from overtaking his expression. There had been better moments to object, but he'd chosen not to because he didn't want to look weak or defensive to the jury. In one misguided motion, she'd obliterated the fruit of his self-control. She didn't know better, and that was exactly why he had hesitated to have her at this table. However, Anneliese relied on her.

She squared her shoulders and raised her chin, the warrior rising up. "The commonwealth's attorney is moving beyond the facts."

"This is opening statement, Your Honor." Allison spread her hands wide, as if pleading with the judge. "I get more latitude here."

"Overruled. You may continue."

"Thank you."

Chase scribbled a note and edged his legal pad toward Margeaux. *Stay seated.*

She barely tipped her chin in acknowledgment, but he'd take it.

Margeaux could barely pay attention over the rushing in her ears.

She knew better than to speak up in this context, but she couldn't let the commonwealth's attorney make a saint of the deceased. Was this what Chase had warned her about? The need to placidly let whatever the state said roll off her as if it was inconsequential? This was going to be an extremely long week if that's what the trial required of her.

Every word felt heavy, every tone nuanced with danger.

She scanned the jury, trying to read their body language. How were they reacting to the commonwealth's attorney? Allison had a way that seemed to resonate with them, guiding them through her carefully woven narrative. How were they responding to Anneliese? And how could Margeaux separate the story being woven from the young woman sitting next to her?

Maybe she couldn't, but she needed to try.

"The defendant moved in, and within a couple of weeks the neighbors overheard loud, angry arguments."

Anneliese stiffened but kept quiet, her gaze firmly fixed on the table in front of her.

"You'll discover how the arguments could be over anything and nothing. What matters is they were nonstop and disruptive. You'll also learn from neighbors that they weren't surprised to learn that violence had erupted. If anything, some were surprised it took so long for the verbal sparring to elevate to physical."

"Objection." Chase jumped to his feet. "This has moved beyond the scope of opening statement and is prejudicial and hearsay." His words were bland, devoid of emotion and yet full of fact-bearing weight. He was good.

"Counsel?" Judge Waters turned to CA Erickson.

"I get more latitude in opening."

"Not this much. Keep it within the facts of what is coming."

"Thank you, Your Honor." She took a shallow breath and turned back to the jury. "There is no question Lauren Payge's life ended violently. And we will lay out a road of evidence from the death to the defendant."

Juror number one, a mom and teacher, focused intently on every word Allison uttered, as if the CA gifted the room pearls of wisdom that had to be captured. The question was how the teacher interpreted them. Did she take them in as the mother of a preteen child, envisioning the pain of loss? The woman shouldn't be on the jury, but she was, so they'd have to find a way to help her see Anneliese as someone who needed protection and understanding.

The retiree next to her had his arms crossed and a grimace painted on his face. His eyes were already glazed as if he couldn't wait to be done, and the trial had only just started. He could be trouble.

Behind him sat a young woman who didn't look much older than Lauren or Anneliese. A recent grad. Margeaux was probably most concerned about her. If she had leadership skills, the other jurors might follow her and weigh her words more heavily since she could bring the perspective of that generation. Or they might ignore her altogether. Margeaux wasn't sure which would hurt Anneliese more.

The whole thing was a logic problem doused in uncertainty that made her head pound.

She never should have answered that first phone call in the middle of the night. Then she would have learned about the murder with everyone else and been concerned, but she wouldn't sit at the defense table wondering what on earth she was doing and how else she would mess up.

Anneliese shifted, her elbow knocking into Margeaux and jarring her back into the moment.

"First, you'll hear from the police on the scene, and then we'll walk you through what happened. Finally, we'll answer why this happened, though we may not answer it satisfactorily." Allison turned and looked at Anneliese. "Sometimes, we can't understand fully. All we can know with clarity is that it happened.

"Your job throughout this trial is to think critically about what you hear. Who do you believe? Why? At the end of the evidence, the commonwealth of Virginia will ask you to return a verdict of guilty against the defendant, Anneliese Richter. Thank you for your time, attention, and service."

As she took her seat, Chase gathered his items, and Margeaux breathed a prayer.

Chapter 43

COURTROOMS USED TO BE A second home to Chase.

Then David Roach died and Chase lost confidence that he could maneuver a jury to the best decision.

Now that Chase was here, he couldn't let his brokenness harm Anneliese. Somehow he had to scrounge up a way to do his job well with what remained of him. He stood, buttoned his suit coat, and gave himself a moment to breathe as he met the gaze of each of the twelve impaneled jurors. Then he set his notes on the podium and stepped away. His ardent hope was the hours of preparation would allow him to walk away without relying on the paper.

He needed to connect with the panel. Here and now, they needed to forget the commonwealth's misdirection and begin to trust him. Instead of seeing him as the enemy, they needed to believe he was a guide here to help them find the truth. That journey began in this moment.

"Over the next week you will listen to two stories. Two very different versions of what happened the night of March sixteenth. The one from the commonwealth will paint a picture of roommates in a war that exploded into a disaster and ended in a horrible tragedy.

"We will tell a different story—one no less tragic, but one that could end with two victims.

The Accused

"A year ago, Anneliese Richter arrived in Virginia eager, over-whelmed, and a bit naive. She was here to pursue her version of the American dream while enjoying a year on study abroad. She'd live here while working toward her undergraduate degree through an exchange program. It was an opening afforded to her that no one else in her family had experienced. That meant no one could prepare her for what she was about to encounter. But she came ready to engage in the fullness of the opportunity. In the process, she hoped to expand her cultural and language skills. If she could do that, it would be a successful year."

He turned and took a moment to let the jury look at Anneliese. His client acquiesced and cooperated by looking back with a small smile, one that indicated shyness rather than haughty indifference. Her insecurity was hidden in this moment, and he could have celebrated but instead tried to appear as if he expected nothing less. After a pause, he turned back to the twelve and two alternates.

"Imagine a place where everything is oversized and intimidating. There are no corner stores, so a trip to Walmart for milk feels like a daily run to IKEA." A woman on the second row—Dara?—grinned at the comparison, and he felt a small bit lighter. He could engage with the pool and help them see what Anneliese had experienced.

"The differences are vast but not as foreign as one might expect. The language? It takes work, but she knew she'd get the hang of it thanks to years of English in school.

"Her greatest challenge? Loneliness. She'd never considered how one could be surrounded by people on a campus of four thousand students and yet feel so utterly alone. She'd thought she was the lucky one because she'd been matched with one of the popular students. A student athlete who initially seemed interested in knowing her. But when Anneliese didn't understand lacrosse, Lauren's curiosity waned. The other roommates were even less concerned about their imported addition." He stilled his pacing and looked at the panel. "That's where reality took a hard turn from the dream and hope.

"During the course of the trial you will be tempted to take all the evidence that the commonwealth gives you, and if you simply accept the testimony without critically engaging with it, you may decide there is no other option than to find guilt." He paused. Would Allison rise to the bait?

A moment of silence passed—enough to let him know she was too professional for that.

Fine. He'd keep going.

He'd always loved that moment when the magic happened and he truly connected with the jury. If he had to try this case, then he wanted to feel that jolt of knowing he and the jury were communicating at a deep, thorough level.

"Instead, I invite you to keep an open mind. Don't reach any decisions until both sides present evidence. Until you hear from both the commonwealth and the witnesses we'll present."

Don't oversell. He reminded himself now was the time for confidence and a bit of showmanship, but not selling to the point he didn't recognize the case. He wanted the jury to trust him when they walked into their room to deliberate.

"Every coin has a second side. Every story has another perspective. All we ask is that you remember that as you listen to every witness and as you review every document. Does Lauren Payge demand justice? Absolutely.

"But so does my client, Anneliese Richter.

"To turn around and commit a wrong against my client won't suddenly lessen the weight of the terrible evil that befell Lauren. We can do better, and we must."

He took a moment to review his notes. Then he looked up and connected with the gaze of each member of the jury. He let himself take the time to feel a real moment of eye contact. "Thank you for your service on this jury and for your attention to all the information you're about to receive. It may feel like a lot in the coming days. However, both justice for Lauren and Anneliese's future depend on you." He made a sweeping gesture toward Anneliese as she looked from him to the jury like they'd planned. He allowed himself one more glance at the jury. Most leaned forward slightly.

Time to end.

"Thank you."

And he sat.

The judge looked over her glasses at the jury. "We will take a thirty-minute recess to give you a chance to stretch your legs and make any needed calls. However, I remind you, you are not to discuss what happens in the courtroom with anyone. Bailiff, you may take the jury." After the jury filed from the courtroom, she turned to the attorneys. "I'll see you in my chambers in five minutes."

Then she stood with a swirl of robes and exited through the back.

Chapter 44

JUDGE WATERS HAD HER GLASSES off and was massaging the back of her neck when the court reporter ushered Margeaux and Chase into the judge's chambers. She quickly sat up and replaced the glasses. Her blue eyeglasses drew attention to her brown eyes, which searched behind the lenses. "Allison with you?"

Margeaux tucked her hands behind her back. "No, ma'am. Do you want me to go find her?"

"She'll find her own way here." She waved to the chairs in front of her oversized desk. "Have a seat. We'll give her a minute, then get started."

The court reporter hurried to the door. "I forgot something on my desk."

The judge barely seemed to notice as she flipped through some papers on the surface in front of her. "What are the odds we'll get through the case this week?" She didn't look up, but there was no question she focused completely on Chase.

"It depends on the commonwealth."

"Don't give me that."

"A week. Maybe two."

He opened his mouth, but before he could say anything else, she held up her hand. "We'll wait to say anything else until the court reporter's back. We'll get everything on the record so there's no question we avoided ex parte communications."

Margeaux didn't know where to look or what to do. While this wasn't her first time in chambers, it was her first time having to wait in them. This week was going to be excruciating if filled with moments like this. She scanned the closest bookshelves, but the books lining them were volumes of dusty old law reporters that the judge probably hadn't touched in years. Most reporters had been digital for decades, so there was no reason to maintain the volumes other than show. "Do you research primarily online?"

Judge Waters glanced up, curiosity sparking her eyes. "Why do you ask?"

"All the books. I can't imagine you really use them."

"You'd be surprised. Sometimes it's nice, if old-fashioned, to have a book in front of me rather than a screen."

The door opened and the court reporter walked in, followed by Allison. Allison carried her briefcase and, other than tightness around her eyes, looked unconcerned.

"Have a seat, Allison." The judge's formal tone returned as the court reporter settled in a chair to the side of the desk. "We have twenty minutes to reinforce the ground rules. Just in case you forgot, I will run this trial on a tight schedule. There's no room for either side to lob accusations at the other. We will stick to the testimony and what the evidence shows. I will allow limited latitude, only when it is warranted and for a strict time. This is not a trial that will be handled in the media if I can restrain it."

She paused long enough to study Chase and Allison before turning to Margeaux. "I understand that this is a high-profile case and one that represents personal connections. However, neither gives either side the grounds to move beyond the bounds of propriety. This will not be a trial that puts witnesses and defendants in the news. Are we clear?"

Allison nodded with a detached air. "Of course."

"Yes, Your Honor." Margeaux would do whatever it took to be an asset, not a liability. If only she knew what it would take.

Chase affected an indifferent air, steepling his hands in front of him as he leaned back. "We have no plans to do anything but represent our client effectively."

"There's no need to posture." The judge swept the room with her gaze. "The jury isn't here."

"True, but I want to be clear we're ready to counter evidence the state presents to the jury that can't be substantiated or borders on hearsay." He leaned forward and put his elbows on his knees. "My client's future and possibly her life are at stake. So while you're concerned for the sake of the court's image, I'm worried about her." He slapped down a file from his bag. "That's why I'm requesting that all witnesses be sequestered until it's time for their testimony." He handed a copy of the motion to the judge, then the court reporter and commonwealth's attorney. "Our arguments are in the attached motion."

The judge spent a minute scanning the document, her pen flying down the page, then looked up with a frown. "Why did you wait until now to present this to the court?"

"I like to see the jury before I make a decision."

The commonwealth's attorney shook her head. "And waiting makes a difference how?"

"Children." Judge Waters's voice stopped the bickering. "We will not devolve." She scanned the order again. "What do you think this will accomplish?"

"The usual." He held up a hand and ticked items off his fingers. "Make sure witness testimony isn't coordinated. Ensure the jury hears the truth. Keep everyone honest."

Margeaux stayed quiet as the two attorneys volleyed back and forth, the judge bending forward with a pinched expression. There was nothing Margeaux could add other than confusion.

"Y'all are worse than my teenagers." Judge Waters shrugged her shoulders, then released them and straightened. "I'd like to take this under advisement, but considering it was just handed to me and we start the trial in ten minutes, that's not an option. The law is clear that I can do this with or without a motion at any point in the trial." She gave

Chase her full attention. "While I'm going to grant your motion, I want you to listen closely to this next sentence. I don't appreciate eleventh-hour filings. When you have an opportunity to file something on time or early, take it. Everything will proceed more smoothly for all of us. Understood?"

Chase nodded. "Yes, Your Honor."

The judge glanced at the clock on her wall. "Then as long as we remember I'm the judge and run the show, we're ready to get started. All witnesses other than the defendant and the victim's parents will be kept from the courtroom until after they testify. Once each witness has been cross-examined, I will allow them to remain in the courtroom."

"What about redirect?" Chase lobbed the question like he was prepared to run the other direction.

"I will allow redirect in the moment, but I will not keep a witness out on the possibility of a redirect at some point in the future." She glanced at the court reporter. "Make sure the bailiff knows of the change. We will also need to coordinate with the sheriff's office." She focused on the commonwealth's attorney. "How long will your first witness take?"

"No more than an hour."

"You're certain?"

"As certain as I can be."

She focused on Chase. "And your cross-examination?"

"No idea until I know where Allison goes in direct."

"Fair enough." She tapped a pen against her mouth as she considered the time. "It will be three o'clock when we bring the jury back. Let's get the first witness through direct and possibly cross today. If we need to recess between the two, we will." She made a shooing motion. "I'll see y'all in the courtroom in five minutes."

As they left, Margeaux leaned closer to Chase. "How did that go?"

"We just won an important volley."

"How so?"

"Watch and see."

He didn't know her very well or he'd know those three words were some of her least favorite.

Chapter 45

ANNELIESE WAS SITTING AT THE defense table when Chase and Margeaux returned to the courtroom. Margeaux checked with her, but Anneliese didn't want to talk while they waited for the action to restart. When the jury had returned to their box, the judge turned the courtroom over to the commonwealth's attorney.

Allison rose, and with a quick straightening of her jacket, called her first witness. "The commonwealth calls Detective Brian Alterhaus."

Margeaux leaned toward Chase. "Why not call Detective Phillips?"

"He won't make a good witness." He made a point of ignoring her.

"That doesn't make sense." Grouchy Detective Phillips was the one at the scene. He was the one who should be on the witness stand. Instead, Detective Alterhaus approached, raised his right hand, and was sworn in. There was something about the way he walked, with assurance and calm, that made him seem authoritative without being demanding, and whispered *trust me*. He was average height and seemed fully comfortable with himself as he approached the witness chair and took a seat. A minute later the ladies in the jury were sitting a bit straighter and on the edge of their seats.

He gave the room a big grin as if he was delighted to be with them and had nowhere better to be.

She didn't like this.

At all.

It didn't feel right. The energy was all wrong, and Margeaux didn't know what to do to change it. So she watched with the sneaking suspicion the case was going to commence in a way that would favor the commonwealth.

And there was nothing she could do to stop it.

Tension radiated off Margeaux in every stiff line of her body, and Chase knew the jury could read it. Worse, Anneliese could too. Rather than adjusting to show strength for their client, Margeaux transmitted that their cause was doomed.

He couldn't afford to go there. Now that the trial had started, he had to believe they had a chance and somehow convince the jury and his client of the same. Either he would save Anneliese, or he'd leave criminal work behind. Maybe he'd manage to do both.

Somehow, he would win the jury over.

Convince them Anneliese could not have killed her roommate.

He quickly scribbled a note and passed it to Margeaux. *Relax. They're watching.*

Margeaux dipped her chin to read, and then realization snapped through her and she pasted on a smile that would fool anyone but him.

That hurdle cleared, Chase turned to the second—the man sitting on the witness stand right now.

Allison shifted her notes on the lectern. "How long have you been a detective?"

"A little over two years."

"And when were you assigned to this case?"

"I was added to the team after the scene was cleared."

The commonwealth's attorney paused and considered him with a tilt to her chin. "What does that mean? After the scene is cleared?"

"Just that the crime scene techs have collected the evidence."

"Is that unusual? Getting assigned after that part of the work is finished?"

"I wouldn't say it's typical, but it's also not that uncommon. I was finishing another case, and my colleague Detective Phillips handled the scene. After that I was assigned to help with the next stages of the investigation."

"Did you work with the crime scene techs?"

"Yes, ma'am."

"Did you receive their reports?"

"Yes, ma'am."

"What did you learn from the scene?"

"Objection." Chase shot to his feet the moment the word left his mouth. "Detective Alterhaus has already admitted he wasn't at the scene at the time of the investigation. Anything he says would be hearsay."

Judge Waters tapped her reading glasses against her mouth as she considered, then looked at Allison. "Ms. Erickson?"

"I'll connect it, Your Honor."

"I'll give you a minute, but make the connection quickly." She turned to the jury. "From time to time, the attorneys will make an objection. The fact they do should not sway you one way or the other. I will let you know what the law permits." Then she turned back to the commonwealth's attorney. "You may proceed."

"Thank you." Allison took a moment to glance at her notes and then stepped away from the podium. "With which aspects of the investigation were you personally involved?"

The detective leaned forward and made eye contact with Allison and then shifted slightly so the jury could take in his boy-next-door good looks. "After the night of the murder, I interviewed witnesses, watched the autopsy, and interfaced with the campus police."

"Why would you work with them?"

"While they are talented, they don't have the resources to handle evidence created by a murder. At our agency, we work hard to facilitate good relationships across the law enforcement community in case of an event like this one. That means we work with campus police as well as the sheriff's office and other agencies to make sure that in the event of a crime like this one, all tools are available to solve it."

"Were there procedures already in place between your agencies in the event a murder occurred?"

"On paper, but this was the first time we utilized them. It's the classic situation where you want to prepare for every eventuality and hope you never need it. Unfortunately for Ms. Payge, we did."

The jury seemed to lean into his every word, and Chase couldn't decide whether to rise and object or let the detective keep talking so his words could turn into a drone of background noise. Neither seemed the best choice, so Chase did nothing. But he hated watching the jury sit forward collectively, charmed by the good-looking detective who relaxed in the witness box.

"How did the partnership with the Monroe College police department work?"

"The campus police secured the scene, and we conducted the investigation."

"Objection. Hearsay. Detective Alterhaus by his own testimony wasn't there the evening of the investigation."

"Upheld." Judge Waters looked to the detective. "Stick to the parts you were personally involved with."

"Yes, ma'am."

Chase sank back to his seat but kept his feet positioned so that he could spring back up if needed, all while trying to look casually indifferent to the testimony. He scanned the jury box, and his gaze stopped when it landed on James Thompson. The retired Marine looked at him and gave a small nod, then glanced down at Chase's feet. Chase didn't look away. So the man saw through him. It didn't matter.

"What role did you play in the investigation?"

"Detective Phillips and I worked closely on the case. After the initial crime scene investigation, we divided the witnesses and work. It's typical to do that in an investigation. We take parts and do the work together." He must have caught something in Allison's expression, because he stopped abruptly.

"What lines of investigation did you take?"

"It was a pretty typical start. We talked with each of the roommates and any neighbors that we could find. Each of them could give us a more complete picture of the victim. That allowed us to piece together what happened that night."

"Who did you speak with?"

"Is it all right if I look at my notes?"

"How and when did you create them?"

"During the investigation. These are my personal notes and formed the foundation for my contributions to the reports we filed." He patted the slim notebook. "I keep a separate notebook for each investigation of everything I learn and see. I write the notes as I'm investigating. To keep me organized."

The man was going on too long about his notes. "Objection. Move to exclude the notes unless the notebook is tendered as evidence."

The judge looked to Allison. "Ms. Erickson?"

"Your Honor, Detective Alterhaus should be able to use his notes to refresh his memory. That's standard practice."

"He should have already done so," Chase retorted.

"I'm going to allow it." Judge Waters looked over her glasses at him and Chase reluctantly sat.

Allison walked the detective through his interviews. Chase took down notes of who Alterhaus had met with, and most of the names matched people he and John Charles had either tracked down or tried to find. He needed a thread to explore.

"No further questions."

Judge Waters looked at him. "Mr. Crandall."

"Thank you." Chase approached the podium. "What was the general reputation that Lauren had?"

"She seemed well-liked."

"Any enemies?"

"Not that concerned us."

"Any that did concern you?"

"No."

"She was a bit of a partier."

"Like some college students."

"And there were reports of police calls to her apartment."

"Yes."

"Domestic disturbances."

"Yes."

"Related to a boyfriend."

"Yes."

"Did you interview that boyfriend?"

"We did."

"Did you?"

"Yes."

"What was his name?"

"Dominic Strand."

Allison had started to move, but the detective answered too quickly, so she stayed seated.

Chase took a moment to weigh the risk of what he was about to ask. "Did you consider this man as a possible murderer?"

"Objection, Your Honor." Allison leapt to her feet, cheeks reddening as her nostrils flared. "This is beyond the scope of direct."

"It's not. When the detective testified about the boyfriend it opened the door to the possibility, and a moment ago he answered the question about the domestic disturbances."

The judge looked at Allison. "Are you prepared to enter the police reports?"

"I reserve the right."

Judge Waters studied both of them as she thought. "I'm going to allow it. The door has certainly been cracked through the questions that were asked and testimony given." She turned to the detective. "You may answer the question."

"We did not."

"Why not?" Chase kept his stance relaxed.

"We didn't find him credible."

"Did he have an alibi?"

"You'd have to ask Detective Phillips."

"Why?"

"He's who conducted the interview."

"So you both worked the case, but you did not talk to Dominic Strand. Is that correct?"

"Yes."

"So you have no firsthand impression of whether or not he was . . . credible, is that what you called it?"

"Yes."

"Yes, you have no firsthand impression or yes, he was credible?"

Allison was back on her feet. "Objection, argumentative."

"It's cross-examination."

Judge Waters considered a moment, then nodded to the detective. "You may answer."

The detective turned slightly from the jury and rolled his eyes. "I did not interview Mr. Strand."

Chase glanced at Margeaux and she shook her head. He had to think her instincts were right. Stop while they were ahead. "No further questions at this time." He fought not to sag. That hadn't won the case, but it had opened a tiny crack. As he turned back to the desk, Margeaux's face reflected her relief.

She understood the small victory they had just won.

Chapter 46

THE SECOND DAY OF THE trial, Chase rearranged where they sat at the table. "Anneliese, you sit at the end." She glanced at him and slid into the chair. Then he gestured to the next chair for Margeaux. "You're sitting next to me."

Margeaux looked at him like he had lost his mind. "Why?"

"Because the jury notices every time you reach over to slide me a note or whisper a question. Having you next to me will cut down on those." And he'd steel himself not to notice the way her scent wrapped around him.

"You don't know me very well." The hint of a smile teased him closer, but he resisted.

"Actually, I do. We've worked together a lot over the last couple of months." And he was grateful for what she'd added to the trial prep, but Anneliese's future depended on how Margeaux responded now. "Smile and look like we're thrilled with how the case is going."

"Why?"

"Because the bailiff is about to bring the jury back."

For a moment a flash of hurt shadowed her face, probably from his tone. But then she did as he asked. Her cooperation made him believe there was hope for this partnership after all.

Did he see her as a liability to the trial? Margeaux knew there was a lot of pressure now that it was underway, but she wanted to help, not make the burden worse.

Margeaux glanced at Anneliese and noted the tightness around her mouth. The young woman looked exhausted, dark purple bruising the skin beneath her eyes. It couldn't be easy trying to sleep in jail. The bright color of her blouse only made Anneliese look paler. Margeaux could see the effort she expended to keep her chin up and eyes forward even as she looked ready to collapse into herself.

She wanted to hug Anneliese but resisted, concerned with how Chase and the jury would interpret that gesture.

The commonwealth called the medical examiner. Margeaux tried not to lose her breakfast as the doctor testified about the injuries and how Lauren wouldn't have died immediately, though it was questionable whether she could have survived them. Margeaux scanned the jury and noted several of them watching Anneliese. What did they see? Hal Jenkins couldn't seem to take his eyes off Anneliese, as if he could see through her to the truth. He squinted, and Margeaux wondered where his glasses were. She scribbled a note on the paper in front of her. Would his lack of glasses impact his ability to reach a decision in the case? Or maybe he didn't wear them when listening.

When it came time to cross-examine the medical examiner, Chase barely asked any questions. "What kind of force would be needed to cause the thrusts you found on the victim?"

"The attacker would either need to have some size or adrenaline."

"What do you mean by size?"

"At least five eight, by my best guess."

"Your best guess or your professional opinion?"

"My professional opinion."

"Thank you." And he ended there. Margeaux hoped that he had planted some doubt that the petite Anneliese could have committed the thrusts without prolonging the potentially damaging testimony.

Then Allison called Renee Jacobs to the stand. The roommate made a show of being best friends with Lauren, and Margeaux fought valiantly not to roll her eyes or jump to her feet to protest.

Allison walked her through the normal preliminary questions, then jumped into the roommates' relationships. "How would you describe how Lauren and Anneliese got along?"

"It started well, but Anneliese's a bit odd. She lurked a lot. You'd think you were alone and then she'd appear. I think Lauren got tired of her always being around. They fought when Lauren had friends over and wanted time alone with them."

"What were these fights like?"

"Loud. Uncomfortable. It didn't used to be like that."

"What do you mean?"

"The three of us roomed together junior year." She gave a small smile as if it was a fond memory. "We would hang out after Lauren returned from practices. We also hosted parties for friends. It was a lot of fun. This year wasn't."

"Why do you think it changed?"

"The only difference was her." Renee pointed at Anneliese. "If she hadn't come, Lauren would still be alive."

"Objection. Conjecture." Chase didn't bother standing as he made the statement.

"Sustained." Judge Waters looked at the jury. "You will disregard the witness's last words. Ms. Erickson, control your witness."

As Allison continued asking questions, Margeaux watched the jury. Several watched Anneliese with suspicion. It looked like they accepted Renee's position that Anneliese was the only thing that had changed in the last year.

"Your witness."

—————

Chase stood, ready to change the narrative. "Miss Jacobs."

"Hello."

"When we spoke, you didn't mention parties at your apartment."

"I don't remember."

"Don't remember what?"

"What we talked about."

"Do you remember us meeting?"

"Sure. It was a few weeks after Lauren died. You came to the place I was staying."

Chase paused a moment to give the jury a chance to understand what she did remember. "I asked about Lauren and her friends."

"Sure."

"But you didn't mention hosting parties."

"Like I said, I don't remember that."

The judge cleared her throat and he got the message.

Chase thought about how to tease the information from her. "What happened at these parties?"

She shrugged. "The normal. College kids having a good time."

"Was there ever alcohol at these parties?"

"Only if people were twenty-one or older."

He looked at the jury with a raised eyebrow and caught a few knowing looks back. "And what about other vices? Any drugs?"

"No."

"Ever?"

"No." She looked horrified. "We'd never do that."

"Did Albert Trales ever come to your parties?"

"Who?"

"Albert Trales. A Monroe College student."

"Maybe."

That was a good enough connection to his old drug-dealing client for now. "What about Dominic Strand?"

"Sure, he was there all the time."

"Why?"

She rolled her eyes. "He and Lauren were an on-again, off-again item."

"Were the police ever called to the apartment?"

"No."

"Never?"

"No."

Margeaux handed him a folder as if they'd practiced the action a hundred times. He smiled at her and loved how a bit of color stained her cheeks. He slipped the first police report from the file. "What about the night of February fifteenth? A Saturday."

"Of this year?"

"Yes."

"I don't think so." But she eyed the paperwork as if concerned about what words filled it.

"What if I told you this paper was a police report filed after a call to your apartment on February fifteenth?"

"I would say I wasn't home."

"Where were you that night?"

"Not there."

"How do you know?"

"Because if that is a police report, I could not have been home, because I was not there when the police were." She smiled as if she'd made a brilliant point.

Chase hid his amusement that she was talking in circles. The situation wasn't a slam dunk, but it looked evasive, and it would plant adequate suspicion in the mind of a juror looking for reasonable doubt. And that's all he needed.

He tugged out the next page. "How about January fifteenth? Were you home that night?"

"I don't know. That was a long time ago." She eyed him as if he held a snake rather than sheets of paper. "Is that another police report?"

"It is."

"You see, the thing about Lauren is she was passionate. She felt everything in big ways."

"Is that why the neighbors called the police?"

"I don't know why people do what they do."

"So you don't deny the police were called to your apartment?"

She stared at him and swallowed. "Look, I don't know who did what or why. What I do know is that Lauren died, and that woman was covered in her blood. If you want me to look at police reports, I will. But Lauren didn't like her, and I think Anneliese got tired of it."

Chase stared at her as her words settled in the courtroom. "Why didn't Lauren like Anneliese?"

"She never liked competition."

"What's that mean?"

"Lauren wanted everyone to love her. As long as she threw parties and scored in lacrosse, she was a campus darling. All the men fell over her. But then this mysterious international student arrives with a sultry accent, and things began to change." Renee shrugged and crossed her arms. "Fill in the blanks."

"No further questions." He sat, but as he did Margeaux nudged him.

"You can't end there," she whispered.

"We're not going to win by letting her say more."

"But she's making Anneliese look terrible."

"Renee could make her look worse."

"How?"

"Ms. Erickson?" Judge Waters looked at the prosecutor's table.

"Just a moment, Your Honor." Allison jotted another note, then stood. "Miss Jacobs, when you heard Lauren and Anneliese fight, what did they fight about?"

"Men. Fights were always about men."

"Anyone in particular?"

"One. Dominic Strand." Then she hesitated. "Then at the end there was a second." She shivered dramatically.

"Who was that?"

"I tried to forget his name because he was older and always made me uncomfortable."

"Jordan Lewis?"

She swallowed again, then gave a short jerk down of her chin. "Yes. That's the one."

"What about him made you uncomfortable?"

"He always looked at Lauren like he owned her. I'd ask Lauren why it didn't bother her, but she just laughed. She said she got the royal treatment from other men. Sometimes she wanted someone who would fight back. She called it competition. I called it crazy. But after Christmas, she really acted nuts. Something had changed and everything was different."

"What?"

"I don't know." Renee looked at Anneliese. "All I can think is it had something to do with her and what she did when she came back early." She twisted her hands as she continued to stare at Anneliese. "I always wondered what happened, but I didn't dare ask."

Anneliese stared at her lap, shoulders hunched as if she could hide.

"No further questions."

As Margeaux watched the jury, she didn't know who had won that round. Questions filled the air—and the questions surrounded Lauren and Anneliese.

Chapter 47

BY THE TIME THE SECOND day ended and they returned to the law firm, Margeaux was ready to give up. No square blows had landed, but all the prosecution had to do was keep building its case bit by bit.

"We can call Blake, and then we'll have to call both boyfriends," Margeaux said.

"No." Chase shook his head as he stared at an image of the two men on a monitor.

Margeaux put her hands on her hips. "What do you mean, 'no'?"

"Exactly that. I want to save Blake until I know if the jury needs her testimony. We don't know enough about Jordan Lewis. I wish John had found more on him, but the man is elusive. We'll make a decision later. Dominic is already on our list."

The tension pulsed through the room as Margeaux and Chase stared at each other across the table.

"Why are you so stubborn? We need to call both of them as witnesses." They needed to call everyone as a witness. Confuse the jury. Make them desperate to go home and do whatever it took to end their role. "We listed both Jordan and Dominic on the witness list. We can't think about it anymore. We have to call them."

"You aren't thinking clearly. Call them and the jury could as easily vote guilty to make it end."

"Not if they aren't convinced beyond a reasonable doubt."

"What's that even mean, professor?"

"That they know she's guilty."

"Know? And how would you define that?"

"That she did it and there's nothing that makes them question it."

"'Beyond a reasonable doubt' doesn't mean one hundred percent certainty."

She slammed a hand on the table, fighting back tears as his words stung. "I know that. I'm not some idiot, Chase."

"We agree on that. But all your knowledge is book smarts. That's great in a classroom, but that's not going to save *my* client in a courtroom." His chest heaved as if he'd been sprinting up and down flights of stairs instead of sitting in the conference room. "It's going to take so much more than knowing the law to save her." He pointed at the images of the two men on the screen. "Calling either of those men is a huge risk."

"But it could have a huge payoff."

There was a soft knock on the door, and then Emma slipped in. "Leigh told me to come on back with the sandwiches. I hope that was okay."

"Sure." Chase looked at her with a quizzical expression. "Chase Crandall. You are?"

"Emma Robbins. Her kid sister." She smirked at Margeaux. "Our parents' best surprise." She looked between them. "Is it okay I'm here?"

"Sure." Margeaux forced calmness into her expression. This was the break she needed from a conversation that was spiraling nowhere helpful. "Thanks for bringing these."

"Mom was concerned you wouldn't eat today if she didn't send food. You know how she gets."

Yeah. Margeaux did. And unfortunately, she'd given her mom plenty of reasons to be concerned. But that had been seventeen years earlier, before . . . Margeaux's gaze brushed over Emma. Before Emma had saved her life. "Do you want any, Emma?" Margeaux dug through the bag. "It looks like Mom sent plenty. Still trying to feed an army."

"I'll go grab plates." Chase sidestepped Emma and left the room.

Emma's nose went through a series of wrinkles, and then she pressed a hand to her stomach before shaking her head. "No, I couldn't eat." She glanced at the table. "What are you working on?"

"Nothing much."

She rolled her eyes. "I know you're helping with Anneliese's case. Is she going to be okay?"

"I'm not sure yet, but we're fighting hard." Margeaux patted the chair next to her, and Emma slipped into it. "Where did y'all hang out over Christmas?"

"Her apartment mostly. Sometimes other places."

"Did you meet any of her friends?"

"I don't know, maybe. Does it matter?"

"I'm still trying to figure out who her friends are, and she's not talking much. Even with the trial in process, we might still find someone who could help."

"She didn't seem to have many friends. I think that's why she liked spending time with me. I mean, really? What college student is going to hang out with a high schooler? Yet she'd call and ask if I could."

"And you did?"

"Yeah. I like her. She seemed lonely, and I understand that. School can be hard, and I got the sense that coming to the US wasn't easy for her. That maybe it was a lot harder than she expected it to be. I was happy to be her friend."

Chase returned with a few plastic plates and handed one to each of them. Then he grabbed a sandwich and moved back to his computer. With a flick of the mouse, the screen came back to life. As it did, Emma turned to look at it, then her cheeks paled and she stopped breathing.

"Emma?" Margeaux reached over and tapped the girl. "You okay?"

She blinked at the screen, then slowly turned to Margeaux. "What's he doing on the screen?" Her words were barely a whisper.

Then she bolted to the trash can and threw up.

Chase stared at the girl and then at his sandwich before wrapping it up.

He wouldn't be eating anytime soon.

Margeaux looked at him with wide eyes before grabbing a wad of tissues from a box on the table and hopping up to join her sister. "It'll be okay." She rubbed slow circles on the young woman's lower back and glanced over her shoulder at Chase. "Can you get her a glass of water? Maybe some wet paper towels?"

"Sure." He tore from the room and away from the scent. So many reasons he went to law school rather than medical school. When he reached the reception desk, he took a deep breath of clean air. "Leigh, clean up in the conference room."

"What did you do in there?"

"Margeaux's sister just lost her lunch, and I'm not sure why."

She frowned at him. "She was fine when she got here. You had to have done something."

"Me?" He slapped his hands against his chest. "I didn't do anything, but I've been sent out to get water and wet paper towels."

"That poor baby." She bustled to her feet. "You handle the phones. I'll take care of her."

As she brushed him into her seat, he didn't fight her. She was right. Something had happened to send Emma from fine to throwing up in a matter of minutes.

What changed?

He played back through what had happened when he'd returned to the room.

She'd been normal. Then the computer awoke from hibernation and the image of the two men returned to the projection screen.

He considered the pictures.

Had she reacted to seeing the men?

That seemed crazy . . .

But . . .

That was the only thing that had changed.

He returned to the conference room. Someone had removed the

trash can and sprayed some type of air freshener in the room. It didn't totally camouflage the stench but covered most of it. Margeaux sat on the floor next to where Emma lay, her feet propped on a chair and a wet cloth on her forehead. Emma's eyes popped open as he took a seat.

She struggled to her elbows, but Margeaux kept a hand on her shoulder. "Stay down another few minutes. Let's make sure you're settled."

"I'm fine, Margeaux. Embarrassed but fine."

Chase watched the two of them, then decided to test his theory, knowing his co-counsel wouldn't like it. No, she was going to hate it. "I think you're more than embarrassed."

"I don't know what you mean." Emma's words didn't have any force behind them since she wouldn't look at him.

"Which of those men upset you?" She stared blankly at him, and then he glanced at the screen and growled. He jiggled the mouse, and the image came back to the screen. "Which of them?"

"Chase?" Margeaux's word had a warning edge.

"Emma, I need to know."

"I don't have anything to tell you." Her chin jutted a bit, but her words trembled.

"If you're scared of one of them, let me know, and I will get you protection."

"I don't need protection."

"Then you wouldn't be so afraid you threw up."

"I'm not afraid. I'm pregnant." The words erupted from her, and then she clapped a hand over her mouth.

"That wasn't what I expected," Chase muttered, then looked at Margeaux. Her cheeks had drained of color and she swayed before launching to her feet.

"Excuse me." Then she slipped from the room.

———————————————

All her sacrifices had been wasted.

The pattern was repeating and she couldn't do anything to stop it.

Oh, but she wanted to find the man and kill him. With everything in her, she wanted to find him and rip him to pieces. She was so angry that she vibrated with venomous energy.

Emma was pregnant.

Her worst fear had come to pass.

And if it was one of those losers on the screen, she would find him and kill him.

End of story.

"Margeaux?" Emma's voice reached her as if traveling from a long distance.

She took a breath and held it. Released it slowly. She had to get back in there and pretend everything was okay. Well, as okay as it could be considering the bombshell Emma had just released.

She could do this, because Emma needed her to be strong and poised. Even if adrenaline thrummed through her in waves, she couldn't act like a deranged person flying into a rage.

"Margeaux?" Emma's voice pulled her back to the room.

She squared her shoulders, grabbed a tissue box as a thin excuse for her departure, and returned to the conference room. "Hey."

Concern filled Chase's face. "You okay?"

"Sure. Just grabbed these." She waggled the box in front of her.

Leigh looked at the box on the table. "Definitely needed another one of those."

Thanks for stating the obvious. They clearly needed to work on the feminine solidarity. "I wasn't expecting to hear your news."

"Can't say I wanted to have it to share." Emma struggled to a seated position. "Why do you have his picture up there?"

"Which one?" There were two men up there, after all—neither of them a winner in Margeaux's book.

"Jordan Lewis." Her eyes widened. "He's not involved in the trial. He can't be."

Margeaux put her hands on her hips and glared at Emma. "He cannot be your baby daddy."

"What a great way to phrase that. Thanks, Margeaux."

"There's no way it's love." Not based on what they'd learned about the man.

"How would you know? You've never been in love."

Chase snorted. Actually snorted. Neanderthal.

"There's a lot you don't know about me, Emma." *She has no idea how much she doesn't understand.*

"Yeah, I know. There's a sixteen-year age difference. Blah, blah. But you also don't know Jordan."

Chase cleared his throat. "I do know he's an adult, so it's a legal issue for him."

"I won't testify." Emma crossed her arms.

Chase mirrored Emma's posture. "You won't need to."

Margeaux groaned. "Let's calm down."

"I'm not the one who started all of this." Emma grabbed the bag of sandwiches. "Mom can bring the food next time. Let her run her own errands when she's worried about whether you're eating. I've got enough to worry about without caring about you." The girl stomped from the room, and Margeaux didn't know whether to follow her or collapse.

"Yep, that went well." Leigh looked toward the door. "Maybe you should go after her, Margeaux." Then the outer door closed.

Chase studied the images on the wall. "Maybe not. We just learned some very important information about one of our two boyfriends."

Margeaux fought to keep the tears at bay. "What's that?"

"He doesn't care about the law. Statutory rape isn't something to play with, and if he's the father of Emma's baby, there's no question he could be charged with that felony." He turned to Margeaux. "Makes it more likely he'd do other dangerous activities, doesn't it?"

Chapter 48

CHASE STARED AT THE BOARD, a grin spreading across his face, and she could tell it was finally happening. The defensive strategy was finally clicking into place, almost too late but not quite. But she feared it would be at Emma's expense.

"I need to go after her." She checked the Find My app and saw that Emma was well on her way home. "I'll call her later." Maybe they both would benefit from cooling off.

Or maybe Margeaux was just a coward.

He rubbed his hands together as if he couldn't wait to get to work. "It's simple. The commonwealth will rest, probably tomorrow. We'll put up Dominic and then Jordan. We'll add Emma if we need to. And then, only if we have no choice, we'll put Anneliese on the stand." Margeaux stared at him, her heart in her throat. From the moment Emma had said she was pregnant, Margeaux had felt the pressure building.

"You can't do that." Her own voice sounded far away.

He watched her carefully from his side of the table, a cautious set to his body as if he was ready for anything. "Why not?"

"Emma is off-limits."

"She can't be." He sighed. "You can't have it both ways. Before she came in with her bombshell, you were the one pushing me to put Jordan on the stand."

"Exactly. It's the perfect way to distract the jury from Anneliese."

"It won't work."

"I don't care. Do whatever you need to, but leave Emma alone."

"I can't and you know it." Frustration had crept into his voice, but empathy still played in his sad smile. "Part of what makes it work with Jordan is that if he would do something like this with a kid like her, it's more believable he would do other questionable and dangerous things. Maybe even murder."

Her thoughts darted, scrambling for a way out. There had to be a way to protect Emma. She'd made a mistake, but it didn't need to be compounded by making it part of a trial that was garnering international attention. "She's sixteen." The words barely whispered past her lips.

"Lauren was twenty-two. Anneliese is twenty-one. No one involved in this is old. You and I are only early thirties. We aren't exactly ancient."

"I feel that way now." She pushed to her feet and paced her side of the table.

Chase cocked his head. "What aren't you telling me, Margeaux?"

Panic swept her skin. The job of a criminal attorney was to ferret out the real story. "I don't know what you're talking about." She crossed one arm over her stomach and nibbled her thumbnail on her other hand.

"Something is killing you. Get it off your chest. If you murdered Lauren, just slide me a dollar, and it'll be covered by attorney-client privilege."

His words grabbed her attention. "What? I didn't stab her."

"Oh good, I was getting concerned."

"Why on earth would you think that?" She sank to the table. "I can't let Emma anywhere near the trial. Not without knowing what happened. If she's connected to Jordan . . ."

"What?"

"What if . . ." She couldn't finish the sentence.

"What if . . ."

"What if she knew about Jordan and Lauren? What if she was jealous? What if Jordan was manipulating her? He had to be. She just turned sixteen. She's a baby, and he's an adult. It's so easy to be manipulated at that age."

"That's why we'll make sure he's prosecuted as soon as we can prove he's the dad."

"But to use her in the murder trial . . ."

"You wouldn't want to, even if it gets Anneliese off? It could create reasonable doubt."

"Emma's my daughter. I was that sixteen-year-old. I can't—" Margeaux covered her mouth with her hand and lurched to her feet. "I'm sorry." Then she bolted from the room. Running away from the one question that had taken over her mind. *What if Emma is the murderer?*

That was a bombshell he hadn't expected.

How would that impact the trial? The next few days?

Chase had watched her face drain of color and the way she swayed on her feet.

She obviously hadn't planned to detonate that bit of information, and now she wanted to retract it but couldn't. There was no way to unexplode something.

And he couldn't ignore it if he wanted to. Information like that impacted every piece of the web they'd created on the whiteboard. Now Emma had to be woven into the threads of the web because, if she was that connected to Jordan, she was connected to Lauren and the rest. What would she do if she felt jilted by the man she loved? The man who was the father of her child?

How far would she go?

He couldn't answer that, because he didn't know her.

But as he watched Margeaux bolt from the room, he realized she was running the same calculations he was.

And the results terrified her.

What had Emma done?

Margeaux dashed to the restroom and closed the door, locking it behind her. She rushed to the sink and splashed cold water on her face, desperate to shock herself free from the nightmare she'd tumbled into.

What have I done?

Margeaux had endured sixteen interminable years, never once spilling the secret that had broken her heart day after day.

She had pretended it was enough to watch her daughter grow up, letting the illusion exist that she was merely the doting big sister. At the time it had felt kinder than adoption, but then she'd realized it might not have been. Who was it kinder to? Her? Not at all, because she wasn't allowed to be her true self—ever. Her parents? Not when they were asked to parent another generation. Emma? She'd hoped so, but now she wondered. Would Emma have thrived in a family that wasn't encumbered by the secrets surrounding her origins, or would she have simply been surrounded by different secrets?

Margeaux's head pounded, and she thought she would be sick.

How could she even contemplate that her daughter could have committed murder?

True, her parents might have been too lenient with Margeaux, but they were decent parents. If anything, they became too strict with Emma in a vain attempt to keep her from repeating Margeaux's mistakes. A fruitless effort, because they never tried to understand the root cause of Margeaux's own teen pregnancy.

Margeaux inhaled sharply. They would be devastated if it became public that Emma was really Margeaux's daughter. What drastic action would her father take this time to save face? She couldn't think about that now. She had much deeper problems to solve first.

She studied her reflection in the mirror, grimacing at how pale her skin was, the dark bruises under her eyes. She had to think logically about other explanations, because she could not believe that her daughter had killed a woman.

Emma might be sixteen and too young and foolish to know better than to get tangled up with a man who turned her head, but she could not be capable of murder. Margeaux refused to believe it. Just like she refused to believe Anneliese had done it.

There was another explanation, and she had to find it. Too much was at stake now not to do so.

She looked up and stared into her own eyes.

"We have to solve this for Emma."

She had no choice.

When she exited the bathroom, she had reapplied her lipstick and eased her shoulders back. Time to find the connections they had missed. They were there. They had to be.

There was something different about Margeaux when she reentered the conference room. She looked under siege but not destroyed. There was a determination to the set of her shoulders that seemed almost fierce, like she stood ready to wage a battle.

"You okay?" Chase's hands fisted and released next to his sides, a nervous gesture that he couldn't quite tame.

"I will be when this is behind us, so let's end it."

"Okay." He stepped next to her and stared with her at the whiteboard. "What do you want to do?"

"We're missing something obvious."

"What?"

"I don't know." The words were tight.

He reviewed what they'd built, wishing there were something to add to it. The moment stretched, becoming taut. He glanced toward her from the corner of his eye, and a tear trailed down her cheek. His heart cracked open, and he wanted to stop her pain but didn't know how. How did he stop this before it became a flood of waterworks? "Margeaux?"

She held up a hand and sniffed. "Don't."

"How can I fix this?"

"You can't." She refused to look at him even as he turned to face her, ignoring everything on the board.

He needed to figure out what to do next in preparing for the trial he hadn't wanted. But all he really wanted to do was take her in his arms and comfort her. Make sure she knew everything would be okay. That they would find a way. But the one thing he knew about Margeaux was that she never wanted to show weakness, could never depend on anyone else. Given what she probably had gone through, he absolutely understood. Maybe they were more alike than either realized.

He turned back to the board but leaned into her shoulder. He could let her know she wasn't alone, but he wouldn't take over. And maybe that would be enough. For now.

The whiteboard had a picture of Anneliese next to a picture of Lauren separated by the space of a couple of feet. Coming out from each photo were lines creating a web of connections.

The first connection was Dominic Strand. He had been Lauren's boyfriend, but Anneliese had known him through Lauren. Anneliese claimed not to like him, but neighbors overheard arguments focused on him between Lauren and Anneliese. Unfortunately those disagreements could be taken either way—disputes because he was a bad influence or because both women wanted him. That meant the testimony wasn't helpful or dispositive in either direction and could be interpreted however the jury wanted.

The second set of connections was the suitemates, Renee and Jillian. Neither seemed to like Anneliese and both seemed firmly in camp Lauren. What he couldn't figure out was why. What had Anneliese done that had turned them against her? Why not remain ambivalent toward her rather than develop this antipathy?

He couldn't shake the instinct that Anneliese could be a fall guy for someone. But what was the motive? Why choose her? Was it solely about the opportunity? Isolated and a loner, she would be easy to frame for the murder because of her penchant for late-night walks on her own. Those removed her chance to have an alibi and made her easy prey.

Maybe that was enough.

But as he stared at the board, he wondered how they could get anyone on it to admit that had been their plan. Because nothing he was throwing at the wall was sticking.

Unless he added Emma to the board. It would break Margeaux to see her there, but he mentally added the girl. Emma was connected to Anneliese. She had spent time with the college student. A bit odd on its own that an undergrad willingly spent so much time with a high school sophomore. During those visits, had Emma interacted with Jordan? Was that how she'd met her baby's father?

He stared at Jordan's photo. The man should have known better than to get involved with Emma. And while he was involved with Lauren. What kind of game was he playing?

The ultimate taker.

What else had he taken?

Chapter 49

MARGEAUX COULD FEEL CHASE'S THOUGHTS spinning almost as fast as hers. So much spiraled through her mind she could hardly grab hold of one idea before it slipped her grasp and the next stormed in.

She was going to be a grandma.

At thirty-two.

The world was such a broken place.

She couldn't pull in a breath.

She closed her eyes, tried to remember the breathing technique her counselor had taught her during her darkest days, and then gave up and prayed instead—the one that had always helped her before. *Father, help me.*

God should never be her last resort, yet he often was. She needed to work on that. As her lungs finally began to loosen, she prayed the words again on a slow exhale. Slowly she sensed his peace flowing into her, reminding her that even when she forgot to turn to him first, he was still working and waiting for her to remember. She was never built to be an island. And even if she was alone, she wasn't ever alone.

I do remember, Father. Help me lean into you.

She opened her eyes but continued to temper her breathing as she took a snapshot of the feeling. She would need to remember it in the coming days. She knew that from her own journey. There would be too much to handle on her own, no matter how tempted she would be to do exactly that. Still, she knew God was always faithful, even if it took her looking back to see the ways he was present in the middle of her pain and questions.

A moment later she was able to look at the board again. Then she slowly walked to it, picked up the pen, and added one word.

Emma.

"You didn't need to do that."

"Yes, I did. We both know she has to be there until we eliminate her." As her lungs tightened again, she breathed out another prayer. "But I'm going to do everything I can to prove she didn't kill Lauren."

"I expect nothing less." His words were an attempt to soothe her.

She knew that logically, but her anger railed to be let free. "Don't be nice to me." She gritted the words out between clenched teeth.

"I'm being honest, Margeaux. I'm not nice." He turned toward her and put his hands on her shoulders, light yet firm. "You should know that by now. I'm stubborn and fierce. Direct and cutting. But *nice* is not a word many people use to describe me."

"Then they haven't taken the time to see you." The words choked from her, but she saw something change in his expression as if she'd surprised him with what she'd said.

"You're dangerous."

"I'm honest, and I'm scared." She swallowed and then licked her lips, noticing the way he watched the motion. Maybe that hadn't been the smartest move, but suddenly she wanted him to hold her and tell her it would be okay because he would make it that way. If he said it, she knew it would be so. He wouldn't rest until it had been accomplished. He was that kind of man. Honorable and committed, even if he couldn't admit it.

He'd do the hard things for others that he'd never do for himself. He just needed someone to recognize that in him. Maybe she could do that.

No.

She could never be that for anyone. She wasn't that type of woman.

She didn't call men to be their better angels. She never had, and that's why she had to always hold herself apart. He deserved so much better than she could give him.

"Don't do it." He growled the words, as if he could somehow read her mind. "I won't let you disappear again." He tightened his grip on her, but instead of hurting, it somehow felt protective—as if he were calling her to him. "Anneliese and Emma need you to stay fully here. Right now."

"Do you?" The words slipped out and she wanted to melt through the floor. How could she be so weak as to let him into the question? She couldn't let anyone see her need.

He opened his mouth, and then he closed it. But there was a flash of longing, and she bit her lower lip as she waited to see what he would decide. When the silence stretched, he blinked.

Could she trust that, or was she just willing it to be so? She leaned up and placed a kiss on his cheek. Then she stepped back, her hand on her lips, and took another step back. "I need to go."

And then, like the coward she was, she fled.

Chase watched her go, his limbs frozen and his mind sluggish. The whisper of her lips lingered feather soft on his cheek, but she'd stepped back before he could turn it into a real kiss.

What had just happened?

One minute they were talking about the suspects and the trial. The next they were talking about them.

Did she want him to need her?

Or did she need him to walk away?

Was the kiss a request or a good-bye?

Why were women so confusing?

He ran his hands through his hair and then shook his hands as if that would somehow jolt his brain. None of this changed the fact that tomorrow morning he had to walk into the court with a brilliant strategy.

Emma.

Margeaux had done it. She'd written her daughter's name on the board. Now that he saw it up there and didn't have to imagine it, he looked for connections and patterns. Because she was friends with Anneliese, she could have interacted with every other person on the board. He had no choice.

He picked up the phone. "Can you get Emma Robbins back in here?"

There was a moment of stunned silence. "Margeaux's sister?"

"Yes."

"Margeaux just stormed out."

"Yep."

"I hope you know what you're doing, boss."

"Me too."

An hour later, the teen sat in front of him at the table. "Where's my sister?"

"She needed to work on something else."

Emma grimaced, an expression that mirrored one he'd seen Margeaux make a number of times. "She does like to work."

"It's helpful for paying the bills."

"I guess."

He carefully probed the edges of her experience with the women of apartment 321. She'd liked Anneliese and been surprised when Anneliese seemed to like her too. It hadn't taken long to realize that Anneliese was simply lonely. "For whatever reason, she struggled to make friends. I didn't understand why though. She was quiet but kind."

"Did you ever interact with her roommates?"

"Not much. Anneliese didn't like staying at the apartment, but there was a weekend she invited me to stay. I think it was because she thought Lauren would be gone for a competition, but it must have gotten canceled."

That was the weekend Emma met Jordan. The man had returned to the apartment with Lauren but had left her bedroom the next morning and focused his attention on Emma. The girl hadn't known what to do with it. Her cheeks colored and she couldn't meet Chase's gaze as she described Jordan's heavy pursuit. "He made me feel beautiful and desirable. I was an idiot. No man would be interested in me. I'm still in high school, just a kid. But I wanted to believe him. Look at me now. Who's going to want someone who's a mom at sixteen?" She rolled her eyes even as her hands went protectively to her still-flat stomach. "I should have known better."

"Earlier you defended him pretty hard."

"Did you see Margeaux's face? She looked like she was going to kill him . . . or me, if she couldn't get to him."

"I'm pretty sure you're safe." Chase couldn't tell her how safe. It wasn't his place.

"Maybe." But she sounded unsure.

He got it. Family was complicated.

He understood Margeaux's reaction, and if Chase had anything to say about it, he would make sure Jordan saw jail time. He was the adult who had taken advantage of the teenager. Preyed on her insecurities. "We'll hold him accountable for what he did. If he pursued you as hard as you say, then that's something we can address once we do a DNA test on the baby." As her eyes flickered, he realized what he'd said, and course corrected. "The law doesn't care. All that matters is your age and his."

"Would there be a trial?"

"If he decides to fight? Yes. But with a DNA test, the trial would be pro forma. It's hard to dispute DNA."

"I guess. But somehow, he'll try." She nibbled her lower lip, a gesture so similar to Margeaux's. "He'll make it about me."

"Doesn't matter. The law is really clear on this." Chase made a note for follow-up. "What was the dynamic like with Anneliese and Lauren?"

"I didn't see them together much, but Lauren didn't seem very nice."

"Why?"

Emma described scenes Anneliese had told her—scenes of a young woman who would make Anneliese leave so that she could have her teammates over or who would have them over without caring if it inconvenienced Anneliese. "Anneliese didn't feel like she could stay at her own apartment. It's why she walked the campus all the time. That was more comfortable for her than to stay at her own home. Can you imagine?" She harrumphed. "I was glad Margeaux invited her to join us for the holidays after I learned that. It's sad to not be with your family, but then to feel like you aren't welcome at your own apartment?"

"What about the other roommates?"

"Anneliese didn't know them well. The apartment was really two sets of suites connected by the living area in the middle. It was weird."

He'd noticed the arrangement and had wondered how much interaction they had with each other.

"Anneliese said she felt more comfortable spending time with me. Isn't that sad? I mean, I'm great, but I'd think she'd want to hang out with people closer to her age."

"Did you like the people in her apartment?"

"I didn't really know them, but I didn't think they were that nice." Emma crossed her arms and her face hardened. "Lauren seemed horribly selfish. She seemed to think everyone should love her and do everything she said. All the time. She didn't like that Jordan wanted to be with me."

He could get that. The relationship wasn't good. In any way. And a healthy person would immediately see that. There was something twisted and broken in the way Jordan had pursued Emma. And the way Emma talked about Lauren in that moment had an edge to it that Chase didn't like either.

He'd considered calling her as a witness, but now, as he watched her body language, the hard edge to her chin, and the glare in her eyes, he rethought that. Cross-examination could probe in bad directions and put information on public display she might not be ready to reveal. What was the right thing to do? For his client? And for the young woman sitting in front of him?

He didn't know if he could do right by both.

Maybe he'd keep her in reserve and call Jordan on his own.

Chapter 50

WHEN DAY THREE OF THE trial began with the commonwealth's attorney calling Detective Phillips, Chase didn't know whether to be relieved or concerned. The man sauntered to the witness stand like it was his second home, and as a police detective it probably felt that way. You couldn't be a detective without being called to testify frequently.

Chase tried not to fall asleep during the early testimony, ticking off questions he would have asked as Allison walked the detective through the scene. He perked up when she got to the investigation into the murder.

"Why did you focus on Anneliese?"

"It's not unusual for the investigation to start with people close to the victim. The fact that the defendant found Lauren and was covered in her blood was a strong signal she should be a suspect."

"That alone isn't sufficient. What else made her a suspect to you?"

"As we talked to neighbors, it was clear there were frequent arguments that involved Miss Richter and the victim."

"How did they know it involved those two? Four young women lived in the apartment."

"They claimed they recognized the voices." He sighed as if this were too much to ask him to divulge. "The roommates also gave important context on the relationships in the suites." Then he looked at Anneliese, and his expression took on a sinister cast. "We also found a necklace in the victim's hand. It was one that the roommates told us belonged to the defendant."

"Objection." Chase felt anger pulse through his body. "Your Honor, this is the first that any necklace has been mentioned."

"It's just been brought to my attention, Your Honor." Allison said it with a serene demeanor, but Chase wanted to yell foul.

This wasn't right. Someone had hidden this evidence—if it even existed.

"Approach." The judge glared over her glasses at both of them as they approached. "What is going on?"

"The police just made me aware of the necklace last night."

Chase turned on her. "And you didn't make us aware? Your Honor, that's worthy of a mistrial. The jury has been tainted by this testimony."

"I don't know that we can go that far, but this doesn't look good. Why would you give the defense an appealable issue?"

"Clearly I disagree on that." Allison leaned closer to the bench. "I only have a duty to list evidence I know about."

"So if the police hide it from you until the trial's underway, no harm, no foul." Chase wanted to rage but kept his emotions under wraps as much as possible since the jury still sat in the box. "Your Honor, this is prejudicial against my client."

She considered both of them, then turned to the commonwealth's attorney. "I will not allow any more evidence on the necklace until it is made available to the defense. I will also instruct the jury to ignore the testimony regarding it."

Chase had to lodge another protest. "Your Honor, they can't unhear it."

"That's true, so we'll do the best we can, and your objection is preserved for the record if you choose to appeal." She lasered in on Allison. "Any more stunts like that and the commonwealth may face sanctions. Am I clear?"

"Yes." The CA's posture tightened, indicating her displeasure with the reprimand.

"Good." After the attorneys returned to their tables, the judge took off her reading glasses and looked at the jury. "You will ignore the detective's statement about the necklace. Ms. Erickson."

Allison pushed to her feet with a soft sigh and then walked the detective through the police reports. "Did you investigate the men listed in those reports?"

"We didn't need to because I'd already talked to the officers called to the scenes."

"And what did you learn from them?"

"No charges were filed on the men."

"Is that sufficient to tell you there was no domestic violence?"

"Not necessarily, but I know the officers who reported, and if they believed domestic battery was occurring, they would have pursued the matter with or without a victim complaint." While he said the right things, Chase noted the way his body language tightened. Interesting, considering he and Allison would have run through the testimony a few times in preparation for the trial.

They kept talking until it was finally Chase's turn.

"Detective Phillips, when did you focus on the defendant?"

"Pretty quickly."

"Did you really look at anyone else?"

"Sure."

"It's a yes or no question."

"Yes."

"Who?"

"Jordan Lewis."

"Who?"

"A boyfriend."

"But you just told the commonwealth that you didn't investigate the men in the police reports."

"Sure, but that doesn't mean we ignored the boyfriends. They remain people of interest until they aren't."

"Why did you drop them?"

"Because we had more evidence against your client."

"Like what?"

"Like her DNA at the scene. Like her clothes covered in the victim's blood such as would occur if she leaned close enough to stab the victim. And let's not forget she was ready to flee the country. Innocent people don't flee."

Chase turned to the judge. "Objection, Your Honor."

Allison lurched to her feet. "He opened the door with the question."

"I'll overrule. Consider your questions carefully."

He gritted his teeth against the unsolicited advice even as he made a note to remember this if he needed an appealable issue. "Why did you arrest Miss Richter?"

"Because she killed Lauren Payge."

"When did you Mirandize her?"

"When we arrested her."

"After you interviewed her several times."

"I don't remember the sequence."

"Isn't it true that you focused on her and kept harassing her until you broke into her phone and created evidence?"

"No." The answer was short, but his color heightened. Good.

"And isn't it true that you also harassed her professor Margeaux Robbins, showing up in her classroom and other places? Accusing her of being part of a murder scheme?"

"I didn't accuse her of anything."

"But you harassed her."

"No. I interviewed her. Let her know what others said about her."

"And caused her to be put on administrative leave." He turned and grabbed a sheet of paper from a file. "When did you leak those allegations to the press?"

"I didn't."

"When did you leak them?"

"I didn't."

"I have evidence that you did."

"I can talk to whoever I want to."

"Not if you're violating the privacy of an investigation. And not when it becomes harassment of innocent people."

Detective Phillips worked his jaw from side to side as if trying to keep from speaking. Then he lost the battle. "I will speak when someone is going to get away with murder. And I will do what it takes to make sure my grandniece is avenged."

Gasps from the gallery pulled all the oxygen from the room.

Judge Waters banged her gavel. "Order in the court." After a few minutes the room quieted down. "Bailiff, I would ask you to escort the jury from the room." After he had done so, she turned to Ms. Erickson. "Did you know about this?"

Allison kept her posture absolutely erect. "No, ma'am."

The judge turned back to the detective. "I recommend you consult with an attorney before you say anything else. I'm going to call a recess for an hour. If that is insufficient time, then we will need to reconvene."

Chase raised his hand. "I have no further questions for Detective Phillips at this time but would like to reserve the right to call him in the future."

"Allison?"

"I'll hold redirect."

The judge considered them. "I don't like this, but I also don't want to declare a mistrial. It doesn't rise to that level . . . yet. I'm still calling a recess, and then we'll call the commonwealth's next witness."

Allison considered her notes. "I believe I'll be ready to rest."

"Will the defense be prepared to go?"

Chase looked at Margeaux, then back at the judge. "We anticipated the state filling the day."

"Fine, we'll restart after lunch. Be ready to call your first witness then. I want no more delays, and no more bombshells." She studied Detective Phillips. "Go see an attorney."

He smirked but kept his mouth shut.

The bowl of cheddar broccoli soup cooled in front of Margeaux as she stared at Chase. "You want to start with Emma?"

"I don't think we have a choice, unfortunately. What's your idea?"

"Put up Dominic and then Jordan. Maybe even put up your former client who can talk about drugs. As a last resort put on Anneliese. Under no circumstances would we put Emma on the stand. She's sixteen, Chase."

"We have to deal with the necklace."

"No, we have to hope the jury will forget about it."

Chase snorted. "Then you didn't pay enough attention to the jury. Mr. Thompson took copious notes again, and all through the sidebar too."

"So you want to put Anneliese on the stand, then? That's even worse than Emma. Then the commonwealth can cross, and I have no idea how she'll hold up to that."

"You're contradicting yourself, Margeaux, and we have no choice."

Margeaux gritted her teeth. "We always have a choice."

"We have to counter the phantom evidence of the necklace."

"Clutched in Lauren's fingers." Margeaux groaned. "That is pretty damaging evidence."

"But we don't know how it got there. We don't even know if it was really there."

"They're going to say it got yanked free while Lauren fought for her life."

"Then there would have been a wound on Anneliese's neck, and there wasn't."

"They didn't know it was Anneliese's and didn't know to photograph her neck for injuries."

"But she was their top suspect, so they looked for defensive wounds."

Margeaux shook her head. "No, I didn't let them. They hadn't made a custodial arrest. It was only an interview. So I wouldn't let Anneliese give them that kind of access to her. They had to either arrest her or wait."

Chase considered her. "That's right." Did it change anything? It messed up their defense that there weren't any wounds. That was annoying, but he couldn't fault the way she'd defended her student. "That was quick thinking."

"Thank you."

"Did you notice anything?"

"What?" She seemed startled by the question, though she shouldn't have been.

"You could be a witness. Did you notice any marks on Anneliese that could be signs of an altercation?"

"No?" The word was hesitant, more of a question than a statement.

"Are you sure?"

"Yes." She thought, then nodded. "I'm certain I didn't see anything."

Chapter 51

Wednesday, June 4

"THE DEFENSE CALLS DOMINIC STRAND." Chase waited as the deputy opened the door and Dominic made his way slowly across the bar and to the witness chair. After being sworn in, he answered the basic questions and shifted in the chair as if he couldn't get comfortable. A date with the truth could be that way.

"What was your relationship with Lauren Payge?"

"At one time I thought we had something special and could be together forever. But that wasn't our story."

Okay. The guy was laying it on thick. "Why not?"

"Lauren decided she didn't want to be exclusive. Another guy homed in on my girl."

Good, the possessive note was already creeping in. "What did y'all like to do together?"

"Have a good time."

"Did that ever include parties?"

"Sure. She was old enough to have a good time."

"Did that good time ever include alcohol?"

He shrugged.

"We need a verbal answer for the record."

"Sure." Dominic didn't seem to care about the reaction he got from the grandma on the jury.

"What about drugs?"

"Well, I can't say for sure, but a hair test might have shown a good time was had."

That comment definitely elicited a reaction. It was enough, so Chase moved on. "Did you ever partake?"

"It's rude to let one person have the good time by themselves."

This guy was an idiot and really needed an attorney. He hoped Allison was taking notes. "Who sold the good time to you?"

That stopped Dominic. "I don't know."

"Really? You don't have any idea?"

"I said I don't know." He thrust his chin out, looking belligerent and defensive.

Didn't know or wouldn't say. "Were you and Lauren dating at the time of her death?"

"Not exclusively, though I still had hopes of a full restoration of our relationship."

"Who else was she seeing at the time?"

"Jordan Lewis was one of the men."

"How did you find out about him?"

"I used an app on my phone to see where Lauren was. I wanted to make sure she was safe." He paused and looked at the commonwealth's attorney's table. "He'd be a good one to look at for drugs. Wherever he is, drugs tend to follow. I actually wondered if he used Lauren to get access to the college scene, but I didn't have time to prove it to her before she was killed. I tried to make her see reason, but she told me I was just jealous." He sank back with a harrumph.

"How'd her treatment make you feel?"

"I don't know."

"Angry?"

"Nah."

"Ticked?"

"Not really."

"Frustrated?"

"Sure. We were good together. That Jordan was just a user, but she wouldn't hear it."

Chase paused as he felt a niggling. "Why do you think that is?"

"I'm not sure, but he had her under some sort of spell. It's the only explanation." He glanced nervously around the courtroom, gaze darting. "He's not in here, right?"

"No." Chase considered another moment. "Last question. Where were you the night of March sixteenth?"

"Out with friends. We were watching a March Madness game."

"No further questions at this time." Chase just hoped Dominic's admission that he'd stalked Lauren was enough to plant some doubt in jurors' minds.

"Ms. Erickson?"

"I just have one." She looked at Dominic with a hint of disdain on her face. "Why was Lauren interested in you originally?"

"I knew how to make her feel loved and special. She was all about that." He looked at the ceiling as if searching for her in the heavens. "She was a very selfish person who wanted the world to revolve around her. When it didn't, she'd do something to make sure it did."

The CA grimaced as if disgusted with him. "Nothing further."

After a short recess, Chase called Jordan Lewis to the stand. This man exhibited the opposite characteristics of Dominic. He exuded a bad boy, James Dean vibe that would have the college coeds swooning. The recent grad on the jury recoiled as he took a seat, almost as if she knew him, but she stiffened and looked at the gallery rather than the witness. Chase filed the reaction away and fired off his questions.

"How did you know Lauren Payge?"

"I knew her big brother." He leaned back in the chair. "We played football together in high school."

"When did you start dating?"

"Off and on in November."

"Was it serious?"

"No. Neither of us had any interest in a long-term relationship. We both were clear we could see other people if we wanted. We were about the fun. Lauren was graduating and moving to the city, and we both thought it was premature to get tied down."

Chase wanted to ask about Emma, but he also wanted to protect her if possible. He'd hold that question for now. "Where were you the night of March sixteenth?"

"With a friend."

"Which friend?"

"I don't think she'd like me to say."

"You need to if you don't want this panel to consider you as a possible murder suspect."

"If you want a name, I can give you one. She's a sweet thing. Emma Robbins."

Chase froze. Why would the man admit that in open court? Now they would have to call her. He didn't dare look at Margeaux.

Margeaux forced her lungs to expand and deflate.

There was no way she would let Chase direct Emma. He'd created this mess. Margeaux would get them out.

And that was how she found herself standing at the podium, staring at her daughter. The young woman looked at her and the commonwealth's attorney with an air of defiance.

After the easy, preliminary questions, Margeaux released a breath and moved away from the podium. Time to rip the Band-Aid off. "How long have you known Jordan Lewis?"

"Since approximately late December or early January. I met him when I hung out with Anneliese during winter break."

"At the time, did you know he was also seeing Lauren Payge?"

"Yes. It was an interesting relationship to watch. They liked to fight, almost like it was part of their banter." She shook her head. "Anneliese and I would often leave when they did that."

"Why did you and Jordan date?"

"I didn't want to, because I'm not into stealing people's boyfriends, but he assured me it was okay with Lauren. I should have been more careful, because he's a lot older than me, but I found it all flattering. I guess I'm really naive."

Chase slipped her a note, and she glanced at it. *You're doing great. Don't forget to breathe.* She smiled and took a breath. "How old are you?"

"Sixteen." Emma raised her chin and squared her shoulders.

"How old is Jordan?"

"A lot older than that. And yes, before you ask, I am pregnant and he is the father."

Margeaux closed her eyes as gasps swept the room. It felt like so much of her past coming back.

Emma continued with only a faint tremble in her voice. "I probably should have known better, but I believed him when he said he loved me. Like I said, I'm naive. Anneliese tried to stop me, to make me see what he was doing, but I didn't want to see." Emma put a hand on her stomach as if protecting the tiny life inside. "I'll live with the consequences of my choices the rest of my life, but I also know Anneliese didn't murder Lauren. It's true she and Lauren had a strained relationship, but it wasn't because Anneliese didn't like Lauren. It's because Jordan had made moves on her too, but Anneliese was smarter than me and stayed away. Lauren didn't believe her, though. I was the reason why Anneliese wasn't home March sixteenth. She was with me. Helping me get a pregnancy test." Emma looked at Anneliese with a sad smile. "It's also why she couldn't tell you. It wasn't her story to tell." Emma blew out her breath. "You see, Anneliese was protecting me. She didn't need to, but she was."

Margeaux stared at her daughter as two tears tracked down Emma's cheeks. She didn't brush them away but instead kept her face high as if daring anyone to judge her.

She looked at Chase, and he gave a small twitch of his head.

"No further questions."

Allison looked at the sixteen-year-old, apparently wondering what could possibly leave her mouth next. "Your Honor, no cross at this time."

"All right. We'll take a brief recess."

As they waited in the hallway outside the courtroom, Chase turned to Margeaux. "You have to call Anneliese. You have to let her explain the crazy triangle"—he gestured as if trying to figure out what the shape was—"or square with Jordan. This could be enough."

She paced the hallway where they hid.

He could be right.

But if he was wrong, it could be an unmitigated disaster. "What if we only open the door for the state to cross-examine her?"

"It's always possible, but you saw how Allison didn't have the heart to cross Emma."

"I saw how she deferred it."

"She won't be able to do that twice. The jury won't let her even if Judge Waters somehow does." He looked at her. "It's my turn to hand you the list. I've had it for a week."

"Then you ask the questions."

"No, you're the one who's believed in Anneliese from day one. You're the one for the direct."

That's how Margeaux found herself standing at the podium again, this time staring at her student. "Anneliese, can you tell us where you were the evening of March sixteenth?"

Anneliese swallowed but met Margeaux's gaze. "I did not want to be the one to tell you. Emma had to share the news when she was ready."

"I understand. But can you tell us now?"

"After Lauren made it clear I was not welcome at the apartment because Jordan was returning, I left. About that time, Emma called in a panic and asked for help. I could tell something was wrong, so I had her pick me up. We went to a pharmacy and together figured out the pregnancy test. After the result was positive, I stayed with her for a couple of hours as she tried to decide what to do. Then I left to go home at about midnight."

"Why didn't you tell the police this?"

"They never asked where I had been." Her statement fell in the room. "I thought they would. But I did not want to tell them information that was not theirs to know either." She sighed. "I know Jordan well enough to know he will not accept responsibility. Emma needed space to decide how to proceed without people telling her what the right answer is."

Margeaux understood just how true this was. "It sounds like you were a good friend to Emma."

"If that was true, I would have never introduced her to Jordan. The way it happened was accidental. She was visiting me. Jordan visited Lauren. At the same time. I wish I had known to warn her to stay away. I did not know he would do what he did."

"Surely you interacted with him. He was seeing your roommate."

"Yes, but I did not think he would invest time in someone so much younger. She is a minor and he is past college. There are laws."

Yes, and she would make sure the law held him accountable. "How did you and Lauren get along?"

"Okay, until Jordan tried to interest me. After that, terribly. I tried to move, but there was nowhere to go."

Chapter 52

MARGEAUX CONSIDERED ANNELIESE. WHAT INFORMATION did she need to get out of Anneliese to make it clear to the jury that she was not the murderer? The question had haunted her for weeks.

Get it on the record.

"Anneliese, did you kill Lauren?"

Anneliese's eyes widened and she shrank back. "What? No."

"Everyone in here believes you did."

"You do not."

"Unfortunately, they don't care what I think. Why should they believe you?"

"I have an alibi. When I came here, I wanted to experience the United States. There is so much to learn and so many ways to take the knowledge back to my country. That was my hope." She straightened in the chair and met the gaze of the jury. "You have an amazing country. It is still the dream of so many to come. Yes, it was my dream, but my dream has always been to take what I learn and return home. This"—she gestured around the courtroom—"was not part of any dream.

"Lauren dreamed of changing the world by working for the State Department. I think she would have been good at it. But someone took that from her. It was not me."

"The necklace. Was it yours?"

"I do not know. The police never asked me about a necklace, and I do not think one is missing. But Lauren and I shared initials. Her name was Lauren Anne and mine is Anneliese Liane. Depending on the style, it could have both our initials but be hers."

Margeaux looked at Chase and he shook his head. "No further questions." She'd kept the scope as narrow as possible.

Allison stood but stayed behind the table. "If you didn't kill Lauren, who did?"

"I do not know. I am not the police."

"Surely you have a thought."

"I would not want another innocent person to be accused."

No matter what question she asked, Allison couldn't get traction, so after ten minutes, she finally said, "No further questions."

Chase stood. "The defense rests."

Judge Waters looked at both tables. "All right, we will take a recess and then it will be time for closing arguments. The jury should get the case before five."

After the bailiff removed the jury, Allison walked over. "I can offer you a plea of five years plus time served."

Chase looked at her. "It's too little, too late. I'll let my client know, but I have a feeling she'll take her chances with the jury." That's what he'd advise, anyway.

When Allison launched her closing argument, she looked serene as she walked the jury through the state's evidence. "Don't let the posturing by the defense counsel distract you from the truth. On March sixteenth Anneliese Richter was the only person home when Lauren Payge's body was found. She is the only roommate who had any known issues with Lauren. While the defense has tried to create issues between Lauren and other people, the universal perception is that Lauren was well-liked. No one denies she liked to have a good time, but that does not mean she should have been murdered.

"Regardless of the attempted smokescreens, it is clear that Anneliese is the only person who was in the apartment at the time that Lauren

Payge died. Lauren's blood was all over Anneliese and her clothes. Anneliese also tried to wash the evidence away and then purchased a ticket to flee the country. Those are the actions of a guilty woman.

"I ask you to follow the evidence and convict Anneliese Richter of the murder of Lauren Payge."

Chase popped to his feet as soon as Judge Waters indicated the floor was his. "We've reached the end of the evidence. And now the hard work begins for you." He walked them through the testimony, highlighting where reasonable doubt could be found. "As you can see, it's not as clear as the prosecution would like you to think. Instead, this is a complicated and tragic death.

"The law is clear. If any one of you doubts that my client is the one who killed Ms. Payge, then you cannot convict her. Two detectives and the medical examiner were witnesses. The medical examiner suggested the killer needed to be at least five feet, eight inches tall. Anneliese is not. You also learned the first detective did not interview many of the key individuals, but instead relied on information obtained second-hand. And Detective Phillips has a bias baked into the investigation since the victim is his grandniece. He never should have been part of the investigation."

Chase took a drink of water before continuing. "Through the testimony of Renee Jacobs, Dominic Strand, and Jordan Lewis, you learned more about the victim. She liked to party, and those parties may have had drugs in addition to alcohol. She also wasn't ready to settle down with any one person, but instead engaged actively in the dating scene when she wasn't focused on athletics.

"And from the testimony of Emma Robbins, you learned more about the victim, Jordan, and Anneliese. We learned that Jordan is willing to break the law in many ways and that Anneliese did indeed have an alibi after all. When Anneliese testified, we learned why she didn't share that alibi, a reason that many of us can understand.

"With all of that testimony, you get to choose. Who do you believe? Is there any reasonable doubt in your mind that Anneliese Richter could be the person who killed the victim? Remember the medical examiner indicated it needed to be someone who was taller than Anneliese."

He took another sip of water as he let the words settle.

"Anneliese did not commit this murder, and I ask that you acquit her. Thank you."

An hour later, after the jury instructions had been read, the jury was ushered back to their room.

"Now the waiting begins." Chase looked at Margeaux, who looked ready to explode. "We can go walk around the building a couple of times if that helps."

"It might. I'm not used to this much adrenaline combined with forced sitting." When they left the building and were alone, she stopped and looked up at him, lower lip pinched between her teeth. "How did it go, really? Should I have convinced Anneliese to take the plea?"

"We combined to give her a really good shot. Now we just have to wait and see."

Friday, June 6

The delays turned into a second and then a third day. The time dragged, and Margeaux felt like it would kill her—she couldn't sleep and could barely eat. She didn't know what to do with the delays. She wanted to believe good news was ahead. Someone was holding out in favor of Anneliese or else there would have been a decision. But it could be just as likely that the delay meant nothing.

At 4:00 p.m. on Friday, Judge Waters called in the jury. After receiving the jury foreperson's report that they were deadlocked, the judge turned to each of the jurors. "I'm going to poll you to see if you can reach a verdict."

Most thought Anneliese was guilty. But when the judge reached the recent graduate, the woman refused to cave. "I don't believe Ms. Richter is the killer, and no matter how they argue and yell at me, my mind won't be changed. I believe it's one of the boyfriends. Probably that sleazeball who got the teenager pregnant. I sincerely hope the commonwealth is going after him for a number of things." She folded her arms as Judge Waters watched her.

"You are certain you can't be persuaded by more time."

"Absolutely convinced."

"Then I will accept that this jury is deadlocked, and the jury is free to go." She turned to Anneliese. "Ms. Richter, because the jury is dead-locked, you are free to go for now. However, the commonwealth may decide to pursue additional charges."

"What does that mean?" Anneliese looked with a panicked expression from the judge to Chase and back.

The judge pinched the bridge of her nose. "It means the common-wealth can choose to try you again if it likes. But it may choose not to."

"I want to go home."

"You may still get to." The judge returned to her chambers, leaving Margeaux and Anneliese staring at Chase.

"What now?" Margeaux needed him to be their guide and help them understand.

"Let me talk to Allison." He stepped to the table, and Margeaux listened to part of the conversation.

Broken phrases reached her. "I'm not making any promises," "might retry," "shouldn't leave the country."

"It's not over, is it?"

Margeaux shook her head. "I don't think so." She looked toward the hallway. "Let's see if we can take you home yet. There's got to be a bailiff somewhere." She could work on that while Chase figured out the next legal steps. Right now, she wanted to get away from the courtroom and determine what was next. If Anneliese wasn't acquitted, did that mean Margeaux wasn't cleared either? She didn't want to think about that, but she needed to, because they embarked on the fall semester in two months, and Margeaux didn't know if she had a job to return to or not.

She spotted the last uniform exiting out a side door, so moved to fol-low. "Let's go this way."

When they stepped into the side hall, a contingent of media waited at the entrance to the rotunda. Lights flashed as reporters yelled questions at Anneliese. The din was astonishing as the noise ricocheted off the stone floors and walls.

Margeaux tucked Anneliese's head against her shoulder as she frantically looked for a way through. She turned to slip back into the courtroom, but the way was blocked by reporters who had circled behind them.

She couldn't think.

Couldn't breathe.

Couldn't see.

Then something sharp pressed into her side.

"Move." The one dark word was almost as terrifying as the item shoved into her torso.

She twisted to see who it was but couldn't, so she let go of Anneliese and shoved the young woman to the floor, hoping that move would launch her to safety. Anneliese yelled, and Margeaux used the shock of the noise and the slight release of pressure on the weapon to spin, finding herself face-to-face with Detective Phillips.

"You?" What was he doing?

"I won't let you get away with your role in Lauren's death." His expression was taut, a mask of controlled anger.

Margeaux squeezed her eyes closed and then opened them again. This was a nightmare. The man surged closer and jerked her against him, his face morphing to concern. "Make way, everyone. I've got to get her to safety."

The reporters looked confused but complied. Many had been in the courtroom over the week and knew he had testified. She made eye contact with several, mouthed *help me*, but they ignored her. Clearly they believed him over her.

She looked around for Anneliese, but the young woman had disappeared behind the wall of reporters. Had she gone for help?

"Let me go. I'm not who you want."

He yanked her closer. "Be quiet. You'll pay for every time you made someone think Lauren wasn't an angel."

He led her down one hallway and then another until they reached a freight elevator. He hit the button, and as the doors opened, he shoved her in. It was only as he stepped in that he dragged her to a stop—squinting into the corner. Margeaux followed his gaze and spotted a dark shadow, then launched toward the doors, hoping to take advantage of his distraction. Instead they slid shut and Detective Phillips yanked her back against him.

"Oh no, you don't."

She tried to wiggle free. "Please let me go. I didn't do anything."

His grip tightened.

The shadow stepped forward, and she yanked her arm but couldn't break away from Phillips's iron grip. Jordan Lewis stepped toward them. Margeaux used her right arm to reach behind her, feeling for the elevator buttons. Somewhere she had to find the one that would call for help or open the doors. There had to be a way to leave this small space and two crazy men behind.

"Detective Phillips."

The man's eyes widened slightly, and then he narrowed them. As he took a step back, he collided with the wall. "What are you doing here?"

"Making sure you don't get away."

"From what?"

"I'm tired of paying for your services." And the man raised the gun and shot the detective in the forehead.

Margeaux screamed as a small puff echoed in the space. She crouched low, feeling the spray and not wanting to name what it was.

"Why?" She hated the way the word whimpered.

"He exceeded his usefulness, and he was going to get caught. If he did, I couldn't have him implicating me." He towered over her, stroking her hair. "Don't make me kill you too." He grinned at her. "In fact, I'll take you with me as insurance. Soon I'll be far away from here and the mess this town is."

He grabbed her arm and she screamed as loud as she could—writhing and twisting, then collapsing all her weight down as the elevator doors opened. Swearing, he pointed the gun at her, but she screamed again, and someone answered with indistinct words. He spun, shooting wildly before sprinting away.

Margeaux scrabbled from the elevator and kept screaming for help. She couldn't go back into the elevator with Detective Phillips's body. But that didn't mean she felt safe exposed in the elevator lobby. Footsteps pounded toward her, the vibrations rolling through her as she covered her head with her arms.

"You're safe now."

When she looked up, a female officer crouched next to her.

An hour later, after she'd taken a shower in the judges' locker room and given her statement to two sheriff's deputies, Chase broke through.

"Are you okay?" He pulled her into a hug, and she sank into the comfort.

"No." She shuddered, and his arms tightened around her. "But I'm better now that you're here." She tipped her face to look at him. "Did they catch Jordan?"

"Not yet, but the elevator's video shows him killing Detective Phillips. It's clear it was him, so there's an APB out for his arrest. He's not getting away."

She hoped not, but it had taken police agencies weeks to catch the man who had threatened Janae when she became embroiled in the murder of a local attorney. Margeaux didn't know if she could handle wondering if Jordan would show up to hurt her. "I hope it doesn't take long."

"Law enforcement is highly motivated to catch him. He killed one of theirs." He tried to ease away, but she leaned in closer, only relaxing when his arms squeezed around her again.

"Please don't go." She straightened as a thought hit her. "Is Anneliese safe? I had her, and then we were surrounded by media and it got crazy."

"She's fine. Last time I saw her, Janae had her."

Margeaux's thoughts continued to spin. "Where's Emma? Is she safe? What if he decides to use her as a hostage?"

"The police assure me she's protected. And taking hostages only happens in books."

"It happens in books because it happened in real life somewhere." She shuddered. "I'm going to have to tell her the truth."

"Someday. But probably not today."

She nodded. Too much had happened today.

Right now Margeaux wanted to trust in the fact Chase was here and she was safe.

Chapter 53

MARGEAUX LINGERED OUTSIDE THE LAW office of Chase Crandall and Associate, wondering if this would be the last time she would be here as an employee. What a bittersweet feeling. As much as she had enjoyed helping with the trial, she didn't want to do that work full-time. She missed her students and the classroom. That was where she was called to serve, and she needed to find her way back there.

And, if she didn't work with Chase, maybe she could explore the tug she felt toward him.

She wanted to, and that was the cause of her uncertainty in leaving the firm, even though her future at Monroe College remained unsettled too.

Notoriety didn't have to be a negative. Maybe she could convince the administration of that.

If not, then she'd trust that God had another place for her to invest her time and talent.

She opened the door and walked inside.

Leigh looked up from the computer. "I wondered if you were coming in or standing outside all day."

"It's nice out there."

"If you like hot and humid at 9:00 a.m. Ready for the meeting?"

"I'm not sure." She wanted to appear strong and sure, but the words popped out before she could stop them.

"Allison will arrive in the next ten minutes." Leigh nodded toward the hallway. "Marcus is already in the conference room setting up. He and Chase already met this morning, planning for our next cases."

Margeaux let her jaw slacken. "They're speaking without you as mediator?"

"Wonders never cease."

The door opened and Anneliese stepped inside. The petite student had a bit of color in her cheeks, as if she'd spent her weekend of freedom outside. Margeaux gave her a big hug. "It's good to see you."

"You too." Anneliese shifted from the embrace. "Are we ready?"

"Let's find out what Chase knows."

"All right." Anneliese strode into the room and took a seat as if she were a warrior prepared for any news, good or bad.

Margeaux barely recognized the conference room now that the materials that made it a war room had been removed. Instead of being covered in a spiderweb of possible connections, the whiteboard was bare and pristine. She walked over to the small fridge and reached inside, but even the iced teas were gone. "I guess the trial really is over."

"And it won't be coming back." She startled as she turned to find Chase standing behind her. He stepped closer. "I think we can convince Allison not to refile. It's too messy with the new information they've uncovered. After Detective Phillips was murdered, they dug into his background. You'll want to talk to her, but they now know what we do. He's the one who leaked to the press about you and the murder."

"Stealing my thunder, Chase?" Allison strode into the room. She placed a briefcase on the table and sat.

"Sorry." He looked anything but contrite.

Margeaux took a seat next to Anneliese and clasped her hand under the table, a mirror of what they had done at trial. "Just like that? She's the wrong person and free to leave?"

Allison snapped open the locks and pulled out a file. "We've found evidence that Detective Phillips received payments from a local businessman to keep the focus on a student. Already enraged with grief, Phillips was pushed over the edge by the payments. Lauren was his grandniece and the pride of the family. Harming her was harming the family. He should have recused himself from the investigation, but didn't disclose the family connection."

"What did you mean when you told him you weren't ready to interview me?" Margeaux shouldn't have interrupted, but she'd needed an answer to that question for a while.

"That was another part of the investigation I couldn't figure out. Our initial investigation suggests he created evidence that connected you to the murder, but I wasn't convinced. It was too convenient, so I had another detective fact-checking it. He found some holes." Allison closed her eyes, and her shoulders rounded for a moment before she straightened her posture. "Before I could confirm one way or another what was off, he had brought you in and made you a focal point of the investigation. For that I am sorry."

Margeaux bit back the words that wanted to explode from her. She looked at Chase and he gave a small nod, so she pushed the words out. This time she would use her voice and be heard rather than be a silent victim. "Your silence makes you part of the problem. Thanks to Detective Phillips's 'investigation' and the commonwealth's complicity, I was put on administrative leave at the college. I don't know if I'll get my position back." She met Allison's gaze. "I need a letter from you to my dean and the vice-provost outlining what Detective Phillips did and that I am cleared of any whiff of wrongdoing."

Allison considered her a moment. "I can do that if you'll agree that clears the commonwealth of any wrongdoing."

Chase leaned into the table. "I think you'd better help her get her job back first. Fortunately for you, she's been paid. Otherwise, that wouldn't be enough." He turned to Anneliese, who had stayed silent throughout the exchange. "Now let's finish talking about Anneliese. For clarity, Anneliese is no longer a suspect in the murder."

"I don't know that you can say that, Chase."

Anneliese's hand tightened on Margeaux's.

"Then what can we say?"

"That we are looking hard in many other directions. Primarily Lauren's boyfriends. Detective Phillips and the businessman muddied the investigation significantly, and no, I can't tell you more, because it is an ongoing investigation. I'm here as a courtesy, and because we owed Ms. Robbins an apology." Allison met Anneliese's gaze. "Ms. Richter, you are free to leave the country. At this time I do not anticipate reopening the investigation against you or refiling the charges."

Chase's mouth tightened. "Maybe it's like not calling every witness at a trial. You might be satisfied, but this isn't a pretty package decorated with a bow."

Margeaux nodded. "In my experience life doesn't work that way. But I need to know if it's safe for Anneliese. Will the commonwealth retry her?"

"As long as I'm the CA, that won't happen. Not without new evidence." Allison glanced at her phone. "TSA just arrested Jordan Lewis at Dulles. Somehow he thought he could hop a flight out of the country." She nodded to Anneliese. "You truly are free to go."

"With my reputation in tatters."

"And the knowledge that if the case against her is reopened, I'll focus all of my efforts on making Phillips the fall guy." Chase grinned wolfishly at Allison. "I might even make it stick. Jordan made some payments to him. We're still not sure what for, but that makes the rest of the police's evidence suspect too. I'd find the connection." He shoved his hands in his pockets.

"Message received." Allison collected her file and left.

Silence enveloped them for a moment, then Anneliese shifted. "The nightmare is finally over?"

"Yes." Chase leaned back with a grin, plopping his loafer-clad feet on the table. "It's over."

"Then I can go home and finally be safe." She leaned into Margeaux. "Thank you for all you did."

"Thank you for being Emma's friend."

Anneliese looked at her. "She will be okay."

"She will."

After Anneliese left, Margeaux collapsed in her seat. "Wow. It really does feel like the Amanda Knox trial."

"Let's hope Anneliese doesn't have to go through the same number of trials and appeals." His gaze seared through her. "You're going to be okay."

"I'm just glad I don't have to look over my shoulder wondering if Jordan's there." She exhaled and stood, relieved all over again. "It feels like that chapter really is over now."

"Good." He rose and studied her. "How's Emma?"

"She's good. She says she knew I was her mom, but I don't know if I believe her. We're slowly working to build a new foundation for our relationship." She sighed as she imagined the road in front of Emma. "It's going to be hard for her."

"But she has you."

"Yes." And that might make enough difference to matter. "I'll enlist other people to help her too. I don't want her to ever feel alone." Not like Margeaux had in those early days and months, when her dad had forced her to disappear and then brushed such a thick veneer over everything that she'd been trapped behind the lies. So much of her life had been a continuation of that first twist of truth. "It's going to take a lot of thought and prayer to navigate this well."

"You can do it."

Margeaux took a step closer. "I'm glad you and Marcus are talking again."

"Me too." He paced nearer to her. "Holding on to my frustration isn't worth it. Good help is hard to find."

"So I've heard." She slid another foot toward him. "I don't suppose you've talked to anyone at Monroe College?"

"About you?" He looked down at her now that they were nearly standing on top of each other. "No, but we'll get that fixed, if that's what you want."

"It is. I enjoyed working on a case with you, but just like you're called to help people in legal binds, I'm called to students. I miss them. I even miss grading." She huffed an embarrassed laugh, but he grinned in understanding.

"It's like me and the piles of paperwork. I hate it until someone threatens to take it away."

"I want teaching back."

"Then we'll get it for you." He stroked her cheek with a featherlight touch. "I guess if you're not going to work for me anymore, I can do what I've wanted to for a while."

He leaned closer, but hesitated once, twice, three times—seeming to invite her in while allowing her to step back. She needed to make the choice.

In that moment she felt so seen and protected that she could have cried.

Instead, she leaned in and melted into the kiss. And as his arms encircled her, she knew that at long last she had found a place to belong.

Acknowledgments

EVERY BOOK TAKES A UNIQUE journey. This book was one I originally started thinking about in January 2020, when I attended the American Library Association meeting in Philadelphia. I was at a dinner with my friend Tricia Goyer and others, talking about what was next. Readers had asked for a book set in Italy since I'd spent parts of four summers there, but I wasn't sure that was quite right. My then-editor Jocelyn Bailey suggested the Amanda Knox case. That set me on a journey. I didn't want to write a fictionalized version of her story. It's too recent, and it's her story. But I did start wondering: What would it be like to be in another country and suddenly find yourself confronted by a legal system you don't know or understand?

Then I started thinking about who should fight for the accused. I hope you enjoyed Margeaux and Chase and their story. Law is a harsh mistress, as Chase has discovered. Even when you love it, you can wonder if you're still in the right place. And teaching is an equally challenging—and rewarding—field. Some of my love—and sometimes fatigue—for what I do in my other jobs may have bled onto these pages. There's something wonderful about being able to pour yourself out for others. That place where passion and talent connect is wonderful, but it doesn't mean people don't struggle. Both Margeaux and Chase wonder a bit if the grass is greener on the other side even as they know they are good at what they do.

One thing I don't have to wonder about is that I work with a talented

Acknowledgments

team. Many thanks to the incredible team at Kregel. From Janyre Tromp, who helps me peel back to the depths of the characters and make plotlines sing, to Kayliani, Rachel, Catherine, and all the others who help market, edit, sell, and publish this book, and so many others, thank you. It's truly been a privilege to work with you on crafting this and other stories. Many thanks to my agent, Rachelle Gardner, for her continued guidance in the complicated world of publishing. My family continues to be my biggest cheerleaders, and they are the ones who give up time with me for these books to see the light of day. Thank you for believing that this dream is worth it.

And thank you to each of you who read my books. I am so grateful. Without you, these would be simply words. They need you in order to come to life. I hope you enjoyed them.

About the Author

SINCE THE TIME SHE COULD read Nancy Drew, Cara Putman has wanted to write mysteries. In 2005 she attended a book signing at her local Christian bookstore and met fellow Indiana writer Colleen Coble. With prompting from her husband, Cara shared her dream with Colleen, who encouraged her to follow it. Ever since, Cara's been writing award-winning books.

Cara is an active member of ACFW and gives back to the writing community through her service on the executive board. She has also been the Indiana ACFW chapter president and area coordinator.

Cara is also an attorney, a full-time clinical professor at a Big Ten university, and an all-around crazy woman. Crazy about God, her husband, and her kids, that is. She graduated with honors from the University of Nebraska–Lincoln (Go Huskers!), George Mason Law School, and Purdue University's Krannert School of Management (now called Mitch Daniels School of Business). You can learn more about Cara at caraputman.com.

Facebook: facebook.com/cara.putman
X: x.com/cara_putman
Instagram: instagram.com/caracputman
BookBub: bookbub.com/authors/cara-putman
Goodreads: goodreads.com/author/show/939004.Cara_C_Putman

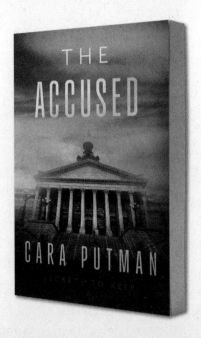

YOU CAN KEEP THIS BOOK MOVING!

Give this book as a gift.

Recommend this book to a friend or group.

Leave a review on Christianbook, Goodreads, Amazon, or your favorite bookseller's website.

Connect with the author on their social media/website.

Share the QR code link on your social media.

KREGEL
PUBLICATIONS

2450 Oak Industrial Dr NE | Grand Rapids, MI 49505 | kregel.com

  Follow @kregelbooks

Our mission as a Christian publisher is to develop and distribute—with integrity and excellence—trusted, biblically based resources that lead individuals to know and serve Jesus Christ.